Joy Martin was bo journalist and worke
moved to writing n
Corporation and the
She has also broadcast
Africa and Britain. N
as a freelance journalis

By the same author

A Wrong to Sweeten

JOY MARTIN

The Moon is Red in April

GRAFTON BOOKS
A Division of the Collins Publishing Group

LONDON GLASGOW
TORONTO SYDNEY AUCKLAND

Grafton Books
A Division of the Collins Publishing Group
8 Grafton Street, London W1X 3LA

Published in paperback by Grafton Books 1990

First published in Great Britain by
Grafton Books 1989

Copyright © Joy Martin 1989

ISBN 0-586-20436-9

Printed and bound in Great Britain by
Collins, Glasgow

Set in Times

For Maurice and Catherine Hennessy
with my gratitude and affection

Acknowledgements

I could not have written this book without the kind assistance and previous research of a great number of people. In particular I would like to thank Maurice Hennessy, Alain de Rochechouart and Mme Marie Geneviève Jonauret of Société JA^S Hennessy & Co., Cognac; Mme Pauline Reverchon, Conservateur, Musée de Cognac; Eugene Gillan, Assistant Curator, Kinsale Museum; Fr Liam Sword, Beatrice Ducasse, Micheline Kerney Walsh and Frank Delaney; and to acknowledge the following writers: John Cornelius O'Callaghan, Richard Hayes, Pierre Gaxotte, Robert Colle, René James, Louis Suire, Nancy Mitford, Alfred Cobban, Nicholas Faith, Herbert Spenser, T. A. Layton, Padraic O'Farrell, Patrick Logan, David Dickson and John Edward Walsh.

The Charentais will tell you that,
for one month after Easter, the moon is sure
to be red.

BOOK ONE
1744–1745

1

There were those who described Ellen Nagle as an exceptionally honest person and others who thought she was artless. Her four brothers told each other that she was too outspoken for her own ultimate good and unlikely, as a result, to catch a husband.

But everyone agreed that Ellen Nagle had courage. Not man nor animal nor superstition intimidated her. Not her father, certainly not her brothers, nor a young horse that had not yet been broken. She was not even afraid of old Ned Meagher who, having been begotten before his parents were wed, had the power of the Evil Eye.

She was five foot eight inches in height, too tall for a woman, and her hands were too big, with clumsy knuckles and square-tipped unfeminine fingers. The beauty spot on the left side of her wide mouth bore false witness to her looks although, on the positive side, she had thick dark brown hair and large green eyes fringed with long, heavy lashes. But her forehead was too high – at sixteen, she had not yet learnt to adapt her *tête-de-mouton* coiffure to hide it – and her snub nose did not conform with her otherwise generous features.

On the morning of the thirtieth of April, 1744, a time when every man, woman and child in Ireland went abroad in trepidation, Ellen, to her brother Rory's way of thinking, was proving her usual contrary self, remaining unperturbed by the story he had just recounted, to underline the significance of this day.

'It isn't the kind of thing a man would imagine – a hare sucking the milk out of the tit of a cow. It's a bad sign seeing such a thing this morning. If I'd gone after the creature you know full well it would have cut itself on the sharp grass and left a trail of blood behind it.'

'So why didn't you then and wouldn't we know for sure whether what they say is true about the hare turning into a woman with magic powers?'

'I had to see to the cow. It was all in a tither,' Rory said, raising his chin and lowering his eyelids in an attempt to regain his dignity.

There were times when he positively disliked his older sister and wished that one of the fairy people who roared up and down the country chanting low music and uttering mystic incantations would take it into his head to teach Ellen a lesson in diablerie and enchantment. Everyone knew that supernatural forces were abroad after sunset on May Eve until sunrise the following morning, when summer began. To ward off the effects of sortilege, green bushes, strewed over with yellow flowers, would be set up at every door before the day was out. A time when sensible men were cautious; when metamorphosing women stole milk in order to work heinous spells. When a hair collected from a cow's tail, or the clay taken out of its cloven hoof, or wisps of straw from the roof could be most amazingly potent. And when, if you were unlucky enough to lay eyes on a hedgehog, all you could do was kill it and hope for the best while a shiver of fear went along your back and your fingers turned into icicles as you mulled over what might conceivably happen to you.

Unless your name was Ellen . . .

Oh, his sister was a bold thing, Rory decided. It would not surprise him one whit if, on the morrow, she was amongst those daring girls who undressed and rolled naked in the dew, the way they could secure immunity from freckles and sunburn and chapping and wrinkles

12

during the coming year. Still, Ellen had freckles enough already, so maybe the treatment would help.

He opened his mouth to suggest it, but Ellen cut in first.

'I have to be going. Tell Mother not to be worried. I'll be back well before 'tis night.'

Rory sniggered.

'So you can look for a white slug to lie on a bed of flour, the way your lover's initials will be traced for you in the morning,' he said, and knew by the colour rising in her cheeks that he had found a chink in her armour. 'I'd say you had it in mind to ride over to Kilawillen.'

'So what if I have?'

'Then you'd better be careful on your way home not to look at the May Eve bonfires lest the *sidhe gaoithe* get hold of you and take the power of speech off you. Though what would be wrong in that, may I ask?'

But Ellen only shrugged: 'You and your wind fairies!' before turning and walking away. Rory, regarding her back view, noticed with disapproval that, typically, she had neglected to wear a pannier under her skirt and *pet-en-l'air*, and that her head was gracelessly bare.

'Much good that slug will do *you*!' he shouted after her, but Ellen did not respond.

On the other side of the Blackwater River, Richard O'Shaughnessy, always known as Dick, was also irascible, but only with himself.

Anticipating this morning, he had long imagined his elated self quivering to be off, like a potential winner at the start of the Mallow Races. Instead, his excitement had come upon him prematurely, keeping him awake in the night so he was now stupid with sleep.

And now he was late! In dire need of the excitant that would whip-lash him into action, he sat up in his feather

13

bed yawning and stretching and scowling, furious that this crucial day should have so inauspicious a start.

He had not bothered to put his nightshirt on and as he extended his arms his broad chest, with the sprinkling of very fine, very fair hair, puffed out. His shoulders were wide, too, but otherwise his body was thin, though the long legs, half-concealed by the blanket he had thrown impatiently aside when he first woke up, were muscular enough.

He shook his head and his straight, milky-blond hair swung out and fell back into place forming a curtain for the long, narrow face with the well-defined features: the straight mouth, the dominant nose, once broken and slightly out of true ever since, the deep blue eyes with the surprisingly dark lashes, and the thick, dark eyebrows. It was not a classically handsome face, but it was much more than merely interesting, even now, when its owner was looking cross.

What was it his father said – Good luck is better than early rising?

And long sleep makes a bare backside.

Gems of Irish wisdom . . .

At that he leapt up, and grabbed a hold of his clothes, the loose ruffled shirt, the hand-embroidered waistcoat, the knee-breeches which closed with a smart ornamental buckle, scrambling into them, squeezing his feet into his new and still uncomfortable top boots, buckling on his stock, all with the speed of a purposeful whirlwind.

He had two coats, one long, close-fitting to the waist, with a flat turndown collar and no lapels, suitable for all occasions, from riding to dancing, and a great-coat, called a wrap-rascal, which he rejected as being too heavy to carry as well as too warm to wear at this time of the year.

He picked up his hat, three-cornered, made out of

14

beaver, its wide brim edged with braid, and set it triumphantly on top of his head. And with this gesture he felt
relaxed, believing himself suitably attired for his magnificent adventure.

At this point in the affair he had envisaged himself
taking solemn stock of his surroundings, reminding himself sadly that he might never again set foot in Kilawillen.

Might never stand by this window looking across to
where the Nagles lived, over in Ballygriffin, no longer in
one of their seven ancestral castles, the outlines of which
he could scarcely trace, with the mist reaching down from
Heaven to tint the landscape silvery-green, as delicate a
shade as the toothed leaves of the silver-birch trees that
grew below him in the garden.

The trees . . . As well as the birches there were the tall
thin elms and the alders with their small woody cones,
their odd flat-topped leaves which, since they were supposed to bring bad luck to a traveller, he would do better
now to ignore; the massive grey poplars, the yews with
their branches pointing gracefully upwards, and the huge
oaks, the tree out of which the True Cross had been
formed.

Once these trees had made up a minute part of a giant
wood covering and protecting the whole of Ireland. Until
the British government had dictated that houses and ships
must be built. And so woodcutters had gone out, and the
big, raw, throbbing heart of the Isle of the Yellow Woods
had been shamelessly exposed – *Tá deire no gcoillte ar
lár.*

The Lords of All the Seas could not conquer the river,
mist-shimmeringly gentle, so that you would never suspect
the capacity it had for flooding, the devastation it could
wreak in the valley, as if it wanted to make its own furious
statement about what had happened to the trees. Queen
Elizabeth herself had feared the Blackwater, had called it

a dangerous water. It flowed within fifteen feet of the house: with a long enough line in his hand he could fish for salmon and trout from his bedroom-window.

The house. So the O'Shaughnessys lightly referred to the ancient castle, quadrangular in shape, sixty feet in height, with walls five-feet thick, to which a three-storey, ten-bedroomed structure had been added, backing onto the river, in more recent times. Many bullocks had been slaughtered prior to this construction and their blood mixed with lime to make a substantial mortar. The result was a sturdy country house with dormer windows in the high-pitched roof and three well-proportioned chimneys.

Misled by the imposing exterior of the castle façade, visitors arriving for the first time at Kilawillen House were invariably disconcerted to discover that the ground floor consisted, not of palatial, luxuriously-furnished chambers, but of a cavernous kitchen, comprising larder, scullery and pantry. To reach the reception rooms they were obliged to pass under the censorious eyes of the servants and go up a winding staircase which led to two stuffy and gloomy parlours on the first floor, and onwards up to the bedrooms and the backroom where the bathing tub was stored.

The fineries of the house, the mirrors, the velvets, the carpets, had all been smuggled into the country, together with tea and tobacco, and lace for trimmings, so that the gowns worn by the O'Shaughnessy women could be refurbished and made to look as good as new.

Smart enough his mother and sisters had looked, setting out of the house at his own suggestion! There was much additional good to be said for the healing properties of the Mallow spa, where people took the waters early in the morning before breakfast, and again in the afternoon. The women of the family, eager to try the new and healthy juices, to be in the fashionable stream of those

16

who did, had been easily prevailed upon to pay a crown each for a chamber and stay in Mallow for a week, enabling himself to avoid the inevitable tearful scene that would have followed had he told them what he was planning to do.

And his father and Willie were safely out of the way, as well, staying overnight with friends near Mitchelstown so they could attend the hiring fair in that town on the following day.

Still, there were others he had to evade, or deceive. Looking as innocent as possible, as if it was normal that he should leave the house at seven in the morning so impeccably dressed, Dick sauntered casually down the stairs, whistling, until he was diverted by the tantalizing smell that came up to him from the kitchen.

Game, and with it the promise of a pie. In his excitement the night before he had only pecked at his dinner but he was hungry enough this morning.

In spite of which he would have to rush through the kitchen as swift as a hare lest old Annie the cook get hold of him and demand where he was going, and why.

But – it was the most delectable of smells. Oh go *on*, he said to himself, and was down the last of the steps and through the kitchen so fast that, afterwards, Annie could not say for certain that she had seen him leave the house.

He was out of the front door, and round the side heading for the yard and stables.

Here a whole host of people could be seen going about their work. The pump-boy, off to draw water. Milkmaids with pails on their heads coming in from the dairy. Padraic Meagher, cousin of Ned of the Evil Eye, who worked in the stables, leading out one of the horses for exercise. And high above all of them, on the roof of one of the outhouses, the thatcher, with a twisted length of sally in one hand and a long needle in the other, and a spangle of

17

straw around his legs just below the knees. The men would be busy in the fields, as well, he knew, though not as fully occupied as they would be on the morrow, on May Day, when they would be moving the sheep and dry cattle into the summer pastures; docking lambs' tails and castrating the young rams, and all the while keeping an anxious eye out for signs of frost or of the east wind, which could presage hard times to come.

His father and Willie were anxious enough already, although their nervousness had nothing to do with the weather. Since February, when reports of an intended French invasion of either Ireland or England had first begun to circulate, the Vice-Regal had been intensifying anti-Catholic measures. It might not be long, Willie said gloomily, before these measures were extended to cover the legislation against Catholic property owners. Even bearing in mind that his elder brother was a terrible fuss-pot, Dick's heart had sunk at these words.

It was bad enough already the way the share of land owned by Catholics was slipping inexorably away. The O'Shaughnessys, like the Nagles, had been lucky, holding onto much of their land despite a law which stated categorically that, as a Catholic, you were entitled to retain only five per cent of it.

The alternative was to convert and side with England against ever more powerful Catholic France. But despite the legal incentives, less than four thousand Catholics had registered formal conversion.

Much of their own luck – of the luck of the Nagles – lay simply in being so far from the authorities up in Dublin castle who knew little of what went on in Munster, what went on in County Cork.

And there was more luck in the fact that most of the Protestant settlers who had been sent over from England were kind people, ready to give to the collections made

18

on behalf of the poor of Ireland even if they could not understand the ways of the Irish themselves and could be heard, on occasions, saying so.

Not the sort who would be killing themselves to let the castle know about the odd bit of land that had been bought back by their Catholic neighbours, or to bring into sharper focus the deliberate fuzziness of the borders of Catholic land.

No, thank God the settlers were too taken up with enjoying balls and ridottos and music meetings, and frequenting the Spa Long Room, over at Mallow – consuming the best teas and coffees and chocolates, the way they would have done, had they stayed at home in Bath or Tonbridge or Scarborough, instead of being used by the government to balance the scales in Ireland – to betray their incomprehensible Catholic friends.

'Master Dick!'

He had been spotted, singled out for conjecture, as he might have known he would be before he left the estate. Tadg Finn the coachman, his beady eyes burning with predictable curiosity as they registered the fancy waistcoat, the ruffled shirt, stopped him dead in his tracks.

'Are ye riding out, Master Dick?'

Dick sighed. You could not move an inch in the Blackwater Valley, he thought, without being the focus of unapologetic surmise.

'I am.'

'Over to Mallow, is it?' Tadg persisted. 'To join your mother and sisters? Mallow is a daza place all right for the likes of yourself to be at.'

Dick cleared his throat, pretending not to hear.

'*Is* it Mallow ye're heading for?' the unabashed Tadg tried again.

A man would be tempted to let him into the secret as a reward for sheer indefatigability.

19

But not too tempted . . .

'I haven't the time to tell you now,' Dick got out of it. 'It's a long story and I'm in a great hurry. I'll saddle Midir myself.'

'Ah, sure, I'll do it,' said Tadg, resisting to the end being driven off the scent.

Taciturnity was the only remaining weapon. When he had finally extracted himself from the coachman's clutches, Dick cantered down the prim straight avenue, and turned sharp left by the big gate, so he was riding between the river and the Nagle Mountains.

This was a stretch of road he traversed almost every day of his life without once being able to shake off the memory of that occasion, four years earlier, when he had been sixteen years old.

When frost had destroyed the crops and more than an eighth of the population had died of hunger.

When he had seen in the ditch a dog devouring the corpse of a man who had waited too long for food.

Instead of lashing out at the dog, killing it for its temerity in feasting off human entrails, he had left it to finish its gruesome meal. For what use was there in intervention? he had asked himself. The soul had gone out of the man and the dog was ravenous, too.

Sometimes it seemed as if the soul had gone out of the country, under the Penal Laws. The people had grown lazy, because they had nothing for which to work, and lawless, because for them the law was an enemy responsible for the ruination of their own Brehon Laws; of the bardic schools, of poetry, literature and language. Of trade. The law was a tyrant prohibiting Catholics from attending Catholic schools, or going to school abroad; from entering the army, or studying for the Law, or practising their own religion. Under the viceroyalty of the Duke of Devonshire there was little comfort to be found in reminding yourself that you came from noble Irish stock.

The trees were beginning to thin out and through what was left of them Dick could see the ruins of Moninimy castle, once owned by the Nagles and since his childhood the site of a hedge-school set up so Catholic children could learn their own religion, language and culture in secret. Mr O'Halloran, the teacher who ran it, was a brave man, risking flogging and transportation to a West Indian sugar plantation, should the authorities catch wind of his activities. Dick and Willie and the girls, and the Nagle children, had been among Mr O'Halloran's pupils, and schooled well in Latin and mathematics, to boot.

But he had not learnt French from Mr O'Halloran. That most esteemed of languages had been taught to the O'Shaughnessy children by their mother, so effectively that all of them spoke it surprisingly well.

He had virtually reached his first destination. There was no clue that might lead an outsider to it, only rocks covered with sallow moss, surrounded by spiky grass, the kind that could give you a nasty cut, and yellow pimpernel and dark blue bugle.

Reining in, his eye was caught by a flash of scarlet through the amassed viridescence. The vision clarified, turned from a patch of pigment into the depiction of a girl on horseback, a young girl in a red tent-like mantle with a deep wrap like a cape. Her head was bare and her dark hair, dew-wet, was pulling out of its ringlets in a way his mother would have disapproved.

'Ellen Nagle!' he called out, pleased, in one way, to see her although her arrival at this place could not have been worse-timed.

She pulled in beside him, her face flushed with her exertions so that she looked prettier than she really was.

21

'Where are *you* off to so early in the day?' she greeted him.

'I could ask the same of you,' Dick replied.

'*I* was on my way to see you,' Ellen said in her frank way. 'I heard that your mother and the girls were in Mallow and I thought to myself that I had a good chance of having you all to myself for a while.'

The nerve of her. Still, they had always been close, he and Ellen. From childhood she had been one of his favourite people although he sometimes wondered why. She could hardly be described as a relaxing companion. She was argumentative and alarmingly independent. It was impossible to deflect her once her mind was made up. She did not offer unconditional love to anyone and if you got into an argument with her she could be openly critical of any views which did not coincide with her own.

And now she had pushed him into a corner, since he could not say that he was in a hurry and ride on, leaving her there, not without collecting what he needed for his journey.

'So where *are* you going?' Ellen asked again, every bit as persistent in her way as Tadg Finn had been in his.

But a different person altogether. Ellen would never, ever betray you . . .

'I'll tell you,' he said, reaching a decision. 'Get down and come in here off the road. There's something I want to show you.'

He was sure he was the only one who knew about the caves, having stumbled on them years before, playing at this end of the land. He had been on a solitary excursion, following the imaginary footsteps of the young warrior Naoise, wandering through the woods, about to fall speechless at the sight of beautiful Deidre.

His fall – an awkward one, over a jagged rock – while

22

less spectacular, had nonetheless yielded much that was of interest.

There were several caves, he had discovered, some quite extensive, all of them well-concealed by the larger rocks and the flowers and grass.

Although the first cave was musky and damp, in the last twelve hours it had made a perfect cache for the bag containing wheaten bread, herb-flavoured butter enclosed in a wooden vessel, cheese, and the makings of *scailtín*, all of which he had neatly secreted out of the pantry while old Annie's back was turned.

He said to Ellen: 'Tether Pooka over there. Midir can graze alongside her,' and when this was done he took her hand and led her to the mouth of the first cave, pushing aside the longer grasses and motioning her to crouch down and squeeze her way through into the darkness.

'Be careful. It's slippery.'

'And full of bugs and beetles, I'd say,' said Ellen, unmoved by this prospect. 'To think that none of us knew it was here.'

'And no one should know,' said Dick severely, for even if he might never need to use the caves again he felt strongly that his secret should not be passed on to anyone else who might avail himself of it, and usurp his previous dominion.

Anyone other than Ellen.

'No one will know, or not from me,' she said. 'What have you got in that bag?'

'It's food for my journey. Ellen, I'm going away – to France! I'm riding down to Kinsale and when I get there I'm planning to board a ship bound for Le Havre. Then I'll make my way to Paris.'

'Is that so?'

'It is. I'm going to finish my studies at the Collège des Grassins – you know that's part of the University of Paris,

23

do you? – and as soon as I have learnt there how to use a musket and a sword I'll join the Irish Brigade and fight for the king of France.'

'You'll be hanged if you're caught,' said Ellen, matter-of-factly. 'You, and the agent who will try to recruit you.'

'Naturally, I am aware of the risks,' said Dick after a moment's silence, and, although he did not know it, in the way he tilted his chin he looked much as Rory Nagle had done less than an hour earlier. 'They will be worth it. If I get to France I will be amongst the élite of our country. Think of the diplomats who have gone there, the counts and the barons, Knights of Saint Lewis and Saint Leopold, of the White Eagle and the Golden Fleece. Not to mention the generals and soldiers of all ranks who perform deeds upon the battlefields of Europe which make the name of Ireland ring with honour round the world!'

'You'll never get out from Kinsale,' said Ellen, unimpressed by this speech. 'It's too busy a port. The English have a large fleet in the Channel. They must be patrolling Kinsale all the while. Why don't you try Bantry, or Glengarrif, or Tralee? The French war corvettes must go into those ports as well, looking for volunteers for the army. 'Twould be safer than Kinsale anytime, being further west.'

'I want to leave from Kinsale,' said Dick, coldly.

A port famed in battle and story and song. Scene of heroic siege. From which town, in 1690, after both of its forts had been lost to the Williamite forces, the Jacobite soldiers had marched onwards to Limerick. And afterwards – as the first of the Wild Geese – had duly set sail, to become mercenaries, far away from home. There had been dreadful scenes at the quaysides, with the poor women who were to be left behind lamenting the loss of

24

their men, some of them plunging into the water in an attempt to follow the boats, and subsequently drowning.

Those women had not been insensitive to the risks about to be taken by their men.

'I think I'll come with you,' said Ellen, in the way of one who was suggesting an excursion over to Mallow.

'I've never heard such ridiculous nonsense,' said Dick, shocked. '*You* – taking part in such an adventure!'

'Why not?'

He had never in his life come across so impudent a girl. His mother would have a blue fit if she could hear what Ellen was proposing.

Not to mention his sisters.

And it was quite ridiculous that he should waste precious moments discussing the issue with her.

On the other hand, if he did not make her see sense at once, she was quite capable of riding alongside him to continue the discussion, all the way to Kinsale.

'Look – '

'*Dick, there's someone else in the cave.*'

'What!'

'Ssh,' she said, softly. 'Listen.'

And she was right. Now he, too, could hear the sound that had alerted her to the alien presence. A moaning, mewling kind of a sound that was still unmistakably human.

'There he is,' said Ellen. 'Over in that corner.'

Dick blinked, as he had a habit of doing in times of crisis, remembering what Ellen and he had been saying earlier on. Incriminating talk, to say the least of it. But who would have expected to find an eavesdropper in this, of all places?

He, Ellen had said. But it could just as easily have been a woman, the bag of bones hunched in the corner. Bones, with great hollow eyes staring out of a sunken face.

25

'Is there whiskey in your bag?'

'Yes, and milk,' said Dick, thinking of the *scailtín* he had intended to make, with butter and sugar and cloves to give the drink a better flavour, when he stopped on the road that night.

Feeling in the bag for the whiskey, kneeling beside Ellen as she knelt before the bones, he said: 'I suppose he isn't licensed. Can you see whether he has a badge on him?'

'It's hard to see anything properly in here,' said Ellen. 'But I don't think he is. The licensed fellows would probably have beaten him out of Mallow, so he wouldn't be encroaching on their territory. His clothes are all in tatters, Dick. Help me off with my cloak, and I'll put it over him for a blanket.'

'Keep your cloak. Give him my coat, rather. Hold back his head and we'll see if he won't take a sip of the whiskey.'

Holding the flagon up to the parched lips, Dick cursed himself for having confided in Ellen at all. What if the man blabbed before he himself reached Kinsale, and he found the authorities there waiting to arrest him?

Although the way the beggar was he might not live long enough to talk.

If he were to die they would have no witness to the conversation.

But he did not want the man to die. There had been too many deaths from hunger.

'Try to drink this,' he urged the beggar, cradling his head in his hand.

The dry lips parted, sucked, although much of what they attempted to imbibe trickled down the chin.

'His throat is sore, I'd say.'

'We could put a Hairy Molly into one of your socks and

26

wrap it around his throat,' suggested Ellen. 'Or maybe if you breathed on him, that would make it better.'

'I haven't the time to wait while you go searching for caterpillars. And breathing only works if a man does it who never saw his father. We need to give him some honey, Ellen. We must take him back to the house.'

'*I'll* take him back to the house,' Ellen corrected. 'You must be on your way. Just help me to get him out of the cave and strapped up on to Pooka's back and I can manage then without you.'

The irritation Dick had felt for her faded away completely.

'Good girl. Come on. He'll be light enough to carry, God knows.'

Not speaking, saving their breath, they hoisted the sick man on to the waiting horse. All through their manoeuvres, the stranger, too, had been silent. Settled, he managed: 'Sir – '

'Don't trouble yourself with trying to talk, man.'

But the sunken eyes were focused on Dick, pleading with him to listen.

'What is it?'

''Tis only – my brother lives in Kinsale. The house in The Mall on the corner with the Blind Gate. He would – be able to help you.'

'That's very kind of you.'

'Crowley – Vincent Crowley. Tell him – Liam sent you.'

'I will. Get him back to the house, Ellen, and Annie will assist you.'

'And *you* – go,' Ellen said.

Knowing that he could trust her, liberated, exultant, Dick stepped forward and kissed her jubilantly on the cheek.

'*Oh!*' she said, caught off-balance and – to his delight –

actually blushing. 'Dick – that is – goodbye. And God be with you.'

'He's bound to be,' said Dick, confidently. 'For isn't He on our side?'

2

So Ellen, who had set out to spend that day with Dick, found herself on the way to the O'Shaughnessys' house in the company of another man.

Enlisting old Annie's assistance in the matter of Liam Crowley's welfare proved a more complex operation than she had expected. It was less than an hour since Dick had set out from Kilawillen House but already the place was buzzing with rumours, put about by Tadg Finn, that the younger O'Shaughnessy son was running away to a foreign country, he being so well-dressed before he started out.

'Spain, I'd say it would be,' Tadg was observing to old Annie as Ellen and Liam and Pooka reached the backyard. 'A lot of them Wild Geese does be going out there these days.'

'*Spain!*' exclaimed Annie grumpily. 'And he leaving this house without saying goodbye to meself?'

Deeply hurt at the way Dick appeared to have deserted her, she was busy wrapping anger over her wound, and adding meanness to it, refusing Tadg, the bearer of her bad news, his customary cut of oaten bread which she had baked on a hardening stand in front of the fire just before he had come in to the kitchen.

Then Ellen appeared at the door.

'Listen, I have a dying man with me and I need your help,' Ellen announced, waiting for Annie to make the appropriate sympathetic comments and rush to make up a bed for Liam Crowley.

Instead, Annie glared at her.

29

'Who told you to bring a dying man to this place, Miss Nagle?' she demanded, not budging an inch to help.

'Master Dick, who else?' said Ellen innocently, unaware that, by the mere mention of Dick's name, she was piling additional fuel into the flames of ire blazing high inside Annie.

'Is that so? Herself and the girls is over in Mallow, as you may well know, Miss Nagle, and I have no authority to make up a bed for the creature here, and he may be bringing the pox into the house, as well as the other maladies that we have no name for.'

'Master Dick did say that you would help me.'

'And where *is* Master Dick, to confirm that he ever said such a thing? When you can tell me that, Miss Nagle, then maybe I can get Tadg Finn to put some straw into one of the stables, and you can position the creature in there.'

It was not at all easy to get around her.

'Ah, please,' begged Ellen. 'Come out and see for yourself how sick he is, the poor man. Will you not let me leave him here for the night and I'll come back in the morning with the carriage and fetch him home to Ballygriffin.'

Old Annie sniffed, but she peeked around the door.

'The carriage, is it?' she said, raising her eyebrows in mock surprise. 'For *this* wizardy wart of a weasel? There isn't that much flesh on him that would make a pickey, may God have pity on him for I can't, not with the threat of the pox on the house.'

'*Please*,' wheedled Ellen, knowing that most of this talk could be discounted, and that Annie was soft inside.

But when the cook relented and gave the necessary directions to Tadg Finn, it was still with an ill grace.

'Only until tomorrow,' she insisted.

And with that Ellen had to be content. She supervised

30

the transfer of Liam Crowley from the yard into his makeshift bed in one of the empty stables, satisfied herself that Annie would provide him with food and drink and, under the latter's hypercritical eye, climbed into the saddle.

She was half-way back to the caves when she heard an eerie, resonant croak: 'Pruck!' Looking up, she saw what she did not wish to see, a massive black bird with a diamond-shaped tail, rolling and tumbling in flight in the sky above her head.

A raven. Ellen crossed herself quickly, her green eyes clouding with anxiety. It was one thing to mock Rory's stories – one way to survive as a lone girl in a family of boys was to challenge and deride her brothers before they could do so to her – but everyone knew that the raven was an ominous bird, the form assumed by a goddess of war, or a harbinger of doom, or a messenger of the gods with bad news to relate. The great warrior Cu Cuchulainn, who had defended the province and honour of Ulster against the men of Connaught, had been able to defy death in battle even after he was badly wounded, strapping himself on to a pillar and fighting on, until a raven had perched upon his shoulder and his enemies had dared to draw near to him.

And, on top of that, it *was* May Eve, when the forces of evil were more than usually active.

Fly with *me* to Ballygriffin, Ellen willed the massive bird. Let your next site be *there*.

Don't take wing for the road that leads south to Cork and Kinsale.

Don't show yourself to Dick.

It was twenty miles from Kilawillen to Cork, and another eighteen miles to Kinsale; since at the start of his ride Dick did not look up, he would not have known if the

31

raven had paid heed to Ellen, or if it was soaring over his blond head. But as the mist lifted he began to relax and he saw that there were plenty of jackdaws in the sky, and chattering opportunistic magpies, and starlings, and, as he drew nearer to the coast, stonechats with orange breasts perching on sprigs of yellow gorse.

There were lambs and calves with their mothers in the fields, and pedlars and packmen, coaches and carriages and waggon-loads of travellers on the road he took, and a vast crowd of beggars, many of them blind.

The beggars, Dick knew, would not find it too hard to get lodgings for the night. The cottiers, not knowing when they might be put out on the roads themselves, had a vast store of sympathy for beggars but, as Dick approached Cork, he himself had to give thought to where he might rest his own head.

Dick had been to the city only once before and on that occasion he had marvelled at the number of waterways and the way the ships came into its heart to load and unload their cargoes. It was still light but it was chilly and he could have made good use of his coat. He had eaten all the food he had brought with him, and he was hungry and thirsty, and the excitement that had sustained him during his long ride was beginning to fade.

Without too much difficulty he managed to find the inn where he and his father and Willie had stayed on their previous visit to Cork three years before. It was not far from the tall limestone tower, grey in colour but curiously known as the Red Abbey, which had housed Augustinian friars in the thirteenth century. The inn itself must once have been the boathouse of a merchant, who had ascended to his sturdy front door from stairs that led up from the waterway. Dick knocked, was admitted without ado and given a room for the night. Having eaten well he climbed into bed, put his blanket over his head, and fell into a jaded sleep.

In the morning he crossed the Lee and set out for Kinsale, thankful that his journey was continuing uneventfully, that he had encountered neither highwaymen nor the curious wanting to know his business, only, next, a gathering of barefooted children who had made a fire out of bones and were amusing themselves by dancing around it. Two of them, in an effort to impress him, ran over the embers, trying not to wince as they did.

Just after, it began to rain. At the beginning it was only a light shower but it settled into a vindictive downpour that soon had him drenched to the skin. Cursing himself for not having replaced his coat in Cork, vowing to buy another one when he got to Kinsale, he hunched his shoulders and pressed on until at long last he reached a muddle of cabins and realized that he was on the outskirts of the port, in the area known as Irish Town where children and chickens ran wild.

'Have you got some money for us, mister?' a boy shouted hopefully, taking a good look at Dick.

He added more daringly: 'Aren't you the rich man, the kind that could spare us a pig?'

The common name for a sixpence was also the sweet word used by nurses for the babies they held in their arms. 'Dear little pig, sweet little pig,' they would croon, as French women, so his mother had taught, said *mon petit rat*. He would have to get accustomed to French being spoken daily.

He would also have to harden his heart to requests for money since he needed all he had for the trip, especially as he had to buy himself a coat.

'One day I'll come back rich and give you a pig. I'll give you a hog then!' he shouted to the boy who had

33

asked for money, thinking – one day, from my own efforts, I will be a wealthy man.

But the boy, disillusioned, was turning away. With his own dreams intact, Dick went through Cork Gate and into the street of the same name.

In spite of its steep and narrow nature, it was bustling with life and, the rain having ceased, there were plenty of people around, a number of men wearing tricorne hats and wigs plastered with pomatum and powder, with long malacca-canes in their hands, the well-to-do of the town.

As he had reasoned it, his mission was to go down to one of the quays and wait around, looking, on the one hand, as unobtrusive as possible and, on the other, like a would-be recruit, until a French agent made an appearance, at which point they would negotiate his passage to France. He was hopeful that the voyage would cost him nothing more than a promise to serve the king of France in the Irish Brigade, after his studies at the Collège des Grassins had been successfully completed.

Many young men in similar positions, relied not upon being enlisted by an agent so much as upon family connections – uncles or brothers or cousins who had gone on ahead to France, and who were already in the Brigade. He could have done it that way. He could have asked his father to write to an influential relation, and been secure in the knowledge that help would be forthcoming on the other side.

Except that he wanted to be independent of the family, to conduct the adventure himself.

Still, he should have no trouble persuading an agent that he would make a good officer. And the French were reputedly avid for Irish soldiers.

On his right was what he realized must be the castle of the Earls of Desmond, with its mullioned windows and stopped battlements and the Geraldine arms, depicting bees on a quartered shield, emblazoned over the door. A once-powerful family, with their origins in the very land to which he was escaping.

He turned into Market Square, the centre of the town. From this point a number of streets veered off, one of them, he supposed, leading down to the quays. Because a number of other people were already making their way down one of these streets, he followed them, tapping his heels lightly against Midir's flanks, thinking – soon, maybe this evening, I will have to sell you, my old friend, since I cannot take you with me.

Edging the horse between the pedestrians, he marvelled at the gregarious nature of the Kinsale people who seemed to gather in talkative groups wherever he went in the town. At the end of the street a crowd was laughing and drawing each other's attention to something that was going on at the water's edge.

By then Dick had realized that, although he was by the sea, he was not actually on the quayside. But he was gregarious himself, attracted by festive public occasions and this one seemed to be fun. He moved out into the forefront of the crowd to see what was exciting it. As he did so a woman screamed loudly, making him blink in surprise.

She was a heavy, red-haired woman and she was strapped into a chair that was secured to that end of a long see-saw which hung out over the sea. As Dick watched, a man tipped up the other end of the plank to precipitate her into and under the water.

A ducking-chair. He could keep silent no longer.

'What has she done to deserve such treatment?' he asked an elderly man.

'They're dipping her for slander,' the other said, his eyes riveted on the water.

Horribly fascinated himself, Dick wondered how long

the wretched woman could remain immersed without actually drowning.

Dick looked at his informant. A repulsive fellow. But all the same a man who would be likely to know his way about the town.

'How do I get down to the quays from here?' Dick asked, relieved to see that the woman's head had reappeared out of the water and that she was still alive.

The elderly man glanced sharply at him.

'That's your way, so,' he said, pointing. 'Aren't you the crackawly to be going abroad soaking wet without a coat on your back?'

'I suppose I am,' said Dick ruefully.

'You may be full of giddum today, but 'tis bate you'll be in the morning,' the man predicted gloomily, his eyes shifting back towards the red-haired woman as the see-saw tipped again. 'You're a stranger in town, I take it. Will you be staying long in these parts?'

'Not long,' said Dick cautiously. 'I don't suppose you know of a horse dealer by any chance? I'm keen to sell my horse.'

'Indeed I do. Indeed I do,' the elderly man told him.

He had a mean, white, pinched face and straggly hair that looked as if it had never been closer than this to water.

'Go down the way I shown you and ask at the quay for a fellow called Flor Feehan. He has a neck on him like a bull and big thick legs like tree trunks. You won't be able to miss him.'

Up and down went the see-saw. To the accompaniment of vigorous screams, Dick retraced his steps and this time, after paying his toll at the water-gate, he got on to Market quay.

When he had seen in his mind's eye his departure from Kinsale the quay had been deserted, except for one or two picturesque vessels at anchor. All the sailors had been below decks and asleep. Night had sheltered him, and out of its embrace had stepped a French agent who had known without being told that he would be waiting, Midir sold, a decent coat on his back, ready to set sail for France and his brilliant career.

Maybe it would be like that later on in the evening but, for the present, there were more than half a dozen ships at anchor and innumerable sailors above deck or on the quayside, and women with low-cut necklines to their dresses and sardonic expressions on their faces, and children with bare feet and old eyes, and pedlars and passers-by.

Forced to make his second inquiry, this time for the man called Flor Feehan, Dick asked a girl in a red skirt and a bodice loosely tied with laces who had been looking him over with apparent interest since his arrival on the quayside.

'Flor Feehan, is it?' she said. 'That's him over there, cutting a great scatter in his new clothes, and his hair manky with the dirt.'

'Thank you.'

The girl had the effect of making him feel even younger and less experienced, more vulnerable than he was. Conscious of many eyes watching his progress, he rode to where the man called Flor Feehan was making a point of not seeing him advance; his huge hairy fingers adjusting his white cuffs, brushing at the sleeve of his black frock coat.

'Good day to you.'

Flor Feehan cast a quick look at Dick out of narrowed eyes, and looked away, as if he had been offended by what he had seen.

'It's a strange thing that a fine gentleman would be out without a coat, I'd say,' he observed in a sing-song voice.

37

'I'm preparing to pay two hogs for a new one. Nothing more,' said Dick, hoping he sounded like a man used to such bargaining. 'And if the price I'm offered is right I'd be willing to sell my horse.'

'Maybe I can help you and maybe I can't,' Flor Feehan said in his atonal voice. 'He's looking poorly, the creature. Not worth a *tráwneen*. You'll have a hard time of it getting a good stocking there, I'd say.'

'Is that so?' replied Dick. 'I'm lucky then that a man made me a good offer earlier in the day. I'll go back to him once you've found me a coat.'

Flor Feehan grew more alert.

'What was the offer you got, may I ask?'

The bargaining had begun.

It was concluded half an hour later, by which time Dick had pulled on the nearly new coat which Flor Feehan had sent a young boy off to find. It was too big and had probably been stolen, Dick thought, but it was fair quality, with a flat turndown collar and no lapels, and would suit his needs for the present.

In one of the pockets he deposited the coins exchanged for Midir, while Flor Feehan grinned at him, revealing a row of rotten teeth.

'Look after yourself so and don't be falling into the hands of the brassers,' he said, nodding his head to where the girl in the red skirt was waiting along the quay. 'A gutty creature that would be hobbling your money, the moment she got the chance.'

'I can look after myself.'

He stood looking after the horse as Flor Feehan led it away, feeling despondent instead of happy. Midir had served him well. More than that, the horse had been a vital part of his life at Kilawillen. For the first time since he had left his home, Dick began to miss it.

To miss those that lived in it, and others. Ellen came

38

into his mind, and with her the black river and the rich valley, and the hills that were draped with clean-smelling heather.

And the trees.

Ah, you're tired and hungry, he said to himself – that's all it is. Find an inn with a room for the night where you can dine well, after which you can go back to the quay, to complete the second half of this business.

By the time he had reached Market Street his new boots were pinching and when he saw a coffee house he grunted with relief. Coffee was a real treat, banned at home by his mother who maintained that all heating beverages had a detrimental effect on the intestines. The Irish, she had said, were hot-blooded enough as a race without needing to warm themselves any further, and the men of the house had to content themselves with drinking coffee only when visiting friends.

As he crossed the street he thought that he saw the elderly man who had directed him to the quay. The curious crowd must have dispersed, and the red-haired woman been unstrapped from her ducking-chair.

'The Green Dragon', said the sign over the coffee house door. Dick pushed it open and found himself in a tiny hallway. The door slammed behind him leaving him in semi-darkness. Stumbling up a short flight of stairs he entered a big room full of gesticulating men, drinking, smoking clay-pipes, all of them talking in the quick, nervous way of his people. Instead of coffee, the room smelt primarily of tobacco. But a fire burnt in a hearth over which hung a huge coffee-pot.

Served with his coffee, he edged his way to a corner by one of the velvet-draped windows and sat down, sipping the hot beverage greedily. Feeling his fatigue diminish, he gazed down at the people passing by in the street below.

One of whom looked familiar. Dick frowned, recognizing, this time without any doubt, the elderly man with the mean face. The fellow seemed to turn up wherever he went.

And having done so was now taking a rest for himself, leaning against a doorway on the other side of the street, contemplating the goings-on around him.

Perhaps waiting for someone. For himself? But that would make no sense. They had no point of contact other than a woman ducked in the sea, a request made and granted.

Therefore why feel uneasy? Don't be foolish, Dick told himself. The man is nothing but an innocent stroller taking a walk in his own town.

All the same, when he emerged from The Green Dragon half an hour later he was relieved to see that the elderly man had vanished from his post. Nor did he put in an appearance when Dick, going in search of dinner and a room for the night, discovered a suitable inn on the other side of the square.

He forgot the man with the mean face. He wolfed down a good meal of fat mutton rubbed with salt and honey and roasted with juicy old bacon; ate cheese made out of sheep's milk, and washed it all down with a pint of ale.

As he did so he waited impatiently for darkness to fall. Eventually the rain-washed sky darkened to violet, and to purple and to darkest grey, and he knew that it was time to return to the quay.

'I'll be out for a while,' he said to his landlady. 'I have an appointment with a friend.'

'But it's a crime to walk abroad at night,' the landlady said, shocked. 'The nightwatchman will be doing his rounds by now and the gates of the city will be locked.'

'I'm not proposing to go far.' He searched around for an excuse that would placate and reassure her. 'A friend of mine is leaving Kinsale early in the morning and it's my one chance to catch him.'

'A sailor, is he?'

'He spends most of his time at sea.'

(Unless he's standing on the quayside, keeping an eye out for potential soldiers.)

A wind had come up from the sea and there were clouds across the moon and no lights in the town. Like a blind beggar he felt his way down to the water.

There was no warning. The clouds moved off the moon and the men seemed to come out of the very walls of the houses around him and before he had time to run they were upon him.

Four of them, and all of them large, armed with sticks, and one of them raising his weapon to bring it down on Dick's back.

He twisted instinctively so that the blow, only partly-deflected, caught him full-force on the shoulder, knocking him to the ground.

Four of them. Two to hold him down. One to threaten, to brandish his club again. A fourth to tear at his clothes, to search his pockets for coins, to grin when his vile hands found them.

Burning with anger, his shoulder on fire, Dick tried to fight them back, catching at the restraining hands when he could loosen one of them, biting at a finger, having the satisfaction of drawing blood while his assailants slapped and punched him back.

'Showery!'

A voice from nearby, giving a warning shout. Someone was coming. The nightwatchman? But he posed another threat.

The men on the ground leapt to their feet, affording Dick space to see the man who had stood guard.

An elderly man with a white face, pinched and mean, with grey hair streeling. A right *sceilpéir*, he.

Dick ran from them. Ran with the fire burning hot in his shoulder and the blood from his nose pouring onto his ruffled shirt.

He veered right, going uphill where a less agitated man would have chosen a pathway down.

Veered again to the right, gasping for breath and swallowing his own blood and sobbing with savage fury.

He ran until he could run no further. With a great gulp he sank down by the side of a wall, propping himself against it, listening out for the sounds of pursuit.

There was no sound other than that of his own uneven breathing.

And why should they pursue him? He knew (he did not have to reach into his pockets to check) that all his money was gone.

I am a right eejit, he thought bleakly. A fool who had asked an elderly man the way to the quay, and how to sell a horse.

And the elderly man had marked him out for a fool, following him, spying on his movements, letting his younger, stronger friends know that there was a stranger in town who had completed a deal with Flor Feehan and that money had been exchanged.

And now he had no money with which to pay for his room or to use on his journey to France. He blinked, confronting his woeful predicament, facing the humiliation of it.

No money. And no friends in Kinsale.

Unless.

My brother lives in Kinsale, the fellow in the cave had said. *He would be able to help you.*

His mind ticked over. His name is Vincent Crowley.

His house is in The Mall on the corner with the Blind Gate.

He winced, remembering his own arrogance when the information had been given to him, how he had patronized his informant, telling him that he was kind when in reality he had just wanted the man to stop talking, so that he could ride on.

The moon was well clear of the clouds. Looking around, he saw that he had retreated into an affluent street. Fashionable houses had been erected all the way up a very steep incline.

The Mall was on the fashionable side of Kinsale. He remembered his mother saying so, remarking that the smart ladies of the town paraded in The Mall to show off their pretty clothes: 'Down the hill – and all the way up it again! That's vanity for you!'

He was – he had to be – in The Mall already.

He forced himself to his feet, wincing at the pain in his shoulder, gritting his teeth, telling himself that he had set out from Kilawillen intending to succeed and that he was not going to be thwarted.

That he would never be thwarted again.

Swearing under his breath he walked further up the incline.

And he found a tall and elegant house with undrawn curtains through which a blaze of candle-light illuminated a well-kept garden.

A house on a corner. How easy it had been! All that was puzzling was that such a smart abode should belong to the brother of a sickly beggar.

Unless that beggar was an eccentric member of a well-to-do family who had taken to the roads out of misplaced sympathy with other vagrants, and had fallen into adversity. Such things did happen occasionally.

He stood at the gateway and peered at the corner

house, at a withdrawing room where two people, a gentleman sporting a white wig with a queue hanging down behind and a lady in a blue *pet-en-l'air*, were engaged in conversation.

Mr Crowley? Mr Vincent Crowley, talking to his wife?

He tried the gate and found that it was unlocked. A sign, maybe, that Saint Christopher, the patron saint of travellers, had not let him down.

He pushed open the gate and walked up the pathway to the front door and raised the knocker. He told himself that maybe Mr Vincent Crowley, on hearing what had been done for his sick brother in Kilawillen, would be happy to reciprocate, as Liam had said he would.

The door was wrenched open. On the other side of it stood a very small housemaid with a spotty face and eyes set too close together in her head.

'What do you want?' she demanded, taking in Dick's dishevelled appearance and the blood on his face and shirt. Her voice was shrill and hostile. 'What time of night is this to be knocking on the door of decent people?'

'Is this Mr Vincent Crowley's house?' he asked mildly.

'It is not!' said the housemaid indignantly. 'Did you ever hear the like!'

More foolishness. To trust the ramblings of a man found starving in a cave.

'I'm sorry to have troubled you,' he said to the housemaid. 'I must have misunderstood.'

She pursed her lips, giving him the full benefit of another deprecating look.

Then: 'Vincent Crowley doesn't own so much as a rack in his top pocket,' she said with a sniff. 'Let alone a house like this. He's only the coachman. You have to go round the back for *him*.'

'The coachman – ?'

And then another voice interjected.

'What is it, Mary?'

And the gentleman with the white wig came into the hall.

3

In Paris that same evening two young men left the Collège des Grassins in the rue des Carmes, walked past the little church with the dome and the double doors that curve inwards, and turned into the wider but less inspiring rue des Écoles, on their way to the room on the top floor of the house where one of them was living.

The taller of the two young men, being the guest, was waved to the only chair. Folding himself into it, he tilted it on to its back legs so that he could more easily stretch out his own very long ones.

He was a tall, very thin young man, with blue eyes, the pale complexion of his Irish father, and the dark, thick, luxuriant hair that he had inherited from his French mother. His name was Philip Cantillon and he was twenty years old.

Partly because of his natural pallor, partly because of the lassitude he affected to cover his shyness, Philip always seemed to be tired, an artifice that deceived all but the few people he permitted to know him well.

As Philip reclined, his companion, Roger De Lacy, leaned forward to speak expressively, not only with words, but with his brown eyes, and with the long elegant hands which he sometimes ran through his dark red hair, sometimes held out with the palms upwards.

Roger, too, was half-Irish and half-French, proud of the fact that his father, and several other members of the De Lacy family, had been Wild Geese. His great uncle had been colonel and commandant of the Prince of Wales' regiment in Ireland during the Jacobite wars. Roger often mentioned that this uncle, having entered the French service, had given his life for France at the battle of Marsaglia, hinting that he was capable of following in these illustrious footsteps.

The De Lacys had come from County Limerick. The Cantillons, with their origins in France, had later moved to Kerry where one of Philip's ancestors, the eighth baron of Ballyheigue, had forfeited his title and estates for his fidelity to the Stuart cause. Retracing familial steps to France, he had fought so bravely at the battle of Malplaquet that his courage was the subject of a tableau.

Roger was not sure whether he envied Philip this ancestor more, or the one called Richard, the astute Parisian banker who – ensuring that the blood of the Cantillons yet again mixed with that of the noble O'Briens of Thomond – had married a sister of Lord Clare, commander of Clare's regiment.

But when he mentioned Richard Cantillon's name to Philip, the latter shrugged, saying that not all his banking relations had been successful, one of them dying a bankrupt.

'Only because he had permitted King James, and Queen Mary of Modena, to overdraw so extensively. What style!' Roger said, but Philip only looked bored.

The contrast between prosperity and poverty in France was a subject closer to his friend's heart, and so Roger went on to say: 'The peasants' lot will never improve unless they themselves grow more daring. They must learn to accept new agricultural methods,' in order to regain his attention.

'They need fertilizers above all. As long as there is a shortage of cattle and horses and sheep in the country what are they to do?'

Roger said: 'Naturally, it is a ridiculous policy to keep taking new, poorer land into cultivation, and to try to spread the same quantity of manure over a wider area. Thank God I'm going to be a soldier, ready to fight for a country in which I believe, in spite of its poor agricultural performance. And ready to die for it, as your father did at Dettingen.'

'Do you have any feeling for Ireland, Roger?' Philip asked suddenly.

Surprised at the abrupt change in topic, Roger frowned.

'I'm curous about the place, I suppose. It must be dreadful to live there. The people in the big houses losing heart, becoming as slatternly as the peasants in the cabins with their dung-pits at the door. Pigs pissing all over the streets. Culture, education, castles, pride destroyed. Only the dead and dying remaining.'

'You believe there is nothing of value left?'

'That's what I hear. I imagine that I would loathe it. No country in the world could ever compare with France, just as no city can compare with Paris. We live in the centre of the civilized universe, Philip. Painting, architecture, writing, theatre, opera – everything begins and ends here.'

'Paris *is* the best city in the world to improve your mind,' Philip nodded.

He pulled in his long legs and sat upright, straightening his chair.

'I must go. Otherwise neither of us will be fit for an early start.'

'I suppose not,' Roger agreed, getting up from the bed on which he had been sitting. 'You should have arranged to sleep here.'

After a momentary silence Philip said: 'I should say goodbye to Maman, you see – and to Catherine, for that matter,' and watched Roger's expression light up at the mention of his sister's name.

'How is lovely Catherine taking the news that your mother wishes to return to the Charente?'

'Badly! Still, we all knew that Maman would only want to retain the apartment in Paris until Catherine had finished her education at the convent of Chartreux. That's not for another year. Catherine has had time enough to get used to the idea of living in Cognac.'

Roger laughed.

'She's a Parisienne through and through. She'll never adapt to life in the Charente.

'She loves city life and what it has to offer. And why not? She's young and beautiful. I always think of her as having stepped out from the canvas of one of the Baroque painters of Italy. There is that wonderful depiction of Judith by Cristofano Allori; the exquisite face, the rounded cheeks, touched discreetly with pink, framed by the dark hair that melts into the background. So unashamed, that face. And yet its owner is holding in her hand the head of Holofernes! Study the picture and you will note that it is the *attendant* who looks distressed!'

And how am I supposed to do that? Philip thought irritably. He doubted if Roger had ever studied the picture either. To his knowledge his friend had never been to Italy.

Most likely, Roger had never seen any of Allori's work. He had read of the painting of Judith, or heard someone else speak of it. What an impostor he was!

But I, too, am spurious, Philip thought. I, too, pretend to be a man that I am not . . .

'However, what better w´y to die than in the hands of a beautiful woman!' said Roger, reinforcing this opinion with the use of his own eloquent hands. 'And Catherine *is* the most beautiful woman in Paris. Will you tell her that I said so, and that I asked for her?'

'I will,' agreed Philip, knowing that in his love for

Catherine if not in much else, Roger was sincere. 'I must go. Listen to the din, even in this part of town. I much prefer Paris after dinner, when the cafés are closed and peace is restored.'

As he turned into Boulevard Saint-Michel he was attempting to push Roger out of his mind, at least for a respite. But Roger obstinately stayed put. It had been Roger, after all, who had drawn his attention to the thermal baths of Lutetia, which he was now passing.

On one of their walks they had inspected the baths, discovered the old swimming-pool.

'Fourteen hundred years old!' Roger had marvelled. 'What a pity there is no water in the pool tonight, Philip, so that we could swim. What a place this is for dreams. Whenever I come here I tell myself that the aqueduct is working again and that I have a beautiful girl with me, and that we are swimming naked together.'

'The abbey is far more splendid . . .'

'It also has its erotic aspects! Did you know that Mary Tudor of England was caught here in a compromising position with the Duke of Suffolk by François Premier's spies? One can imagine her – another little dream.'

'I have my own dreams,' Philip had said, and had not added that they were very different from Roger's.

Roger remained in his thoughts as he reached Port-au-Change – Roger, rather than the money changers, the gold and silver smiths who had once set up house by the bridge. He stopped, leaning over the parapet, gazing into the murky water. At this point, the river was wide. He felt more relaxed, better able to contemplate the task that lay ahead of Roger and himself tomorrow.

A dangerous undertaking, but a worthy one. An assignment of which his father would have approved. It was curious how, in connection with so many aspects of his life (but not all) his dead father seemed to live on, directing his son's actions.

A painful imposition. A burden too heavy, perhaps, for his own frailer back?

The river was the colour of mud, polluted and clogged by innumerable nescient horrors, yet struggling onwards to the sea in search of its lustration.

'Monsieur?'

He swung around. A whore, still young, nubile, her blue open robe hitched up to reveal flat shoes, silk stockings. His fear and disgust did not overrule all of his compassion.

'You are not in a hurry. You have need of me?'

With a whore he could afford to be honest.

'*I* have no need of you,' he said.

He thrust a coin into her hand not only out of pity, but to silence her mockery, and walked away quickly towards Palais-Royal.

The house in rue Vivienne, one of a row of fine-façaded mansions which overlooked cool courtyards, had a double door-knocker in the shape of crowing cocks. Philip, having unlocked the door with his own key, mounted the stairs that led to the top apartment, taking them two at a time.

Inside, he saw that although there was a light burning in the *salon* there was no sign of his mother. Catherine's bedroom door was ajar. His sister did not look up from her escritoire when he came into the room.

She was very small and very dainty. Her pointed-toe silk shoes, made specially to fit her tiny feet, had exceedingly massive heels but they still only succeeded in elevating their wearer to just five feet two inches in height. The bell-hoop of her pink open gown, which was oblong and made of seven hoops of cane sewn into a stiff petticoat, made sitting and rising difficult. The gown, with its low neckline, and short frilled sleeves, was open at the bodice, filled in by a stomacher, and open again under the waist to reveal the quilted under-slip in a lighter shade of pink.

'You're home early,' she observed, but sounding as if she did not care one way or the other.

'Mm. Been shopping – or did one of your admirers surprise you?' Roger enquired, his attention caught by the set of enamels painted with four cupids mounted in gilt-chased metal, which stood on her escritoire.

Catherine was an accumulator, adding to her collection of enamels and glass, which she bought from M. Govignon in the Boulevard du Temple, whenever she got the chance. As well as objects, she also collected men, a tendency of which their mother wholeheartedly disapproved. The two women were more like jealous sisters than mother and daughter, Philip thought. His own relationship with his mother was far more stable.

'What do *you* think?' Catherine asked, looking at him in the gilded mirror hanging on the wall. 'Have you been with your friend Mr De Lacy?'

'I have. He asked for you. He says that you are the most beautiful woman in Paris.'

'How flattering,' said Catherine in her most impassive voice and he was no nearer knowing what she really felt for Roger.

'Shall I tell him you're pleased? We're going away tomorrow, he and I, on an expedition. We may be away for some time. Perhaps a month. I'm not sure.'

'You're going to Ireland, aren't you?'

Somehow, in spite of the hoop, she managed to swing around in her chair, to look at him accusingly.

'Yes. You know that I have always wanted to go. Please don't tell Maman. She will only worry. I shall write her a note explaining that Father Plunkett has given Roger and me permission to go to Bordeaux to see Roger's parents – that his father isn't well.'

'What a complicated story. You should tell simple lies, as I do, or act them out. You should have seen me simulate a faint in chapel this last week – the nuns were quite convinced that I needed a complete rest at home!'

'You didn't succeed in duping Maman.'

Catherine's expression grew more guarded. The long lashes fluttered. He had an image of a woman at a window, pulling the curtains together as if to shut out an unpleasant view or noise.

'Maybe not. But she came around to the convent and took me away, full of apparent sympathy, lest the nuns – Heaven forbid! – conclude that she is a bad mother! Does the Prefect of Studies know where you're going tomorrow?'

'Naturally. You know how it is at the college. Students take turns in these trips. I would be regarded as a coward if I refused to take mine.'

'How much of a risk are you taking?'

For the first time since he had entered her room he detected a modicum of emotion. He smiled at her, conscious that she was fond of him and, like their mother, frightened of the militant aspirations implanted in him by the man who had given his life at Dettingen.

'I suppose there's always some danger in these expeditions.'

The eyelashes fluttered again. The window was thrown open. What he saw in her eyes made him expand: 'It can be a difficult run, they say. But French ships go over and back to Ireland in safety all the time. There's no reason why this trip should be any different from the rest. We'll travel by horse to Rouen, of course – to Le Havre by river.'

'And then? Which Irish port?'

'In a fortnight we should be in Kinsale – briefly.'

'Kinsale,' she repeated. 'Well, as he's going so far with you I suppose I should send a message to Mr De Lacy. Tell him – '

'Yes? Don't play games, waiting to make sure you've got my attention before you say any more.'

Catherine sulked.

'I'm not. Tell Roger De Lacy that he is very kind to pay nice compliments.'

'That's all?'

'What more does he want to hear?' Catherine asked, making a little *moue*.

She turned pointedly back to her escritoire, to a letter about to be sent, he supposed, to some other unlucky fellow.

That ridiculous bell-hoop! It made it impossible for one to administer the spanking his sister so richly deserved!

'Ellen, how could you slip away from the house on May Eve, of all times,' Clare Nagle said reproachfully when her daughter got home to Ballygriffin. 'What's more, you could have been carried off. That kind of thing is so common these days. There are abduction clubs, I'm told, with representatives in every home, and details of girls' fortunes taken into consideration.'

'Mama, abduction is a capital felony. I'm sure it's not nearly as common a happening as they say.'

'You know nothing about the wickedness of life,' Clare said sadly.

She was a nervous, melancholy woman, skilled in the practice of making those who loved her feel guilty.

'They draw lots, or toss up, once they've selected a suitable girl.'

'Ah, Mama!'

'And it's no good your telling me that the law is on our

54

side in this connection for it's said to be inoperable. The rogues always maintain that the girls are willing to elope with them. When they capture an heiress they put her onto the horse in front of the man who's won her, to give the impression to anyone watching that the girl was eager to go.'

'What's wrong with those girls that they don't scream and kick under such circumstances?' asked Ellen in exasperation. 'Maybe they *do* want to be carried off!'

'*Ellen!* Charles, there you are. Ellen is causing me such trouble. I'm beginning to feel quite weak.'

'Don't be upsetting your mother, now,' Charles Nagle ordered. 'You must stop imitating your brothers, Ellen, riding wild around the country at all hours, even if it's only for the sake of your mother's health.'

When the Nagle children misbehaved, their father invariably drew their attention to their mother's asthmatic attacks. Under stress, this condition worsened. Confronted with whistling respiration and shortness of breath, miscreants almost always agreed to shame the Devil.

'I'm sorry,' Ellen said, 'I'll try not to worry you, Mama,' and when Clare, pleading an obstruction of the bronchioles, lay sick in bed the following morning, her daughter thought twice about introducing another invalid into the house that day.

I'll bring Liam over tomorrow, Ellen decided, while the men go to the hiring fair, to recruit more milkers and reapers.

'Has the Sign of the Cross been made over the cattle, Rory?' her father shouted next morning, and Rory called back: 'And over the mangers and stalls. Only we used froth from the pails for the cattle and saved Holy Water for the rest of it.'

'Good. Ellen, remember – no cinders or ashes from the

hearth must leave the house this day lest the fairies lay hands on them.'

'I'll remember, Pa.'

Surely old Annie would remember, too, that May Day would be a difficult time for moving about the country, and look after Liam meanwhile?

Sure that this was the case, Ellen took the carriage over to Kilawillen the next day. By then, there was trouble well-brewed on the other side of the river. Contrary to her expectation, old Annie had not taken May Day into account as an excuse for Ellen's absence, and she was more put out than ever.

And that was only the half of it. Hints had been dropped to Dick's mother and sisters that Miss Nagle from Ballygriffin was in the know about his departure. It was even insinuated that Ellen had been instrumental in organizing his flight, and encouraging him to leave the house without so much as a goodbye to his desolate family.

There was animosity instead of friendship in the eyes of the O'Shaughnessy women – Ellen saw that as soon as she got to Kilawillen – and she realized that they were only tolerating her in the place in the hope of extracting more accurate information from her about Dick's whereabouts.

'The rumour is that you may have helped him run away to Spain,' Ida O'Shaughnessy, Dick's mother, began as soon as she got the chance.

'*I* think he's on his way to France,' Eithne, Dick's most intelligent sister, observed sagely. 'Ellen has cousins, Nano and Ann Nagle, in Paris, Mama. Dick could be going over to them.'

'Why would he go and stay with members of the Nagle family when we have our own cousins in France?' Fanny, the youngest sister, wanted to know.

'Aren't Nano and Ann having a wonderful time in

Paris, with parties and dances and musical evenings?' Uny interjected. 'Maybe that's more of a draw than our cousins?'

They all forgot that the O'Shaughnessys and the Nagles had been so close over the years that they thought of each other as cousins, and frequently said as much.

'Is it Spain or France he's heading for?' Ida asked, and finally there was a gap left in the interrogation for Ellen to reply.

'I don't know,' she said bleakly.

She was a very bad liar. It was written all over her face that she did.

'You mean, you're not prepared to tell us,' said Ida in an ominous voice. 'I would never have thought I'd have lived to see the day when one of my sons ran off to Paris seeking frivolity instead of acquitting himself as a man.'

'Maybe Dick *is* going to do something noble,' Eithne said.

She looked at Ellen and gambled.

'I'd say myself that he's gone to France,' she pronounced and, seeing Ellen bite her lip, added: 'To fight for the Irish Brigade. That would be noble enough.'

The other O'Shaughnessys digested this possibility in silence. Then Ida said coldly: 'We won't be delaying you, Ellen, if you want to take the man Crowley and go. I just hope your poor mother won't mind about him.'

'I expect she will,' said Ellen wearily.

It was a relief, at least, to be able to tell the truth about that.

I had better not tell Mama anything, Ellen decided. Liam will have to be hidden in one of the lofts and nursed back there to health.

To her surprise, luck did not turn against her. She got the sick man as far as the ladder to the loft without being observed, and although she was sure that his spindly legs were going to give under him, he somehow struggled without mishap up the steps to the top and pulled himself inside the trap door.

Sneaking back to the loft with blankets and food, Ellen settled him into the farthest corner, behind an abandoned settle table and a broken walnut chair.

'Thank God it's only the start of summer,' she said to him. 'What would we have done if it was October and the threshing over and all of the lofts full? Don't move from here, whatever you do. I'll be over and back to attend to you, but if anyone does come up in the meantime don't mention where Master Dick has gone.'

'I'm no waugh-mouth,' Liam protested weakly. 'I wouldn't sour on him, or on you either.'

'I hope not.'

Struck by a thought Ellen added: 'You never thought of volunteering for the army in France yourself – with your brother so influential and all?'

Liam looked abashed.

'I was against it, Miss Nagle – for myself, that is. Vincent wasn't too pleased with me about that, I can tell you.'

'Is that so? Maybe you shouldn't talk any more for the moment. Are you all right where you are?'

'I'll be better before I'm twice married and once a widower,' Liam Crowley said, and Ellen went away.

4

'You seem well enough for a chat, Mr O'Shaughnessy,' said Mr Thomas Creagh, employer of Vincent Crowley.

Dick had been a guest at the house on The Mall for two days. Under Mr Creagh's supervision, Mary the housemaid had applied a plaster of very fine soot mixed with egg-white in a bandage to Dick's aching shoulder, confirmed Mr Creagh's opinion that none of his bones had been broken, and had made up a bed for him. When Dick woke up he found that his clothes had been whisked away for washing, but, as Mrs Creagh said when she came to check on his condition, he would not be in need of them since he had to stay where he was until he was properly rested and recovered from his ordeal.

Now, cheerful and clean, he sat with his host before an elaborately carved Irish mahogany table, dining off goose eggs and roast badger. There was no sign of Mrs Creagh. But as the conversation proceeded Dick realized that she was most likely keeping a discreet distance so that confidences could be exchanged between her husband and himself.

'Let me put it this way, Mr O'Shaughnessy,' said Mr Creagh, contemplating his well-piled plate, 'French ships come in regularly to Kinsale. I wonder if you would be interested in hearing what we know of their movements.'

'I could be.'

'I thought so. Let me put some facts before you, Mr O'Shaughnessy. My youngest brother emigrated to France as a young man to become an officer in Clare's Irish regiment. He is now Lieutenant-Colonel of that corps. As a result of his appointment, as well as of my own beliefs, I have helped many young men in what I think is your position to make their way to France, with Vincent Crowley assisting. You mentioned his name the night you arrived and the fact that you had come across his brother in Kilawillen. All I'm saying is that if I'm right about your intentions you've come to the right household to help you carry them out.'

'You're very kind.'

'I'm a practical man. The regiment needs men like yourself, young and resourceful. Unless – '

'Unless what, Mr Creagh?'

'I thought that you would be heading for Paris, for the Collège des Grassins, but there's the possibility that you could be a cleric, on the way to the Collège des Lombards. A few of the clerics have been troublesome, the ones that were not ordained when they left. A number of complaints have been received from the Bishop of Killaloe. It seems that some of the lads changed their minds about the priesthood when they got over to Paris and went into the medical profession or set themselves up instead as merchants. The Bishop is none too pleased about that, I can tell you! You wouldn't be one of them?'

'No. And I'm not a newly-ordained priest, either.'

'Ah, they're easy,' said Thomas Creagh. 'They can accept chaplaincies or foundations for Masses to help them defray the expenses of their education. We have no problem with them. Why are you frowning, Mr O'Shaughnessy? Would it be that you're concerned about money – or the lack of it maybe?'

As Dick hesitated, the older man went on: 'I know full well that you have no money on you. I went through your pockets myself in search of coins to put by for you before Mary took your garments for washing, not wanting to

60

leave temptation in the girl's way. The men who attacked you, I'd say, saw to it that there was no money left.'

'They did.'

'Ah, well, there's so much lawlessness in the country these days,' Thomas Creagh said, resignedly. 'Wild days and no mistake. We can help you with money, Mr O'Shaughnessy. Don't be worrying your head about that. And if you bide your time awhile we can get you onto a boat. You must give news of his brother to Vincent Crowley. He likes to maintain there's no good in the man, but he'll be pleased to know that you came across him, all the same. And have another helping of badger. You have to build up your strength.'

'Don't draw attention to your presence. Stay in the house until we get you onto a boat.' So said Vincent, along with a few discontented grunts, after Liam's name was mentioned.

Staying in the house, biding his time was difficult for Dick who was not by nature patient. Soon he was bored and restless.

He decided to ask for pen and paper to write a letter to Ellen, to reassure her of his safety.

As he wrote he began to enjoy the process. He had always found it easy to talk to Ellen. Writing to her, he discovered, was every bit as satisfactory as conversing – even more so in one way, since she could not interrupt.

Vincent Crowley posted the letter for him. But in a week Dick had an urge to write to Ellen again and this time he confided: 'I want to make my mark on the world . . . It is not easy having an older brother who diminishes your accomplishments and makes light of your dreams.'

Writing in this vein was a release for him and he told her much more about himself than he realized. He did not bother to read the letter back. Had he done so, he might have had second thoughts about its contents.

The third time he put pen to paper he had the impression that Ellen was very close to him, her green eyes staring out of her impudent face. He felt a sharp twinge of nostalgia. But her presence was only an illusion. The real Ellen was thirty-eight whole miles away in Ballygriffin . . .

'I wish you were here,' wrote Dick impulsively. 'After all, what a shame it was that we couldn't ride together to Kinsale and journey on to France. I would like that more than anything.'

After Vincent Crowley had taken this letter to be posted he had important news for Dick.

'There's a French ship come in to Sandon quay, Mr O'Shaughnessy,' he said meaningfully. 'In a short time from now there will be visitors to the house. You could do well to make your preparations for a journey.'

They came to the corner house at midnight, a very tall young man with dark hair and his shorter, red-haired friend, and Mr Creagh conducted them in to the library where Dick had been instructed to wait for their arrival.

'It is the custom for students under these circumstances to act as liaison officers between the ship's captain and ourselves and to see to it that new recruits are escorted safely to Paris. Mr Philip Cantillon, Mr Roger De Lacy – Mr Richard O'Shaughnessy.'

'Dick . . .'

'Mr Dick O'Shaughnessy.'

'How do you do?' said the tall young man.

He must have had a wearying journey, Dick thought, the tired way he subsided into a chair. By contrast, Mr De Lacy seemed to be full of energy, drawing attention to himself and to the gifts the two young men had brought for the Creagh household.

'Cheeses, sir. And a barrel of cognac which has come from the Charente.'

'Cognac?' said Mr Creagh, unaware that the cognac in question had been purloined by Philip from his mother's cellar. 'A king amongst brandies! Would you not agree, Mr O'Shaughnessy?'

'I've never tasted cognac,' Dick admitted.

Or even heard of its existence.

'Never tasted cognac? How very strange!' said Roger De Lacy promptly.

Was that pity on his face?

But his tall, tired companion said: 'I envy you, Mr O'Shaughnessy. You're about to have a novel experience,' and cast a scathing look at his friend.

Mr Creagh was pressing a glass into Dick's hand and motioning to him to drink.

A distinctive aroma, soft, rich, mellow. As he sipped, Mr Creagh said: 'Is it not warm and full? With a slight taste of wood that comes out of the oak from which the barrel is made.'

'It's excellent.'

He sipped again appreciatively and Vincent's head came round the library door.

'Mr Creagh, we wouldn't want to be delaying too long. 'Tis time, I'd say, to be going to Sandon quay.'

He had said his farewells to Thomas Creagh and Vincent Crowley and had climbed onto the deck of the two-masted, twenty-gun corvette which had been waiting off Sandon quay, proudly flying the white and gold fleur-de-lys Bourbon ensign.

The ship was quite small, stocky and stubby and painted with black pitch from stem to stern, and only sixteen feet

63

across, but it might have been the greatest sailing ship in the world, the way his heart was pumping.

'. . . ridiculously short visit,' Philip Cantillon was saying, in French. 'If only we could have stayed longer, and been able to see something of the country.'

'The sooner we get home the better for me,' said Roger De Lacy with feeling. 'That is, if we reach Le Havre in safety with the British navy on full alert.'

'It's routine for the British to check privateers raiding commerce in the Channel,' Philip yawned. 'Anyway, although our little lady may be small she can out-run any of their frigates. And she's clean. *Her* bottom isn't tangled yet with seaweed.'

'She can't outmatch their gunpower. And she's hardly a pleasure to sail on.' Roger was not reassured.

'Now that she's unloaded her cargo she'll be faster, as well as lighter.'

'What did she unload?' asked Dick, watching the sailors closing the gun ports in case of heavy seas and sealing the haws and holes as a preliminary to departure.

He, too, had spoken in French. There was a brief pause before Roger, quirking an eyebrow at Philip, said: 'A linguist! Although the accent – '

'There's nothing wrong with Mr O'Shaughnessy's accent,' Philip retorted angrily.

As his two companions glared at each other, Dick looked away, back at the town which had been both cruel and tender in its dealings with him. In the moonlight he could see Compass Hill, once covered by a great oak forest, James's Fort, and Charles's Fort, where the ghosts of a Black Dog and a White Lady were sometimes reportedly glimpsed.

'. . . and wine. I shouldn't imagine that we're carrying cargo back. Potatoes, maybe. Does Ireland offer much more in the way of exports these days?'

Roger had recovered his composure.

'She offers soldiers,' Philip said in his quiet, weary voice. 'The most valuable export of all. You're not the only recruit on board this vessel, Mr O'Shaughnessy – just the only one who has the makings of an officer. There are a dozen or so ordinary soldiers below decks.'

'Crammed in below decks,' Roger corrected. 'Come down to the lower deck, Mr O'Shaughnessy. The headroom down there is so limited that Philip here has either to stoop or sit.'

Ducking under the timber beams and the knees that supported the deck above, the three young men reached that part of the lower deck where a lantern had been placed on a primitive, hinged table that could be folded back against the wall.

'Gloomy. The whole vessel is badly ventilated, too.'

'Why are you in such low spirits, Roger?' Philip wanted to know. 'We have enough illumination for our needs. Do you play piquet, Mr O'Shaughnessy? I brought two packs of cards along.'

'It's one of my favourite card games.'

Dick had always excelled at cards, and been lucky at them as well. Willie and he had often played piquet together. He must write to Willie from France, and to his father and mother and sisters, and tell them he was safe.

'Shall we draw for deal and choice of seat?'

'Why not?'

'*Une dame de pique* – the queen of spades,' said Roger, looking at the card Philip had drawn. 'You're going to face a formidable battle, Philip – and probably lose it! To draw the queen of spades is to declare that you cherish your own injuries.'

'And to draw the king of spades is to cure oneself of such wounds,' Philip said, seeing Dick's card. 'A short-lived victory. After all, the lower card has choice of seat,

65

and it's my deal first. I may do better. Cut the pack for me.'

Watching Philip deal the cards, two at a time, twelve to each player, Dick felt that he was on home ground, in spite of being aboard a foreign ship. The crude, coarse-papered cards, too, were familiar: those used by the family at Kilawillen had also been made in France.

As his opponent spread the remaining eight cards down on the table to form the *stock* he realized that the vessel was actually setting sail. Commands were shouted from the deck above. I hope to God that I won't make a fool of myself by being seasick, Dick thought. He had no idea how his stomach might react to the journey and whether or not it would obey his silent command to behave.

'How much?'

'Thirty-six.'

'Good.'

'I think I'll leave the two of you to your game and go back on deck,' volunteered Roger. 'I don't feel quite so confined up there.'

'Yes, do go!'

'*Tierce.*'

Dick was concentrating fiercely on the game, conscious, at the same time, of the response of the little ship to the undulation of the waves.

Philip, who also had a sequence of three, was observing Dick's game with interest. The man knew exactly what he was doing, he realized, as, playing his next card, he announced his cumulative score. He lost and was rubi-coned. They began to play again.

Engrossed, neither of them heard the shout from the upper deck as a sailor yelled out: '*Prenez garde!*'

The first indication that something was wrong came to them only when Roger, pale-faced, arrived breathless at the table.

It was a full minute before he managed to gasp: 'My God, how can you two go on playing? Can't you hear what they're shouting up there?'

'Oh? What is it?'

'*Philip!* There's a British frigate in pursuit of us. It's flying the Red Ensign. I knew something ghastly was going to happen. We should never have embarked on such a foolhardy mission.'

From where the three of them stood on the top deck they could see the three-masted, full-rigged frigate quite clearly.

'How many guns do you suppose it's carrying?'

'Thirty. Forty. Does it matter? What we're concerned with is its speed.'

'Forty? They're damn' close now.'

'Oh, be calm, Roger. Proximity doesn't mean that much.' Philip was unruffled, his only apparent problem his habitual fatigue. 'Naval ordnance is notoriously ineffective. You'll agree with me when the British begin firing. Roger?'

But Roger had once again disappeared down the companionway, to hide on the lower deck.

'You're not afraid of a British frigate, are you?' Philip said lightly to Dick. 'Although I suppose it's unwise to turn ourselves into targets. Move down here. It's as good a vantage point as any.'

From where they stood Dick could see their own gunners. As the British frigate drew nearer each man estimated his range, elevating his gun by means of a wedge under a threaded shaft.

At the same time Dick felt the corvette pick up speed, ready at once to defend herself and to flee from the frigate's path.

When the first iron shell hit the deck, causing the ship

to convulse so violently that for one dreadful moment Dick thought that it would overturn, Philip's hand dropped casually on his shoulder. Turning to look at the other man, Dick was startled by the expression on Philip's face. It was as if he had been transformed: was brilliant, ecstatic, shining. A man out of a legend. Dick thought of Midir, King of Longford, husband of exquisite Etain of the golden tresses and rowan-red lips; he who had been converted by his own magic in order that he might steal back a wife coveted by an acquisitive High King. After which that other metamorphosis: Midir and Etain a pair of swans, flying forever together.

'Philip?' he said, using the other man's Christian name for the first time.

But his new friend seemed hardly aware of Dick's existence.

A second shell hit the deck. Their own vessel was veering south-west, hampered by the prevailing winds which came from the same direction, yet the corvette increased speed.

In unison, their own gunners returned the enemy's fire and the hand on Dick's shoulder tightened its grip.

'We've hit them – several times.' Philip's blue eyes were burning with an unnatural intensity. 'My God, man, this will be a hard battle! Our gunners are superior – I am convinced of it. If only I could be amongst them.'

But we may be mortally hit – sink – drown, Dick reminded himself, since he seemed to be feeling no emotion whatsoever, neither the fear that had sent Roger scuttling below decks nor the elation of gentle, exhausted Philip.

If I am to die, may God forgive me my sins.

In that state, he saw the high dorsal fin, the rounded head, the nearly uniform glossy back, and he blinked, because that same image was duplicated, and then repeated innumerable times, down there in the water.

Dream images. Eyes with white stripes – enormous . . .

He *was* dreaming. How could he not be, since the creatures in the water were rising to the surface, exposing and opening their nostrils to discharge the exhausted air from their lungs into huge fountains of water?

Surely he was asleep?

Except that the hand on his shoulder was now gripping the cloth of his jacket, threatening to tear it apart in the manner of a man who was wide awake.

And the owner of the hand was laughing so loudly that Dick was sure that the sound could be heard above the noise of gunshot.

'Whales!'

'*What?*'

'Killer whales. There are dozens of them in the water – look – between us and the British frigate. It's a miracle, Dick! They're forming a blockade between us, slowing the enemy down better than any of our guns are capable of doing!'

Another bellow of laughter, to which he seemed to be adding his own rumbustious guffaw.

'Voracious creatures,' said Philip approvingly. 'They're common in these waters. But I doubt that the British navy carries harpoon guns. What luck. See how the frigate is dropping behind. We're going to get away.'

5

So Dick was in good hands. And, having fended her off
when she had suggested riding alongside him, was now
missing her company.

His letters pleased and stimulated Ellen. If only she
could join him! Briefly, she toyed with the idea of saddling
Pooka and setting off straightaway for Kinsale, only to
dismiss the idea since Dick would very likely have left the
port by the time that she got there.

Well, maybe she would go to France anyway. Her two
cousins, Nano and Ann Nagle, had been living in Paris
for some time. They, too, would be delighted to have her
with them – she was sure of that.

As she ministered to Liam Crowley in secret, noting
with satisfaction that he was already on the mend, Ellen
wondered what Papa would have to say if she were to
suggest to him that she spent a year abroad.

She wrinkled her snub nose, pondering. Mama would
be bound to object, protesting that her baby should not
undertake such a dangerous journey. If her mother envisaged ogres lurking on the roads of west Cork, what
horrors could she conjure up on the high seas, and the
streets of the French capital?

Ellen was convinced that no harm would come to
herself on such a journey, but when she considered it she
found that she was worrying about Dick, who must by
now be at sea.

'Here, have this dish of cream. Maybe 'twill make you
fat,' she said to Liam Crowley.

It isn't only me that she has on her mind, the sick man

70

thought to himself. And, his concern mirroring Ellen's, he said: 'I hope himself is well.'

In fact, Dick was soon under threat again. As the corvette reached the active waters off Plymouth, the weather worsened. The sea swelled belligerently. It was as if some powerful and sadistic giant was stirring the contents of a broiling cauldron.

The only good thing, from Dick's point of view, was that his stomach, by then grown accustomed to sailing, had not, after all, let him down.

Others, less fortunate, retched and heaved, spewing out at random all over the ship so that everywhere he went he was in danger of slipping on vomit. The stench, the cramped conditions in which they lived made Roger more depressed than ever, and he outlined his fears of the British ships which, he said, would be bound to arrest them at the mouth of the Channel.

'We'll have to run past at least half a dozen vessels. They're bound to spot us.'

'It didn't happen on the outward-bound journey,' Philip pointed out. 'You can pass within five miles of such a fleet at night without being seen. The storm might even assist us. The sky couldn't be blacker and there's no trace of a moon.'

'There's still the sea to contend with.'

When Roger, looking green, had collapsed into a corner, Philip began to chat to Dick about their mutual ambition to join the Irish Brigade.

'So many things are happening in this war. Until last month, France, as you know, was officially ranged only against England. At least, now, it's out in the open. We have *declared* war on Austria and Sardinia, too. With Spain and Bavaria as our allies *and* Frederick of Prussia,

71

for all that he pretends to hate the French, as a supporter, we are bound to win in the end.'

It was the longest speech Philip had ever made to him and Dick saw that his new friend's eyes were glistening with the same fanaticism they had shown when the ship had been hit by shells.

Before Dick could reply, Philip added: 'The war is gathering fresh momentum. I cannot wait to leave college and join the Brigade. I *have* to fight. It is all I want to do.'

'For the rest of your life?'

Philip looked surprised.

'Of course. Don't *you* intend to make a career in the army?'

'I'm not sure if I want to be a soldier all my life.'

'But if you're not a soldier, what will you be?' Philip asked, disapprovingly.

The answer – 'I'm not yet sure, but I do know that I want to be *successful*' – seemed woefully inadequate, especially in comparison to Philip's clear vision of his own future.

A commotion breaking out below decks came to Dick's rescue.

'A British ship is going down,' Philip said, making sense out of the excited shouts. 'It will deflect the attention of the enemy vessels. Roger, you can come out of your corner! I think the danger has passed.'

And so on to Le Havre. And from there to Rouen, where regimental drummers were beating up for volunteers to serve in the army as they arrived, and where they took rooms at the oddly-named Sign of the British Arms, an inn frequented by the captains of such corvettes as theirs.

Having rested, they set out on horseback for the capital.

'I wonder if the college will assist me to find lodgings?' Dick said.

But Philip insisted: 'Stay in our apartment. It is much more comfortable than anything you will find through the college, I can assure you.'

'Are you sure? Will your mother not mind?'

'She'll think of you as a second son. And my sister will be delighted.'

'I wonder!' Roger intervened darkly. 'Perhaps you should ask their opinions first.'

He scowled at Dick, and, to emphasize his displeasure at the invitation, he edged ahead of the others.

'What's the matter?'

'With Roger? He is in love with my sister. He's jealous of you already.'

'And your sister? Is she in love with him?'

Philip said dryly: 'I very much doubt that Catherine has ever cared for anyone more than she cares for herself. Be warned!'

It was just after seven in the evening when the three young men reached the Palais-Royal district by which time Paris had lapsed into its deepest calm of the day or night.

'What has happened?' Dick asked, perplexed. 'Does everyone here go to bed so early?'

Philip and Roger laughed.

'You won't think that in two hours' time when the spectacle begins,' Roger said knowledgeably. 'This is the period when people are preparing to go out to supper, or to the opera, or to visit friends. It's the most dangerous time to walk about the city. It may appear peaceful, but violence lurks everywhere, believe me. Paris is plagued by thieves and rapists.'

'It's so magnificent. And it seems such a wealthy city.'

73

'Only on this side,' Philip said sadly. 'In the Faubourg Saint-Antoine the people are in rags.'

'But everyone who counts lives in Palais-Royal,' Roger added.

'And most of them are too frightened to see what happens elsewhere,' Philip said, so softly that only Dick caught what he said.

They had turned into rue Vivienne and Roger, becoming more animated, asked eagerly: 'Do you think Catherine's convent will have closed yet for the summer?'

'Most likely my sister will have persuaded the nuns that *her* term should end earlier than that of the other pupils! If you're asking me whether Catherine will be at home this evening, the answer is – probably yes.'

'Then I will call on her – and on your mother,' said Roger quickly. 'How good it is to be back in Paris – although Dick here must be finding it strange. Country people take some time to get used to our ways – and Parisians, I'm afraid, tend to be somewhat intolerant of the provincials. I hope he won't have too bad a time.'

'I think Dick won't find it difficult to adjust,' Philip said sharply, and led the way through the doorway of a house with rose glass windows, upstairs to the top floor. 'Maman – Catherine?'

Dick had just enough time to wonder if the sister would be even half as hospitable and kind as the brother when suddenly there she was. A tiny girl in a yellow wrapping-gown with softly falling sleeves. A creature so feminine, so lovely, so enticing that it was all he could do not to rush forward and take her right into his arms.

He forced himself to stay still. He blinked, then continued to look at her intently.

Horrible, dark thoughts haunted Ellen when Dick did not write again, for surely he must be dead.

74

It was true that if he had been captured on the quay at Kinsale and subsequently hanged, news of his fate would have ultimately reached her in Ballygriffin.

But what if he had drowned in the Channel? Who would tell her about that? Certainly not the fairies who lived in *Tir fo Thuinn*, the land beneath the waves.

When you reasoned it out, the only other alternative was that he had succeeded in getting to France to be set about by brigands who had beaten the life out of him.

None of us will know his fate, Ellen mourned, when six weeks had gone by without a letter.

And then her mother announced that the O'Shaughnessys at Kilawillen had heard from Dick; that he had written to them from Paris saying that he was studying philosophy and the liberal arts at the Collège des Grassins, and staying with wonderful friends.

Ellen was almost as stunned by this news as if Clare had brought confirmation of Dick's demise, and every bit as confused.

'*What?*'

'That's not polite, Ellen. I said I met Ida O'Shaughnessy in Mallow this morning and they're very happy at Kilawillen House, having got a letter from Dick. Are you feeling all right, child? I hope you're not going to take after your mother and have problems with your health.'

'I'm well enough.'

Or as well as she could be, under the circumstances, wondering why Dick hadn't written a similar letter to her.

But Dick, having done his duty by the family in Kilawillen, was too taken up with his new life to give further thoughts to writing to anyone else.

Paris enthralled him. In 1744 it was, as Philip had said, a city of stark contrasts. There was lively, elegant Paris, as typified by the rue Saint-Honoré and the Palais-Royal area: the shops and the *ateliers*, where the most beautiful objects were made so that the wealthy could decorate their homes with wood sculpture and stone figurines and little flower-pots and gadgets. There were the cafés to which you went not only to drink coffee but to be seen by the *beau monde*, not that Dick cared much about that. There was much entertainment – little theatres and the *opéra-comique*, and, on the boulevards, street-jugglers, acrobats, Spanish dancers and even exotic performing animals.

Further out of town there were circuses with dogs and fighting wild boars and lions and tigers in them; and there were firework displays, as well.

But why bother to go out of town, Dick asked, when Philip suggested doing so. There was so much to do in Paris.

They could walk in the Tuileries Gardens; or sit on the terraces drinking lemonade, marvelling at the variety of toys, confectionery, sweets and cakes that were sold in that vicinity.

Or simply gossip. Parisians, Dick discovered, had an insatiable appetite for speculation and that summer there was plenty to feed their curiosity.

The best of it – the most salacious – concerned the king and his mistress, Madame de Châteauroux.

'She is the sister of the Comtesse de Mailly, and of the Marquise de Vintimille, both of whom were his mistresses previously,' Philip explained.

'All *three* of them?'

'Oh, yes. Madame de Vintimille took him away from Madame de Mailly, and then died giving birth to his baby – that's the Comte du Luc. The king went back to Madame de Mailly after that and she adopted the child. But then he fell in love with Madame de Châteauroux who is very beautiful and apparently most unpleasant.

76

She has made King Louis exile Madame de Mailly from the court. The poor thing is known as the Widow.'

Philip enjoyed Dick's company so much that he sometimes even forgot about his shyness and talked much more than usual. The two young men were sitting over coffee in the Café de la Régence and Dick, with one eye on the nearby chess-player, said feelingly: 'The king must lead a very complicated life. I would hate to be him.'

Philip shrugged.

'I suppose he is bored by the queen. He had ten children by her by the time he was twenty-seven, but she is a dowdy woman, very pious and probably not much fun to be with. And love for the aristocrats is a game – no more. Does it offend you?'

'It's God's business to pass judgement, not mine. I loathe earthly moralists, don't you?'

'Naturally. Anyway, here is the latest gossip from the court circles. The king has gone off to join the army on the eastern frontier and not only has Madame de Châteauroux gone with him, but also her *fourth* sister, the Duchesse de Lauraguais! What do you make of that?'

But Dick was beginning to lose interest in the intricacies that could arise out of the passionate Bourbon temperament.

'The French troops – I mean *our* troops – are bound to be inspired by the king's presence.'

'Let's hope so. The French, so brilliant in so many fields, are not, you must understand, natural soldiers. Marshal Saxe, our leader, is the very first to admit it. It's all a matter of discipline. At the beginning of a campaign, he says, our army is well equipped and in fine order but all too often it returns from battle ruined. Our commanders admit that they have difficulty in restraining our men from pillaging and deserting. That's the big difference between the Prussians and ourselves. At Dettingen *their*

77

degree of manoeuvre and of exactness was remarkable – and yet they had no previous experience of war.'

'What was their secret?'

'The men obeyed orders implicitly. *We* must put away our independent thoughts – our imagination, the qualities that in other areas make this nation so exciting, and, as soldiers, develop a precise combination of military talent and efficiency.'

To develop his own military talent and efficiency, it was necessary for Dick to enter another, very different sector of Paris, the scholastic and religious purlieus around the Sorbonne where, as well as the university, there were the Jesuit colleges and houses and a number of convents. At the Collège des Grassins, in the company of a hundred and twenty other students, he was learning to handle a sword and musket, as well as furthering his more conventional education.

He was gratified to be told by his instructor, Father Patrick Corr, that he had the makings of a good swordsman who understood instinctively the importance of thrusting with a sword, thrusting rather than cutting, which produced wounds more likely to heal, and he was warned not to let excitement get the better of him so that he attacked with the flat, instead of leading with the edge of his weapon.

And he was getting along very well with his fellow students.

The priests, Dick soon realized, struggled hard to find money to maintain the college building, and to buy books, although they had general benefactors amongst the French and the wealthier Irish settlers.

But no matter how arduous life might be for the clerics at the college, it bore no comparison to the harsh existence eked out by the Parisians living near the Bastille, where hunger had reduced men, women and children to the level of scavenging animals.

'Go there at your peril,' Philip warned, for he knew poor Paris well, but Dick was determined to confront every aspect of his adopted city.

In spite of the admonition he went to the Bastille district, to witness the savage scenes that took place in the streets as men fought to the death, egged on by screaming women, while child thieves sought indiscriminately for anything to steal. At such times he thought that the service provided by the *falot*, who would escort customers to and from their homes for a modest fee, was indispensable for those who could not afford full-time servants.

'Pouf – I cannot understand why you visit the ugly side of Paris,' commented Catherine, when he returned from one such expedition.

For there was always Catherine waiting to beguile him. Her beauty irradiated the apartment. Sexually, he was acutely aware of her.

In Paris, he thought ruefully, it was all too easy to dwell incessantly upon sex. Whether the details embraced the latest royal amour or an *affaire* closer to one's own heart, the French behaved as if coupling was a natural and vital pastime rather than sinful unless for the procreation of children. Although such artists as Jean-Baptiste Chardin might depict humble genre scenes, Catherine herself introduced him to the work of François Boucher, whose work was often concerned with the female nude in a completely uninhibited way.

His dreams transposed the pearly-white painted bodies with Catherine's. Awake, he struggled to obliterate the fantasy. The Parisian heat conspired with this new sexual awareness to add to his discomfort. The summer of 1744 was particularly hot. When, at six in the morning, the bakers brought their bread into the city to sell and the wives of ironmongers stirred sugar into their husband's café-au-lait, to give them extra strength, Dick was already well awake, hot and itchy from the heat.

'No wonder you suffer from the sun, wandering around Paris when you could be in the apartment, keeping me company,' Catherine teased.

Mme Cantillon, in contrast, made a fuss of him.

'You poor boy, you should be purged and bled and sweated. I will give you an ointment made out of sulphur and hog's lard. Sulphur is excellent for itch. Catherine, poor Dick is suffering from heat-itch.'

'Poor Dick,' agreed Catherine tonelessly, for it was not her policy to show too much compassion to her admirers. 'But, by being unwell, you are in good company. I hear that the king is also ill, at Metz.'

'All Paris knows that,' said her mother scornfully.

'Ah, but does all Paris know that the *dévot* party has driven Madame de Châteauroux away from him? I heard while I was shopping that the king has made a public confession. He has asked pardon for his promiscuity and for the scandalous example he has set. People are saying that the *dévots* and the clergy are alerting the queen to the fact that a new reign is about to begin.'

'When the king recovers he will not be so pious.'

'He may not recover. I will hear more news tomorrow. Dick, you will come shopping with me? *Why* look at unpleasant things when there are so many delights on this side of the city? And as for visiting Les Halles, as you tell me you have been doing, I am told that the smell there is disgusting – cheese and fish and leather and offal all mixed together, and rubbish all over the street!'

'It *is* like that,' Dick admitted. 'But it's lively. The market stalls and the noise and the bustle – '

'Tomorrow you will come with *me*,' repeated Catherine. 'I'm going to Monsieur Maille's shop to buy a lotion for my hair but afterwards I will take you to purchase the best chocolates in Paris. There is a confectioner's at the rue de Neuve des Petits-Champs where they also make liqueurs, and sell brandy for export.'

'Didn't Philip have a plan for Dick for tomorrow?' Mme Cantillon intervened. 'I'm almost sure – '

But Catherine said: 'Dick – you will be late for your lesson with Father Corr. Hurry!'

She had just time to shut the door behind him when her mother spoke again.

'You knew that Philip was going to suggest an outing. You want to spoil their friendship. Even as a child you were always like that, wanting to take your brother's toys just because they were his.'

'And you've always preferred Philip to me, haven't you?' Catherine said bitterly. 'Whereas I was Papa's favourite. He had great love for his baby daughter – more, maybe, than he felt for his own wife . . .'

To her satisfaction, she saw her mother flinch.

Catherine was looking her loveliest. She wore a wide-skirted pink dress with an *échelle* stomacher and her hair was drawn back from her face into ringlets at the back of her neck; Dick was as impressed as she had intended.

'Shouldn't we invite Philip to come with us?' he asked before the two of them set out for the shops, but Catherine shook her dark head.

'Maman is very concerned that he apply himself more to his philosophic studies. She worries that he is only concerned with becoming a soldier. Now, first we must buy my hair lotion . . .'

When this had been achieved and Dick had examined the labels of M. Maille's other bottles – vinegars for virgins and for stopping bad breath; lotions for spots and asthma – they walked together to M. Sauvol's establishment on the corner where the rue des Bons Enfants meets the rue de Neuve des Petits-Champs.

'Good morning, Monsieur.'

'Mademoiselle Cantillon – I am enchanted!'

Throughout the Palais-Royal district the air was redolent of perfume and embrocations, very different from the fetid odours of 'bad Paris'; but in M. Sauvol's shop, as Catherine selected the chocolates, Dick's senses were assailed by another smell, warm, mellow and rich.

Why, all of a sudden, was he thinking of Mr Thomas Creagh's library, on the night when visitors from France had arrived:

'That smell – it's cognac!' he said triumphantly.

'You are correct, sir,' M. Sauvol concurred. 'As well as selling cognac by the bottle I distribute it in bulk for retailing and export. Mademoiselle Cantillon here will be able to tell you all about this fine brandy. Her mother tells me that she comes from Cognac, the town in which it is distilled and from which it gets its name.'

Instead of returning the shopkeeper's smile, Catherine looked sulky.

'I think of myself as a Parisienne,' she said, quite put out at being linked with the provincials. 'Dick, it's time we left.'

'I suppose it is,' Dick said reluctantly. 'Yours must be an interesting business, sir. Perhaps we'll talk again. Catherine?'

Catherine's lips were pursed. The sky, too, was dark. Dear God, but it is hot, thought Dick. He thought ruefully of cool Kilawillen.

The green valley. The shade offered by the trees . . .

Between the trees strode a girl in a red cloak, her hair lifted out by the refreshing breeze.

'Ellen!' he said in his mind, pleased, as ever, to see her.

Alongside him Catherine walked purposefully towards the rue de Grenelle where M. Debois welcomed her obsequiously and asked if he could paint her portrait for nothing.

'How charming,' said Catherine laconically, and, as if to reward him, finally managed to smile.

6

The only letter Ellen got from Paris that summer was the one that her cousin Nano wrote, saying that Ann was unwell and that the sisters were therefore returning to Ireland. Could Ellen postpone her visit until the following year when, hopefully, they would be back in Paris and happy for her to stay with them?

Altogether, too many people sickened that year, although King Louis recovered and, as Mme Cantillon had predicted, promptly sent for Madame de Château-roux to return to the palace.

But the king's mistress was running a fever: she rose from her bed in the rue du Bac, bathed, collapsed, and died.

And although, at Kilawillen, Liam Crowley got better and was found work in the fields, Clare Nagle complained, not of asthma so much, as of a pain in her heart.

That was in August. By September Clare was spending most of her time in bed with Ellen acting as nurse. As the broad, flat-topped leaves of the alder trees turned black, Ellen was a virtual prisoner in the house, watching the autumnal changes only from the window of her parents' bedroom, longing to escape but too concerned about her mother's health to leave her alone for more than a short while.

On *púca* night, when Irish children were forbidden to touch the fruits which the spirits were said to be spitting on, Liam Crowley fixed a plain wooden cross over the entrance to the stables, to ward off evil influences.

Everyone else seemed to be feasting that night, as they

always did on November Eve, drinking punch and eating apple pie, throwing nut-shells into the fire and foretelling many strange things from what they found in the ashes. But though the gargantuan fire made out of black earth was hot enough, throwing out great belches of conversation-stopping smoke into the lower part of the house, the Nagles did not feel festive enough to hold a party.

'All the same, this is the first year ever we have not played Catch the Apple,' lamented Rory, who was only half grownup and still hankered after childish games.

'Ah, none of us has the heart for it, not with mother the way she is,' Ellen said.

She was cross with him, and with her other brothers, and with her father, too, for the effective way they all dodged the sickroom, sneaking off to friends at night instead. Under normal circumstances she would have stood up to them, but she was over-tired lately, not sleeping well now that she had moved into her mother's bedroom to keep vigil with the invalid, while her father slept with the boys.

Ellen stayed at home on *Margadh Mór* when Donagh and Rory went into Mallow to bring home the Christmas fare, having selected the best wines and spices. But Christmas was sombre. When the family went through the customary ritual of drinking three sips of salted water before dinner, which was conducive to good health, they all grew silent, thinking of the sick woman upstairs.

Gruesome January turned into grim February. At the end of that month Clare suffered a sudden failure to the left side of her heart and stagnation of blood to her lungs. Her circulation did not re-adjust. Ellen's term of imprisonment in the house came to an abrupt and tragic end.

It was at her mother's funeral that she heard further news of Dick.

'Ellen.' Nano Nagle, who had come down from Dublin to attend the Requiem Mass, got hold of her. 'I met Dick O'Shaughnessy in Paris before we left and I told him that you had been thinking of joining us there. Give my love to Ellen if you see her, he said, and tell her that she would have a great time over here.'

'Did he now?'

It was disgraceful feeling that way at her mother's funeral, but Ellen was charged with renewed life.

'He loves it in Paris himself,' Nano went on. 'He seemed to be doing well in his studies and he's made good friends. I have his address, for he insisted that I take it. Here it is. Why don't you write to him?'

'Maybe I will,' said Ellen, thinking, wondering if Dick had perhaps used Nano as a means of getting a message through to herself.

Because, all of a sudden, an entirely different perspective on what had happened came to her.

Dick had written *three* letters to her from Kinsale, but she had never answered any of them.

It was true that he had not given her an address in Paris to which to write, but he had sent this to his mother. Knowing that Ellen, in the matter of attending to Liam Crowley, would be over and back to Kilawillen House, he could have taken it for granted that his address would be handed on; that she would have asked his mother for it.

He was probably disappointed not to have heard from her.

Dick stayed in the forefront of Ellen's mind all that day, distracting her from grief, and while her father and brothers were downstairs with the guests in the evening, attempting to drown their sorrows with drink, she went up to her bedroom and took out Dick's letters.

'. . . wish you were here . . . shame it was that we

couldn't ride together to Kinsale and journey on to France. I would like that more than anything . . .'

He had been longing for her company.

She must put things right between the two of them, write him a long letter explaining about her mother's illness the way he would understand how pre-occupied she had been recently.

She very nearly did write. She got as far as taking out her quill pen and a pot of pokeberry ink, and was searching around for paper when a shout from downstairs distracted her.

'Ellen?'

'I'm coming, Pa . . .'

'We have people in the house, girl.'

She would write to Dick later.

But after the funeral a new idea came to her, one that responded to the new surge of life within her.

'Would you not give us something more exciting to eat than dry bread and porridge?' grumbled Donagh while this idea was fermenting.

'It's Lent,' Ellen said tartly. 'You'll have to drink your black tea and put up with it for now.'

Donagh was still grumbling to himself when Ellen went into the fields in search of Liam Crowley.

'Liam,' she said, 'I'm going to France, to join Master Dick. I take it that your brother Vincent could be of use to me, in getting me onto a boat.'

Liam put his illicit mug of buttermilk down on the right side of the squeezy-stile and rested a skinny arm over it, to hide what it contained.

'France is it?' he said weakly, the lines going up and down on his ruddy brow as he digested Ellen's words. 'You – want – to get aboard a boat?'

He spoke slowly, like a man in shock, as indeed he was.

'Yes,' said Ellen. 'Now don't start exclaiming in protest,

87

Liam, because I don't want to waste my time with your gasps and splutters. Have you heard lately from Vincent?'

'I have,' Liam told her. 'Isn't he always after me, to go down to Kinsale and get on a boat meself. Only aren't the English ships keeping watch on the town and the other south-west ports at the present moment. That neck of the woods isn't safe, Miss Ellen – not now. At least wait for a month or two until the English are out of it. There'll be many more boats for you then.'

'I've had enough waiting to last me a lifetime,' Ellen said decisively. 'If I can't get out from the south or the west I'll sail instead from Dublin.'

'*Dublin!*'

'Yes!'

'What would you go to Dublin for, Miss Ellen?' Liam asked, wondering if he could believe his own ears. 'Isn't it miles out of your way?'

'I've always wanted to visit Dublin. And from there I'll travel to England and after that to France.'

'And how would a woman travelling alone manage the likes of a journey like that?' Liam demanded. 'This is a terrible wild country, Miss Ellen, and Dublin is a city of fearful excesses, with drunken men carrying swords and no gentleman taking his station in life until he has smelt powder. You'd be poxed with luck to come out of the place alive, let alone consider journeying on to England and France on your own.'

He paused, pining for a sup of buttermilk. From what he could judge from Ellen's expression his admonitions were falling on barren ground.

'If it's so dangerous for a woman then I'll travel dressed as a man,' she said to his further horror. 'Everyone tells me that I'm too tall for a girl so I'll take some of the boys' clothes with me, and I'll speak like the settlers in Mallow, and no one will dare molest me.'

'They will,' said Liam grimly. 'Oh they will! Unless – '
He stopped, biting his lip.

'Unless?'

'Unless I come with you, Miss Ellen, to make sure that they do not.'

'You? And what would you do with yourself, once we got over to France?'

But Liam was picking up his mug of buttermilk, holding it before him in a defiant kind of a way, straightening his shoulders.

'Vincent is right, Miss Ellen,' he said thoughtfully. 'It's high time I joined the army and became one of them Wild Geese that Ireland is so proud of. *That's* what I'll do in France. And I'll write to Vincent. I'd love to see his face when he knows what it is I've done.'

When her mother had drawn her attention to the jewellery that would ultimately be hers, Ellen had shown little interest in the rings and lockets and pendants that Clare Nagle had owned, and she had not thought of them since. Faced with the necessity to provide travelling expenses for Liam and herself, her legacy took on a new, more important dimension.

I'll sell it, Ellen thought. For what use are these rings and lockets and pendants, being dead things, sad relics from my point of view, although Pa might feel differently. So I had better not sell them in Mallow, lest he catch sight of them in Mr Herbert's window and be hurt by what I have done. I'll take them with me, hidden on my person, and dispose of them in the first big town we find.

Their journey would take them through Cahir and Cashel, Maryborough and Portarlington, and then on to Monasterevin and Kildare and Newbridge and Naas, after which there was Dublin.

'I've talked to people who have ridden to Dublin,' said

Ellen to Liam. 'Seven miles an hour is what we can reckon upon. We must allow for two weeks to get up there, allowing for hitches.'

There were bound to be hitches, Liam thought morosely. Ellen was elated about the forthcoming trip but the more he considered it the more troubled he became, wondering what her father would do to him if he found the two of them on the road.

When he mentioned his misgivings to Ellen, however, she dismissed them: 'We'll wait until Pa and the boys are off somewhere for the day and we'll get a good start on them, just to keep you happy.'

''Twould be hard for me to be that,' Liam said in a melancholy voice, but Ellen took no notice.

The opportunity for which she was looking manifested itself a few days later.

'There'll be a bull-bait at Mallow tomorrow,' Donagh announced. 'All of us men will go.'

He looked over at Ellen as he spoke, waiting for his sister to say once more that it was a cruel sport that permitted dogs to snap at a bull's muzzle or dewlap or penis but, to his surprise, she did not rise to his own bait.

In fact, next day, when Ellen saw the men take out the specially-bred, huge-jawed hound, prior to leaving for Mallow, the sorrow she felt was not for the animal destined to suffer but for her own plight, to be parting from them for an unknown length of time.

'You're all right, aren't you, Ellen girl?' her father asked, a routine question to which no answer was expected.

'*Slán leat!*' the boys yelled, and with a clatter of hooves and a flick of reins they were gone.

Thirty minutes later Ellen was in the caves, changing out of her black sack mourning-dress into knee-breeches, roll-ups, an undress coat, and a sleeved vest with a high, stiff cambric stock which buckled at the back of her neck. Over the stock she arranged a black tie, and she crammed her long, thick, dark hair in tightly under Donagh's big black hat.

''Tis Master Donagh himself you are!' exclaimed Liam when he caught up with her presently. 'Or maybe Master Kevin . . .'

'Is there plenty of food?'

'Isn't the horse destroyed with the load,' he told her, and looked anxiously up at the sky.

It was covered with grey clouds so thick, so low-lying that he wondered if they were not going to roll down on their two heads, and make a dust devil out of their bodies.

There were no fences between the badly-maintained road and the wild green fields. They encountered no carriages, only the occasional block-wheel cart and rough sleigh on which produce was being dragged in the direction of Mallow. For many miles they did not talk, being locked into their own thoughts.

Ellen was considering the possibility that they might not be able to dispose of her jewellery until they got to Dublin.

'We may have to sleep out in the open under a tree or in the ruins of a house or a castle,' she observed to Liam when they got to Doneraile and were riding by the splendid forest park of the St Leger family.

'The two of us in the same place?' Liam's scalp prickled with fear as he thought of her father's anger.

'Or in the corner of a dry ditch,' Ellen went on.

'If we can find a dry one.'

They lapsed back into silence, Ellen thinking how pleased Dick was going to be when he saw her in Paris, and Liam questioning his own sanity in having embarked on a long and dangerous journey in the company of a girl just turned seventeen.

Well into the evening, too tired to go further, they stopped in the rain outside a miserable cabin, not more than the height of a man, badly in need of rethatching, which had been built into the side of a hill.

Ellen knocked on the rickety door and a gaunt woman of about thirty answered.

'*Dia daoibh.*'

Her red petticoat was nothing more than rags and her shawl was filthy dirty. The floor of the room beyond her had been fashioned out of cow-dung. A fire burnt in the middle of it, although there was no chimney and on a heap of straw three small naked children snuggled together along with a pig, a dog, a huddle of hens and one bedraggled duck.

'*Dia duit,*' Ellen said, returning the woman's greeting. 'We are in need of shelter.'

'Come in. We only have *pratas* to eat.'

'We have enough food for the house,' Ellen said, ignoring Liam's raised eyebrows. 'Is your husband out in the fields yet?'

The woman smiled sadly.

'He's gone from us this long while. To France. To fight in the army, and not a word heard from him since.'

'We're also bound for France.'

'Maybe your paths will cross yet,' said the woman.

But there was no conviction in her voice.

Woken on the hard floor by a snuffling pig, Ellen laughed again, this time at the spectacle of Liam lying flat on his back with his mouth wide open.

'Wake up,' she said, nudging him in the ribs, 'it's time to be on our way,' and turned to confront two of the naked children who were gazing at her with big, curious eyes.

On an impulse she reached deep into the pockets of Rory's undress coat where her jewellery was concealed and pulled out a gold pendant with a crystal frame bearing the inscription *Je ne m'attache qu'à toi*. As the woman of the house came in carrying a pail of rain-water Ellen pressed the locket into her free hand.

'You can sell it, maybe,' she said, and wondered how and when.

The woman tilted back her head, drawing herself upright.

'There's no charge for shelter.'

'I know. But who knows but that we might not find your husband on our travels, after all. I'd be able to assure him that you were well . . .'

In a matter of minutes they were back on the road again.

'I wonder if her husband is still alive,' mused Ellen. 'Though if he is, you would think that he would have been in touch with them, so I suppose he must be dead.'

'Or dodging them,' Liam said cynically. 'There are a few men that do use the Wild Geese as an excuse, Miss Nagle, for leaving their children and wives. Don't I know that full well, for wasn't my own father one of them, a tarry-boy by all accounts, chasing after the women and letting my own poor mother, God bless her soul, bring up three sons on her own.'

'Your *father* went to France?'

'He did. To fight, he told her. But he had the reputation of a ranker, a coward, Miss Ellen, and for all that I know he was off out of it again before the first shot was fired in his presence, and not a lop sent back to his family since the day that he went out.'

'But what if he had died in battle, Liam? Haven't you ever considered that?'

'Wouldn't his comrades in arms have let us know if a thing like that had happened?' Liam demanded, his voice thickening with anger. 'No, Miss Nagle, that fellow always had a great lip on him for drink. And wasn't he always knawyshawling and asking for trouble in that condition? Died in battle, is it? 'Tis more likely that he got langers and was in a fight, and landed up dead in the ditch. I'm not like Vincent who prefers to deceive himself in the matter, telling everyone that our Da was a hero. The middle brother, Sean, took it different. Became a Protestant, the way he could join the British army as a private man. That got Vincent altogether. If it's the enemy you're joining, he says, off with you to him tonight, and he chawed Sean out, hoping maybe that he'd think twice about what he was doing. But the next thing we knew Sean was in the Coldstream Regiment of Foot Guards and to this very day Vincent won't hear his name mentioned.'

Ellen shook her head.

'And you? What do you feel now?'

Liam might not have heard. His eyes were fixed on the road ahead.

'Liam?'

He said: 'A lot of it had to do with me Da being there, Miss Ellen. I thought, if I went over and saw for myself what had happened to him, 'twould make it even worse.'

'You're not afraid of that anymore?'

But Liam was actually laughing.

'Not afraid, is it?' he managed, in between guffaws. 'Miss Ellen, I can't cod you. I may be up on me taws all right but I'm still destroyed with the fear of what we're about to find.'

* * *

The hospitality given to them by the sad woman was offered again by others as they journeyed through County Cork into County Tipperary and on to Cahir, at the eastern end of the Galtee Mountains where a castle stood proud on an island in the Suir River.

But one night there was no available cabin and Liam's fears about running into robbers was aroused by the sight of a group of horsemen up ahead.

'We'll pull off the road, Miss Ellen. Terrible tales I've heard of fellows being attacked and their ears cropped and their tongues cut out and they left mangled corpses in the open fields.'

Ellen sighed. But she gave in to Liam's suggestion, following him to a quiet spot by a small muddy stream.

When they had tethered the horses she pushed the thin green spattered reeds aside and eased her tired feet into the cool tawny water.

Isn't she the beautiful creature, Liam thought, watching Ellen paddling. And innocent! The trust she puts in a man . . . What's in the dog comes out in the pup: what if I turned out to be like me Da, a fellow that was a rogue since he was knee-high to a grasshopper?

What if I couldn't resist her charms?

But wouldn't the Da step over ten naked women to get to a pint of ale, he said to himself: take comfort from that if you can.

Look away from her now. When you get lime on your *brógs* it's hard to shake off – and the same boots have a long way to go yet.

Ellen, waking in the middle of the night in her bed on the damp grass, saw that the water was brown no longer but black-blue, the same colour as the sky, except for that part broken by the lemony moon and the straggle of stars which silhouetted the blue-black trees and bushes.

'Isn't that a sight!' she said to Liam.

But his eyes were tight shut.

They had ridden past the Rock of Cashel, seat of the Munster Kings, and high-gabled Cormac's Chapel into Queen's County.

'It's said that Portarlington is like a real French town,' Ellen said. 'Look at the way the gardens go all the way down to the river, Liam. We're getting closer to France!'

On an open space to their left three barefooted boys were laughing and pushing each other around and attempting to kick a ball made out of a pig's bladder.

'And *that* means there must be freshly salted meat in someone's barrel this day,' said Liam reflectively. 'Young fellows, who gave you the ball?'

'Me ma did,' the smallest of the boys grinned gap-toothily. 'We killed the pig two weeks back.'

'And ate it this morning,' one of the others chimed in. 'His granda is two days dead. Do you want to go to the wake?'

''Tis over!' the smaller boy said indignantly. 'Aren't they off to dig the sod.'

'Ulick!' exclaimed a woman's voice. 'I've been calling and calling for you. What have you done with your boots?'

'I have them here,' said the third boy, the well-dressed one of the trio, as an equally expensively turned-out woman with his own red hair and freckled face came around the corner. 'These men are hungry, Mama, I'd say. Can we take them back to the house?'

The woman nodded.

'You look as if you have ridden a fair way, gentlemen,' she said. 'My name is Naomh MacAlester. Are you heading for Dublin? My husband is going there in the morning. If you care to stop over with us, you can all ride on together and I can feel better about his going, knowing he has protection along the road.'

The MacAlesters' house had all the hallmarks of affluence and they were sumptuously fed; but although Liam could rest assured that here, at least, Ellen would not feel impelled to open her jewellery-case out of pity, he found it difficult to relax under Anthony MacAlester's scrutiny and the barrage of questions to which they were subjected.

'You're going no further than Dublin then?' he probed, after Mrs MacAlester had retired and they were passing round the port.

'We may be,' Ellen said cautiously.

MacAlester smiled.

'You wouldn't be travelling to France, I suppose?' he asked, looking up ruminatively from his glass.

Before either Ellen or Liam answered, MacAlester added: 'News is getting round that the French court has resolved on measures to strengthen the Irish regiments in Flanders. That again would be why the English are watching the southern ports . . . If by any chance the two of you are interested, I may be of assistance to you in getting a sailing from Dublin.'

We can trust him, Ellen decided.

'We would appreciate that.'

MacAlester must have reached the same conclusion about his guests. He said: 'I am going to France myself, on a confidential mission in support of the Jacobite cause. The young chevalier, Prince Charles, is back in Paris waiting for support from his friends in Ireland and Scotland in the matter of staging a rebellion in Scotland and a simultaneous invasion of England. I understand that the Macdonalds and many other chieftains are opposed to a rising; but there are others, Lord Clare amongst them, who feel differently. A group of us will be gathering in Dublin to discuss what can be done to assist him. Another man and I will be acting as emissaries of that meeting. Stay with us. We will all travel together.'

What were they getting themselves into, Liam wondered, all the way to Dublin. Other than that, he worried about the lengths to which Ellen's courage might take the pair of them.

He did not relax when they got into the city, being more alarmed than elated by the grand buildings, the number of coaches and carts, the packed taverns and coffee houses.

The insults exchanged between the street traders, who had come in from the country to sell poultry and wild fowl and rabbits, and the regular shopkeepers who saw their presence as a threat, grated on his nerves. While Ellen marvelled at the number of bookshops they passed, Liam winced at the raucous street cries and he breathed a sigh of relief when they had found lodgings at an inn.

Highest on the list of both their priorities was the sale of Ellen's jewels. When MacAlester had departed for his meeting, Ellen and Liam walked down Cutpurse Row, a narrow street that acted as the main thoroughfare from the southern road to the eastern end of the city, on their way to find an appropriate jeweller. They proceeded with difficulty for dirt had been laid all over the horse droppings for the purpose of making manure.

'Clean your shoes?'

'You could if we had the money to pay you,' Ellen told the crippled beggar who persisted: 'I have a special polish of lampblack and eggs.'

'The man is in need of your custom!' interjected a loud voice.

Three students, clad in gowns and caps, all obviously the worse for wear from drink, stopped by them.

'Give the fellow a chance.'

There was something about the first student – the same teasing, almost sadistic look – that reminded Ellen of Rory.

She said crossly: 'Mind your own business!'

'But we don't like to see such ungenerous behaviour!' said the first student.

He hiccuped, and gestured to his friends: 'What do you say we take these gentlemen back to Trinity, to the front court, and duck them under the pump?'

'An excellent idea!' one of the others shouted, sidling up to Ellen. 'The fellows would *want* us to teach them a lesson.'

Liam was not sure whether the student's hand was actually on Ellen's shoulder when she swung around to lambaste him. Before he could try to intervene they were all involved in a fracas, hitting out wildly, and tumbling onto the ground in a jumble except for the shoe-black who ran off, abandoning the tools of his trade.

In terms of savagery and inflicted injuries the altercation bore no resemblance to Dick's experience in Kinsale and it ended abruptly when one of the students wrenched off Ellen's hat, dislodging the hidden hair.

'A *lady*!' he mumbled, shocked.

The first student clambered unsteadily to his feet.

'Gentlemen, desist! Our apologies, Madam. Allow me to help you up.'

'I *told* you 'twas a fierce bad city,' said Liam, self-righteously. 'There's no protection for the likes of us during the daylight and only a Protestant employed as a night-watch. I say it again, Miss Ellen – this is no trip for a lady.'

'I don't intend to be thought of as a lady – not till we

get to France,' said Ellen, marching ahead. 'There's a jeweller's shop over the street. We'll sell my gems in there.'

Doesn't it take a woman to outwit the devil, Liam was thinking, back at the inn. Three hundred pounds Miss Ellen had got for her mother's diamond ring, telling the jeweller that it was a perfect one-carat stone and not being one whit put off when he had breathed on it, to check, he had said, on its colour.

And the oval locket with two pendants, a key and a heart, had fetched a good sum, as well as the emerald brooch and the rest.

One item Miss Ellen had not sold, an étui with an agate mounted in gold on it which she maintained was going to be useful though Liam could not imagine for what.

Or care much. Now that the transaction was completed and his own worries held off for a while.

With a sigh of relief he pulled off his jackboots and rolled down the thick knitted stockings – hand-me-downs from Kevin Nagle – which acted as a protection over the thinner ones beneath.

He was about to climb onto his bed for a nap when someone knocked on the door.

'Come in,' he called, and he looked up to see Miss Ellen, with the agate étui in her hand.

As he said afterwards to himself, the minute he spotted that determined look she had on her face, he might have expected trouble.

For Ellen had shut the door behind her and was opening the étui and taking out the tiny pair of gold scissors that had been concealed within it.

'Liam,' she said, looking straight-faced and stern. 'I'm not prepared to take any more risks. You must cut off my hair so that I'll look more like a man.'

'I can't do that for you, Miss Ellen,' Liam wailed, not taking the scissors. 'I've never cut anyone's hair . . .'

'Then this is your chance to start,' Ellen said, unrelenting.

'If you say so, Miss.'

'I do. What are you waiting for?'

In deep disapproval Liam took the scissors out of her outstretched hand.

'Go on . . .'

With his inexperienced fingers he began to hack at the thick, dark tresses, averting his eyes from the curls that fell like autumn leaves on to the stony floor.

7

'This new regiment Colonel Lally is building up is worth considering.' Roger De Lacy was holding court amongst a group of students. 'They're retrenching forty from each of the other Irish regiments in order to assist him, but he'll need as many as four hundred and fifty men to be ready and trained by April.'

'For battle . . .'

'Of course. And look what we have to gain if we can defeat the English and their allies. The conquest of Flanders and the overthrow of King George. And, finally, the establishment of a Catholic dynasty on the throne of England!'

'You put it so succinctly, Roger!' William Mehegan, a young writer, the son of Chevalier O'Mehegan, Commandant of La Salle in Cevennes, who was visiting student friends at the college, joined in with some amusement. 'Some of us could not have calculated the sum total of our winnings!'

'All the same, Roger is right,' William's older brother, James, interjected. 'Colonel Lally is something of a military genius. An inspiration to fight under. And as well as that the stimulation of joining a newly-formed regiment. Morale would be bound to be high. What do you feel, Philip? Which regiment will you join?'

'Clare's, I'd say,' Philip said monosyllabically, looking as if he was only by the most monumental effort managing to stay awake.

'And you, Dick?'

'The same. Apart from the admiration I have for Lord

Clare, I'm more or less committed to the regiment, because of the introduction I was given to Lieutenant-Colonel Creagh, by his brother in Kinsale.'

'You've been to see the Lieutenant-Colonel?'

'Several times. It was on his advice that I've been taking additional tuition in fencing from Maître Fournier. He stressed the fact that it needs two hours' practice a day to become a good swordsman.'

'And no doubt you've also been along to see Lord Clare, as well?' Roger asked mockingly. 'Or is My Lord Comte de Clare, to give him his French title, busy trying to wrest the estates and honours to which he feels he is entitled back from his Protestant cousin Murrough?'

'But he *is* entitled to them,' a student called O'Neill ventured. 'His cousin, the late Earl of Thomond, offered them to him in England, before the war, *and* forgiveness for his family's opposition to the Williamites, provided Lord Clare was prepared to turn Protestant. He refused to do that but it doesn't make his claim any the less valid.'

'Yes, he probably *is* the best of the lot,' Roger said, anxious not to lose popularity amongst the group. 'I shall be fighting under his command myself.'

'You're joining Clare's?' Dick found it hard to disguise his displeasure in this announcement.

'I'm one step ahead of you already in that,' Roger said, triumphantly. 'The military tailors will have my undress and full dress suits ready within four days. I must say I can't wait. It's a wonderful life in the army. Two hours' drill in the morning, they tell me, and otherwise you're free to do exactly as you like.'

'Unless you're officer for the day,' O'Neill added.

'Or the regiment actually engages – what an unwelcome thought! – in battle,' William Mehegan said sardonically, quirking an eyebrow at Dick. 'What do you say we break up this very serious military discussion and adjourn to the most conveniently situated wine-shop? Or should we go to a gambling house and watch Dick, here, distinguish himself at *biribi* and *pharaon*?'

Dick grinned: 'Another night. Don't tempt me!'

'Let's go back to Philip's apartment,' Roger De Lacy said eagerly. 'He suggested doing that, earlier on.'

'Ah, yes,' said William Mehegan, his eyes glinting with mischief. 'The Cantillons' apartment where the lovely sister waits. I've heard that you were keen.'

But Roger, pretending he had not heard, was scuttling out of the room.

'The way events are leading up to a battle we should enlist as soon as possible,' Philip said to Dick when, headed by the love-struck Roger, they had all ensconced themselves in the apartment in rue Vivienne.

'In that case, perhaps we should ask Roger for the address of his tailor!'

Philip laughed.

'I think we can manage without him. Our lives are going to change dramatically, Dick. Now that I'm actually about to join up I wonder why I waited so long – why I ever bother attending the college. To please Maman, I suppose. But war is what really matters. War, and following in my father's footsteps . . .'

'Personally, I am far more concerned with philosophical analysis,' William Mehegan said, overhearing. 'You are as dedicated a soldier as my brother, Philip. By nature I am a scholar. I find it quite beyond my capabilities to get excited over a war.'

'Do you *have* to talk about war?' Catherine demanded, coming into the room and positioning herself by the *rocaille* commode which Mme Cantillon had purchased the previous week. This piece of furniture, the work of Jacques Caffieri, was supported by drooping masses of flowers and the floral theme was echoed in her own silk sack-dress.

'Not at all,' said Roger quickly. 'We'll talk about whatever interests you – '

But Catherine, gliding rather than walking, using tiny but very fast steps, in the manner of the Court ladies, was moving in Dick's direction. Roger scowled and then, remembering that it was considered polite to look cheerful at all times, hastily re-arranged his expression to simulate happiness.

'If you want to amuse me you must tell me the latest gossip about Madame d'Étioles and the King,' said Catherine addressing the group in general. 'They say she is installed in an apartment at Versailles which used to belong to Madame de Mailly and which is connected to the King's room by a secret staircase.'

'Madame de Pompadour – but let's hope that her husband does not behave as the Marquis de Montespan did, during *his* wife's affair with King Louis XIV,' William Mehegan drawled. 'The poor deranged man arrived at Versailles in a coach adorned with black drapes, with a pair of stag's antlers on the roof, can you believe it! Although it seems that Le Normant d'Étioles is more restrained – or perhaps he is simply too prostrate with grief to take the appropriate action.'

Under cover of the others' laughter Catherine said, *sotto voce*, to Dick: 'You're not amused? What is the matter?'

Dick, she had discovered, was not as easily pinned down in love as her other admirers. In fact, she was no longer confident that he *did* love her, although she was sure that he desired her. Lack of confirmation of eternal devotion from men was an unfamiliar experience for Catherine, something that made her feel uneasy and insecure, and all the more eager to bind Dick closer to her.

'I'm just a bit restless. We all are,' he said, returning her smile. 'We'll feel better when we have actually joined the regiment of our choice.'

'When are you intending to do that?'

'Within the next few weeks.'

It was all Dick had time to tell her before Roger, his jealousy only manifesting itself in his burning brown eyes, interrupted.

'Which regiment do you favour, Catherine, Clare's or Lally's? Which choice do you think *I* should make?'

It was quite the wrong time to ask the question. Catherine, intent on recapturing all of Dick's attention, said dismissively: 'You must make your own choice – as I'm sure that Dick will do.'

Dropping his pretence of good manners, Roger stared with open animosity at his rival.

'You have no *idea* of what is going on in what used to be the Opéra-Comique,' William Mehegan was saying. 'Ever since it became the home of pantomime and light opera Boucher has been in the Foire St Laurent, painting the O'Morphi daughters. Pink-tinted nudes – voluptuous scenes! What would all those whose writings have contributed to the success of the place – Prion, Le Sage, Fuzélier, Dorneval – say about such misdoings . . .'

'Don't think you'll win Catherine from me,' Roger whispered fiercely to Dick. 'You won't – one day I am going to take her out of your life forever.'

That evening the visitors to Dublin were joined for dinner by a young, auburn-haired man whom Anthony Mac-Alester introduced as Count Patrick Darcy, explaining that he was a soldier and scientist of Irish origin who normally lived in France.

106

'He will be travelling with us on the boat,' MacAlester said, glancing around the room to make sure that no one outside their party was close enough to hear.

'How soon can we leave?'

Now that her jewels had been sold, Ellen was impatient to finish her journey.

'I hope tomorrow,' MacAlester said. 'The corporations are staging a procession, a triannual event to mark out the boundaries of the chartered districts of Dublin. The procession will apparently draw up at the Custom-house and proceed to Ringsend where a spear will be thrown into the sea to mark out the eastern boundary. We will go along. When the procession has moved on to Stephens-green, to the division between the city and the liberties, we will stay behind, and wait until a boat docks to pick us up.'

'Tomorrow!'

'Tomorrow. All Dublin will be out on the streets.'

It seemed to Ellen more like the whole world. As well as those who came merely to watch there were those who participated, the weavers, printers, shoe-makers, brewers, merchants and smiths.

Wedged between, on the one hand, a rowdy crowd of young bucks, and, on the other, a portly merchant, Ellen heard the songs and odes and cries of the weavers and the sound of the smiths' anvils and bellows long before she caught sight of the procession itself, and of the gay coloured ribbons which the weavers threw out into the crowd.

And –

'Look at the shamrock,' she marvelled as a huge emblem, exhibited by the merchants, came into view.

Count Darcy, standing behind her, said: 'The ship should be of more interest to you – I mean, that one,' as a huge model vessel which formed part of the merchants' display trundled past the crowd. 'They tell me it is being navigated by real sailors. The man Crowley tells me that you are impatient to get to France so that you may enlist in the Brigade.'

'Yes . . . And you?'

'I have postponed my scientific studies for the present. I shall join Condé's regiment. But there are other battles to be won – '

When they had boarded the brig *La Doutelle* the Count confided in her more expansively.

'When this vessel sails again from France there will be a royal person on board.'

'Prince Charles Edward?'

'Bound for Scotland, with many Irish supporters on board, including myself. We are to be accompanied by a frigate laden with arms and ammunition to assist the forthcoming rebellion.'

The Count's enthusiasm was infectious but Ellen, for the time-being, was concerned with the dilemmas relating to their own expedition.

To her consternation she had been forced to share a berth with the Count instead of, as she had expected, alongside Liam Crowley. In what she regarded as an act of snobbery Liam had been allocated space with what MacAlester referred to as the common men.

'Isn't he used to sleeping with me?' she had protested.

MacAlester had looked surprised.

'The man said he would feel more at ease below decks. Isn't it natural he'd want to be with his own kind . . .'

Tracked down, Liam had been distinctly furtive.

''Tisn't right for you and I to be sharing,' he had whispered.

'And is it right that I should be put with another man altogether?'

'I know you, Miss Ellen. Fortune favours the brave.

You'll have the Count out of there in no time and the cabin all to yourself.'

Ellen had been hard put to it not to box Liam's ears. And now here she was wrestling with the problem of how to evict the Count without arousing suspicions as to the nature of her sex.

On the other hand, maybe she should simply tell Count Darcy the truth. He had been open with her. More than that, he had trusted her to the extent of risking not only his own secret with her, but that of the Jacobite cause, into the bargain.

Looked at that way, she should not even hesitate.

'Would you have a fit if I told you that you're sharing your cabin with a woman?' she said on the instant.

Count Darcy did not have a fit but he was certainly dumbfounded. He even cast a quick glance around him, as if to ascertain whether the woman in question could have come into the cabin unbeknownst to him.

'You?' he said eventually.

But he did not look angry or scandalized or censorious. Quite the opposite. His expression was appreciative, admiring.

'Well, I take my hat off to you,' he said. 'Which reminds me, if I were you I'd keep mine on. Whoever cut your hair made a mess of it. MacAlester said as much to me about it the other night!'

'He did? Do you think he suspects?'

'Not at all,' said the Count reassuringly. 'And I think we won't tell him. He has enough to worry about, where the Young Chevalier is concerned, without our adding to it. And I think I can accept the idea of sharing a cabin with a woman. Tell me, what is your first name?'

It was the beginning of a real friendship. As *La Doutelle* headed for France, Ellen and Count Darcy had plenty of time for talking.

The Count, she realized, was not only a man of integrity, but a highly intelligent and gifted student who, although ready to sacrifice a portion of his life to the Stuart cause, was nevertheless looking forward to resuming his scientific studies.

'And you?' he asked curiously. 'What do you intend to do in Paris? Surely you're not going to pretend to be a man all your life? You'll want to marry . . . Are you in love with anyone? *Why* are you running away to France?'

'It's an adventure,' said Ellen lamely.

She was disconcerted by this interrogation. And when the Count said, 'You cannot base your life upon adventure,' she felt even more thrown off-balance.

'You must think seriously about your life,' her friend went on, but in a concerned rather than a patronizing manner. 'Still I'm sure you'll fall in love with France, even if you do not, at this stage, feel that way about a particular man.'

'It's magnificent!' exclaimed Ellen when, without serious incident, *La Doutelle* reached Brest and she caught sight of the land-locked bay, the steep hillsides of the old fishing settlement and, soon afterwards, of the harbour and the castle, with its donjon and seven towers.

The people on the quayside did not look as foreign as she had expected, being stockily built, with fair compexions and blue or grey eyes. But they were chattering away in a language she could not recognize.

'Breton,' explained Count Darcy. 'They are Celts, like us. Brittany was only annexed to the French Crown in the sixteenth century. It looks as if today is a *pardon* when the people gather to honour a saint, or to pray. Look at the men's embroidered waistcoats and the lace head-dresses – *coiffes* – of the women.'

On horseback, they moved inland from the jagged

coast, with Ellen exclaiming and enthusing over everything from a dish of tripe to a man seen playing the *bombarde*, until they reached the low limestone plateau of the Beauce, where the clayey topsoil is red.

They rode together, as a group of four, until at long last they reached Paris and were forced to fragment.

'You will write to me, won't you?' the Count said quietly to Ellen. 'Here is an address in Paris to which you can send your letters – although my replies may come to you from elsewhere.'

'I will write,' she promised, and the Count and Mac-Alester rode off, leaving Liam and Ellen alone.

'You're quite sure we should call on Master Dick this night?' Liam said at once, although Ellen had long since announced her intention of doing so.

'I am,' said Ellen. 'And won't he be pleased to see the pair of us!'

'I hope so,' said Liam, less confidently, but Ellen's attention was taken by the unfamiliar sights in the boulevards.

'Will you look at that, Liam!' she said, catching sight of a dancing bear.

'And he with a pair of eyes on him like two bloodshot onions!' Liam was edging his horse away.

He was more relaxed when their two horses were stabled, and Ellen and he were strolling along a quiet street.

But when she stopped at a door which had two roosters on it for a knocker, his unease returned.

What on earth would the people they were about to meet think of them, he wondered grimly. Neither could be called clean-smelling, after their long ride, and Ellen's undress coat had a tear on the left shoulder where she had caught it on the low-hanging branch of a tree. Her hair looked even worse than it had done in Dublin, and one of her cheeks was smudged with grime, a fact of which she was blissfully unaware.

Before he had the chance to tell her to at least wipe her face she took hold of both of his hands.

'Liam!' she said happily. 'How good you've been to come with me on this journey!'

She had a great way with her – there was no denying that. At that moment he no longer noticed the dirt on her face, only the joy reflected there.

''Twas nothing,' he said. 'I'd do more than that for you, any day, Miss Ellen.'

And Ellen reached out for the knocker and brought the roosters crashing down.

In the room above, Philip and Dick had been attempting for some time to make an important announcement.

'*Not* if it's to do with war,' Catherine said, putting her small hand up to her red lips as if to smother a yawn. 'You promised to take us to the theatre this week. I want to see *Enfant Prodigue*. I love Voltaire.'

Behind his sister's back, Philip raised his eyes heavenwards in exasperation.

'Maman, excuse us. Dick and I will return in a minute or two . . .'

'Catherine, you are as usual laying down too many opinions and drawing too much attention to yourself,' her mother said sternly when Philip and Dick had left the room. 'Paris has proved too rich a fare for you to digest. It's high time we returned to the Charente.'

'But Maman – '

'Since I control our finances you have no other choice.'

Catherine lowered her eyes and focused her thoughts on the damask shoes with the buckle and dainty heels which she had bought in the afternoon. If only the toes could be pointed. But the shorter, less-pointed section with the rounded tongues were, unfortunately, *à la mode*, and, in that also, one did not have an alternative.

Strange that Maman is so generous with money and so very stringent with love.

'. . . bad habits . . . not a good influence at the convent . . . Reverend Mother . . . your aunt . . . the same . . . *I* am not superficial – did not make fools of young men . . .'

Odd that Maman never, ever mentions Tante Danielle except in the context of a lecture. But then, of course, she is dead.

'. . . Voltaire . . . you are hardly a *philosophe* . . . your level of conversation . . . unlike . . . impress Montesquieu – Vauvenargues – Fontenelle . . . revolutionaries – anarchists. Yes, Angélique, what is it?'

'Pardon, Madame. Two young men are here. They wish to see Master Dick.'

'Show them in, please.'

Then Philip and Dick came back.

Ellen was still in a euphoric state when the elderly maid ushered Liam and herself into a room hung with white taffeta curtains.

That was all she observed of the décor for standing near the doorway were two young men, dressed identically in red coats, and waistcoats edged with white, yellow facings and lace, with tricorne hats on their heads and swords in their hands.

One of whom was Dick.

Ellen's green eyes opened very wide. For at that moment she realized that she could answer at least one of the questions put to her by Count Darcy on board *La Doutelle*.

'Are you in love with anyone?' he had enquired.

'Yes,' she could now say with absolute conviction. 'I am in love with Dick O'Shaughnessy. Perhaps I always have been. Maybe, without really knowing it, that is why I journeyed to France.'

To those closer to her than the Count at this time, however, she said nothing at all, or not then. It was Catherine who spoke first: 'Mon Dieu!' she said, for she was also gazing at Dick – at Dick, rather than Philip. 'You are in the uniform of the regiment of Clare!'

As Catherine made this statement, it seemed to Ellen that she was being slowly lowered from her heavenly cloud into a much less acceptable setting.

The room and its occupants came into clearer focus. She saw that there was a pretty, middle-aged lady sitting on a rococo sofa.

That the other young man in uniform was tall and extremely thin.

That there was a beautiful girl of about her own age present, who wore a white dress with bows on the bodice and a round-eared cap on her head.

The girl who had just spoken.

Who was looking at Dick as if she owned him – as if she had the right to dictate what clothes he should wear.

Suddenly, Ellen was acutely conscious of her own dirty, dusty and torn garments – of her untidy, crudely-cropped hair – her need to wash.

'I – ' she began, and stopped.

For Dick had finally registered her presence. He was gazing at her, blinking and gazing, and struggling, it seemed, for words.

At last he found them. But they were the wrong words . . .

'Ellen!' he gasped. 'Ellen – what are *you* doing here?'

And after that the beauty in the white gown joined in the conversation.

And what she said was worse.

'*Ellen!*' she exclaimed in a tone of the utmost incredulity. 'Ellen, did you say? But surely it is not possible. This cannot be a girl. Look at the hair – the big hands – so ugly. How could this be a girl?'

It was then that Ellen, who had never been afraid in her life, had her first meeting with fear.

8

What was he going to do with her? Dick asked himself distractedly in the night.

Ellen and Liam had been hospitably received by Mme Cantillon – hot water had been brought for bathing; soup and ham and wine put on the table for the guests; beds made up – but they could hardly stay indefinitely in the apartment.

He wished devoutly that Ellen had not heaped responsibility for her welfare onto his shoulders at a time when his only fealty should have been to King Louis and the regiment of Clare.

And there was a battle in the offing, with Britain and her allies, some 53,000 men, already assembling outside Brussels.

In that sense, the question of Liam Crowley was a far more simple matter. Lieutenant-Colonel Creagh would be bound to allow him to take along an extra man, as long as he was worth it, although even that remained to be seen.

Whereas Ellen . . .

She would have to return to Ireland as soon as possible, all the more speedily since Mme Cantillon and Catherine would soon be leaving for the Charente.

He must speak to Ellen, convince her that there was no future for her in Paris.

Searching for her in the morning, he found the doors to the drawing room closed. Hearing a murmur of female voices from within he knocked and was admitted, to find Mme Cantillon and Ellen sitting in matching gilt wood and tapestry chairs, engaged in earnest conversation.

Ellen was no longer dressed as a man. Mme Cantillon had lent her a gown and her hair was brushed into a semblance of order, although it still looked strange. She looked, he thought, rather more serious than usual but hardly repentant for arriving so inopportunely in Paris.

'I slept very well,' she said, although he had not asked her if she had done so. 'And Madame Cantillon and I have been having a long talk.'

As if Mme Cantillon and herself were already old friends!

'Dick, I have persuaded Ellen to accompany Catherine and myself to Cognac,' said the older woman, to his vast relief. 'She will like the Charente, and she will be company for Catherine. We will notify her father of her whereabouts and, of course, if he objects then she will have to go home. But if he does not then I think she should remain with us, at least until the war is over and it's safe to travel again.'

'That's an excellent idea . . .'

'I thought that you would approve of it. And I'm sure Catherine will feel exactly the same.'

But Hélène Cantillon was quite wrong about that.

'I don't want her to live with us,' Catherine said furiously. 'Please, Maman, send her back to Ireland where she belongs. She's not sophisticated enough for us.'

'What nonsense you talk, Catherine. I agree that, at the moment, she is not very *chic* but that can be rectified by the right clothes – when her hair begins to grow in. She has the making of a very pretty young woman.'

'But we have nothing in common,' Catherine wailed, not at all reassured by her mother's final sentence.

117

'In time you will have plenty in common,' said Mme Cantillon firmly.

And that was the end of that.

'We are embarking on a truly noble campaign.'

So said Philip several times as the regiment marched towards Flanders.

It was easy, looking at the gay red coats of the Irish Brigade and at the flags – Clare's a red cross on red-and-white quarterings displaying the royal crown of Ireland; Dillon's, with the addition of a harp embroidered in gold – to be romantic about the forthcoming battle.

But the reality of what war could do to those civilians unfortunate enough to be caught up in it came home to Dick before the Brigade even reached the wood of Barré, on the edge of which they were to bivouac, when he saw the first of the frightened creatures pouring out onto the road from the villages of Ramecroix and Antoin and Fontenoy.

Many despondent men and women walking, carrying small children on their shoulders or in their arms. Others had emptied their huts of their few possessions and loaded them onto carts. All of them were fleeing, their one instinct, to travel as far as possible before the first shots were fired.

'It seems that Fontenoy village is already occupied by a strong body of troops under Marshal Noailles,' Philip reported when, on the seventh of May, they encamped beside the wood. 'Our leaders have just selected the position from which we are to fight.'

'Where – tell us.'

Several officers, including Roger De Lacy, had gathered close to find out what was going on.

'Well, it seems that this position is virtually impregnable. Over there – look – the river Scheldt covers our right. The brigade, which is fortified, secures our communications.'

In his enthusiasm for battle, Philip had laid aside his normal air of fatigue. He went on: 'And from Antoin, on the river, to Fontenoy the valley is very narrow and difficult to traverse. Our left is covered by the wood itself and a strong redoubt has been constructed in there, fortified with breast-works and abatis. And elsewhere in the vicinity of the wood the natural difficulties make it unnecessary to set up field works.'

'The French army is about to regain its pride!' Roger declared. 'We're all set. We will prove yet that we are capable of decisive action.'

As he spoke he looked meaningfully at Dick.

Philip added: 'We have been defeated in the past by lack of discipline – and of cohesion. We must keep reminding ourselves of that.'

'If you are wounded, Dick – Lieutenant O'Shaughnessy – are you going to take up Sarsfield's cry, "Would that this were for Ireland!" or will you be thinking of France?'

'Come off it, De Lacy! We Irish fight like devils. What more do you need, damn you!' a fourth officer shouted, and the others began to laugh.

On the evening of the tenth of May, the day before the battle, the men were less cheerful. Even Philip's mood had changed to one of resentment.

'The Irish Brigade *ordered into reserve* in the morning!' he exclaimed angrily, his pale cheeks burning with furious colour. 'We'll be forced to sit here, at the edge of the wood, like a pack of hounds whose master has been foolish enough to lose his horn! The prospect is unbearable.'

'I suppose it is,' agreed Dick, wearily.

They *were* like kennelled hounds, he thought. All they

119

needed was a killer in the pack and the pent-up frustrations of the last few days would erupt into fighting among themselves.

To get away, however briefly, from the tenseness and the unease, he walked the short distance to the outskirts of the wood.

He stood, urinating, against a sycamore tree, observing how the grasses around it differed each from the other, seeming to dance out of step in the light breeze, some rapidly, others swaying to and fro, the rest hardly moving, as if each blade was determined, in this way, to express its individuality.

The branches and trunk of the young tree against which he was spraying out his effusion were a pale grey. As he looked at the blunt-pointed leaves they appeared to alter in depth of colour, green on the upper surface, bluish-green underneath. Later in May, when the battle was over, the greenish yellow flowers would open and the fruits would hang down in bunches, green to begin with, and afterwards crimson and brown, until the air currents spun them away. And the villagers would be –

He frowned, peering through the branches. Further into the wood, on his right-hand side, in an excellent position from which to take aim, an officer of the Irish Brigade was standing as still as the sycamore tree, his fusil, like an extended branch, pointed directly at Dick.

What – ?

'Jesus, Mary and Joseph!' cried a voice within himself.

For he had been mistaken – deceived by the similarity of uniform worn by the enemy and themselves. This was an officer of one of the *British* regiments, his scarlet dress coat heavily laced with gold. On his right shoulder were gold and crimson aiguillettes, and a silk sash was brought down to tie on his left hip.

His shirt frill was white, with lace at the throat and

wrists, his gorget gilt and engraved, fastened by blue ribbons and rosettes.

Powdered hair, tied with black ribbons into a pig-tail. A black tricorne laced in gold, with a gold-laced tie.

Transfixed, he recorded the details of his enemy's appearance.

He was slender and long legged. His face . . .

The face of the enemy seemed to move towards him, as if it had detached itself from the body holding the gun. It was a pale oval-shaped face with too much distance between the mouth and chin as if nose and eyes had been pushed upwards in the making towards the hairline. The mouth, too, took up less space than one might have expected.

The nose turned up at the tip. The eyes . . .

Hazel eyes, dilated now, like his own eyes, but showing no trace of the panic he felt his own must reveal.

Soft eyes. Eyes which contradicted the militant stance their owner had taken up.

Eyes which provided incontrovertible proof that this was a man dogged by compassion.

The British officer did not fire. Did not want to fire, if Dick could truly believe the eyes, rather than the rational explanation: that a shot would attract the attention of the rest of the Irish Brigade in bivouac by the wood.

Of course he must be a spy. A determined man who had found a way through the natural difficulties of which Philip had recently spoken.

So there *was* a way through the wood. It would be vital for the enemy to inform his superiors of that fact while ensuring that the French knew nothing.

In which case he would have to kill Dick.

But still the enemy did not fire, or move, fusil at the ready, towards him. Like maquettes whom their creator has whimsically attired in fancy costumes, the two men

121

stood, and around their feet the irrepressible grasses danced and trembled and swayed.

And then something – a quickening within the wood, the inaudible scuttle of a small and tremulous rodent – deflected Dick's gaze. Slightly turning, he saw that someone – another officer, armed – was positioned in the wood. Unmistakably an officer of the Irish Brigade . . .

Roger De Lacy, musket in hand. Watching. Smiling.

Waiting for Dick to die . . .

Then a shot rang out. The young Englishman did not cry as he fell backwards onto the gyrating grasses. When Philip, holding a fusil, walked towards the inert body, Dick thought that the spilt blood, seeping into the red coat, had hardly left a stain.

There was no sign of anyone else. As swiftly and silently as he had entered the wood, Roger De Lacy was gone.

'Brilliant!' Philip said. 'Lord O'Brien will commend us for this, I'm sure of it. He should have our message by now. Did you know that the king was holding a grand reception tonight at which all officers of rank will be present . . .'

Dick looked beyond to where the men were moving about the tents, collecting wood for the fires, stirring the black pots, containing the evening meal, which hung from crossed sticks over the burning embers.

The enemy . . . A young man like himself, who had – he was sure of it – shown him compassion . . .

An Englishman – young, like himself . . .

'Damn everything!' he said, to Philip's surprise. 'Damn governments. Damn battle and death!'

On the advice of Colonel Lally, the wood had been secured. At five o'clock in the morning, after a salute from – said Philip – Lieutenant-Colonel Lord Charles Hey of the British First Guards, the cannon broke into a roar. From their position, they could see way in the distance the figure of Marshal Saxe, in a position from which he, in turn, could command a complete view of the enemy's approaching ranks. At a nearby post, the King and Dauphin and cortège nobles watched, confident of success, Philip surmised, and relatively untroubled.

'Over there, on the British right, their General Ingoldsby is attempting to break through. The Dutch, under the command of the Prince of Waldeck, a useless soldier in my opinion, are coming through on their left.'

'But the centre – '

'The British and Hanoverians? A formidable combination, but only ten thousand strong. Dick, I can assure you, they stand no chance against our numbers. It will be a quiet day for the Irish Brigade, that's the only pity . . .'

In the beginning, it looked as if Philip's prediction was right as the Dutch, foiled by the three redoubts and sixteen cannon by which the indefatigable Colonel Lally had secured the wood, fell out of the range of fire, to be followed into retreat by General Ingoldsby's men. While the centre . . .

'They have a front of only forty men, yet they advance in perfect order through the storm of fire,' Philip muttered, divided between admiration and worry as the morning wore on and the British could clearly be seen, on the top of the hill. 'It's almost unnatural, that precision. The way each vacant place is filled quietly and regularly. And they're dragging that damn' cannon by hand!'

'While, on our side, regiment after regiment is being decimated. The Régiments des Gardes Françaises and the Gardes Suisses . . . They say it's a blood-bath up there,' Roger De Lacy, having avoided Dick until this moment, was edging in between his rival and Philip as if he were seeking shelter. 'They're saying that, after all, this could be another Dettingen. For God's sake, the enemy column is right in the middle of our army and without cavalry to assist its advance.'

'They'll call upon us yet,' Philip cried.

I suppose I might have expected the change, Dick thought ruefully, looking at his friend. The intensity in his eyes. The elated voice . . .

'My God!' said Roger De Lacy. 'Do you really think they will?'

Reports that Marshal Saxe had begged the King and the Dauphin to retire across the bridge of Calonne out of the way of danger were followed by confirmation that the King had refused to go.

And there were other reports – that Colonel Lally had pointed out to the Duke of Richelieu the impossibility of employing only musketry against the enemy's twenty pieces of cannon. The answer was simple: to meet cannon with cannon.

The Irish Brigade had volunteered to stop the enemy's march. All troops between Fontenoy and Antoin were to be called up; a logical decision, said Philip, with the Dutch no longer a threat.

Then two men were sighted. The men waiting by Barré wood scrambled to their feet as Lord Clare and Colonel Lally approached.

In a clear voice Colonel Lally issued their orders: the six regiments of the Irish Brigade, accompanied by the Brigades de Normandie and des Vaisseaux, were to advance upon the right flank of the foe. The infantry Brigades du Roi, de la Couronne and d'Aubeterre to march against the left.

'March against the enemies of France and of yourselves without firing until you have the points of your bayonets upon their bellies . . .'

Then the watchword: 'Remember Limerick and Saxon

perfidy!' before the band burst into a loud rendering of *The White Cockade*. Above the strident notes men shouted wildly: 'Remember Limerick – remember Limerick!' marching forward together.

The master's horn has been found, Dick thought, recalling Philip's imagery: the hounds are moving in for the kill. With Philip beside him, he was being carried forward by a frenzied wave of hatred as men whose families had been murdered or dispossessed by successive British governments prepared to take revenge. Some swore volubly about what they intended to do to the foe. Others, as if to remind themselves of their true identity in this alien place, reverted to Irish. On his left, an officer muttered: '*Mhaighdean Mhuire!*' invoking the Virgin Mary, as he stumbled and nearly fell.

By contrast, Dick was detached, not only from his comrades but from his own body, trudging obligingly up the hill towards the inexorable column. How clever, after all, Marshal Saxe had been, he thought, keeping the Irish Brigade in reserve so that their hatred would ferment into a usable and vicious potency. In this so-called noble campaign, we, the Irish – poorly paid, in need both of work and a release for our anger – are nothing more, in reality, than instruments of governmental strategy.

As, too, was the young British officer who died last night in the wood.

They were far up the hill now and he could see the column coming down.

He was in Hell, his ears assailed by the thunder of cannon, musketry, the screams of the wounded, his eyes by the sight of butchery and dismemberment, pleasure in slaughter. He could smell the blood. He thrust his bayonet into the first accessible belly, willing himself not to register its owner's gasp of pain. He killed. He no longer thought of the young officer in the wood – or of men as people.

He did not think at all. A few paces to his right, Lord Clare, struck by bullets, fell senseless to the ground. Dick prepared to kill again.

And was distracted by a sight so horrendous that it was barely credible. And yet – remembering his own error in Barré wood because of the similarity of uniforms worn by the British and Irish, it was only too possible: in the mêlée the *carabiniers* were charging the Irish Brigade.

'Mother of God!' he cried. 'Stop them. They think it's the enemy they're shooting – '

Then a bullet tore into his right thigh and he sprawled, alive, amongst the dead.

Twice the British ranks had been broken and their men had rallied round. But now, at long last, the enemy column was in retreat before the furious Irish, falling back in an order as regular and as perfect as before.

With blood seeping out of the wound in his thigh, Dick staggered to his feet. Men were cheering – throwing hats in the air, shouting: 'Two colours and fifteen pieces of cannon! The trophies we have to our credit!'

Other hats were being raised on the tops of bayonets. He could just see the King and the Dauphin as they rode between the ranks – watched as the Dauphin dismounted, ran forward to greet and congratulate Colonel Lally, slightly wounded, but the first to have entered the enemy's ranks.

'Lord Clare is well enough – he'll live to see another day!' someone shouted out and another man said that Lieutenant-Colonel Creagh, brother of Thomas, would receive a decoration.

'You're wounded, man. For Christ's sake, sit!'

Men were attending to his wound, stretching his leg out, applying flat splints and bandages, raising him onto a litter with long poles which was placed between two horses.

'You'll be all right. Easy now . . .'

The ends of the poles, he noticed, had been passed through leathern hoops suspended from the saddle and covered with flannel wrapping.

'*Vive le roi!*'

In their jubilation, officers embraced.

But they were surrounded by the débris of the dead and wounded. One look was enough to ascertain that the Irish Brigade had suffered heavy losses.

'*Vive le roi!*'

The stench of blood mingled with the odour of excrement: there was nothing noble in death.

But we won.

At what cost . . . ?

The officer leading the two horses halted, waiting for men to pass. From the litter Dick had a clear view of a body that lay on the grass.

Philip – or what remained of his friend. Wounded in the stomach – bayoneted to death.

'We'll have you back in camp in two shakes of an ass's tail.'

Before he was sick he thought clearly: *I must care for Madame Cantillon and Catherine.*

In the comparative peace of the camp he slept and, waking, found Liam Crowley beside him, sitting on the ground.

'Don't you be trying to talk, sir.'

'I'm well.'

'Better. 'Twill be some time yet before you can walk. They say you'll get a citation for finding the man in the wood.'

He blinked, remembering Philip.

'*We won.*'

(Remember that.)

Liam's craggy face crumbled.

'Eight hours of Hell.'

'But we won . . .'

'A strange kind of victory,' Liam said, 'with Irishmen fighting on both sides. Sir, *I found my brother dead.*'

'And I . . .'

His head swam. Liam's face drifted, and seemed to float away.

'Cognac,' he said, or thought he did. 'When I'm well I must go to the Charente.'

'When you're well,' Liam said. 'And I'll be coming with you.'

9

What got into me at all to agree to travel with the Cantillons? Ellen asked herself soon after the three women had set out for the Charente.

Her second, more comfortable journey tired her much more than the first. She was unable to ignore the tension between mother and daughter, intensified by their day-long incarceration in the coach, even if she could not understand all its nuances.

Attempting to converse with them in her own fractured French made her wearier still. Both of them spoke perfect English but Catherine, after saying loudly that it was a most uncivilized language, refused to speak it again, and Hélène thought that Ellen should try to improve her French at once.

More exhausting than anything else was attempting to come to terms with her newly-found love for Dick; her anxiety about what would happen to him in battle, and her uncertainty about his relationship with the obnoxious Catherine.

But when she asked herself what she was doing with the Cantillons, the answer: they can provide a link with Dick while he's away fighting, made her despise herself for her opportunism.

For it was bad enough taking advantage of kind Mme Cantillon, even though she kept insisting what a pleasure it was to have Ellen accompany them, but it was far worse to allow herself to ostensibly be in alliance with Catherine when, in reality, she could not stand the sight of her face.

What a hypocrite I am, thought Ellen unhappily. But

there was no *time* to make another plan which would ensure that I could keep in touch with Dick, she reminded herself. He and Philip had to leave so fast. How could I foresee that there was a battle in the offing and that the one person I knew in Paris would soon be gone?

How was I to anticipate that I would fall in love with him when I saw him inside the door and that, having done so, I could not conceive of being apart from him again?

How was I to foresee that, loving him, I would be frightened of losing him to this girl . . .?

For that's why I am prepared to stay with the Cantillons – tell the truth to yourself, Ellen Nagle, even if you won't admit it to anyone else.

You want to be there – by Catherine Cantillon's side every day – to find out what is between herself and Dick.

The way you can undermine their feelings for each other – if feeling there is between them. Aren't you the despicable one? If you had any decency in you, wouldn't you be away from the Cantillons this minute?

All the same, Ellen stayed where she was and the coach reached Angoulême, in the Charente, with the three women inside it. From this town, explained Hélène, they would travel along the Charente river by boat all the way through to Cognac.

'We are on the old pilgrims' road which goes through the Charente valley to Santiago de Compostela in Spain, so we will stop at the cathedral of Saint-Pierre to say a prayer,' she told the two girls, as the coach wound its way up to the top of the town and stopped in the rue du Minage which led on to the Place Saint-Pierre.

Stepping out of the coach, all three women instinctively put their hands over their eyes to protect them from the intense glare. The sun was white and piercing, the sky very blue. On one side Ellen could see the drop into the valley, the forested hills, the breaks where wild red

130

poppies grew freely in the vivid grass and where purple plum trees and great oaks gave shade to beds of yellow marigolds. Before her was the imposing cathedral with its intricately sculpted façade.

'Ellen, regard the sculpted figures over the door,' Hélène commanded. 'There are seventy-five persons depicted. You see the knight on horseback, the devil with his lolling tongue, the lady who is waiting in safety – '

'Are you going to light a candle to Saint Brice, Ellen, and ask for a special favour?' Catherine asked idly.

'And why not?' Ellen answered, tossing her head.

Now that she was actually in the Charente she was recovering from her lassitude. The sensation she had of being released from a cloister, together with the sunshine and the panoramic view, induced the same feeling of being reborn as she had experienced on the day of her mother's burial.

'Do you think Saint Brice will understand what you are trying to say, if you attempt to pray in French?' Catherine wanted to know.

There must have been something going on between herself and Dick. Otherwise why would the creature carry on as she did?

I'm going to fight for him, Ellen decided. But there was a terrible fear in her heart.

That, too, she fought, trying to batten it down.

She faced Catherine.

'Whatever language I use in prayer,' she said, 'Saint Brice is as likely to listen to me as to pay attention to you!'

The river was wide and slow flowing and white swans swam in it, preening themselves, puffing out their back feathers so decoratively that, unless you were close to them and you could see the swell of the muscles on the long necks, you would never think they were dangerous.

'In Ireland, swans are sacred,' said Ellen. 'Although, like ravens, they can bring you bad luck.'

'You have so many pagan beliefs, Ellen,' Catherine commented.

Molle – the word meaning gentle and soft, which Hélène had applied to the river – did not in any way sum up her daughter, Ellen decided.

'And in this beautiful valley – so incongruous – Calvinism had its headquarters,' Hélène told them. 'Over two hundred years ago, of course, yet, to this day, we are still plagued by Protestantism in this part of the world.'

'Protestants are not locusts, Maman!'

'Protestantism is a great evil. There is a most superb château – you can see it from the river – in the village of Saint-Brice, near Cognac. The very château in which Catherine de Médici tried to persuade Henri of Navarre to return to the true faith. If she had succeeded at that moment, others would have followed his example, and we would be free today of this scourge.'

'Maman, Catherine de Médici was a murderess. Everyone knows that. What an example hers would have been to follow!'

'And Protestants are becoming bolder all the time,' Hélène went on, as if her daughter had not spoken. 'They're even daring to propose marriage to Catholic girls. And some accept, even though they know they will risk their immortal souls by undertaking such marriages.'

'Poor creatures!' Catherine said promptly. 'Be warned, Ellen. I suppose it is as well that I have made up my mind to marry a Catholic. As far as marriage is concerned, I know exactly what I am going to do.'

A statement of fact or wishful thinking? Either way, Catherine must be referring to Dick for the tone she had adopted was challenging and so was the look in her eyes as she gazed over at Ellen.

A shiver ran down Ellen's spine. Catherine was so beautiful. What man could resist her?

Ellen closed her eyes to obliterate that beauty. But a voice inside her head said again: '*Look at the hair – the big hands – so ugly. How could this be a girl?*'

At Cognac, they disembarked at quai Papin and were whisked into a cabriolet to be driven the short distance to the Cantillons' Charente home which, Hélène explained, was on the opposite side of the river from the town.

'In rue Basse de Crouin, although I would myself prefer to live in rue Haute de Crouin which I feel is just that little bit more exclusive. Still . . . In a day or so, when we have unpacked, Catherine will take you into Cognac and show you the town, Ellen. It is 1,800 years old! Once, it was the site of a Benedictine priory and later on, because of its situation on the river, it became a main centre of commerce. We used to export salt from here. And Cognac has always been an artistic and intellectual centre, where poets and sculptors lived. Now, of course, our brandy trade is flourishing.'

'You have omitted the fact that François Premier was born here, in the Château no doubt, although legend insists that it was under an oak tree,' interjected Catherine. 'After he became king, he brought his mistresses back here. Am I speaking too rapidly for you, Ellen? I keep forgetting that you only have very limited French.'

'Unlike your manners, Ellen's French is showing distinct signs of improvement,' Hélène said promptly.

Mother and daughter glared at each other while Ellen groaned inwardly. If they continue to antagonize each other, she reflected, my life in Cognac really will be unbearable.

133

But that was the end of bickering, for they had reached their destination. Ellen found herself staring at the grey, seventeenth-century manor house which Catherine had nicknamed Manoir des Yeux, for it had twelve front-facing windows, four on the ground floor, five on the first, and three more set into the high black roof, all identical and all appearing to scrutinize the formalistic garden.

The house, to Ellen's eyes, was ascetic and stern; the garden was equally devoid of frivolity. In the rectangular flower-beds, which were bordered by a running filagree of trimmed boxwood, red roses grew in profusion. Around these beds ran paths so straight they might have been measured by a giant ruler. Two fountains – positioned equidistant from each other – emitted jets of water of precisely the same volume.

This formalism, Ellen learnt later, extended even into the plan of the vegetable garden – the *potager*, as Catherine called it – where all the vegetables, herbs, plants, shrubs and trees had been planted according to their ultimate sizes as well as to their natures: two tall Cypress trees, of more or less the same dimensions, marked the *allée* which ran through the *potager* towards the back of the house.

But now a middle-aged housemaid had opened the door and was saying: 'Madame, Madame, you are back!' and Mme Cantillon was explaining that this was Yvette, and Ellen was peering around at her new home, thinking how different it was from the big houses she had known in west Cork.

In Ballygriffin and Kilawillen and Mallow and Castletownroche, there had been no attempt made to match or tone furniture, carpets, curtains and canopies: artefacts and cushions, chairs and tapestries had been jumbled together in a haphazard, happy-go-lucky manner, hosts and hostesses being more concerned with conversation and conviviality than with the environment in which merrymaking took place.

But at Manoir des Yeux much thought had been given to the creation of a pleasing harmony. The colours were pale – pastel blues and pinks and yellows, relieved by white and cream. So the sunny shade of a cushion placed on a *bonne femme* armchair blended with a mirror set in a gilt frame, and a hand-painted screen, with flowers in pink and blue and white, complemented a painted blue-and-white *buffet*.

In some of the downstairs rooms, Mme Cantillon had been influenced by the current fad for *chinoiserie*. Soft, comfortable ottomans had replaced the tapestry-covered *canapés* which the previous owner of the manor had favoured, and although other tapestries, of French design, still hung on the walls, the draperies were fashioned from Chinese silk. There was an informally convoluted bronze and a Chinese escritoire in one of the reception rooms, and a Chinese *magot* figure in varicoloured porcelain on the oak-veneered commode in the *alcôve*.

'Yvette will prepare your room,' Mme Cantillon said to Ellen when a whirlwind tour of the ground floor had been made. 'It seems that she did not receive the letter I sent to her from Paris before we left, explaining that you would be with us.'

When Yvette, without smiling at Ellen, had disappeared upstairs, her mistress continued: 'You will get used to the Charentais in time. They are by nature very reserved. They have an extraordinary fear of exposure. You will see that they close their shutters at dusk the moment the lights are lit. Slow people – but sure. Outsiders call them *cagouillards*.'

As Ellen looked mystified she added with amusement: 'It is the name for the edible snails which you find in this part of France.'

135

'Poor Ellen,' said Catherine in her most patronizing manner. 'What a lot you have to learn.'

'I'll learn,' Ellen said, keeping her temper, just.

All the same, it was a relief to postpone any further lessons in life, to follow Mme Cantillon up the graceful stairway to the next floor, and to enter the room that was to be hers.

This room had been allocated to Ellen by her hostess because she felt that the girl would feel at home in its relative simplicity. It contained a painted bed, its head-board sculpted with laurel garlands and pomegranate motifs, and a matching three-drawer *commode*, as well as a tall *armoire* – 'For the gowns you will have to have made.'

A cool room, in which a blue so pale it was almost grey was the predominant colour. The hand-blocked curtains were open, permitting the late afternoon sun to attempt to filter through hand-made lace; the shutters were only half-closed.

'I think we should all rest now.'

'I think so, too,' said Ellen gratefully. 'Thank you for all you have done for me.'

Hélène Cantillon said: 'We want you to be happy.'

Ellen could not help herself.

'I know *you* do,' she said.

For weren't they both aware that Catherine did not give a hoot for the well-being of Ellen Nagle?

But even Catherine the hard-hearted was subdued when, next day, the three women learnt that casualties amongst the Irish Brigade at Fontenoy had been heavy, with Colonel Dillon of Dillon's regiment killed, and Colonel Roth of Roth's.

'If you want to come with me to Cognac, you can,' she said to Ellen, leaving the latter with the impression that, like herself, Catherine did not want to be left alone to think of what might have happened to Dick and Philip. 'I want to buy some chocolates.'

And so they went together into the enchanting old town, dismissing the cabriolet so they could walk up rue Saulnier – street of the Salt Harbour – taking care to avoid the *moulière*, the central gutter, and admiring the fine town houses, one with a Florentine pediment and the little tradesmen's windows on the ground floor, and another in which rainwater was drained through zoomorphic gargoyles on the entablature.

For the first time since they had met Catherine was almost affable, promising to take Ellen to see the medieval Château de Valois, badly damaged in the Hundred Years War, and offering her a chocolate.

'But before we go anywhere else we must stop and say a prayer in the church of Saint-Léger,' said Catherine, and Ellen was sure that she meant – a prayer for Philip and Dick.

Side by side, as if they were real friends, they reached the Romanesque church, built in the shape of a Latin cross, which Catherine maintained had been quite spoilt by the addition of a flamboyant Gothic rose-window, designed to light the nave.

But *I* like the rose-window, Ellen thought, and I love the portal with the signs of the zodiac and the carvings which Catherine explained evoked the work of each month.

'What does that old man sitting down symbolize? He isn't doing anything!'

'That's the point,' Catherine said. 'He symbolizes the idleness of winter.'

It was a pleasant outing, and both girls forgot for the moment that they were rivals.

But not for long. Coming home they passed a group of serious-faced men carrying axes walking along the road.

'Who are they?' inquired Ellen.

'The *tonneliers*? They are coopers,' Catherine informed her. 'They make the casks in which the brandy which is distilled in this area is stored.'

And then, as if she had suddenly remembered that, after all, Ellen was less friend than enemy, she added: 'Really, how little you know. But I suppose that is understandable, as you come from backward Ireland!'

And Ellen took her cue from that.

'We're not backward!' she said furiously. 'And we have a custom at this time of year which might be of interest to you. *Teine Féil Eóin* the old people call it – Bonfire Night. They say it's a good time to exorcize the demons out of women like you!'

Catherine flinched. Quickly recovering her composure she said lightly: 'I don't know why I'm bothering to enlighten you. After all, you won't be staying in Cognac for very long, will you? And in the meantime I doubt if the *tonneliers* of Cognac are destined to play a significant part in your life.'

The day was spoilt. How horrible Catherine was, Ellen concluded.

She said as much that evening when she wrote to Count Darcy.

'You will understand when I tell you that the voyage I took in your company was far preferable to the one on which I am now embarked . . .'

She sealed the letter and addressed it to the Count at his Parisian address. But it was of Dick she thought when she finally went to bed.

'If 'twas my father I had found dead, I wouldn't have minded. They could have given it to *him* hot and heavy

138

any old time, but Sean, now that was a tragic matter,' Liam said, having once again described in gruesome detail his discovery of his brother's body amongst the enemy dead.

Dick blinked. While Liam found apparent relief in talking about Fontenoy, harping on the state of the wounded and the numbers of the dead, Dick skittered away from the subject like a shying horse startled by an unexpected shout.

Only I can't close my mind to the fact of Philip's death, he reminded himself sternly. Or to the fact that I have the news of it to break to his mother and Catherine.

Or to the fact that to Mme Cantillon, who treated me as a son, I now owe the obligation of a son.

I must look after both of them, as Philip would have done.

He felt sick not only in mind but in body, aware that, in his desire to get to Cognac as soon as possible, he had forced himself prematurely into the saddle. The wound in his thigh, which had not healed, was festering, and he was beginning to wonder if he would manage to complete the whole journey.

You vowed that you would never be beaten again, he told himself.

You cannot give in.

So, only half-listening to Liam's incessant chatter, feeling worse rather than better by the day, he forced himself to ride on until, after what seemed years, they saw the fortified manors of the Charente, the high walls and massive gates which nervous Protestant owners had built around their houses to fend off possible attack by Catholic neighbours.

He was very nearly at the end of his tether when he and Liam came within sight of the ruins of the Château de Cognac, partly destroyed in the Hundred Years War.

By then, Liam was talking rapidly to retain his companion's attention, hoping that, by doing so, he might prevent Dick from actually fainting.

'Aren't you the lucky man, Master Dick, to have two beautiful girls waiting for you, Miss Ellen and Miss Catherine?'

'Ellen?' repeated Dick blankly. 'Ellen will be there?'

On this last leg of his journey he was finding it difficult to remain in full command of his senses. Ride to Cognac, break the news of Philip's death to his family were the commands he had given himself at the beginning of every endless day. In those last days his exhausted brain registered nothing.

He repeated: 'Ellen – ?'

He was lying on one of the ottomans in the drawing room and Catherine, not Ellen, was saying rather too clearly: 'Philip loved you, I think.'

'Loved?'

The windows were open. He could smell the roses.

Red roses. Red, the colour of blood . . .

'Surely you knew about my brother? He was a deviant.'

A shaft of sunlight fell on one of the rose bushes highlighting the presence on the sepia-brown bough of a lizard of identical colour. To all intents and purposes, Philip had concealed his true self.

'Surely you knew? Didn't you find it offensive?'

When he replied there was a new, brusque note in his voice.

'I'm not a fool and no, I didn't find anything offensive in Philip. He very wisely kept his feelings to himself. I think they should remain private.'

Catherine said: 'Don't think we're not proud of him. After all, he *was* decorated posthumously for what happened in Barré wood. You must rest. You are still far from well.'

140

He dozed, and woke to find Ellen in the room, holding a tray in her hands.

'You look much better,' she said in a positive voice.

'I feel better. Ellen, I want to talk to you.'

'About what?'

'About the Cantillons. Madame Cantillon is in a bad way. I doubt if she'll ever really get over Philip's death. You're going to have to look after her for me.'

'I am?'

'Because the war isn't over – only one battle. There'll be another – and when I'm well I'll have to fight again.'

'Not so soon,' Ellen said fiercely. 'Dick, not so soon.'

'Maybe. And when that happens I want to ensure that Madame Cantillon and Catherine have you here to comfort them. You're good at looking after people, Ellen. Eithne wrote and told me that you were wonderful when your mother was dying.'

'She did, did she?'

'And you've settled so well in France. Unless you're set on going back to Ireland?'

And leave you – or the chance of being close to you, Ellen thought: is it mad he thinks I am?

And maybe he's right – maybe I can offer comfort to Philip's mother, after all. It's the least I can do for her, after her kindness to me.

'I'll stay here and see what I can do for Madame Cantillon,' she said. 'Provided, of course, she wants me.'

'I'm sure of that,' Dick said. 'You're a great girl, Ellen. I always said you were.'

Visitors came. Monsignor Doussinet, the curé of Cognac, visited him, and Father McMahon, down from Bordeaux, pressed upon him a copy of *The Garden of the Soul*, by the popular spiritual writer, Richard Challoner, and said the contents would give him much to ponder upon. Ladies

141

from Jarnac and Saint-Brice, contemporaries of Madame Cantillon, called in, to wish him a speedy recovery.

In August, he was well enough to go out, to be driven to Saint-Brice or Chatres or Jarnac while the two girls pointed out vineyards and châteaux and Romanesque churches with elegant façades, and tried to mind their manners in his presence; and Hélène said how sad it was that some Charente churches, desecrated during times of religious strife, of necessity had been rebuilt and refurbished without adequate funds so their restoration had not been as effective as one would have wished. But she spoke absently, as she so often did these days, and when she thought no one was looking she surreptitiously wiped away a tear and pretended that she was examining the vista outside the cabriolet.

Dick, too, was detached, Ellen thought, keeping an eye on him as well as on Hélène. The wound in his leg may have healed but it is going to take longer to mend his poor soul.

As a fillip to both spirit and body she brought him a glass of cognac.

'It's a medicament.'

'I don't have to have an excuse for drinking cognac!' Dick said.

Sipping, he thought of Thomas Creagh and his fondness for a good brandy. Mr Creagh would be pleased to hear of his brother's award for bravery at Fontenoy.

I should write to him, Dick thought, and myself tell him of the battle.

But even as the thought flashed across his mind he veered away from it. To write of Fontenoy would be to relive its horrors; to be forced to remember too closely what he had seen from the litter.

But he owed it to Thomas Creagh to make contact – to thank him for his generosity.

142

Blinking, he sipped again. And then it came to him. He would send Mr Creagh what that affable gentleman would most like – a cask or two of cognac.

'Have you heard recently from your father?' Ellen was saying.

'Quite recently.'

And I may as well send a few casks to my father and Willie, he thought – to gladden the heart of one and put some life into the other.

'And from the girls?'

'From Eithne. Listen, Ellen, do you know how Madame Cantillon goes about buying cognac? I'd like to order some as a present to send home.'

'I'll ask her this minute,' said Ellen. 'And Liam can get ahold of them for you, and take them down to the quay, and get them shipped for Ireland.'

In August, too, Ellen heard from Count Patrick Darcy. The letter had not been posted from Paris, but had come all the way from Scotland.

'We boarded *La Doutelle* after he of whom I have spoken followed your example in selling family jewels to buy certain commodities which were taken on board a second ship, a man-of-war, the *Elizabeth*, which sailed in company with us. But four days after setting sail a British man-of-war engaged with the *Elizabeth* for several hours, as a result of which she was so crippled she returned to France and our commodities were lost. We had to start again . . .

'You would like My Friend. He is very handsome with fair hair falling in ringlets to his neck, and light blue eyes . . .

'After much discussion and initial hesitation the chiefs are rallying to our aid . . .'

'You're very engrossed in your letter, Ellen,' Dick said, discovering her in the *alcôve*.

As she hastily thrust the letter inside the bodice of her dress, he added: 'A love letter? Ah, you're blushing!'

And not a sign of jealousy on him! How maddening men could be!

''Tis not a love letter at all.'

(Isn't it you I love . . .?)

And what a fool I am, thought Ellen later on: Catherine would have managed it all so differently.

She would have used the Count's letter to full advantage, in order to *make* Dick jealous.

More post, this time for Dick. Letters – jubilant letters from Ireland, from Kilawillen and Kinsale.

'Thanking me for the gift of cognac.'

'What does your father say?'

'. . . the Nagles were here and the McDonnells from Mallow and the O'Callaghans of Duhallow and they all expressed their appreciation of this fine drink. Could you send by return several more casks . . .?'

'I'll get Liam to attend to it now . . .'

'Wait a minute. I can't continue supplying the whole of west Cork with cognac, even if I was given a gratuity after Fontenoy. It isn't as if I have a regular income from the army. You know, Ellen, how it is with the Brigade – we're employed for the preparation for the battle, and for the fighting itself, and then disbanded till the next time.'

'Then make west Cork pay for what they're drinking!'

'Hmm?'

'Why are you frowning at me?'

'I'm not frowning at all,' Dick said. 'Far from from it. Ellen, you great girl, you've given me an idea. There was a man in Paris – a Monsieur Sauvol who used to sell cognac . . .'

'There was?'

'I'll tell you about that some other time. Ellen, I'm going to export cognac to Ireland. If Mr Thomas Creagh likes it, and the McDonnells and the O'Callaghans, not to mention our own fathers and brothers, then there must be others in west Cork who will drink it, too. Maybe others even further afield . . . And I'm here, in Cognac, where the brandy is actually distilled! Why – tell me – *why* didn't I think of this before?'

'Because you were too sick for that kind of thinking and anyway you didn't *know* what they thought in west Cork . . .'

But Dick was not listening. He had her by the two hands and was shaking them up and down in his enthusiasm.

'I can maybe make a good living out of cognac yet,' he said. 'Ellen, who knows – I could be rich!'

BOOK TWO
1748–1756

1

He was twenty-four and his life had once again altered completely. He stood at the window of a room in the rue Saulnier in Cognac, gazing at but not really seeing the grotesque gargoyles ornamenting each side of the door of a house across the street. The roof of this house was, like most of the roofs and walls in the town, covered with the black fungus which fed on the fumes given off by ageing cognac.

So many changes, he thought, not only in his own life, but within France.

The austere financial methods of Controller-General Orry, who had extended road works and attempted to develop the mines, rejected. His successor, Machault d'Arnouville, left to wrestle with the seemingly insurmountable problem of how to pay the cost of war.

The Secretary for War, comte d'Argenson, also fallen from favour. Marshal Saxe, having impressed the king with his military expertise, permitted to offer advice: attack the United Provinces; pressure Britain to accept peace.

And so, in the spring of 1747, the Irish Brigade had joined the French to prepare for the battle of Lauffelt. He blinked, remembering.

Recalling first the rumour, growing into a conviction, that the Young Chevalier, defeated the year before, after the abortive Jacobite rising, and forced to flee from Britain disguised in female attire, was actually in Lauffelt. An illusion, a flight of somebody's fancy, nothing more, but a myth which had acted as an inspiration to the men

149

of the Irish Brigade so that they had fought like demons, neither taking nor giving quarter, and cutting all before them.

And themselves meeting with very rough treatment: for more than 1700 officers and private men were among the dead and wounded.

Many friends lost forever . . .

But Britain and her allies had been defeated. And this month of April 1748 peace had been signed at Aix-la-Chapelle and the Brigade again disbanded.

A stroke of genius.

Surpassing belief, too, it sometimes seemed to him, was his own *coup de théâtre*: how from the gift of a few casks of cognac he had been able to build up a small but thriving export business.

Of course, the terms of his service with the Brigade, so fluid, had proved an advantage to his alternative career. Over the last three years he had been able to pay several visits to Cognac and to spend long periods of time in the little town. In the summer of 1747, although, with battle in mind, the officers and men of the Irish Brigade had been fully paid, they had not actually been deployed in the field: he had been able to devote those months fully to his own negotiations.

When he had been forced to return to the Brigade, Ellen – as steadfast a friend as ever – had kept the momentum going on his behalf.

He shook his head, thinking of her with admiration. She should have been a man, with her clarity of thought, her strength, qualities largely wasted on a woman. And she actually had a head for figures – that was another point in her favour. His order-books had been meticulously kept all the time he had been away.

Naturally, Ellen had needed help. She could not have survived alone, even with constant postal direction from himself. There had always been Liam Crowley close at hand, with strict instructions which of the growers and distillers to deal with. And it had been Liam, too, who had personally taken the barrels of cognac down to the quay, from where they were transported down the river to the harbour at La Rochelle, and shipped from there to Ireland.

Because the orders had continued to come in from Ireland on an increasing and most satisfactory scale, as the O'Shaughnessys and the Nagles and the McDonnells and the O'Callaghans spread the word around, first in the Blackwater Valley and then beyond it just as he had envisaged that day in 1745, when he had hit upon the idea of becoming an exporter.

Back in the army he had literally fought to save the money to build his business up. He had been obsessed with the concept of developing trade with Ireland. He had longed to return to Cognac. The battle itself had become a stepping-stone to a new career, as well as a hurdle he had to clear before he could embark upon it.

He continued to gaze out of the window, thinking how, having been bewitched, at twenty, by all that Paris had offered, he was now at home in a tiny town, once the site of a fortified camp and castle, which had been built on a hillock in the middle of a valley which was, in essence, a vast vineyard. On each side of this hillock the Charente flowed, sometimes – more usually – good-humouredly, on occasions furiously, always reminding him of his own Blackwater river.

But there was nothing in the narrow, picturesque winding streets of Cognac that recalled Kilawillen, or even Mallow: the ghosts of *his* noble ancestors did not call out to him from the Château de Valois which looked so austerely over the quai de la Charente; the houses of Cognac not only bore no resemblance to the homes of his

151

friends in Ireland but were totally dissimilar, each to the other, this one with its wrought-iron balconies, that with its Gothic arch, another with a modern classical door. And on one occasion when he had stopped to examine the stonework of a building he had seen in it a sign that the Romans, too, had stopped in Cognac, just as, every so often, he came across a carved salamander, like those on which the large oriel window of the Château de Valois rested, monument to François Premier.

Looking back, he wondered at his own brashness when he had first set up his business in Cognac, convinced that it would all be so easy; that he would only have to build up his orders, find his suppliers, visit wine farms and learn just a little about the actual process of distillation. He had known only that the export of *eau-de-vie* as a single distillation was not new; that the Charentais had been making and selling rough brandy hundreds of years before. But he had known nothing of the Cognaçais themselves.

They had been difficult men to understand or get to know well, as different from his own people as it was possible to be. They had taken time to accept him – to work with him. He had learnt that they were patient, discreet, reserved and introverted – people who drank only sparingly of their own product. He had discovered how to speak to them, not only in their own language, but in a way they found acceptable.

Dealing with them no longer worried him. Buying from them, at the brandy market that was held each week in the town, was no longer an ordeal but a challenge. It was to that market that he was going today, along with Liam Crowley.

Having proven at Fontenoy that he was, as he put it, no ranker, Liam had been quite happy not to have to test his

152

new-found courage again. It had suited him very well to stay behind in Cognac when Dick had gone off to the war.

'Better red wine than red blood, Master Dick!' he had commented when asked if he would be willing to work on the new project and Dick had left him to discover for himself that cognac was distilled, not from red wine, but from the acidic white wines of the region.

He could see Liam now coming along the rue Saulnier and he went down and out on to the street to waylay him.

'You're late.'

'I am so,' Liam agreed. 'But wasn't I busy providing a name for the fine grey filly Miss Ellen is after buying?'

'The two-year-old?'

'The same one. Holy Jesus, I'd started to say when she surprised me with the creature, till I remembered 'twas in the company of a woman I was and not back in the army. 'Oley Gee, is it, asks Brigitte, being bad at the spoken English, and Miss Ellen says *that's* the name for the horse, and she the Holy Terror herself.'

'She is,' Dick said, his mind more on the impending market than on Ellen's new acquisition.

Propelling Liam in that direction, he said: 'I'm going to have to look out for larger premises. This room of mine is too small to act both as bedroom and office. Will you keep an eye out in that connection?'

'I will. I suppose you think it's unseemly staying with the three women now that Master Philip is gone?'

'It would be,' Dick said shortly.

Encouraged, Liam would gladly embark on a eulogy of Philip. Dick was relieved when they got to the market without the anticipated oration.

Once there, Liam was in his element. Having learnt to speak French, he could now put his talent for picking up rumour and information to good effect, worming his way into other people's conversations and unashamedly listening in.

Dick left him to it. Around them, blue-suited farmers, their trousers tucked into white socks tied above the knee with red ribbons, wide flat hats on their heads, were resisting the persuasions of the *négociants* to lower their prices for cognac. In many ways, he sympathized with the intransigence of the growers. They were plagued by government taxes, as were all Frenchmen who were considered to be in full possession of the fruits of the earth.

It's so unfair, Dick thought, looking at the farmers. These men who cultivate the land bear the whole burden, those who actually own it are not obliged to pay out.

Now that he knew his way around the market he was aware which distillers were Catholic, like himself, and which were of Huguenot stock and even more resistant to pressure from a *négociant* who practised a different religion.

'Your price is too high for me,' he said, truthfully, to one grower.

The man shrugged, giving the impression that he did not care one way or the other.

Half-an-hour later Dick found himself within earshot of the same grower. With him was a stocky man, obviously a *négociant*. A man in his late thirties with a heavy, square-shaped face and deep blue eyes who, neither by his appearance nor by the cut of his clothes, gave the impression of being French.

To his irritation, Dick heard the grower agree to lower his prices. Two Protestants doing a deal, he concluded.

'There you are, so, Master Dick,' said Liam, sidling up beside him.

'Do you know who that man is?' Dick asked, nodding towards the dark-haired man.

'I do. Mr John Marrett. An Englishman,' said Liam with distaste.

He added vehemently: 'A man that sharp isn't he in danger of cutting himself.'

'You know him that well?'

'*Of* him, Master Dick. *Of* him. An exporter of cognac to England and a fellow that close in business he'd skin a flea for a half-penny.'

Or maybe a decent man, Dick thought. He did not add to Liam's load of anti-British hatred by mentioning that the fellow had done him out.

Instead he said: 'I'll ride beside you this evening when you're returning to Crouin. I'll be dining across at the Manor.'

Long before Dick and Liam left to ride the very short distance to Crouin, Ellen and Catherine had gone to their bedrooms to select what they would wear that evening.

The material of Ellen's wrapping-gown, worn with a pannier and double ruffle-cuffs, was exactly the same colour as the green eyes of its owner, and the gown itself, crossed over in the very low bodice, had been designed to show off her figure to its best advantage, at least above the waist, the skirt being a concealing puffball of fabric. Her shoes were hand-embroidered. Her hair, no longer unevenly cropped but shining and well-dressed, was drawn back off her face and left to hang down the nape of her neck.

On the whole, she was quite pleased with the over-all effect. But then, in the mirror, she saw her strong, practical hands and her confidence ebbed away.

What young man could ever be attracted to a woman with hands like that? Here she was, getting all dressed up to impress Dick when with such a physical drawback, she had no possible hopes of doing so. Ridiculous!

155

Ah, don't be so faint-hearted, she told herself. Reminding herself to buy another pair of long gloves, she turned her back on her own reflection.

Catherine had no qualms about any aspect of her appearance that evening. Her violet-and-rose gown was cut even lower in the bodice than Ellen's green one and she had tied narrow violet ribbons round her neck and through her hair which was piled onto the top of her head.

With the air of an expert who knows perfectly well that she has used two hours to good effect, she gave herself a final cursory glance in the mirror, refusing to allow herself to frown lest it lead to wrinkles.

But she was frowning nevertheless inside. It was, she thought, very objectionable the way Ellen virtually clawed her way into Dick's business, setting herself up as a keeper of his books, and trying to make herself important to him.

And, in that sense, actually succeeding! It was so unseemly – so unfeminine.

One would like to think that, in behaving in this way, Ellen was bringing about her own doom, for Dick, surely, as a result, did not think of her as a woman but more as a younger brother, or cousin.

But who knew what Dick was thinking. For the last two years, ever since Fontenoy, Dick had kept most of his thoughts to himself. Had been preoccupied, detached.

It was true, of course, that he had been engrossed both with his business and with the war, but, even so, he had been not exactly cavalier but certainly not as attentive as one might have expected.

He is still affected by Philip's death, Catherine concluded, saddened by that herself. He is in a torpor.

He must be shocked out of it. Then he will pay proper court to me again.

She heard Ellen coming out of her bedroom and walking down the corridor on her way, presumably, to greet Dick.

Well, let her see how far she could get with him.

Not very far, I am sure, Catherine said to the girl in the mirror. Then *you* make an entrance and deflect the attention onto yourself.

'What kept you – you're late!' said Ellen to Dick.

'I'm sorry. I was working quite hard.'

'Have you got more orders?'

'I have. And Liam and I have been to the wine market. And you – tell me your news. Have you heard any more from your count?'

He knew that Count Darcy, having returned to France from Scotland where he had served with the Young Chevalier and the Jacobite army, had resumed his scientific studies and was in regular contact with Ellen.

But, as usual when he mentioned Count Darcy's name, Ellen looked displeased.

'Now and again,' she said curtly. 'And he's not "my" count – he's just a friend.'

'Dick – you're always so punctual! Come and sit down. Maman will be so pleased to see you.'

'You're looking very beautiful,' Dick said, to Catherine's gratification.

So the violet-and-rose dress had made the hoped-for impression. But, at dinner, Dick's attention still seemed to be wandering.

'Have you heard – they're writing some ugly *quatrains* about the Pompadour, saying how dreadful she is, how much money she wastes on trifles,' said Catherine, fascinated by the gossip circulating about the king's mistress. '*We* know that she directs and inspires artists to do their best work, and I've even heard that she pays some of

157

them out of her own pocket. But the general public does not appreciate that. It is felt that, since her arrival at Versailles, she has had a bad effect on the king, encouraging him to be recklessly extravagant.'

Instead of responding to this information, Dick was helping himself liberally to raw oysters on the half-shell and hot spicy sausages, a speciality of the Charente, and it was left to Ellen to say tartly: 'The general public is crippled by taxes. You can't blame them for being critical.'

'I'd love to go to Paris and see the houses that she is creating. Apparently, the king's private rooms are continually being redecorated.'

'Oh yes?' Dick said vaguely. 'That reminds me. Rooms . . . I'm looking for an office to rent in town. If anyone knows of a suitable place . . .'

'The rue de la Richonne,' Catherine said promptly. 'There's a room about to fall vacant in one of the buildings there. Mr Marrett mentioned it to me only the other day.'

'Mr Marrett? What a coincidence. This very day, at the brandy market – '

But that was as far as Dick got when Hélène, to his surprise, said sharply: 'And where did you meet Mr Marrett, Catherine?'

'At the Breuils, Maman. Don't you remember – I went there to dinner. That evening when you were unwell.'

Her mother said: 'Mr Marrett is a Protestant. I would rather you did not talk to these people.'

'Maman! He is a very nice man.'

'But a Protestant,' Hélène said, pursing her lips.

As Yvette, carrying a platter of partridges and ham, came into the room, Catherine, glad to have scored over Ellen in the matter of assisting Dick in his business, whispered to him: 'I'll explain later about the room.'

* * *

After that the conversation moved on to what interested Dick – the fact that, with the war over, the seas were going to be safe for trade again.

'Do you think the British will permit more Irish exports now?' Ellen asked. 'How *dare* they have placed a prohibition on Irish glass!'

'You know, there may be hope,' said Dick. 'In the 1730s, remember, we struggled successfully for the reduction of duties on Irish woollen and worsted yarn going into Britain. The British are more tolerant of Catholicism these days. The Protestants no longer believe that we will convert to their faith. So few of us actually did so. The Penal Laws were ineffective in that.'

Religion followed by business followed by politics followed by religion, thought Catherine, exasperatedly. Why does nobody talk about light-hearted subjects, like what is going on at the court, what balls are being organized by the Pompadour, what plays by La Chaussée and Dufresny are being produced on her orders at the Théâtre des Petits Cabinets? Don't Maman and Dick and dreary Ellen want to know that the Pompadour actually takes part in these dramatics? Don't they ever wonder, as I do, what the queen thinks about the *affaire*?

Since the answers to all these questions were only too obvious, she had no choice but to sit pretending to be interested in the conversation and comforting herself with the surety that she was looking so much more beautiful than Ellen and that Dick, even in his new vagueness, had been made aware of that fact.

Not until just before Dick left did she manage to catch him alone, and even then only briefly.

'John Marrett rents offices himself in the same building,' she said. 'He told me the name of the owner. Fortunately I have a good memory for these things so I am able to help you.'

2

Within the week Liam was reporting that Dick had taken an office in number one rue de la Richonne and that he would be pleased if Mme Cantillon and the two girls would visit his new headquarters and afterwards drive with him to the area known as Grande Champagne, where the best brandy was produced.

'We can take luncheon with us and eat outdoors by the river,' suggested Ellen.

'How vulgar,' Catherine said, grimacing. 'I can't think of anything worse than sitting out in the open, being bitten by insects, with the sun beating down on one's head, ruining the complexion.'

Even allowing for the fact that any situation in which Dick and the two girls were involved brought out the very worst in Catherine, her rival, Ellen thought, seemed unusually snappy. Perhaps her bad mood had something to do with the letter she had received in the morning?

But when Ellen asked her point-blank if she had received bad news, Catherine shook her head.

'The letter from Roger De Lacy? Nothing *he* could say would ever worry me. In fact he gave me good news of the Mehegan brothers. I may have mentioned James and William to you. Apparently James is distinguishing himself in the army and William, although he can be rather tiresome sometimes, is making a brilliant name for himself in the literary world.'

The absence of young men then? The war had killed or maimed so many of them, although some would be returning now that peace had been signed.

'You'll have a few beaux to dance attendance on you in the next few weeks,' she said to Catherine, speaking her thoughts out loud. 'That will cheer you up.'

'I'm not interested in other men,' said Catherine untruthfully, resuming hostilities in their own personal war. 'As you should know, I get all the attention I require from Dick.'

I suppose you do, Ellen thought, unaware that, in this respect, Catherine felt deprived. More's the pity Dick doesn't know what a cranky creature you are.

The evening before their outing with Dick the reason for Catherine's intensified ill-humour became painfully obvious.

'You've got mumps!' Ellen exclaimed, looking at Catherine's swollen throat and neck.

'I have not!'

But when she looked into the mirror the facts spoke for themselves.

'You'll get them, too, Ellen!'

'I've had them already,' Ellen said triumphantly. 'You only get mumps once.'

'No visits to anyone for you, Catherine,' dictated her mother. 'No protests. Off to bed and stay there until the swelling goes down. Ellen, you can go with Dick since Liam will be there to chaperon you but I will have to look after Catherine.'

'But Maman . . .'

'Catherine – *to bed*!'

A day more or less alone with Dick, marvelled Ellen. Surely Dagda, the ruler of all the gods, had come out of the heavens for the express purpose of sending her to *Magh Mel*, the Plain of Honey.

And Dick himself could well be described as being like one of the warrior heroes of old, sons of kings and queens, with golden yellow manes on their heads, smooth comely bodies and bright blue-starred eyes who marched amid the spears.

Mumps, mumps, she sang silently. To the world at large maybe an infectious disease affecting the salivary glands but, to herself, a heavenly present.

Undoubtedly Dagda was aware that, over the years, her feeling for Dick had strengthened rather than weakened, and was sympathetic towards her love.

And now she would have him to herself for several hours, although he, of course, did not know that yet.

She arrived at number one rue de la Richonne early in the morning at the same time as a pleasant-faced man with eyes as blue as Dick's.

'Good morning,' she said, 'I'm Ellen Nagle.'

The pleasant-faced man – he was in his thirties, she surmised, and had dark hair, slightly greying – looked startled, not used, apparently, to such directness.

After a pause he said: 'And I am John Marrett.'

'Do you also have an office in this building?'

'Yes,' said the dark-haired man, and Ellen because she was in *Magh Mel* already and wanted others to share her happiness there, said: 'Then you'll know Dick O'Shaughnessy. No? Then come in and meet him.'

Looking somewhat bemused, the man followed her into what turned out to be a tiny office, was duly introduced to Dick, and made polite conversation while Ellen peered out of the window and noted that there was a convent nearby.

Then she and Dick, having said their farewells to Mr Marrett, set out for the Grande Champagne, driven by Liam Crowley.

It was an idyllic day for a drive, warm without being hot and stifling, luminous and serene, although if they had travelled through the heart of a blizzard Ellen would not have cared. It was years since she and Dick had been on their own for any length of time, free to talk without Madame Cantillon's and Catherine's intervention, and although in one sense they were not really alone, with Liam being at the reins he could neither hear what they said nor join in the conversation.

'Tell me what we're going to do and see,' she said, tucking the basket of food which Catherine would have scorned out of the way of her feet.

'There's a wine-farmer I know. A good fellow. I asked him if I could bring friends the next time I called on him and he said I could.'

'He's a distiller as well as a grower?'

Dick nodded.

'A *bouilleur de cru* – that means that he distils only his own wine. It's too late in the season now to watch the distillation process.'

'I know that. It starts early in November.'

'Even earlier on some farms. And goes on until early in May. But you'll see today how the grapes are grown and cultivated.'

Ellen leant back, luxuriating in her happiness. Now that she was in *Magh Mel* the countryside seemed lovelier than ever, densely wooded, the trees green down to their very roots, their branches heavy with pheasants. The odour of meadowsweet acted soporifically upon her senses, as if the fairies were trying to drug her. Her mind was filled, not with its normal quota of practicalities, but with fanciful images of spring. Soon, she thought, young men will come in secret to their sweethearts' doorways and leave there flowers or cakes or oranges, the symbols of their love.

They crossed a bridge and passed, under the trees, into La Trache and the road sloped downwards. They were heading in the direction of the old village of Bourg-Charente. Having driven close to the smart Château of Saint-Brice and the village of Chatres, with its exquisite Romanesque abbatial church, the forestry began to give way to farmland. In a field a woman with a striped apron over her skirt and blouse was tending three goats. She held a blue umbrella over her head to protect her from the sun, although on her head was the curious forward-thrusting white bonnet known as the *quichenotte* designed, Ellen had heard, to ward off the amorous advances of English soldiers in the days when they had occupied this territory.

'Shall we stop and ask her if she will sell us some cheese?' Ellen asked, knowing that it would be made from a special secret recipe to which herbs and spices had to be added at just the right moment.

But Dick, keen to press on, was shaking his head. Soon they saw the first vines, sometimes planted in the shape of a diamond, at others in the shape of a square.

'The farmers here grow Balzac grapes, a variety which ripens quite late so they're not affected by the spring frosts which would otherwise kill the shoots and clusters,' said Dick. 'We have a perfect climate in Cognac for grape-growing, gentle and temperate, with misty rain.'

'Irish rain.'

'Yes! But, here, that rain means that the grapes can ripen slowly and regularly in *tamisée* – filtered light. And here in Grande Champagne we have the best *terroir* of all. Look at it. It's white and crumbly and soft. Cretaceous soil. It's because of that soil that the wines are acid. But from that acidity the best brandy is distilled.'

Liam was turning off the road to stop by a farmhouse, surrounded by black stone walls. Standing waiting for them was a middle-aged man with a round cheerful face and black curranty eyes.

'Captain O'Shaughnessy, good day.'

'And to you, Monsieur Merlet.'

They followed the farmer through a gate into a cobbled yard and a short, sullen-faced woman, whom Ellen presumed was Mme Merlet, nodded to them and disappeared into the house.

'My wife,' M. Merlet corroborated and then, as if Dick already appreciated that Mme Merlet was not an easy woman to live with, the farmer smiled at him in a conspiratorial way.

'Don't concern yourself,' Dick said. 'We'll walk around the farm and see how your vines are progressing and talk together later.'

The rapid shoot, as he knew, was due only to peak in early summer but there was much, all the same, to point out to Ellen. And he was rather looking forward to teaching her about viticulture, explaining the importance of pruning to her, a job already done by the men in late winter, when the sap was at its lowest, and amusing her by describing how some of the saplings were burnt in the kitchen fire, to give a unique flavour to any food cooked over it. And she would surely be interested in the part that women played in the vineyards, tying the fruit-bearing branches in a traditional, prescribed manner that only they understood, once the pruning was done.

'Viticulture is a very, very old occupation,' he began. 'The Phoenicians carried the grape into France in 600 BC. And even Noah is said to have planted a grape-vine.'

'Yes, I read about that in the Old Testament,' said Ellen, ruining the start of his dissertation.

'I might have known that you would!' Dick said to her. 'Now will you *listen* without interrupting!'

She did, more or less. After that, he had a business talk with M. Merlet and the latter, as a parting gift, gave them a cask of cognac.

And then they made their way down to the river bank, selecting a spot which looked across to the Château de Bourg on the other side of the Charente.

Liam, on the pretext of examining the church at the top of the rise against which the village of Bourg-Charente had been built, tactfully left them together. He was acutely aware that both Miss Ellen and Miss Catherine had designs on Master Dick, and was determined to do all he could to boost Miss Ellen's cause.

Miss Catherine he rated as crooked as the horn of a ram and no right partner for a man like Master Dick.

But Miss Ellen, on the other hand, struck him as a mere beginner in the – to him – wholly incomprehensible game of love, knowing no more about it than a pig did about an armchair. He hoped devoutly that the gods would deal her a good hand.

Having dutifully surveyed a Gothic mural representing the Adoration of the Magi, he made his way back to the river, glad that he had filled his pockets with refreshments before setting off, and sat down in a secluded spot under a tree which enabled him to see without being seen. He took his position as chaperon seriously, although it did not occur to him for a minute that Master Dick, that great gentleman, would harbour in his mind the evil thoughts that had once plagued his own about Miss Ellen, on the road to Dublin.

Munching on a piece of ham, he focused his eyes on the pair of them. By the looks of things they were about to have a drink.

The cask of cognac which M. Merlet had given Dick as a present was only a miniature but it was as perfectly made as a full-size barrel.

'*Sláinte!*' Dick said, toasting Ellen's health in Irish.

'*Sláinte!* Do you know that this is the first time I've ever tasted cognac, or any strong spirit at all, come to think of it?'

'And do you like it?'

'It's strong . . .'

'Sip – don't gulp, Ellen, for goodness' sake. It's brandy, not water.'

Dick felt blissfully at ease, as he always did when he sat by the river in the shadow of the trees, the poplars, their foliage dark green at the top but white and dense and pubescent below, and the weary willows which seemed to him more languid than gloomy.

The shapes of these trees and their colours were reflected in the lazy river. On this day in late spring the mood of the Charente was so serene, so easy-going that it was difficult to believe, let alone remember, its more volatile dimensions, the havoc the river could cause when its mood changed and it flowed dark and angry over the green banks, as it had done this winter past.

He liked both phases. Unbroken harmony, he thought, would be boring. Contrast and change was not.

'Doesn't the Charente remind you of the Blackwater?' he said idly to Ellen. 'When I sit beneath the trees I always think of Kilawillen.'

He passed the cask to Ellen and she drank from it again and as she did so he suddenly knew that, one day, he was going to live beside the river.

'When I have made a lot more money than I am making now I am going to own a fine château on the bank of the Charente,' he said.

'You are?' said Ellen, and of course, the fairies promptly put an image into her head of herself, married to Dick, living alongside him. A definite cause for celebration! Before passing the cask of cognac back to Dick she sipped from it again.

* * *

167

Liam, from his position of vigilance, saw her take another sip from the tiny barrel and he frowned in disapproval. What did Master Dick think he was doing, encouraging a young girl to drink as freely as that?

What would Mme Cantillon say to him if he were to bring Ellen home drunk, he wondered, and pondered the wisdom of getting up and joining the picnicking couple, to put a stop to their carryings-on.

It was then that he saw the red deer standing nearby. A stag with proud soaring horns, looking, he thought, as lithe and as fleet as a *luarach* – except that the creature, far from gliding into the water and sailing off, did not budge an inch.

Nor did he dare to stir himself. A quiver of fear went down his spine, in spite of the warmth of the day, and as if he had thus been turned into a block of ice, he remained motionless.

For there was no point in getting up and attempting to run away. He had only to look at the stag's antlers to appreciate the foolishness of drawing attention to himself by moving.

Then he realized that the stag had already seen him. Must have done so long before he had become aware that it was close. Its huge brown eyes – the colour of Miss Catherine's eyes, Liam thought, distracted – contemplated him with interest, as if this trembling stranger sitting under a tree was one of the sights of the forest, like a wild flower or shrub.

Unable to take his eyes off the stag – it was as if it would not allow him to do so – Liam sat motionless, not daring to move an inch.

After a while his fear began to ebb away. Unblinking, the stag continued to gaze at him and, in spite of himself, Liam came to the conclusion that it had no intention of charging: that he and this wild animal were exchanging nothing more ominous than a natural communication between two of God's creatures.

The stag turned away first, as if their silent conversation had exhausted itself. Treading with dainty hoofs, more reminiscent of a woman in high-heeled shoes than a beast of the forest, it retreated along the bank, away from Liam and Dick and Ellen, and disappeared into the trees.

'An angel's born!' Liam said to himself, chuckling aloud with relief.

Instinctively, he looked to the river bank where Master Dick and Miss Ellen were sitting. What he saw caused him as much consternation as he had experienced when he had first laid eyes on the stag.

Ellen was feeling deliciously tipsy. She would have liked to have lain back on the grass, as Dick was doing, but the heavy boning of her silk bodice did not permit such laxity. Instead, she moved closer to Dick, so near that through the layers of her full-skirted gown her thigh touched his.

'Will your château be very imposing?'

'Of course. But the garden will not be too formal. An avenue lined with trees and in the centre of a grand square a circular *bassin* with a jet of water rising straight up from its centre.'

He had the bluest eyes in the world. Eyes that might have been painted with a potion made out of bluebells by an artist who had only completed his work minutes before, a careless craftsman who had not noticed or cared that the colour of the irises was running, and shading the corneas blue . . .

Dick did not move towards her. He simply looked up from his supine position into her emerald eyes. It was Ellen who did the kissing, leaning over him and pressing her full mouth onto his straight one, caressing him with her soft supple lips.

An unfamiliar glow seemed to filter through her body, as if a representative of the *Sidh*, the Fairy People, had transformed her into a ray of sunlight. She closed her eyes, parting her lips as Dick parted his and the tip of his moist tongue began its tentative exploration.

And it seemed to her that their bodies were floating; that the *Sidh* had lifted them effortlessly and was transporting them to a fairy palace where they would lie naked on a downy bed and drink from cups made out of white silver.

But first Dick had to undo the fastenings of her gown and remove her cumbersome bodice.

'God between us and all harm!' an all-too-human voice exclaimed loudly and the startled *Sidh* at once let go of the two of them, bumping them back onto the bank of the river.

Reluctantly, she opened her eyes. Standing over them was Liam Crowley, his own eyes huge with alarm, and he waving a piece of ham at them as if it were a weapon.

'Master Dick – Miss Ellen!' he was wailing. 'If herself gets to know about what's going on, I swear she'll tear me asunder!'

'She might at that,' said Dick soberly.

Gently but firmly he pushed Ellen away and leapt to his feet.

'Come on,' he said, his voice not that of a lover at all, but rather reminding her of Mr O'Halloran the teacher, from the hedge-school at Ballygriffin.

And when she looked up at him she saw with her heart sinking that his expression too was not loving but stern.

'You're quite right, Liam,' said Dick in Mr O'Halloran's voice. 'And we must be going back.'

In the carriage they sat far apart and they did not look at each other.

170

And what have I done to merit such disapproval? Ellen asked herself miserably. I love him. I kissed him. And why should that make him cross?

And he kissed me. He seemed to like it at that time, and was wanting to go on.

Is it embarrassed he is at Liam's intervention? Is that why he turns his head away and looks out of the carriage window?

Or does he find me repulsive, now he's had time to look at me again?

To look at my big ugly hands . . .

So unlike Catherine's dainty little hands. So maybe it's Catherine he wants – and always has wanted. Catherine who is destined to share with him the château of his dreams on the bank of the Charente.

She pulled her lips in tight to stop herself crying but all the same two large salty tears trickled out of her eyes and fell onto her folded hands.

Onto her horrible hands . . .

Oh, she had no hope with Dick. She would go through life with only the memory of a kiss, prompted by herself.

And her head was beginning to throb.

'We're almost in Cognac,' said Mr O'Halloran's stern voice. 'It's late in the day. Liam can set me down at my office and take you straight home to Crouin.'

3

Ellen believed herself at fault as a woman; Dick, in his own eyes, also stood condemned.

His, he believed, was the unpardonable crime of having survived two battles in which valued comrades of his own age had been slain or maimed.

He was drenched in guilt, as they had been in their own blood. Only by immersing himself in work could he find ease, then, from his self-hatred.

Anyone who knew him would have told him, with truth, that he was free from blame; that, despite having learnt to loathe war, he had fought extremely bravely in those two battles, but the conviction that he was suspect was so entrenched, buried so deep inside him that he would not have believed them.

In any case, he confided in no one. On the face of it, he was a perfectly normal, even cheery young man with initiative, who had set himself up as a broker and exporter of cognac. The wine-farmers, the shippers, even Liam Crowley, accepted him as such; the Cognaçais were too reticent by nature to ask him any questions about his war experiences and Liam's attempts to discuss Fontenoy Dick successfully parried.

In the daytime he worked hard. At night he found it difficult to sleep. When he dreamed it was often of battle – of a British officer dead in a wood, of Philip's lifeless body. And when he woke after such dreams, dry-mouthed, those who had died seemed still to be present in his bedroom, accusing him of living.

Convinced of his own worthlessness, he fought shy of

romance, punishing himself, since no one else saw fit to do so.

The day after the disastrous picnic with Ellen he went to La Rochelle on business. He travelled not by horse but by boat, boarding one of the small barges, known as *gabares*, which were used to transport brandy in barrels to Tonnay-Charente, a few miles inland, where they were loaded onto *cogues*, the larger craft which took them on to La Rochelle, for shipment to Europe.

He stood on the deck of the *gabare* enjoying the sensation of travelling by water. The river was unruffled except for the little waves set up by the boat; its banks, lined by clumps of reeds at the water's edge, were thickly encrusted with trees.

When he looked at the river he found himself thinking of the Blackwater again, and of the valley, speculating idly about his parents and sisters and Willie. Now that peace had been signed, now that he was out of the army, he could visit Ireland without fear of being arrested. One day he would do so. France and the French had been good to him but he was, always would be, an Irishman at heart even if it was necessary for him to earn a living outside his native land.

His thoughts were still in Ireland when, through a clearing in the trees on the right bank of the river, he saw the partly-ruined château, a long low building with a tower beside it, set back from the water's edge, on a hillock, in a tangle of overgrown garden. Closer to the building trees, which had been planted in a double avenue up from the water's edge, looked blackened and lifeless. The château, too, had been extensively damaged on one side. Fire ravage, he thought, and wondered how it had been started.

'What is that place?' he asked the captain of the *gabare*. The man grimaced.

'The Château de Pericard? They say it is unlucky. Twice there have been fires.'

'And now it is deserted?'

'You can see. In the last fire there were deaths. No one will live there.'

The boat continued to drift downstream. The Château de Pericard vanished into the verdancy leaving Dick with a memory of shattered elegance and neglect in a perfect riverside setting.

If he could buy the château . . . He was not in the least deterred by the knowledge that it was considered to be unlucky. He was not superstitious about such matters. A merchant, after all, dealt with facts and figures, not in spells and omens and chance. He was only prepared to believe in luck as it related to gambling.

But the preoccupation of others with doom and predictions could work in his favour. If the Château de Pericard was considered ill-fated, he might well acquire it for little or nothing; have it repaired, rebuilt; restore the chapel; turn it all into a beautiful dwelling on the river bank, reminiscent, in that way, of his old home at Kilawillen.

When he returned to Cognac he would make inquiries and see if it was feasible to carry out these ideas.

In the meantime, he had something else, another distraction, as well as work, to take his mind off war.

Dick's journey to La Rochelle, to meet the shippers, was not strictly necessary, but when he saw the three gigantic medieval towers set out in the sea in front of the enchanting old port he thought that, for the sight of them alone, it had been worth his trip.

'Tower of the Lantern. Tower of Saint Nicholas. Tower of the Chain,' the captain, a native of La Rochelle, explained proudly. 'The chain – it was placed between the

174

chain tower and the tower of Saint Nicholas – was, naturally, to prevent the pirates coming in.'

'Interesting.'

Although, Dick thought, perhaps not as fascinating, from his point of view, as the other idea taking shape, now, in his mind.

Rich landowners, he knew, often stored their brandy after distillation until they were sure that they could obtain a high price for the whole consignment. Although brandy was popular with men of all classes, rich and poor alike, the more discriminating were beginning to observe that some vintages appeared to be better than others.

If he, as a *négociant*, a merchant who shipped directly to his customers, could save enough money to buy up a reasonable percentage of a good year's production and store it against a bad year's vintage, he could fill the gap in the market with a product that was already tried and approved.

In between seeing his shippers he bandied the idea around in his mind, liking it more by the minute. Its one drawback – that he did not at present own a house of his own, let alone a *paradis* or cellar – would fall away if, as he hoped, he acquired the Château de Pericard and restored it.

He had wanted to prove himself energetic and innovative and successful. Here was a way in which, by working hard and operating shrewdly, he could succeed in his ambitions.

He strolled around the harbour, looking out at the deep bay, lost in thought with the sun beating down on his head until, realizing that he was thirsty, he paused to drink from a fountain.

'No, don't do that!' a man advised and he turned to see John Marrett standing behind him.

'Monsieur O'Shaughnessy – or perhaps I should say

Captain O'Shaughnessy,' said Marrett in his rather husky voice. 'My apologies for intruding but it is unwise to drink from fountains in La Rochelle.'

'In that case please don't apologize for doing me a good turn! What a coincidence meeting you here.'

'Perhaps not, as we are in the same line of business. Are you alone? If so, perhaps you would like to join me for luncheon? There is an excellent inn, I believe, in the rue Saint-Jean.'

'That would be pleasant,' said Dick, and felt his over-worked conscience nudge him once again.

Since moving into the office in rue de la Richonne he had, as a matter of course, spied upon his neighbour, watching how many wine-farmers came to see him, asking Liam to find out who they were and what price they were wanting for their *eau-de-vie*.

John Marrett, of course, probably did likewise – was bound to have done so. Had not Liam said explicitly that the Englishman was a canny fellow?

If he was as mean as he was reputed to be then his purpose in inviting Dick to luncheon, so far from being hospitable, could be his way of insinuating himself into his neighbour's confidence to find out about his business.

In that case, thought Dick, I had better keep up my guard.

But when they were seated opposite each other in the inn and had selected what they wanted to eat and drink Marrett made no attempts to probe and pry.

'Here's to your good health,' he said, and smiled rather shyly at Dick.

'I hear you deal in commodities other than cognac,' said Dick, thinking that, if John Marrett was not making inquiries, he might as well make some himself.

'That's correct,' said Marrett. 'I buy tanned hides and clover-seeds for export to England. But I'm primarily

176

interested in cognac. Thank God for the Dutch, I always say. Without their demand for *brandwyn* this market might never have been opened up. They may have put in a poor performance in battle in recent years, but it was the Dutch who established stills in the Charente and passed on their expertise in distilling to the Cognaçais. These fat snails are very good, don't you think?'

In spite of Liam's warnings about Marrett's parsimony, Dick was beginning to like the man. He was a gentlemanly fellow, and, more than that, he was eating luncheon with every indication of being a *bon vivant* rather than a miserly recluse.

And he seemed to have an eye for the ladies. With amusement he saw Marrett cast an admiring glance at a pretty serving girl bending over an adjacent table.

'We have similar tastes!'

Marrett looked abashed, like a small boy caught by his father in an act of mischief.

'A lovely wench.'

'Isn't she?' agreed Dick, watching the girl straighten and smile in their direction before disappearing again into the kitchen.

The girl reminded him of Catherine, although she was not, he thought, as attractive.

Marrett said, 'She reminds me of someone I know . . . You know Mademoiselle Cantillon well?'

'I do. She mentioned that she had met you.'

'Then you have seen her recently?'

'A fortnight ago. She has been ill, I believe, with mumps.'

It was as if he had announced to his companion that Catherine was dying of an incurable disease. John Marrett looked stricken.

'But that is terrible,' he said. 'Is it – very serious?'

'I don't think so. Just uncomfortable.'

'Are you going to visit her?'

'I would like to. I had mumps as a child, so I can do so safely.'

At this John Marrett looked even more miserable. The devil! thought Dick. He's in love with Catherine. And he's been pumping me for information about her.

That's why he asked me to luncheon!

'Red roses for me – *and* a letter!' said Catherine contentedly.

The swelling in her face and neck had gone down and she was feeling very much better. And now here was Ellen handing over the kind of tonic that made every girl better, even if she was not sick.

'From Dick, I suppose,' she said, and had the satisfaction of seeing Ellen wince before she left the bedroom.

The writer had printed her name on the envelope. It was only when she drew out the pages that Catherine saw that they were not written in Dick's rather slapdash scrawl, but in unfamiliar, small, neat handwriting:

. . . I am writing to you with some trepidation, having learnt from Captain O'Shaughnessy that you are ill . . .

What is this all about, Catherine wondered crossly, and what does Dick think he is doing, telling people that I have mumps?

Without reading anymore she examined the signature on the third and last page:

. . . Your humble servant – John Marrett.

'*Merde!*' said Catherine aloud, using the worst word she knew, an epithet so frightful that its use shocked even herself. 'Why is *he* writing and sending me flowers and Dick is not?'

She was so distraught that she hurled the letter to the foot of the gilded wooden couch, its mattress covered with pink satin, on which she had been resting, and the small white dog which had been considering leaping onto her lap rapidly changed its mind.

So much for thinking that Dick O'Shaughnessy, that most elusive and most irritating of men, would have made a romantic gesture.

And to think that she had boasted about his having done so to Ellen! Her cheeks burnt with rage at the realization that she had made a fool of herself.

But a little later, when her anger and disappointment had partially ebbed, she found consolation in the fact that John Marrett had written to her, and sent her such lovely red roses.

She reached down and retrieved the scattered pages of his letter, and put them back into logical order:

. . . enjoyed meeting you so much. Hoped that we could meet again . . .

He was certainly in love with her. Catherine's former good humour was almost completely restored.

Her new admirer was quite old – perhaps as old as thirty-three or -four – but he was captivated by her charms – that, with such a dearth of young men in the Charente, was of more importance than his age.

And, since John Marrett might be offset against Dick in some way, he could yet have his uses.

'Come, Mou-Mou,' she called to the little white dog. 'Come and let me stroke you.'

In the matter of making inquiries about the Château de Pericard Dick once again employed Liam Crowley.

''Tis for sale all right, Master Dick,' Liam reported. 'It seems that 'tis still in the hands of the descendants of the fellow who built it long ago.'

'And who would that be?'

'A right upstart, they tell me, who made money out of

179

trade with the East, and wouldn't that be a warning to you, concerning the taste of what he constructed.'

Dick grinned covertly. Liam, under the influence of Hélène, was becoming a bit of a snob. Maman, he thought, had much to say about the social changes which had created financial difficulties for the landed aristocracy. The men of commerce had done well for themselves. Despised as vulgar by the old *noblesse d'épée*, they had adapted themselves to fluctuations and even found them beneficial, and when the establishment had formally recognized *rentes*, loans guaranteed by the city of Paris which paid a high rate of interest, the *noblesse de robe*, as the newcomers were called, had become more omnipotent still.

'When was the château built?' he asked Liam and when the latter told him: 'A century or two ago, Master Dick, but, mind you, there was a castle there before that,' his interest was even further awakened.

Like the man of commerce – presumably, Monsieur de Pericard himself, for surely a member of the *noblesse de robe* would not have lost an opportunity to link his name with his château? – he, Dick, was an upstart in France, even if he had come from an ancient Irish family. What could be more fitting than that he should acquire a château which combined the dream of a medieval knight with the aspirations of the *noblesse de robe*, since he had connections with both?

Liam was looking less enthusiastic.

'Don't you know there's a curse on the place because of the two fires?'

'Ah, curses,' said Dick dismissively. 'I suppose you found out how the fires happened, as well?'

'I did. 'Twas love that caused them both – or passion. Didn't the first fellow – the one that built it, who would cheat the devil in the dark – make off with another

180

fellow's woman and he left with a heart of holly and a great desire for vengeance.'

'And the second fire?'

'That was more recent. Wouldn't a jealous woman make trouble between two breast-bones?'

'A woman did it?'

Liam said: 'So they tell me – so they tell me. And wasn't the owner's son and his two sisters burnt alive in the conflagration?'

All the same, Dick made an appointment to inspect the château, which was at Chez Landart, about eight miles from the centre of Cognac. To reach it he had to ride past Manoir des Yeux.

Dodging Ellen, he did not call in, as he would normally have done, or even glance in that direction, but rode on along rue Basse de Crouin and rue Haute de Crouin, through Jarnouzeau and Douzillet and Chez Chassat.

The man who was to show him over the property was waiting anxiously for him at the gates.

'A beautiful setting, sir.'

'Indeed.'

'The original castle commanded a strategic position, as you will see, on the bend of the river. As for the château, it was, you understand, a *maison de plaisance*, built specifically for King François himself, and for the most beautiful of all his mistresses.'

Dick shut his mind to such inventions. Behind him the silver-green river; emaciated trees peering perilously out of the flood meadow; before him – perhaps – his future home.

Directly in front of him was a gateway which, he supposed, gave way to the *corps-de-logis*, or central court, around which the ground floor rooms would be arranged. Over this gateway were inscriptions in honour of François

Premier and reliefs in the form of the salamander: to the left of it, an exterior staircase, to the right an open arcade.

'. . . most desirable residence – '

'Could we go inside?'

'Of course. But, monsieur, first, this staircase. It leads, you understand, to the chapel. The frescoes depict the Passion and are most remarkable. The principal staircase is inside the *corps-de-logis*, between the hall and the parlour.'

They stepped into the court and Dick looked curiously around. To his left and right ran arcaded galleries over which, in low relief, he could see carvings of mythological subjects, animals and birds. Eased forward and left by his companion he found himself in a parlour in which a monumental stone fireplace depicted a wolf carved in the round. Further left again he discovered all that remained of the medieval château fort, the high, round, thick-walled tower which, with the *donjon* or keep in which the *seigneur* and his family would have lived, would have formed the all-important defence of the moat, long since filled in.

Doubling back, the agent skilfully propelled him in the direction of the straight stone stairs, above which were ribbed ogive arches.

'Wait – I want to see what is over here, on the right.'

The agent shrugged: 'The buttery. The kitchens. A passage for servants. It is of little importance.'

'All the same, I would like to see.'

No wonder the man was steering me away from this wing, Dick thought, completing his investigation of the ground floor and taking in the blackened walls and crumbling surface of what had once been white plaster-work. In the kitchen he looked upwards and saw that there was a hole in the ceiling.

'Upstairs, it is a miracle,' the agent was insisting.

'It would need to be,' Dick said, 'to counteract what has happened down here.'

He had no intention of revealing his growing interest in the property to this man and made a point of tentatively testing the stability of the staircase, preparatory to exploring upstairs.

In the gallery, mullioned windows interspersed with stone tabernacles depicting what Dick decided must be the original owner and his family, all of them dressed and coiffed in the manner of François Premier. In the largest of the bedrooms were further frescoed murals relating the history of long-dead knights.

'You see, from this window, the garden. It would be easily cleared and replanted.'

'The other rooms on this floor?'

The agent sighed resignedly.

'Slightly damaged by fire again, monsieur. You understand . . .'

'Slightly' was an understatement, Dick found, when he went to see for himself. Only one of the three bedrooms in this wing still retained its door, its thickness considerably reduced by the onslaught of fire. When Dick shouldered it open, he noticed at once that the interior walls were bulging and blackened by smoke.

The rest was an agent's nightmare. Fallen plaster exposed half-burnt timber lathes and cracked stonework. The floor of the room looking, literally, down to the kitchen was severely eroded.

'There's been extensive structural damage to these walls.'

'But, no, monsieur!'

'I'm afraid it's true. Now shall we go and look at the chapel. You were telling me about the frescoes . . .'

His companion had the air of a beaten man, having no

183

inkling that, in Dick's mind, the bargain was already clinched.

As he followed the agent along the gallery towards the chapel he was saying to himself that the château was ideal not only because it was – or could be in time – charming, but because on this site he would be able to store all the cognac he could buy over the current year.

'Here, there is a floor made from Italian marble. Monsieur, what are your feelings about the property?'

'For a start, the price is far too high,' said Dick airily. 'Perhaps you would tell the executors that, although the place has certain potential, I'm not even slightly tempted to buy at the figure you've mentioned.'

It was difficult to keep a straight face, not to show his jubilance as the two men rode back to Cognac together. It was going to be all right – Dick was sure of it. The executors *would* reduce their price. From the agent's behaviour, and the rumours of a curse on the château, it was easy enough to deduce that they would be glad enough to dispose of it.

I think I'm in luck, he said to himself.

'I hear that the fires were deliberately started, as acts of revenge,' he remarked to the agent.

The man looked shocked.

'Monsieur, against François Premier, who would seek a revenge?'

He had been too preoccupied earlier to notice the run-down cottage, built from cob and straw, set into the trees on his left. Seeing it now, and the peasant farmer at work outside it, Dick suddenly felt ashamed.

The farmer, typical of so many in France, was so poor he might have been Irish. Such people knew nothing of luxury – of fine châteaux by the river – except as a far-off view. They lived on buckwheat, rape and oil of rape, and instead of wine they drank water. They wore clothes made of wool gathered from their flocks and kemp out of their gardens – if they were lucky enough to have access to flocks and gardens. Many, too many, lived in the coastal swamps and the woods and in filthy potholes, and all were plagued by disease and epidemics.

And by taxes. That was the other form of pestilence. Both direct and indirect taxes. The loathed *gabelle*, or salt tax, the *traites*, the customs duties, the *aides*, excise taxes on items ranging from tobacco to leather; and on top of those innumerable local variations, all designed to refill the depleted coffers of the royal treasury at the tragic cost of the common people.

And here was he in high old humour, at the prospect of the fine house he was about to possess – the comfortable life he would live in it.

But not at the expense of others. One day in the not-too-distant future he would be employing peasant labour. When that time came, he vowed, the men would be justly treated and paid a decent wage. All his life, from a position of comparative security, he had been acutely aware of poverty and suffering. Was it therefore so unusual that he should want to reach out to those in need, even if they were not his fellow countrymen? Ellen, who expressed herself so forcibly on the subject of taxes and injustice, would surely understand his thinking.

Ellen, whom he had been consciously avoiding. He could not dodge her forever.

Only for a while.

For a month or two, until he felt he could face her with equanimity.

Until he was again in control of his emotions.

* * *

185

In the meantime, he was in something of a turmoil.

Ever since the day he had spent with Ellen at Bourg-Charente he had become more and more reluctantly aware of his own sexual needs.

It was all her doing! Since then he had found himself covertly looking at women, noticing the attractive things about them: the satin smoothness of skin disappearing into the neckline. The fine hair on their arms when they rolled up their sleeves. Their smell. Their hands and fingers. The shape of their breasts inside their *pets-en-l'air* as they turned their bodies or stretched.

In Confession, Monsignor Doussinet put it to him bluntly: 'You are being tempted by the Devil, Dick,' he said. 'You should be married. If you are to remain in a state of grace, find yourself a wife.'

But Dick was not yet ready to face that truth, having to contend with the memory of a harsher, more painful concern.

In his dreams the two matters merged. In the early hours of one morning two women seemed to be beside him, Ellen and Catherine.

'*I* am the right woman for you, Dick O'Shaughnessy,' Ellen said, coming straight to the point at once. 'You know that I love you. Why do you not return my love?'

He struggled to find the words with which to answer her, but he could not speak. His voice was gone and it came to him that he had been struck mute, and would never again be able to converse with Ellen.

'In Paris, before Fontenoy, I was quite sure that you, like all the other young men, had fallen in love with me,' said Catherine to him, sulking. 'Why have you withdrawn from me since then? I demand an explanation!'

'Remember, Dick, what I told you,' another voice, equally familiar, warned. 'You are under an obligation. Be sure that you carry it out . . .'

'You may be asking too much of me,' he wanted to say to the third voice.

But that speaker had gone away and only the girls remained.

'It's pointless going to Ireland to ask Willie to settle the matter. What about my business?' Dick said to the two of them, for his voice had just come back.

Between them, they would ruin his career. He was sure of it, and woke covered in perspiration, annoyed with himself and his dream.

He threw the bedclothes aside. But he remained, for the moment, concealed inside another cocoon, knowing that – sooner or later – he would have to emerge and face the reality of which Monsignor Doussinet had spoken.

But then the agent for the Château de Pericard approached him again and diverted him by further nego-tiation. After some protracted dealing, Dick became its new owner. For a short time his attention was diverted from women to property.

Instead of visiting Manoir des Yeux, he wrote to its occupants explaining that, for the time-being, he would be extremely busy but that he would be in touch with them in due course.

Playing for time, he immersed himself in the business of restoration. And so the summer slipped by.

It was well into autumn before Ellen realized that Cath-erine was involved in some intrigue.

There was an air of suppressed excitement about her, her cheeks were flushed and her brown eyes were sparkling.

Hmm, Ellen thought – and why is she wearing her new mantelet with that low-crowned beaver hat, and carrying her cashmere shawl, if, as she maintains, she has only been to the market?

Then Catherine said something which Ellen believed to be the all-too-obvious explanation for her radiance.

'I met Dick in town today. He wants us to visit his new château and to advise him about décor and furniture.'

'Does he?' said Ellen sadly.

But, at least, he has extended the invitation to include myself, as well as Catherine, she tried to comfort herself.

There was little consolation in the probability that Dick and Catherine had met in Cognac not once but several times during the last few months which would explain Catherine's frequent absences.

If only I hadn't made such a fool of myself that day at Bourg-Charente, Ellen thought again.

'You'll come to Chez Landart?' Catherine asked in the voice of one who hopes that the reply will be in the negative.

'I will indeed,' Ellen forced herself to say.

It was not a cold day and indeed Catherine, in her warm clothes, was incorrectly attired. All the same, Ellen realized, her feet were chilly as ice.

It was harvest-time, and the grapes were being picked before they reached full maturity since the low-alcohol wine from which the best brandy would be distilled required a low sugar content. If he were to ride into the wine slopes Dick knew that he would see the women picking the white grapes and putting them into huge baskets.

Instead, he stayed at the château, with his band of hired helpers, rebuilding, replastering and, in the case of the kitchen and buttery, tearing down walls in order to replace them.

As he worked he made discoveries. When he inspected

the ceiling beams of the bedroom in which he intended to sleep he found that it was decorated with arabesques and flowers, each one accompanied by a Latin epigram referring to its nature. In that side of the vaulted kitchen which had escaped the worst fury of the fire was a flat-arch fireplace and a bake-oven with a spit for roasting meat, neither of which he had noticed on his initial visit to the château. And in the grounds was an empty pond through which, when refilled, horses could be driven to clean their feet.

Restoration was still far from complete but great strides had been made, enough to make him aware that he should be giving serious thought to colour schemes and furnishings.

But, in that respect, he was out of his depth and he knew it.

'Will your château be very imposing?' Ellen had asked him (on that disastrous day at Bourg-Charente) and he had said blithely: 'Of course,' as if he would fill it with all manner of costly things, to maintain its Renaissance splendours.

Now that the château was beginning to emerge, phoenix-like, from its ashes, he was beginning to think of it as a home rather than the house of his dreams.

And homes – surely – should not be pretentious, but comfortable and functional, as Kilawillen House had been. The beamed ceilings of the château lent it a rustic character. He could see that, although it had been the creation of an upstart, a man from whom Hélène – or Liam – would have expected the ostentatious, the over-all effect was gently formal, unfussy and serene.

All the same, the château was a challenge. The more he worked upon it the more it seemed to be quietly urging him to reach a decision about its final refurbishment.

But what did he know about carpets and cushions and

189

tables and coverlets? That needed a woman's touch. When by chance he met Catherine in Cognac he knew that she would be just the right person to advise him.

It seemed, too, a good opportunity to see Ellen again and to attempt to get back to their former understanding.

If that was all that came out of their visit he would be pleased, but he was sure that, when they left, his problems with furniture and colour would be finally resolved.

'I can see it all clearly,' Catherine said, looking around the parlour. 'Red satin chairs and sofas. A linen wall-covering with a painted pattern of red and white and blue Indian liana-blossoms and a black-and-gold lacquer commode. And in the master-bedroom a bed with a canopy of embroidered Persian silk.'

'That would be horrible!'

'I beg your pardon, Ellen?'

'It's much too ornate. This is a country house, not a palace!'

'It is a Renaissance château, built in the classical *mode* of the great Loire châteaux,' Catherine said, managing, even from her less-elevated height, to look down her nose at Ellen. 'There were strong Italian influences at that time. You need to re-create that feeling of luxury and opulence.'

'Why? Dick isn't a prince – he's a merchant. He wants a home to live in, not a palace.'

'He would like, I am sure, to live in a modicum of style . . .'

Dick said: 'And how would you decorate my château, Ellen?' more out of diplomacy than because he expected her to put forward any suggestions.

Ellen, he thought, was a doer rather than a creator. He did not think she had an artistic bone in her body.

But then she surprised him.

'I'd want to put the colours of the earth and the flowers and the sky into it,' she said. 'And the silver-green of the river. Don't you want to see the blue Canterbury bells on your bedroom ceiling more clearly – and the yellow in the breast of the blue-tit which is carved out on the gallery? And how could you do that if your attention was caught by too much opulence? You wouldn't look at the wolf over the fireplace in this room if there were red satin and gold lacquerwork to distract you, but you would if you had simpler, country furniture carved in the same sort of style.'

'What strange taste you have,' Catherine said before Dick could speak. 'And I suppose you'd have rush-seated chairs, or maybe you'd even paint them green?'

'And why not? I think they'd be lovely.'

Afterwards, Dick thought their visit had been well worthwhile. Ellen, far from being an awkward guest, had been too engrossed in her plans to paint and furnish the château to be ill-at-ease in his presence.

The colours of the earth and the flowers and the sky, and the silver-green of the river . . . Who would have expected Ellen to come up with such ideas?

I should forget once and for all about Dick O'Shaughnessy, Ellen thought: you only have to see Catherine and himself together to realize how taken he is with her. I was asked to the château to act as a chaperone – or out of politeness. If I had any sense in my head I'd go back to Ireland this minute.

Except that, if I did return to Ballygriffin, Dick would be there in my mind, living across the river, the way he did in the past. There would be no escaping him.

And you stay here, my girl, she said to herself, and one of these days you'll be invited to attend his wedding, when he marries Catherine.

191

She had got no further than that in her thoughts when Hélène and Catherine had one of their disagreements.

'You're never at home. You spend your whole day in town, sitting in the coffee-house, shopping, and wasting too much money.'

'It's dull at home. If I were in Paris . . .'

'But you're not!'

'But I will be soon!' Catherine said, with the air of a victor. 'See this letter, Maman? It's from Roger De Lacy. He wants to marry me. And when I'm his wife I'll live permanently in Paris.'

Hélène shook her head.

'I've never trusted that young man. You would make a dreadful mistake if you married him.'

'You don't know him as I do, Maman. He worships the ground I walk on.'

Catherine had no intention of marrying Roger De Lacy. Secretly, she, too, distrusted him, although she was quite happy to lead him on by letter, just as a matter of course.

But let Maman think that I have accepted his proposal, she thought. Let her worry. It will serve her right for being so unsympathetic about the way I behave.

Had Hélène known just what Catherine did on her frequent visits to Cognac she would have been even more concerned.

Catherine's relationship with John Marrett had developed over the summer months. He adored her. She thought him mannerly – a man who rigidly observed the *civilités*, sat down with his hat on, guarded against too-candid criticisms of others, and swallowed his wine slowly.

It was not always easy for the two of them to meet since, if they were to do so in public, Maman's friends, Catherine knew, would be bound to see them and report what they had seen. But with Dick so often at Chez

Landart at work upon his château she was able to meet John in his office in the rue de la Richonne without too much risk. This necessitated being set down from the carriage by Liam in another part of the town and making her way back when she knew that he had gone, a nuisance and tiring on the feet, but worth it all the same.

On the day when she had declared her intention of marrying Roger De Lacy in the presence of her mother and Ellen, Catherine made her way to John's office and sat there demurely, waiting for a visiting wine-farmer to conclude his deal and leave.

But it seemed that the two men were discussing, not brandy, but the latest tactic of the Controller-General to raise the necessary finance to pay for the recent war.

'A tax of one-twentieth on all incomes without exception,' said the farmer.

'What good will it do? The *noblesse*, naturally, have refused to pay. The clergy oppose it and they are supported at court by the *dévot* party and by everyone from the Queen and the Dauphin to the Jesuits and the Secretary of State for War . . .'

'They say that the Pompadour is backing the Controller-General.'

Catherine reached out for another of the mouth-watering chocolates provided by thoughtful John.

How lucky she was to have these unloved but useful admirers, like John and Roger.

While Ellen was much too outspoken and vulgar, by comparison, and would never attract a civilized man. One only had to consider the way she broke into extravagant praise each time Yvette brought her favourite dish to the table to conclude that, no matter how long she remained in France, the girl would never develop manners.

Poor Ellen, she thought, and, seeing that John was looking at her, she flashed him a charming smile. If anyone had told her that 'poor' was the one adjective that was being applied to herself at that moment, she would never have believed it.

Poor little girl, John thought, looking at Catherine.

The knowledge that she lacked confidence did not make him love her any the less. If only she could be taught to trust, he said to himself, then her strengths and her resources, her determination and persistence and her true abilities would be seen in a much more positive light. Given real power I doubt if she would misuse it. She needs to marry, to be in charge of her own home, to be acknowledged, protected and loved.

All of which would fall into place as soon as the two of them were wed. He was determined to marry Catherine in spite of her mother's prejudices against Protestants, and he did not intend to renounce his faith before the wedding to please her or anyone else.

It was true that there had been a new wave of anti-Protestant feeling in the country. In Bordeaux, only the week before, *Parlement* had ordered forty-six people who had dared to marry out of the Catholic faith to leave their husbands or wives. But the Cognaçais were, in the main, tolerant people: he had an advantage in that.

It was less the difference in their religions that was of consequence, he thought, than the matter of persuading Catherine that she loved him, rather than young Captain O'Shaughnessy. Although she had not confided in him about her feelings for the other man they were, to John, obvious, although in the end he did not pay too much attention to them. Catherine was still very young – not yet twenty-one – and Dick was close to her family. It was an easy step from proximity to imagining oneself in love, especially at a time when there were few other eligible young men to meet.

Still, Dick was rather forceful; a potent rival. Now that he owned the Château de Pericard he would be bound to have a decent *paradis* and quite possibly a substantial stock of cognac. He must move quickly before Dick managed to do so.

Knowing nothing of what was in John's mind, Catherine sat waiting for him to finish his conversation. In her pocket was a little mother-of-pearl box which contained a mirror, some rouge and a supply of little patches in a variety of shapes, square, round, star-shaped, and others in the form of animals and birds. And a heart-shaped patch – that was the most important. These patches, according to where the wearer positioned them, spelt out a message to a lady's lover, telling him that she was passionate (if placed on the forehead), impertinent (on the nose) and discreet (on the lower lip).

If, on the other hand, she desired to be kissed a patch could be placed on the corner of the mouth, a most vital message.

But not one she intended to send this day, although sheer villainy tempted her to do so.

Instead, while John was seeing his visitor to the door, she took out her mirror and peered into it, approving her appearance. A little flushed perhaps, but that was all to the good, obviating the need for rouge. On the whole, she was satisfied with what she saw.

'You look perfect to me!'

'I wasn't really looking – ' Catherine began, annoyed at being caught out, but John said: 'Why not – you are so beautiful to look at.'

It was a small incident but it disturbed Catherine's composure. She pushed the mirror back into her pocket and sat upright, so that she might appear taller. Still, John was admiring her hat and her new mantelet and stressing how glad he was to see her. After a few minutes she dismissed the suspicion that he and not she might be in charge of the day.

Then he said: 'I wonder why you are so unhappy, when you have so many advantages?'

She was so surprised that he might as well have slapped her face rather than hit her with phrases. Her eyes widened in shock and her mouth opened as if she was about to speak, although no actual words came out.

While she was still deprived of the power of speech he reached out for one of her hands and held onto it firmly.

'I'm very sorry. I didn't mean to hurt you.'

Silence.

'On the contrary, I would like to protect you from harm. You know, I'm sure, that I love you, although I love what I think you are, what you are capable of becoming, rather than what you pretend to be.'

The hand fluttered like a startled bird but still she did not speak.

'And loving you I want to marry you. *Would* you consider becoming my wife?'

This was more familiar language, as far as Catherine was concerned. Resignedly, John saw that she was preparing to slip back into her customary role, doing her best, now, to assume the predictable attitude of a sophisticated young lady who has just received a proposal.

He could have spoken her next lines before she did so herself: 'I'll consider your proposal.'

'Please do,' he said. 'And then let me know what you have decided to do.'

All the same, Catherine, by the time she got to the rue Magdelaine, where she had instructed Liam to meet her, was in a state of considerable confusion. In a matter of minutes John Marrett had succeeded in intruding into her

196

mind and she was stunned by his impertinence and stung by his accuracy.

Something's nettled her, Liam thought, when he saw her approaching: she's as nervous as a bag of cats.

The devil got into him, too, that day: 'By the hokey, you seem to have done a fine lot of shopping, Miss Catherine!'

Catherine, looking dazed, did not reply. Instead, she climbed into the carriage, and shrank back on the cushions, refusing to utter a word.

That same day, Dick, after one of his sleep-lacking nights, made a decision about his future. To implement it, he rode to Crouin where he found Hélène alone.

'You're worried about something?' he asked when he had kissed her on both cheeks. 'Is something wrong?'

'It's Catherine,' Hélène said, clicking her tongue. 'Catherine and that wretched man Roger De Lacy. She's going to marry him.'

'My God!' Dick said. 'It can't be true.'

'It is. She told us this morning.'

Dick, she thought, looked stricken. The poor, poor boy was doubtless in love with Catherine, as all the young men were, and had probably hoped to marry her himself, once his château was ready to live in.

'Sit down,' she said. 'Dear Dick, you know I think of you as a son. I would have been so happy for you to be truly part of the family.'

'She's determined to marry him?' Dick asked. 'She's absolutely determined?'

'So it would appear. She wants to return to Paris – that is her real purpose. She finds Cognac very provincial and frequently says so. I suppose it was too much to expect that she would ever settle here.'

'I suppose so,' said Dick, looking so woebegone that

Hélène wanted to take him into her arms and comfort him like a baby.

But what he really needs is some practical advice, she decided. It's time I spoke my mind.

So when Yvette had served refreshments she reached forward and took one of his hands, rather as John Marrett did, a little later on, seated with Catherine.

'*I* would have been happy to have you in the family but, in the end, I wonder if you would have been. She's a difficult girl. She always was. Whereas Ellen – '

Dick, she noticed, blinked. She wondered, thinking how much she disliked the way Catherine encouraged men only to drop them when it suited her, if he was going to cry.

'Ellen is the right girl for you,' she said, firmly. 'The happiest of marriages grow not from the attraction of opposites but from the matching of like to like. Ellen, having been brought up in the country, sees the value in life in the Charente. She's a wonderful girl, Dick – so honest, so brave, so loyal. And she loves you, I know she does. Forget Catherine. I tell you that only because I care about you so much. Marry Ellen instead.'

'You think I should do that?' Dick said, looking minimally more cheerful.

'I do. I do. I'll go upstairs and let you talk to her on your own. Try not to think too much about Catherine's decision. I know it's painful – '

At the mention of Catherine's impending marriage Dick looked stricken again.

'Think of Ellen,' Hélène said, and tactfully went away.

Ellen had been in the *potager*, gathering herbs and idly wondering what kind of a garden would emerge at the Château de Pericard when Dick had finally cleared away the overgrowth.

With a sprig of tarragon in one hand and one of bergamot in the other, she sauntered along the *allée* towards the back of the house. Then she saw Dick's horse tethered by the outbuildings.

Isn't it as well I have my good dress on me, she thought at once. She had made it herself, under Hélène's guidance. The bodice laced up over a false front and both the skirt and the petticoat had side-pocket slits concealed in the gathers. She was less certain of the colour, known generally as Burnt Opera House in the new terminology relating to shades.

Her hair ribbons and her Louis-heel shoes were also red and she was sure that her face was now the same colour.

She went into the house, still holding the tarragon and bergamot, eager, as always, to talk to Dick.

'What are you visiting here for when we only saw you yesterday?' she demanded when she had tracked him down.

He was looking every inch a man of commerce. He wore a burgundy coat with a cloth waistcoat woven with a floral design and black breeches and his hair was lightly powdered which it had not been in the past.

But with all her brave talk instead of looking at his face she fixed her gaze on his black, red-heeled shoes, his white boot hose, waiting for his explanation.

'You look nice in red,' he said just as Ellen was reminding herself that this was the first time they had been alone together since that embarrassing day by the river.

She was not used to compliments from Dick. What had got into him to be flattering her? she wondered. At the same time she noticed that one of his feet was pawing the floor as if it was the hoof of a restless racehorse.

'You never said things like that to me before,' she said to him, and thought that she heard him sigh.

'Ellen,' he began. 'I have something to ask you – ' and paused, although his restless foot did not.

'What is it?'

'Will you marry me?' he said.

She dropped both sprigs of herbs. There was not a sound out of her. Asked the most important question of her young life, Ellen, most uncharacteristically, was completely lost for words.

Dick, worn out by lack of sleep and a surfeit of emotion, had gone by the time that Catherine got home.

By then, Catherine was in a mood that was altogether strange to her: she was desperate to talk to Ellen about John Marrett's proposal. She had never felt the need to confide in anyone before, let alone a woman, and the realization that she wanted to reach out for a confidante confused her even more.

She found Ellen where Dick had left her, in the *alcôve*, and because she was thinking of her own situation she did not notice that Ellen was looking strange.

'Ellen,' she started to say.

But it was difficult to take even a tentative step into real friendship. She had not the faintest idea how to begin.

So –

'I've just had a proposal,' said Catherine.

'Another one?'

'What? Oh, *Roger* . . . *He's* not important.'

'But you're going to marry him. You said so only this morning.'

'No, I'm not,' said Catherine.

Small and foolish and young she might have felt in John

200

Marrett's presence, but she had no doubts of any kind about Roger De Lacy.

'So who else has proposed to you?'

It was extraordinary how hard it was to explain oneself – to describe her state of confusion. Why wasn't Ellen more helpful? Why couldn't she make it a little easier to talk to her – smooth the path of confidence, instead of asking so many questions?

Feeling unsure of herself again, Catherine said: 'The Englishman – John Marrett.'

'Did he?'

But Ellen sounded quite pleased. *Was* glad, it turned out, because she went on to add: 'He's a nice man. I like him.'

'You know John Marrett?'

'I met him going in to Dick's office when you were sick with mumps. We had a bit of a chat.'

Catherine thawed again.

'Ellen, you mustn't say anything about this to Maman. John is a Protestant, after all. Even the mere mention of his name makes her angry.'

'He can always convert,' Ellen said. 'If he does we can have a double wedding.'

'He wouldn't convert . . .' Catherine said.

And paused, frowning.

A double wedding? Was that what Ellen had said?

'What did you say just now?'

'A double wedding. Catherine, I have something to tell you, too. You can never imagine what happened to me today . . .'

'Dick asked *you* to marry him?'

Catherine could hardly speak for shock. Surely – oh, no, it could not be true.

Except that Ellen was nodding her dark head. Ellen's

green eyes were dancing with happiness. Ellen was looking most attractive even if, Catherine thought darkly, her face was as red as her dress.

'Isn't it wonderful? I was beginning to think – I mean, I thought he'd marry *you*.'

'So did I,' Catherine said sourly.

She felt raw all over, as if a brutal hand had ripped off the crust of her existence.

'But now you're going to marry this nice man and – Catherine, I'm so happy for us!'

I didn't say I was going to marry John Marrett, Catherine shouted silently – I was trying to tell you that his proposal has confused me – that I simply wanted to talk.

Why don't you understand that it's Dick, not John, that I love?

Dick – whom you're going to marry . . .

'Ellen – Catherine, are you there?'

'Coming,' Ellen called, eager, no doubt, to herald her good news.

And she did rush out of the room leaving Catherine with only Mou-Mou, peering out anxiously from underneath a table, to offer the necessary solace.

Catherine sat limply on one of the ottomans, absently gazing at the wall. Hélène and Ellen, talking animatedly about Dick's proposal, forgot all about her.

Finally, in their absence, Catherine came to a decision.

'Liam,' she said, a few minutes later. 'I have more shopping to do. Take me back to town.'

202

4

Catherine, sitting serious-faced in the carriage, had no idea that the man at the reins was as worried, in his way, as she was, in hers.

Having not thought about his father this long while, Liam was now being forced to consider the possibility that the fellow could well be alive.

More than that, could be far too close for his own comfort.

It had started when Father McMahon, revisiting Cognac, had called upon Dick and heard mention that Liam's surname was Crowley.

'There's a fellow by that name doing odd jobs at the Irish college in Bordeaux,' said the priest. 'He wouldn't be a relation of yours by any chance?'

Liam's heart had taken a massive leap.

'What age would he be, Father?' he had asked, marking time.

'Old enough to be your father and maybe an uncle . . .'

Divil a thing, Liam had said to himself. I bet my life that's him!

'I hear there's been a proposal to close up the college in Paris and hand it over to the clerics,' Liam said, by way of diversion.

'There was – but didn't the Bishop of Killaloe write from Ennis to the Archbishop of Dublin and he managed to stop it.'

Liam thought he had been saved but not a bit of it. After a gap of several months he had just received a letter from Father McMahon: '. . . would have written to you

before but I have been in Paris at the Collège des Grassins
. . . sure now that the man I mentioned to you is your
own father . . . tells me that he had a son called Liam,
but that he unfortunately lost track of his family after
coming to France . . .'

And whose fault was that, Liam wanted to know.

And here was Father McMahon suggesting that he
should pay a visit to Bordeaux, the way father and son
could meet!

Liam was raging as he drove back into Cognac.

'Bad cess to that auld fellow!' he muttered under his
breath. 'And he the crawthumper, along with all else he
is, insinuating himself into the good Father's books in a
hypocritical manner after the years of neglect to his wife
and sons!'

I won't answer the letter, he decided. But that wasn't
the solution, either, he knew, since Father McMahon had
stated that he would be returning to Cognac within a
month or two and would be bound to be hot-foot after
him, nagging him about taking his father back into his
life.

If only I could be out of the place when he comes, Liam
thought, the matter could blow over.

The way that father of mine has led his life he can't be
long for this world. God is good. Maybe He'll take him
over the next year.

But where could I go, in the meantime?

There were good things and bad things about being
engaged, Ellen was learning.

Anything directly connected with Dick was naturally
positive. In a way that she privately considered miraculous
they had not only reverted to their old, easy relationship
but had added a depth to it that had not existed before.
Their dreams and ambitions, relating to the expansion of

Dick's business and the final restoration of the château, seemed to be interwoven, Dick talking at length about the orders he could take when he had stocked his own *paradis* with really good cognac and Ellen telling him how glazed tiles would improve the kitchen floor and the way she planned to fill enamelled pots with roses and violets once the garden was cleared and to plant beds of artichokes and strawberries.

When Dick reported that the workmen had unearthed a statue holding a vase of water in one hand and an inscription in the other, she was as excited as if they had found gold; but she was even more pleased when Dick gave her a book about the history of distillation to read because it meant that he wanted her to be truly involved in the business.

And so she learnt that, while the Egyptians had practised the art of distillation before the coming of Christ, the French had first heard of it from a Spaniard, Arnaldus di Villanova, a teacher of astrology and alchemy in Montpellier and Avignon.

Then, in 1636, heavy wine taxes had so angered the people of Angoumois, along with the *députés* of Cognac, Jarnac and Merpins, she read, that they revolted and said that they were not only going to distil their wines but to denude the forests of trees in order to do the heating.

Distillation *à la charentaise* was different from ordinary distillation, involving the separation of volatile elements in the original liquids.

'It's very complicated,' Dick said. 'You'll never understand it just by reading. I'll take you to see for yourself.'

'To Monsieur Merlet's?' Ellen asked, hoping that Dick would not be as disapproving of her on their next visit to Bourg-Charente as he had been on the last.

'Yes – and this time I promise that I won't spoil the day for the two of us,' said Dick.

205

So that was all right.

He must have warned M. Merlet in advance that they wanted to watch the distillation process because the minute they arrived they were escorted into the barn and shown an old furnace-fired still-house in a stone square in which an open fire burnt.

There was a very strong aroma of fumes. Ellen gazed up at the still, shaped like a giant onion and made up of several pieces of red beaten copper soldered together with tin and zinc.

'We call it the *chaudière à eau-de-vie*,' said M. Merlet. 'And it is very important that we keep it clean or our cognac will taste *rimé* – as if it has been burnt.'

At the top, the onion swept up into a smaller but also rounded shape which was called the *chapiteau*. It, too, had an extension, known as the *col de cygne* – the swan's neck – from which the trapped vapours would trickle down into the *serpentin*, or cooler, and afterwards into a double-bottomed circular tub, the *bassiot*.

To be a distiller, a *bouilleur*, you had to be vigilant and patient and meticulous, M. Merlet said pointedly.

'The temperature of the fire must be controlled throughout the distillation – high at the beginning, then lower, and then high again.

'Every two to three hours the *bouilleur* has to refill the furnace, during the night, as well as during the day.'

'During the night!' exclaimed Ellen, looking at M. Merlet sympathetically. 'But what if he over-sleeps?'

'He wouldn't dare to. He knows very well that if he did and a fire spread he would be burnt to death. For that reason the still-house – the *brûlerie* – is always built as far as possible across the yard from the farmhouse.'

Dick and Ellen exchanged glances. She knew that he was wondering how Liam was going to cope.

For, as a result of hints thrown out by Liam and a talk

206

Dick had had with M. Merlet on a previous visit to Bourg-Charente, the former tramp would not be returning to Cognac at the end of this day or for some time thereafter.

Neither Dick nor Ellen could imagine Liam's reasons. First, Liam, looking shifty, had mentioned that he would like to find employment out of Cognac for a while and that maybe Dick could help him.

'Perhaps work on a wine-farm, Captain O'Shaughnessy. It's not that I want to leave you in the lurch, understand, where deliveries to the quay are concerned . . .'

When Dick had said that, with the numbers of men out of work these days, he could easily find a temporary replacement, Liam had looked relieved.

'Because I'd want to come back again. 'Tis just for the moment I need to be away . . .'

At the time Dick had wondered if Liam was wanting to be out of Cognac because he was in some kind of trouble. It seemed unlikely that he owed money since he was proud of living frugally and saving most of what he earned.

A woman after him, from whom he wanted to escape?

But Liam was terrified of women and would hardly have got to know one intimately.

Beyond that, he could not conjure up any explanations. In any case, it was none of his business.

'I'll see what I can do,' he had said.

And then M. Merlet, too, had confided in Dick.

If only, he had started off by saying, he had married a Cognaçais instead of a woman from Bordeaux, a woman who, ever since they had wed, had been wanting to return to the place of her childhood.

And now she had succeeded in firing their son, Louis, with the same ambition, filling the boy's head with notions of grandeur, telling him that he would be better off working in her father's business than training to be a *bouilleur de cru*, a distiller, as the Merlets had been for generations. It was true that her merchant father could do with help in his shop but was that a reason, M. Merlet had asked Dick, for his wife and son to go against his wishes and re-instate themselves in Bordeaux?

'My only remaining son,' M. Merlet had said sadly and Dick, then, had learnt for the first time of the two Merlet sons who had lost their lives in the war, one at Fontenoy, the other at Lauffelt.

When M. Merlet had gone on to bemoan the fact that he was now short of trusted assistance Dick, with some difficulty, had persuaded him to let Liam act as an apprentice *bouilleur de cru* for as long as it suited both of them.

There were, said M. Merlet, continuing his lecture, not one but two distillation processes employed in the making of cognac.

'In the first – *la première chauffe* – the wine is turned into a *brouillis*, that is, a half-strength spirit, not drinkable because it will contain impurities. The second distillation is called *la bonne chauffe*, but that you will not be able to see today. The first process takes a long time, as much as eight hours. The second is longer still.'

When M. Merlet was quite satisfied that the *chaudière à eau-de-vie* was perfectly cleaned, Liam helped him to carry the fermented wine into the *brûlerie* and to pour it into the copper boiler.

More wood was thrown into the furnace.

Then M. Merlet said: 'Captain O'Shaughnessy – Mademoiselle Nagle, you will not be able to stand all day in front of the furnace, I can assure you! Much has yet to happen. For me, it will be necessary to wait until, at the right temperature, the alcohol which is at the heart of the cognac turns into vapour. Go out and walk by the river.

Come back at intervals to see how we are getting along. The process of distillation is something that can never, never be rushed!'

A distiller was truly a scientist – a bit like Count Darcy, Ellen decided when M. Merlet explained that his function involved separating the water-white spirit known as the *coeur* from the other matters which escaped from the wine as the temperature continued to rise. These included the *tête*, the milk-like product that came out of the grapes and their skins, and bits of twigs and yeasts.

Her head was beginning to ache as she attempted to assimilate all this information and she had no idea how Liam was going to do so.

But, at long last, the first distillation was complete.

'And this is the *brouillis*,' announced M. Merlet.

There was a long way to go yet – the *brouillis* was not yet a pleasant, let alone a delectable liquid.

But M. Merlet was content.

Forced to leave because of the late hour, Dick and Ellen were told that they would not be able to watch the second stage of this particular distillation because it could not be postponed until the following day but must be carried out at once. 'To prevent oxidation during storage. We will arrange for you to come again when the second distillation is being carried out in daylight. But I warn you, be here very early. *La bonne chauffe* can take up to twelve hours to complete.'

All important, in distillation, Ellen learnt, was estimating the point of separation.

'You have to know exactly how much *tête* to leave in,' said M. Merlet when they came again to watch him. 'If it is a bad year you leave more because, if the solids are not good, the *tête* will act as a neutralizer. But this has been a good year. I can afford to leave more nutrients in the spirit than I would otherwise have done.'

When the process was virtually complete they watched in fascination as he applied what he called the rule of the *trois perles* – putting a small quantity of the newly-distilled brandy into a glass which he then shook.

'See – three bubbles have appeared on the surface. That means that the break has been made. You may taste what we have just produced if you wish. It will be pleasant. But, remember, this is not yet real cognac. In the making of great *eau-de-vie* the wood of the cask is almost as important as the vine. We in the Charente maintain that our cognac owes all of its colour and half of its taste to the wood in which it is allowed to mature.'

He held out the glass.

Dick said: 'Liam, you taste it, and tell us what you think.' While Liam was sampling the colourless liquid, he continued: 'You're very particular about which wood is used for casks, aren't you?'

'The oaks which our *tonneliers* use come either from the forest of Tronçais – from those trees which grow on the very edge of the woods where the timber is more tender – or from the Limousin oak-tree which grows alone in the middle of a field. Each has a very different texture,' M. Merlet said, watching Liam's face. 'But what do you think of the spirit at this stage, monsieur?'

Liam winked at him, and shook his head in appreciation.

'Fiery to the tongue, Monsieur Merlet!' he grinned happily. 'And to the throat, with a taste of flowers and fruit to it. And you say it will get better yet! Tell me, when is that likely to be?'

* * *

'Do you think Liam will succeed in learning the art of distillation?' Ellen asked Dick on the way home. 'He's certainly enthusiastic enough.'

'He might,' said Dick cautiously. 'And it would be good if he did. One day I would like to buy land and grow my own grapes, from which my own wine could be produced. But that's far in the future. In the meantime I could just buy wine from local farmers, and set up a *brûlerie* at the château. How useful it would be then, to have a *bouilleur* amongst us!'

There were so many plans to make.

Ellen wanted to be gone, to share this stimulating new world with Dick.

Less exciting were the constraints Hélène was putting upon Ellen at home, now that she was engaged.

Maman will keep lecturing me about the necessity to behave like a *châtelaine* already, Ellen groaned inwardly, and I am not even wed yet.

And when I do live in the château I don't want to behave like one of the land-holding aristocracy, cutting myself off from people.

If only Maman was less snobbish. If only she would stop talking about the importance of maintaining a division between us and the peasants.

I don't think she realizes that people in this country are hungry – *that* is what is important; the fact that the tax system now is chaotic; that, as well as the *tailles*, there are taxes on utensils and equipment; on subsidies for waifs and strays; on personal dues.

And there are so many struggling widows as a result of the wars.

Yet the people vent their anger, not on the nobility, who have created this chaos, but on the tax collectors employed by the state.

And, if you listen to Catherine, you hear that, in Paris, Madame de Pompadour is spending the king's money like water, building houses and pavilions; renewing the flowers in her gardens each day.

Hélène said: 'And, Ellen, you really should not receive anyone who has grown out of the *roturier* class. Doctors, for example.'

'But it takes years of study to make a doctor.'

'But the surgeon, one has to remember, used to combine his trade with that of the barber. You only have to look at the way some of them dress! Men who wear suits adorned with lace, as if they were officers in the gendarmerie, should not be invited to supper. Nor people who give names like Jacquon and Pierrot to their children. It is very easy to tell a gentleman. The way he bows in the streets, with his hat sweeping the ground and his body bent double, is an indication in itself. Just remember that the bourgeoisie are socially ambitious and anxious to marry upwards, so they may try to attach themselves to a young couple like Dick and yourself, in order to better themselves.'

One afternoon, Ellen, having endured this kind of conversation for far too long, was trying to steer Hélène onto the more welcome subject of the wedding itself.

'Would it be possible, do you think, for us to be married in the château chapel, now that it has been restored?'

'I don't see why not,' Hélène said, 'I will speak to Monsignor Doussinet and see what he has to say.'

Then the door to the parlour opened and Catherine, who had been missing all day, stood on the threshold, as if she was not sure whether to come in or go out.

'Where *have* you been?' Hélène demanded crossly. 'I don't know how many times, Catherine, I must tell you to spend less time in town.'

Catherine shrugged.

'You won't have to tell me again, Maman,' she said, yet she did not sound in the least repentant.

Hélène frowned, puzzled at the discrepancy between her daughter's words and the actual tone of her voice.

'That's good news,' she said eventually. 'But you ought to apologize, all the same, for having been out of the house all day.'

'There was good reason for that, I can assure you,' Catherine said clearly.

'There was?'

'There was indeed, Maman. You see – I was being married.'

'*Married?*'

I must be imagining this conversation, Ellen thought. I am obviously asleep. I must be. Catherine, who likes order and ritual, who has many a time expressed a preference for a coloured wedding gown, although some women these days favour white, who would never – surely? – get married without an enormous fuss – could not possibly have done so in private.

Only in a dream . . .

So presumably, in reality, Hélène is not saying in a cold voice: 'Is that intended to be amusing? Are you making a joke?'

And Catherine, who is not smiling, who is, on the contrary, positively stern in her manner, has not said by way of reply: '*No!* Don't you want to know who my husband is?'

It might be a nightmare, Ellen thought. Suppose – suppose he is Dick . . .

'I cannot believe this,' Hélène said in an icy voice. 'But if you are determined to play foolish games, very well, I will ask you – what is your husband's name?'

It was not a dream. But it was not a nightmare, either.

'It's John Marrett,' Catherine said.

And, holding out her right hand, she pointed to the plain gold ring adorning her third finger.

'He is a Protestant!' Hélène said. 'You are not married. This heretical marriage counts for nothing, in the eyes of the Church. You will be extremely lucky if you are not arrested and imprisoned. How could you be so foolish?'

'I am married in *my* eyes,' Catherine said, tossing her dark head. 'And in the eyes of my husband. At my suggestion, Maman, John has rented a delightful manor for us in the rue Haute dè Crouin. I shall be close to you – to all of you. In fact, Dick will have to ride right past my gate every night, when he is going home . . .'

'Your children – if you were unlucky enough to have them – would be illegitimate, Catherine, and incapable of inheriting property. Oh, what made you do it! However, it's not too late. The marriage has not yet been consummated. I will speak to Monsignor Doussinet. He will tell me what to do. In the meantime you must stay here – stay away from that man!'

'From my husband?' Catherine said. 'Now you, Maman, are trying to make a joke. And I'm afraid that it is too late. John and I are lovers, as well as man and wife.'

'Lovers . . .!'

Ellen had not noticed until then that the evening had drawn in – that a wind had come up from the river. She shivered, looking at Hélène and Catherine, aware of the lack of love between them.

Then the pendulum clock outside the doorway chimed and Hélène said: 'I am going up to my room. I will stay there for an hour. When I come downstairs again, Catherine, I will expect you to have gone.'

* * *

214

When she had left the room Ellen said weakly: 'How did you arrange it?'

Catherine shrugged her shoulders again.

'There is a preacher. The Cognaçais are tolerant people. I assure you we don't expect persecution from anyone else but Maman.'

'And John? *Were* you lovers before you wed? Are you *passionately* in love with him?'

'No and no again!' said Catherine. 'A girl would be foolish to make love before she marries. What if she were to become pregnant? But afterwards . . . Anything is possible in society for a married woman. Who knows – perhaps I'll take a lover later on. Madame de Pompadour had a husband – but it didn't prevent her from seducing the king!'

Without Catherine an odd almost abnormal peace seemed to descend upon the manor. Her departure saw an end to the virtually daily bickering between mother and daughter, and Ellen now felt more at ease.

Because the truth was, with Catherine to remind her of the sheer power of physical beauty and of what she felt to be her own shortcomings, Ellen had continued to feel uncertain; convinced that some abberation had taken hold of Dick prior to his proposal and that, sooner or later, he would regain his sanity and, having broken off his engagement to herself in a gentlemanly manner, ask Catherine to marry him instead. When Catherine had slept in the house Ellen had sometimes woken in the middle of the night and asked herself what had possessed Dick to propose to her at all when he had such an attractive alternative.

In Dick's company she tended, even now, to avoid talking about Catherine although he mentioned her himself from time to time, saying that he had met her in the

215

offices in the rue de la Richonne, when she came there to see her husband.

Neither Ellen nor Hélène had seen Catherine since the day when she had announced her marriage. And that was bad of the two of them, Dick said: 'I know you two weren't great friends, Ellen, but you, at least, should not cut her off.'

'I'll go and see her one of these days,' said Ellen, putting it off.

But one evening Dick arrived with the news that Catherine had been seriously ill, having had a miscarriage.

'Madame Cantillon should visit – '

'She won't. She says Catherine is living in sin and that she will not condone it.'

'Then you go. It's not right to neglect her like this. It's very cruel.'

'I'm not meaning to be cruel,' Ellen said truthfully, knowing that it was a kind of cowardice that kept her from visiting Catherine, rather than unkindness.

It was April by then and pouring with rain.

'*C'est profit pour tous quand il pleut en àvril,*' the Cognaçais said, pleased with the weather, relieved that there was no likelihood of frosts which might adversely affect the vines.

And at night the moon was red, as it always was after Easter in the Charente, or so everyone insisted.

In the rain Ellen walked the short distance from the manor to John and Catherine's house in rue Haute de Crouin. As Catherine had stated, her new home was delightful, exquisitely furnished, as Ellen might have expected, even if, to her taste, it was all rather ornate.

Catherine lost no time in telling her that the lacquer work was by Robert Martin whose name occurred constantly in the Royal accounts at Versailles.

'I do love marqueterie, don't you?' she said. 'Boulle, I

know, does some wonderful work in tortoiseshell but I prefer marqueterie in different coloured woods, violet, or pink or purple. You know the kind of thing.'

'No, I don't,' said Ellen, looking at a mechanical table which, Catherine explained, obviated the necessity of having servants wait at meals.

Back in Catherine's company she felt her confidence ebbing again. Catherine did not look as if she had been dangerously ill, but as lovely and as composed as ever. In her presence Ellen felt large and clumsy. When she looked down at her hands they seemed to have grown, to be not only larger but also uglier and redder than ever.

'What are you going to wear at your wedding?' Catherine wanted to know.

'I thought – white satin. With a long train. And maybe a small French cap to match. Or a wreath of orange blossoms.'

'And your hair unconfined in ringlets.'

Catherine sounded quite friendly when she made this suggestion.

Remembering that she had lost a baby and that sympathy should be expressed, Ellen said: 'I was sorry to hear about your miscarriage. Was it very bad?'

But Catherine's expression had hardened. She said coldly: 'It was nothing to make a fuss about. I am perfectly well now. I hear you're going to be married in the chapel at Chez Landart. John and I are looking forward to it.'

Seeing Ellen looking nonplussed she added: 'Didn't Dick tell you that he had invited us? He absolutely insisted that we should be there . . .'

'Why didn't you tell me that you had asked them? It made me feel a fool, not knowing.'

'It slipped my mind,' Dick said, 'between one thing and another. Anyway, we *had* to invite Catherine.'

217

'It will upset Maman. She doesn't want to see Catherine.'

'Well, *I* do,' said Dick.

And, indeed, why should she not come?

. . . wish we could all be at the wedding, wrote Rory from Ballygriffin. *Donogh, as you know, will be married the month before you. The other news here is that Nano Nagle, who went back to a cloister in France after Ann's death, is planning to return to teach poor children in Cork. If the city authorities catch her with a catechism in her hands who knows what will happen? Good luck to the pair of you. None of us can believe that you are marrying Dick . . .*

When Hélène had stressed the importance of a long engagement Ellen had known perfectly well that Maman was simply lonely, trying to hold onto her surrogate daughter for as long as possible.

On the morning of the wedding she regretted having given in. It was a bleak November day and rain clouds were gathering overhead.

We should have married in the summer, like everyone else, Ellen thought, drawing on her garter. It was blue, the colour associated with the Virgin Mary.

She had changed her mind about what she was going to wear. Her wedding gown was not white, as she had originally intended, but made of silver tissue trimmed with silver, and it had a train nearly six feet long. On her head was a cap fashioned out of purple velvet.

It was half past ten. At eleven o'clock she was to leave for Chez Landart. To be married to Dick. To be happy forever after . . .

'Ellen,' Hélène said. 'Stay still. I want to put scented powder on your face.'

'Madame,' said Yvette. 'Liam Crowley is here from Bourg-Charente, to drive Miss Ellen to church.'

'Aren't you the sight for sore eyes!' said Liam when she was finally ready to leave.

Would it rain? Would Maman snub John and Catherine? Was there anything that could possibly go wrong?

It was as well for Ellen's peace of mind at that moment that she knew nothing of an omission of Dick's.

In making his arrangements for the wedding to be held in the château chapel it had not occurred to him to mention to Monsignor Doussinet that John and Catherine would be present.

Nor was Dick aware of a recent clash between the *curé* and John.

Monsignor Doussinet was acutely aware of the fact that the Church had a weaker hold on the Charente than on most of rural France. He knew that Protestant services were frequently held in secret in lonely country barns, yet, no matter how often he complained about this to the authorities – no matter how many times soldiers were sent out in pursuit of the heretical preachers, the culprits were never found.

This, he knew, too, was entirely due to the sympathy shown to Protestants by the Catholic Cognaçais. The *curé* reminded himself that such tolerance could be suspect. So many of the old ideas were already being threatened. At the Academy at Dijon there was worrying talk of a new morality which challenged the Catholic belief that man, in order to attain eternal happiness after death, must conquer his worldly desires and ambitions.

Not that most men were convinced that a successful union could be formed between virtue and materialism. Many of those who had spent too lavishly on earthly possessions later felt that they might have gone too far, leaving large bequests to the Church when they had gone to face their Maker.

Still, there was a strong case in favour of a firm reversal to sterner codes, especially where marriage was concerned. Monsignor Doussinet had been horrified to hear of the secret marriage that Catherine Cantillon had made with the Protestant, John Marrett.

And so he had tracked down Mr Marrett, to see what pressure could be brought upon the man to make him convert. At worst, a symbolic Catholic ceremony could be held for the purpose of legitimizing any future children.

But, to the *curé*'s surprise and indignation, John Marrett had refused either to convert or to go through a ceremony which, he said, would only exist in name.

'God considers that we are married. That is all that matters to me,' John had said.

'You are jeopardizing your wife's immortal soul by taking this attitude,' Monsignor Doussinet had warned.

'I don't think so.'

Monsignor Doussinet had decided that he could do no more for the moment beyond adding Catherine to the long list of those sinners for whom he had to pray. Her dastardly husband, he thought, would have to intercede with God for mercy for himself.

He was therefore upset when, shortly after arriving at the Château de Pericard on the day of the wedding, John and Catherine drove up.

The man in him acknowledged that Mme Marrett was a very beautiful lady, that her décolletage was very low, and that the heretic who had seduced her must have been sorely tempted to lure her into sin.

The cleric thought differently.

'I cannot conduct a wedding ceremony in the presence of heretical guests,' he said to Dick who, in a suit of clothes with brass buttons, his cravat trimmed with lace, his hands encased in white gloves, was about to greet the pair.

'But they're my friends,' protested Dick, knowing, all the same, that he was wasting his breath; that Monsignor Doussinet, a good but obstinate man, would never alter his views.

Other guests were arriving. And Ellen's carriage, with Liam at the reins, was turning in at the gates.

'They must *go*,' said Monsignor Doussinet, surveying John and Catherine.

Or there will be no wedding, his expression implied.

'I'll tell them what you think,' Dick said miserably, and went off to do so.

John Marrett could not have been more understanding. He went so far as to apologize for having put Dick into an awkward position by accepting his invitation in the first place. With dignity, he took his wife's arm and ushered her away.

Ellen, descending from her carriage, saw Dick gazing in a disappointed way at Catherine's retreating figure.

He looks as bitter as thick milk, she thought. We are about to be married and he's looking at Catherine, regretful, I would say, that he did not have his chance with her.

Having only been mildly nervous up to then she felt as if she had been shot by fairy darts, and all her joints made swollen.

She tried telling herself that there were only two things that could never be cured – death, and want of sense – but it made no difference. Instead of the darts inflicting lasting pain they were inducing a strange numbing effect. As she walked into the chapel for the Nuptial Mass she was responding to no emotion at all.

* * *

'*Deus Israel conjungat vos.*'

She was a married woman. There was a diamond ring on her finger.

Despite this evidence Ellen remained insensible. She might have been asked to take part in a masquerade, required to move and speak according to alien commands.

Dick, looking solemn, bent to kiss her circumspectly but he seemed as much a stranger as the guests who watched him leading her out of the chapel to the hall for luncheon and the cutting of the Bride Cake.

Perhaps one of the dart-shooting fairies had taken her out of her body and inhabited it herself because she had the distinct impression that she was floating above it, watching herself behaving like a bride – smiling and chatting and sipping wine and eating a piece of her own cake.

Everybody seemed to be pleased with her, even Dick no longer looked miserable and actually appeared to be enjoying himself immensely.

Finally, the guests tipsily departed and she was left alone with her husband. It was not yet night but the grumbling grey clouds which hung over the river had darkened the château prematurely and candles had already been lit.

'Isn't it as well you only get married once in your life?' Dick commented cheerfully. 'So many people – I thought they'd never go!'

In the candlelight his familiar face was distorted and changed. He looked older and harder: there were shadows under the blue eyes.

In Ireland, she remembered, only certain people could remove the darts which the fairies inflicted on their victims. But where, in France, did such physicians exist . . .?

They were in the room off the parlour, the one that was

flanked by the ancient tower. From where she was sitting Ellen could see the narrow, left-turning spiral stairway built into the massive thickness of the wall, and one of the slit windows which had been cut through for air.

Following her gaze Dick said: 'In the old days those walls would have been hung with tapestries and the ramp would have been lit with torches. And if I was a *seigneur* and you were my lady we would have found it much easier to have had our privacy than we did this day.'

When they had been children in Ballygriffin and Kilawillen he had spoken to her many times in this storyteller's voice with a hint of the tease in it, but then he would have been speaking of Etain, daughter of Etar, more akin to the *Sidh* people than to those of the human race, beloved of Midir of Bri Leith, or of Deirdre and the love she had for Naoise and the treachery and death that came after it, but in those days, too, Dick had put his arm around her shoulder, the way he was doing now, and pulling her close to him.

'The moat would have been filled and the minute we saw people approaching we would have pulled up the drawbridge or – if they were over it already – we would have lowered the portcullis and closed them off on the entrance to the courtyard.'

Storytelling, Ellen thought again, and one of the darts that had numbed her mind must have been plucked out of it because she was beginning to feel again.

Although what she was experiencing was neither an intense surge of love for Dick nor entrancement with his story but a rush of indignation that – instead of taking her more seriously at this moment – he should be telling tales and teasing . . .

'. . . or if we were very eager to get rid of them we would cut loose a heavy stone and let it fall down on their heads.'

'What kind of a thing is that to be saying to me this night?' Ellen demanded suddenly.

Dick blinked, but since she was pulled into his chest she could not see his face.

'Isn't that just like you!' he said, sounding annoyed. 'What's wrong with what I've been saying?'

Another dart must have been plucked away.

Ellen said: 'Aren't I your wife? Stories are for children. What have they got to do with the likes of you and me?'

'Mine has,' Dick said and the teasing note had gone out of his voice altogether, although the anger in it remained. 'Because I was going to tell you about the way married women used to be glorified in chivalric culture. Do you know what *Minnedienst* is? It was the homage that was paid to women in this country long ago.'

Ellen's reply was drowned out by a rumble of thunder. Through the slit window she saw the lightning flash.

'In those days many women were better educated than men,' Dick said. 'And more clever. You're clever, too, Ellen, but you let your tongue cut your throat!'

When she was not expecting him to move, he took his arm from her shoulder and held her away from him, looking into her startled face. He was looking as cross as he sounded, but her own anger had ebbed away and with it the last of the numbness.

When you looked directly at Dick, full-face, not in profile the way you could notice his crooked nose, he was a beautiful man, Ellen thought, and she forgot about the kindness that was in him, and the bravery and the explorative side of his nature, the qualities that attracted her to him, and thought only of the darkness in his eyes, and the shape of him, the breadth and the leanness of him, and the enticing smell of his sweat.

He stared at her as if he, too, was seeing her in a different way, with anger and something akin to hostility

224

and they had never been so apart, and so close, in wanting each other.

'Come on,' Dick said and pulled her to her feet to lead her inside the tower; and an image came to her – from a book she had read, from Dick himself? – of how the knights and their families had lived in times of siege, in their castle keep, sleeping together in one great bed, man and woman making love under a pile of furs.

'I – ' Ellen began impulsively, wanting to say 'I love you', but Dick was tired of words.

He pulled her in to him, kissing, probing, stroking, tugging impatiently at her clothes, guiding her hands to assist him, finally drawing her down to the floor.

Ellen was not in a tower-room at all, but in a long tunnel and there was no consistent light. She was travelling slowly through the tunnel which was illuminated only occasionally by a glow she could barely discern.

'Ellen,' Dick said, faraway, at the end of the tunnel, and she hastened to catch up with him, and the mysterious and intermittent glimmers grew brighter and closer together until they were one continuous blinding, radiant light.

Burning and self-glorying, in adoration, her body was carried on.

'Dick,' Ellen said, when he did not mind if she talked. 'Listen, it's pouring down. All those people in your story are on the outside of the portcullis. Would you think of asking them in?'

'If I did,' said the familiar, kind, teasing and totally accepted storyteller, 'they'd keep us awake all night feasting and cardplaying and dancing and asking us to watch the travelling *jongleurs* with them. Let them stay outside in the rain!'

5

Now Ellen could wake in her own home and be proud of what she and Dick had created. In Catherine's scornful presence she had spoken of using the colours of the earth and the flowers and the sky and the river in redecorating the château and of forsaking opulence for rustic simplicity.

But then she had fallen under the influence of an Italian craftsman who had travelled to the Charente in search of work, and had learnt that it was possible to introduce romantic and slightly richer elements into her colour scheme without losing its basic purity. So there was a touch of gold in the soft sun colours of the walls in the various rooms which still harmonized with the curtains and cushions which she had made herself out of hand-blocked *Indienne* fabrics.

These fabrics – although freely available – were illegally bought, being banned by the Crown to protect the local silk and wool factories. Ellen wished that she was clever enough to duplicate them, having heard that it was possible to produce dyes that did not run if you mixed mordants, metallic salts, with vegetable dyes, thickened with gum arabic, on natural fibres.

Instead, she had contented herself with watching Signor Lorenzetti make furniture to her specifications.

Some of these pieces – the most prized – were carved from golden walnut, a tree so special that it was used as a bride's dowry and, in some places, was only cut before a crowd of onlookers when the moon was full. From this tree, the *noyer*, Signor Lorenzetti had made the huge

226

armoire, designed to last forever, or so he said, in the main bedroom, embellishing it with eglantine flowers, the symbols of conjugal love, vine-leaves and grapes. Ellen liked just as well the furniture made from *chêne or oak*, whatever anyone else might say about it being humble.

It was strange living in a house so large that there were parts of it she did not visit for days on end. It would be fine when it was over-run with children – the many children that she and Dick were planning to have.

For now, in May 1750, Ellen was six months pregnant.

Although she had Brigitte, the new maid, to help her in the kitchen she was dressing a brace of pheasant herself, at the same time wishing that the gamey smell was less overpowering. Pregnancy seemed to intensify a woman's sense of smell. She looked at the wasted beauty of the male bird, the richness of the green neck feathers, the black-spotted cinnamon plumage, the long elegant tail, and the simple task of removing the entrails filled her with repugnance.

It was not only the high smell of the pheasant that was making her queasy, she knew. Having finally gone over the household accounts she had realized that Dick had spent far more on the restoration and refurbishment of the château than he had originally planned to do.

He's not as good with money as I am, Ellen thought. He's over-generous. He gives it away, or lends it and is not always repaid. And he does not press for outstanding debts. It is just as well that I am going to take over his books again.

And even so it will be some time before he can realize his dream of adequately stocking his cellars with the best cognac – not to mention building his own *brûlerie* and distilling his own *eau-de-vie* here, at Chez Landart.

But I suppose those days will come . . .

Having denuded the male pheasant of its plumage Ellen

looked down without enthusiasm at its mate. Both birds were to form part of the menu that evening when John and Catherine were coming to dinner, to atone, as Dick had put it, for the way Monsignor Doussinet had behaved towards the two of them on the day of the wedding.

Along with the brace of pheasant Ellen was going to serve a dish of kid cooked with sage and white wine and allspice. But although she had enjoyed planning the menu she was dreading the evening itself.

She rubbed her forehead with the back of a bloodied hand and thought of Dick's regretful: 'We shouldn't have left it so long without seeing Catherine.'

Who is bound to be her insufferable self, Ellen thought darkly.

With her strong hands she stripped the female pheasant of its plumage.

'*Catherine!*' she said aloud, and, with her sharpest knife, she cut off the pretty brown head.

Until the evening Catherine came to dinner, Ellen had imagined the château to be inviolate and impregnable, so secure in its restored state that no intruder, no matter how powerful, could threaten the tower of strength which she and Dick had built.

But when Catherine looked around at the furnishings, seeming to sneer at the hand-thrown *faïence* which Ellen had bought from a local potter, it was as if Ellen had been swung around and forced to contemplate her familiar environment from another aspect. Within ten minutes of entering the château Catherine had contrived to make her see her rustic haven as being somehow unworthy of Dick. When, before dinner, they had led her into the tidy but haphazard garden, Catherine had remarked that although she had heard that there was a new vogue for the *jardin anglais* surely – since the château had been built in the

228

time of François Premier – it should have at least a vestige of form.

In her presence Ellen felt hugely pregnant. Every so often she felt Catherine eyeing her swollen stomach as if she was marvelling at its obesity.

And then they went in to dinner.

'Oh, *kid*!' said Catherine, looking down at her plate. 'I hope it *is* kid and not *bouc*. Billy goats do have a very unpleasant taste as they mature.'

'It's kid!' said Ellen, furiously.

Later, when John had left the room to relieve himself, Catherine added: 'When you come to dine with us I shall serve you black truffles. They are a great delicacy. Quite incomparable and – ' she paused, and looked pointedly at Dick – 'a well-known aphrodisiac!'

'She's not coming here again!' Ellen said when the Marretts had finally gone.

The enemy had stormed the castle – her home had been penetrated and reviled.

'But why not?' asked Dick, mystified.

Then he looked down at his wife and smiled.

'You're dead tired, aren't you?' he said kindly. 'It will be fine when the baby has come.'

The baby was two weeks late.

Hélène looked unperturbed.

'It happens sometimes that a baby is lazy,' she said. 'It was like that with Philip.'

'And Catherine?'

'With Catherine? No – Catherine, I think, was on time. Philip was such a beautiful baby, Ellen – so handsome, even then! His eyes, so blue, and so much hair you would not believe . . .'

You would think she had never given birth to another child, Ellen thought, so effectively has she cut Catherine

229

out of her life. Even bearing in mind how poisonous Catherine can be she's still her daughter. Doesn't she miss her at all?

'Maman – '

She stopped, sure that she had felt the first contraction. It was very short, lasting only for about forty seconds, and when it was not immediately repeated, Ellen was sure she must be wrong.

'Are you feeling all right, Ellen? You're looking pale.'

'It's nothing. Just a slight pain in the small of my back.'

Hélène smiled knowingly.

'I don't think it's nothing,' she said, in the voice of experience. 'It seems to me that your lazy baby is just beginning to stir.'

But it was nearly another half-an-hour before anything happened again.

The first stage of labour seemed to Ellen to last forever.

But it was no time at all for a first baby, Hélène insisted – only eight hours.

'What time is it?'

'Six o'clock. Perhaps you will have the baby to show to Dick when he comes for dinner.'

'Yes – yes. It's going to be born now!'

'Not yet. In one hour – maybe two.'

'But it is not possible to continue like this!'

But Ellen had no alternative.

And then, at seven, when she was muddled from pain and exertion, Brigitte, who had been lending additional support, reported: 'Madame, she is fully dilated. I can see the head.'

'Push!' Hélène ordered. 'Now the shoulder! Brigitte, we need water – quick.'

It was over.

Or must be because Hélène was saying excitedly: 'It's a boy – a boy, Ellen!'

But she was still in pain.

'*Push!*' Brigitte said, pressing her hand on Ellen's stomach, to force the after-birth out, while Hélène cut the umbilical cord and began to cleanse the child.

A boy –

James . . .

'We must swaddle him,' Hélène said. 'We must do it in such a way to include his arms and feet.'

'The best boy in the whole world,' said his father when he saw him.

With such happiness it was impossible to conceive that anything could ever go wrong.

That was the best time, Ellen would think later on.

Because, inevitably, along with the advantageous things that happened over the next few years were setbacks and blighted hopes.

It took Dick longer than he had expected to stock his cellars with precious cognac. Just as he was beginning to prosper, a ship carrying orders for Ireland was lost at sea and he suffered a serious loss.

And after that came the bad year when, instead of the hoped-for rain in April, heavy frosts damaged the vines. The juice of that year's grapes was neutralized, the wines thin and flat, a fault intensified in distillation.

In February 1752, a second son, George, was born to the O'Shaughnessys. But in the following year Ellen lost a baby and she thought of Catherine who had been through the same experience and was still without a child. In her grief she was tempted to write to her. But she did not and the two women did not meet. When, in July 1754, Dick the white-haired, nicknamed Bawnie, was born, Ellen gave barely a passing thought to her old rival.

231

As 1755 came round all seemed to be well at the château. Dick's cellars were finally stocked. Although he was not yet able to buy land on which he could grow his own grapes and produce his own wines for distillation, he had built a *brûlerie* at Chez Landart and had bought wines in from a local farmer.

For Liam was back, to act as his *bouilleur de cru*, Louis Merlet having ultimately become disillusioned with life in Bordeaux and come home to assist his father.

'Doing our own distillation is in the nature of an experiment,' Dick said to Ellen. 'If it works we can produce our own label. But in the meantime our real riches lie over there, in the cellars. All our savings are in that *paradis*. With the demand for good cognac increasing all the time what we've got over there is a gold-mine!'

6

In the first week in April Ellen saw John Marrett as she was walking along the rue de l'Isle d'Or on her way to the Cognac market.

'It is so long since we have met,' he said, sounding as if he regretted the lack of communication, and Ellen at once felt guilty for having come up with spurious excuses when the Marretts had issued invitations to dinner, and for deliberately allowing time to come between them.

John was such a nice man! He could hardly be held responsible for his wife's personality . . .

'You should visit Catherine,' he urged Ellen. 'I am away so often, on business, and she spends too much time alone. She would love it if you called to see her.'

'Is that what she said?' asked Ellen, surprised.

'It's what she thinks,' John insisted. 'She is lonelier than you realize.'

No wonder, the way she behaves, Ellen almost said. For John's sake she bit back the words, and left it at that.

She was four months pregnant and with three obstreperous boys to look after she had little time to herself. She thought it would make a change to talk to a friend of her own age. What a pity Catherine was so objectionable. It was probably true that she was in need of company for, apart from the fact that she must have driven other women away, too, by her carry-on, some people probably snubbed the Marretts because they were not married in the eyes of the Catholic Church.

Even in tolerant Cognac there had been reports of

attacks on Protestants lately. Dick had said that Protestants were burying their dead by night to avoid being set upon by ill-wishers and that they were selecting sites for this purpose under existing Cypress trees, lest new gravestones be deliberately defaced.

When she thought about these things Ellen felt sorry for Catherine. Maybe I will go and see her after all, she thought, but I haven't got time this week.

It would have suited Liam quite well had Ellen gone to see Catherine, as long as she took the three boys with her. That way, James and Bawnie and George would not have been in the *brûlerie* every time they got the chance, distracting him from the serious business of distillation and asking him unnecessary and repetitious questions about what was going on.

It was his own fault for encouraging them in the first place, he knew. But away from the *brûlerie* and the furnace, when he was not performing his vital role as *bouilleur*, the boys seemed to him a fine little trio, with whom he enjoyed having a bit of hack.

Liam was relieved when the *tonneliers* arrived at the château and the boys' attention was on them, instead of on himself.

Sitting solemn-eyed on the ground, watching M. Vergniaud and his five sons cut planks of similar length and thickness to fashion the casks into which their father's newly-distilled *eau-de-vie* would be poured, the O'Shaughnessy boys would, with luck, be engrossed for several hours!

James was trying to remember what his father had told him about the oak trees from which the planks had come. After they had been felled their branches, which were of no value in the making of casks, had been severed and set

234

aside for firewood and only the trunks floated down the Charente, as far as Chez Landart. Then the planks, the staves, had been sliced off and let dry in the open, in stacks, to be seasoned by air and rain. To James, it sounded almost mystical. Every aspect of his father's business enthralled him.

There was not a sound out of the three O'Shaughnessy brothers as the *tonneliers*, in their red trousers and white shirts and knee socks, having cut the trunks into planks of similar length and thickness, slotted them between strips of metal.

The planks were stacked tightly, side by side, so that, from where the boys were sitting, it looked as if they had already been turned into barrels.

Only James was old enough to understand that this was not, in fact, the case.

For the exciting part was still to come. Inside each cask-to-be a fire was being lit from the heat of which the planks would be soldered together without the assistance of nails.

This fire had to be consistently maintained so that the planks could become malleable and curve perfectly inside the hoops that bound them.

It was almost as good, James thought, as when the *voituriers* came with their carts and horses and mules to transport the cognac Papa brought to the *gabares* on the quays in Cognac.

This year, Papa had promised that, if he was good, he would take him on one of the little barges as far as Tonnay-Charente, and maybe even to La Rochelle.

James was thinking about that excursion when Brigitte came out of the château with wine for M. Vergniaud and his team to drink. Even at not quite five he was aware that the young maid was pretty. She was small and slender, with sooty eyes and hair that was more auburn than brown and Maman said that she looked more Irish than French, like Queen Maeve, maybe, who appeared in some of her stories.

When Brigitte came up to the *tonneliers* they all looked at her but only one of them, Gérard, the one with the ugly face, stopped working and made as if to follow her when she had passed around the wine and was about to go back to the kitchen.

James did not hear what they said to each other, but he did catch sight of Gérard Vergniaud's face when the *tonnelier* came back to tend the fire inside the cask. The expression on it made him shiver.

Brigitte might resemble Queen Maeve, but Gérard, he thought, looked like his own idea of an angry and vengeful Devil.

In the parlour Ellen was talking to Father McMahon who, having called to see Hélène earlier that day, had ridden out to Chez Landart.

'It's a troubled world we live in,' the priest said heavily. 'France and England at loggerheads again over colonies and trade.'

'You were saying earlier that the *parlements* have refused to obey the Pope in condemning Jansenist thinking in the Church.'

'I was. Do you see now, Ellen, what will happen? The *parlements*, in taking this stance against Rome, will spread a spirit of opposition to the Church throughout the country, undermining respect for it, and for the monarchy. Indeed, it isn't so much Jansenism we're talking about here as Gallicanism, the *parlements* trying to lay claim to power in ecclesiastical matters . . .'

After a while Father McMahon asked if Ellen would like to make her Confession.

Examining her conscience, aided by the priest, she was forced to confront her attitude to Catherine.

Was it not uncharitable? Father McMahon wanted to know; hadn't Christ Himself reminded us to turn the other cheek . . .

Ellen had to agree.

'Go and see her,' urged Father McMahon. 'Maybe it's part of God's plan that you help to bring her back into the Faith.'

Privately Ellen doubted that He had any such thing in mind. But having come round to the view that she had been lacking in Christian decency she thought that she should see Catherine.

I may as well strike while the iron is hot, she said to herself. Dick said he would be late home. I'll go to Crouin this evening.

'Was that the man Crowley I saw in the garden earlier on?' Father McMahon, struck by a thought, said just before he left.

'I'm sure it was. I'll ask Brigitte to look for him.'

But, with an inscrutable face, Brigitte came back from a search of the grounds to say Liam could not be found.

He must be the only man in this place who hides from Brigitte, Ellen thought, amused. The girl *did* look more Irish than French and her hair was really quite red.

But, in Ireland, a red-haired woman was often avoided, being said to be unlucky, reminding the superstitious that Judas, who betrayed Jesus, was red-haired himself: a man who met such a woman on his way to work might well turn back from his labours.

Perhaps that was it. Liam, having serious work to do in the *brûlerie*, was taking no chances with fate.

'I'm sorry we couldn't find him for you, Father,' Ellen said.

Privately, she thought Liam was getting carried away with folklore.

Brigitte unlucky, indeed!

* * *

237

Riding beside the river on her way to Crouin, Ellen was in such a good mood that she was even able to convince herself that Catherine and she would be friends in a few hours.

It was the kind of evening, balmy and serene, in which it was quite impossible to have pessimistic thoughts. She rode beneath majestic grey poplars and golden willows, their erect catkins not yet ready to burst open. Under the irreverent hooves of 'oley Gee beds of anemones grew. In the gentle green river white swans drifted disdainfully near unseen nests in the reeds.

Concealed, too, tucked away behind the trees, were the miserable huts of the poor.

How lucky I am, by comparison, Ellen thought, and saw, in the distance, the house in which Catherine lived.

Most Protestant houses were surrounded by high walls and looked as if they had been turned back to front, with their gardens hidden behind, so that the curious and intolerant, peering through the locked metal gates, could gauge little of what went on within.

But Catherine's house, as if to defy and stand up openly to prejudice, was not hidden away. Its façade stared boldly onto the river and although there was a wall, newly-built, and a gate, it was quite possible to see into the terraced garden.

This garden, as Ellen saw once more when she reined in, had been designed with painstaking precision, planted *en broderie*, with mirror-like ponds and basins with high-jetting fountains. Long, straight *allées* were lined with clipped trees.

What she was looking at could not have been more different from her own familiar, wilder garden at Chez Landart.

Yet the dissimilarity, she thought, was not only because one garden was formal and one far more natural, but

238

because, in Catherine's garden, no children had ever played: there were no signs of discarded playthings, no footprints in the schematic flowerbeds.

But Catherine's garden was not totally deserted. Along one of the *allées* two figures were strolling, their arms entwined.

A man and a woman engrossed so deeply in conversation that, although they were walking in the direction of the gateway, they remained unaware of the rider and horse outside it.

John and Catherine? More than anything in the world Ellen wanted the couple in the garden to be John and Catherine. She would have desired nothing more than to have slipped discreetly away from the gate rather than intrude into what was obviously a very personal conversation between a loving husband and wife who were enjoying a quiet evening stroll.

Only the couple in the garden were not husband and wife. As they approached she could verify that only too clearly.

'*No!*' Ellen whispered. '*No . . . !*'

But she could not hide from the facts. The couple who walked with their arms entwined were Dick and Catherine.

She could not move for the pain. For a time it seemed inevitable that Dick and Catherine, having reached the gate, would look up and see her gazing at them through the metal bars.

She was already certain that she could hear Catherine speaking to her, reminding her of the impression that she had made when she had so gauchely arrived at the apartment in rue Vivienne.

'Such big ugly hands,' Catherine said again. 'How could *this* be a girl . . . ?'

But although Catherine still seemed to be mocking her, no direct confrontation took place. Instead, Dick and Catherine, without once looking up, turned and began to make their way back towards the house.

As they did so Ellen reacted with the instinct of all badly wounded animals, her heels urging her horse to head for home in a gallop.

She gasped for breath as she rode and the air got into her mouth and dried the back of her throat and her cheeks were soaked with tears.

And all the way Catherine taunted her, whispering: 'Ugly – ugly – ugly!' and, in a louder, more triumphant tone, called: '*You see – I took a lover, after all!*'

Ever since Brigitte had rejected him, Gérard Vergniaud had been in a foul temper.

That evening he, too, heard a voice in his mind, Brigitte's voice, and it was also taunting, reiterating what she had said before.

'*Dégoûtant!*' she said, scornfully. 'You are disgusting, Gérard. You have the face of a gargoyle – ugly . . .'

One of his brothers, overhearing, had laughed: '*Fais-te là, Gérard!* What else can you do!'

Rape her.

Gérard spat furiously. By the door to the kitchen Brigitte was talking to Liam Crowley. Gérard's face grew uglier still.

Under his breath he said, viciously: '*Pute!*'

Liam went into the house.

By the time she had reached the gates of the château, Ellen's emotions had multiplied: she was flooded with anger as well as grief, a rage so terrible that she was frightened of herself, sure that she could kill.

Her instinct now was to rush inside the house and lock

herself into the nearest room, until the madness had passed.

But as she rode round the right-hand side of the château to the stables, she saw Gérard Vergniaud embracing Brigitte, kissing her passionately, running a hand through the back of her hair . . .

Love reciprocated. Or so it seemed until Brigitte screamed, and Ellen saw that her face was striated with blood.

In her right hand Ellen was still carrying, out of habit, the riding-crop she never used on a horse, believing that an expert signals with his heels, rather than blows or hands. But she had a use for it now. As Gérard Vergniaud swung round Ellen struck him across the face.

'He bit me!' Brigitte wept. 'On the mouth, and pulled out the back of my hair. *C'est un brute*, Madame – a beast!'

'He's gone – he's gone,' Ellen said, reassuringly.

But she was quite wrong. Gérard Vergniaud was still in the château grounds, standing beside the cask on which he had earlier been working, touching the wound on a face which was so contorted with anger that it did, indeed, look like a hideous gargoyle. Had James been there to observe the narrowed eyes, one lower than the other, the bared yellowing teeth, he would have fled in terror, but James, like George and Bawnie, was tucked up in bed asleep.

The fire which Gérard had lit to solder together the slats of his new barrel was still burning. And inside the warped mind of the *tonnelier* another fire – a furnace of rage – was flaring up.

As Gérard stood contemplating the visible fire, the two conflagrations seemed to him to fuse and blaze together.

241

He swore with the fluency of a bitter man consumed with hatred of all women, thinking of retribution.

And still he looked at the fire . . .

It was already quite dark when Dick left Crouin: at Chez Chassat he thought that the red moon had run into the sky and tinted the golden willows and he marvelled to himself at the beauty of the scene.

Closer to home he realized that he had been deluded; that it was not a lunar overflow that had coloured the night sky but flames, leaping high from a blazing building.

Flames over Chez Landart . . .

It was his own house that was blazing.

Ellen, he thought frantically – the children – and he rode at a full gallop with fear and love in his heart, hoping and praying that somehow, by a miracle, the family would have been alerted to the fire, and be out of the house in the grounds.

When he reached the grounds he saw no sign of his family although other figures were scuttling to and fro dragging hastily severed branches of trees to use as beaters, holding them low to drive the sparks back into the flames. Amongst them were various members of the Vergniaud family and Liam to whom, as soon as he got within earshot, he yelled: 'Where are they?' and Liam shouted: 'Inside, Master Dick. We'll have to get them out.'

The fire, starting in the kitchen, had raged through the buttery and hall to the parlour and through an open arcade to the staircase, blocking off access there.

'The wood will be acting as tinder,' Liam lamented.

'Not necessarily,' Dick said, hoping that the thick baulks of timber he had put in during restoration would be reasonably fire-resisting.

But there was no time for talk. Pulling a branch out of the hands of one of the *tonneliers*, Dick went round by the left court towards the ancient tower where he and Ellen had first made love.

It was not of love he was thinking now but of the possibility of being able to go up the spiral steps to the top; and from there getting onto the château roof to climb downwards into a bedroom window.

To his immense relief he found that the fire had not yet reached the tower. It stood as it had done for centuries, threatened but impervious to threat; throwing down his branch, Dick ran up the steps to the top floor, thankful that he had once had the presence of mind to widen the slit windows which would now enable him to climb through, and, ultimately, reach the first-floor landing of the château.

To his amazement he did so without anything going wrong. There was no smoke, no hint of fire at this level, but all the same he sprinted towards the bedroom he and Ellen shared and flung open the door.

Ellen lay in the big bed. In her arms, snuggled against her body, were his three sons. Amazingly, with all that was going on, all four were asleep.

Ruined. This word, which James heard over and over during the next few days, was applied by his father not only to the condition of the severely burnt château but to the state of his financial affairs.

By then they were all staying with Grand-maman at Manoir des Yeux, a situation that was apparently going to continue more or less indefinitely.

James had been under the impression that Papa, as a matter of course, would be living there with the rest of the family. But then Papa said: 'I won't be able to stay in business. Everything went into stock and it's gone – all

243

gone,' and James remembered what he had heard before, that cognac was highly inflammable which meant easy to burn.

'So what will you do, Papa?'

'A good question,' Dick said bitterly.

He got up suddenly and walked away from James to the window and looked out into the garden, lost in thought.

'Papa? For you are quite old, I think. Maybe more than thirty even. What are you going to do?'

And Dick finally answered.

'I'll have to rejoin the army, James. It's all I'm trained to do.'

'But will they have you? Don't they want *young* men?'

His father laughed although he did not look in the least bit cheerful.

'They'll have me all right,' he said, and he sounded not happy about that but cross. 'France and England hate each other as much as before, you see. They're in conflict over Canada and India so, even if they're nominally at peace at home, that won't last for long. You'll see, another war will start and Lord O'Brien will need the services of Irishmen who have already proved themselves in battle to rejoin the regiment of Clare.'

'Oh,' said James, not understanding very much of this, only the first sentence. 'So you *will* be wanted for fighting. When I grow up, Papa, I will also be a soldier.'

Dick said: 'When you grow up you'll probably decide, as I did, that war is a futile and destructive matter, and that kings and politicians make terrible use out of the dreams of boys.'

But that, too, James found difficult to comprehend.

BOOK THREE
1760–1765

1

By 1760 the Irish Brigade was garrisoned on the Ile de Ré, off the coast of La Rochelle, as near to home as he was likely to be without being able to go there.

Dick was frustrated by the sensation of being at once in his element, and yet out of it. The people of Ré were very different from the rest of poverty-stricken France, with impressive agricultural production and respectable exports, wine, brandy and vinegar being sold not only to the French coast but to visiting foreign fleets from Sweden and Denmark, Saint-Dominique and the East Isles which, in turn, provided the island with fruit and other imports at very acceptable prices. Men were making fortunes out of the gold, property and ship-building industries and, in some cases, conducting highly profitable illicit trade, for Ré was a smuggler's haven.

And he was on a soldier's salary, most of which was needed to support Ellen and the boys and Biddy, their daughter born after the fire, leaving him nothing to invest.

There *were* compensations: the island was very attractive, its name aptly derived from *ratis*, meaning fern. Its wild and lonely beaches reminded him of the Irish coast. The port of Saint-Martin, with its beautiful buildings, comfortable inns and pleasing private houses was an amusing place to visit with his friends.

And the *camaraderie* was good: he had always enjoyed the company of men.

But the war was going badly for the French. Defeats at home in successive years – by Frederick II of Prussia at

Rossbach, Ferdinand of Brunswick in Hanover and West-phalia, and, after an abortive attempt to invade the Rhineland, at Minden – were equalled only by overseas disasters: Senegal and Goree falling into English hands; French influence in India supplanted; in Canada Quebec gone, and the strong points of Louisburg, Fort Duquesne and Fort Frontenac lost. West Indian possessions captured by British naval expeditions. The Toulon and Brest fleets routed at Lagos and Quiberon.

And on top of all of this a dagger attack on the king by the half-mad Damien who was duly executed in front of a vast excited crowd.

But not before first being tortured . . . Dick shuddered at the recollection, having himself been in Paris on that day. The executioners dressed as if they were on their way to a festival or a ball. The condemned man stretched on a scaffold, and secured with iron thongs. In his right hand, the dagger.

And then that hand placed on a stove in which sulphur had been burning. Boiling oil poured on to his muscles and skin.

And – in the presence of three priests – Monsignor d'Orleans, Monsignor de Paris and Monsignor de Lyons – the stretching: his arms and legs secured to horses. The horses lashed – the bones cracking . . .

And *still* he was alive, conscious when they cropped his limbs and threw him into a fire, or so Dick had heard later, having long before turned and left.

After all this, morale in the army – throughout the country – was low. Away from Ré, the people were poorer than ever, expected to pay out of their own pittances for a war into which France, without the court being aware of it, had been dragged by Maria Theresa, Queen of Austria, to help her recover Silesia.

A war which had gone on for far too long, and showed

no sign of abating. A war which parted husbands and wives . . .

Even on his infrequent leaves he felt apart, these days, from Ellen, who seemed less spontaneous – withdrawn, as she had been on the night of the fire. Perhaps it was the shock of that which had changed her – that and the strain of bringing up the children while her husband was at war. At least Liam was there, more in the capacity of odd-job man these days than distiller, to lend her moral support, to take James and George and Bawnie off her hands.

Write often, Dick had said to her, about to depart after his last leave, but even her letters seemed detached, passing on routine information about the children but containing little news of herself.

Between one thing and another, he thought, life was damn' depressing lately. To cheer himself up, he decided, that evening, to go into Saint-Martin with some of his old companions. But even that got off to a bad start: outside the old church, a fortress during the Wars of Religion, he met by chance his least favourite comrade, Roger De Lacy himself.

Perhaps the most irritating of all Roger's recent traits was his insistence on treating Dick like a valued friend instead of an old rival and enemy, as if he had never stood in Barré wood waiting for him to die.

Or am I being too harsh, Dick wondered, misjudging the man, forgetting that he was, to all intents and purposes, in the throes of an intense and youthful passion, and that this, now, had passed.

'Come and join us!' Roger cheerfully hailed him and his companions. '*Your* friends, of course, I know, since we are all in the same regiment but mine may be strangers to you, although you may have heard of them by repute. Dorigny le Dauphin – François Choderlos de Laclos.'

Two young men, one in his mid-twenties, the other younger, possibly only eighteen or nineteen years old.

'Good evening.'

Dick was aware that his own friends were exchanging discreet glances for Dorigny le Dauphin, as everyone knew, was one of the king's illegitimate sons, the result of a passing love affair with a pretty housemaid, and himself an art dealer of some distinction. His presence on Ré emphasized a second scandal, for he was doubtless paying a visit to his half-brother, the Jesuit Père Ignace Joubir des Maricres, Louis' other natural son, a man who devoted that part of his life which was not consumed by his vocation to the development of Saint-Martin.

'I wonder how many more royal bastards will make their way down here!' Colm O'Neill said, *sotto voce*, after Roger, having invited them all to join him for drinks, began striding ahead with his friends. 'The Parc aux Cerfs is seemingly fully occupied by prostitutes who have moved into that little villa in Versailles to give birth to the king's children. I gather even we Irish have a royal connection since *La Morphil* climbed into bed with the king!'

'Well, they do say Madame de Pompadour can't keep up with his demands. Perhaps she has had too many miscarriages . . .'

But the subject did not really interest Dick. The king, he thought, was venal. The behaviour of the girls, making love, having babies in order to be able to retire with a modest dowry, seemed, in the face of national poverty, far more comprehensible. *La Morphil*, Louisa O'Morphi, had, like other members of her family, been painted by Boucher in lively and voluptuous settings on the orders of Madame de Pompadour, to titillate the king. At seventeen she had been taken to Le Trébuchet – the bird-snare, the king's love apartment – later giving birth to a daughter in one of the Presentation convents before being married off to an officer from Auvergne who had died at the battle of Rosbach.

'They say Louisa is a delectable thing,' Colm went on. 'How old would the daughter be – five? If the war goes on we'll still be garrisoned here by the time *she's* old enough to pay her respects to Père Ignace. I'll look forward to that!'

There were times, sitting across the table from Roger, when it was possible to believe that there had been no intervening years since they had first been together in Paris, Dick thought. As if he had never owned his own export business or the Château de Pericard.

Except, of course, that Philip was not there. And that he, Dick, was in his mid-thirties, with a wife and four children.

'I intend to be a great writer,' the younger of Roger's friends, Choderlos de Laclos, was announcing to the room at large. 'I will write something out of the ordinary, eye-catching, something that will resound around the world even after I have left it!'

'A modest fellow!' Colm O'Neill said, out of the corner of his mouth.

'And are you writing now?'

'A few elegies for the dead, who aren't likely to find out about them, and some epistles in verse, most of which will never be published, fortunately for the public and even more fortunately for me . . .'

'If you're ready to be friendly to the other one, perhaps he'll give you one of Boucher's paintings!' Colm said to Dick. 'One of the Pompadour perhaps. That would be a *coup*!'

'Mr De Lacy here tells me that you play cards, Captain O'Shaughnessy.' Dorigny le Dauphin had a rather high-pitched grating voice and a condescending manner designed, presumably, to make his listeners aware of whose son he was.

'Every now and again.'

'. . . and that you are a fairly competent player.'

A bantam-cock, if ever I saw one, Dick thought, less irritated than amused at the careless manner and deliberate disrespect. He drank long and slowly, putting his empty glass back on the table before he replied.

'Fairly competent, I'd say. And yourself?'

'I am extremely skilful.'

'We're going to have some fun!' Colm O'Neill said softly. In a louder tone he added: 'Would you like to qualify that? Where do your skills lie – in quadrille – or piquet or lansquenet maybe?'

'All of them equally,' Dorigny le Dauphin said, yawning as if to intimate his boredom. 'Or Faro.'

'You play Faro?'

'Naturally. It's one of the oldest card games – and one for highborn gamblers so, of course, I would play it. But I must warn you that my friends and I are all very experienced players . . .'

The trouble with yawning, Dick thought, was that it was catching, especially if one was bored. And he was immensely bored all of a sudden, bored with banal talk about the king's concubines, bored with Roger De Lacy's insincere friendship – for it surely was nothing more – bored with youthful bravado. He was beginning to regret having come into Saint-Martin at all. How much more pleasant it would be to be at Chez Landart, with the family, or in his old office in the rue de la Richonne. The rueful comparison jogged his memory of a recent conversation – with whom? O'Neill? One of the others? – at all events with someone who had been down in Cognac and by chance had met John Marrett. And John Marrett, still operating out of *his* old office, was, by all accounts, doing

252

extremely well exporting cognac to Europe. To Ireland? Picking up the business that he, Dick, had lost? It was quite possible and perfectly ethical. From John's point of view, Dick was out of the game – the Irish market was his, if he cared to exploit it.

But the mere suggestion that he might have done so was just like a knife in the guts. If only I had some capital, Dick thought desperately: just enough to start again, and build up my business.

'Captain O'Shaughnessy, would you care for a game or do you feel you would be out of your depth with us?'

Dick blinked, returning from contemplation of his ruined career to his comrades round the table, all of whom were looking at him expectantly.

'What did you say?'

Slowly and with contempt in his voice Dorigny le Dauphin repeated his former question. Slowly, Dick registered the insult.

He still had no intention of spending the rest of the evening playing cards with this objectionable young man.

But then, looking up suddenly, he was surprised by the expression on Roger De Lacy's face – a look of equal hate and hope, and for a split second he was back again in Barré wood in the spring of '45.

So he has *not* forgiven me for depriving him of Catherine, Dick thought, startled. It is not friendship that Roger is looking for when he invites me to join his friends, but an opportunity to see me humiliated, as he once was, by me. I should have realized that desire for a woman fades long before the memory of rejection and defeat.

Having intended to announce that it was time that he returned to barracks, that perhaps he and Dorigny le Dauphin might play another evening, he found himself catching Roger De Lacy's eye and answering with his own

253

– So you want to see me defeated in cards by this arrogant braggart?

Roger looked away.

'I don't think I would be out of my depth with you at all,' Dick said to Dorigny le Dauphin, and in his anger he forgot that he could not, in truth, afford to risk losing even a small amount at cards. 'As you're such a skilful player, I suppose you've brought some cards?'

Colm O'Neill was acting as banker. In front of him a shuffled pack of fifty-two cards lay, placed face up, in the dealing box. The complete Spades suit had been placed upon the table. It only remained for players to signify their bets by placing chips on the cards.

'Captain O'Shaughnessy, *I* have access to unlimited funds. Whereas *you*, on army pay – '

And suddenly Dick was very angry indeed, with the insouciant young man across the table, with life for having dealt him such a bad hand on the night of the fire at the château. He had been diminished in his own eyes for long enough through the loss he had sustained then and he, who had vowed to succeed in life, gaining respect as well as more material rewards, was, in that moment, not prepared to be diminished in any other's. He looked up, confronting each of the faces around the table in turn – the expectant face of Roger De Lacy, willing him to lose; the arrogant young faces of Dorigny le Dauphin and Choderlos de Laclos; the mischievous faces of Colm O'Neill and his other friends, waiting for Dick to put the king's bastard truly in his place.

'Don't worry about me,' he said icily.

At the same time he recognized that he himself had plenty to worry about since, in theory, Dorigny le Dauphin was perfectly right: he could not afford to get involved in a betting game. Be honest, he urged himself, you should not risk a *sou* and yet here you are allowing yourself to be challenged by a rich young man who, for all you know of him, could be as disreputable a cardsharp as Apoulos the Greek was proven to be by his grandfather after being admitted into the court circle. Unlike the Greek, Dorigny le Dauphin is not going to allow himself to be caught *in flagrante delicto* and condemned to the galleys whereas I, if I lose even the small amount of money I have on me tonight, will not be in a position to make the occasional trip to Saint-Martin with my friends for the next couple of months.

And if I win . . .

But in recent years I seem to be consistently a loser, in business and in war.

As if he had been reading Dick's thoughts Roger De Lacy said: 'You're right, my friend, to give Captain O'Shaughnessy here the option of refusing, even at this late stage. I can remember a time when he was considered an excellent player but in recent years he has been somewhat down on his luck.'

To hell with it, Dick thought furiously, I'll risk the little I've got.

'We're wasting time,' he said curtly. 'Does anyone object if I deal and cut?'

Luck is a changeable lady, Colm O'Neill said to himself lightly as, after each turn, when the bets settled were paid and collected, Dick continued to win. At midnight, the other players looked nonplussed. Choderlos de Laclos, in particular, seemed to be out of his depth.

His friend, Dorigny le Dauphin, was better able to maintain a nonchalant façade, but only just and his stock of insolent comments had long since run out.

'Do you want to continue?'

Dick's question, put in a hard, unyielding voice.

'Naturally.'

But Dorigny le Dauphin had a cornered look about him now. Where, at the beginning of the game, he had exchanged conspiratorial glances with Roger De Lacy – a man Colm himself disliked – as it progressed he carefully avoided catching the older man's eye.

And Colm had the distinct impression that the king's illegitimate son did not have access to unlimited funds, as he had earlier claimed – that his money was running out . . .

'In which case, Monsieur, go ahead and bet.'

With a long, slim hand Dorigny le Dauphin placed a chip on the four of Spades and Colm turned up two cards. Neither was a four.

'Your bet remains unsettled.'

'Turn again.'

'The four of Hearts. The four loses. I take your bet,' said Colm, grinning, knowing that if Dorigny le Dauphin had bet on the four to lose he would have had to pay him.

Soon, only three cards remained on the table, and it was up to a player to bet on the exact order in which they would come up.

'I'm calling the turn,' Colm announced, meaning that he would pay the betting player four to one if he was correct.

'I'll bet.'

Dick, out for a final fling.

In that moment, Colm saw him not as a close friend who was experiencing a run of unprecedented good luck, but, rather, as an enemy, a man who was winning much more than anyone deserved.

'Whereas you, on army pay – ' Dorigny le Dauphin had sneered, forgetting that others – Colm amongst them – were in the same position and, unlike Dick who had owned his own business and still had to his credit a château in Cognac, unlikely to move beyond it.

While Dick, after pulling off tonight's *coup* . . .

If two of these three cards turn out to be a pair, I will only have to pay him two to one, Colm thought, letting resentment take over.

Turning, he saw with a twinge of envy, that Dick had won again.

'Captain O'Shaughnessy?'

At this rate, I could treat all of us to a *chaise à porteurs* to take us back to barracks, Dick was thinking, when Dorigny le Dauphin, panting, appeared out of the darkness behind him.

'Captain O'Shaughnessy, could I have a word?'

A different approach altogether, with the hauteur and insolence gone.

'What is it?'

'In private?'

'You want to be careful. He might not be alone,' Lucan O'Keeffe, one of Dick's own party, warned. 'We'll wait for you up the road.'

'What did you want to talk to me about?' Dick asked Dorigny le Dauphin when the others had moved on.

It was a clear enough night – clear enough for Dick to be able to see the young face, intelligent, spoilt and, it seemed, vulnerable now and abject.

'Well?'

Dorigny le Dauphin said: 'That money – most of it was not mine.'

'So?'

'So I have a request to make. There is a painting. By Boucher – of the O'Morphi girl. You know that she fell from favour?'

'I know there is a rumour.'

257

'She asked my father what terms he was on with the old lady – meaning the Pompadour. That was the end of her affair with the king. The painting, too, was removed from Versailles. It fell into my hands. I – brought it to Ré to sell along with several others.'

'Then sell it – sell them. And pay your creditors back.'

'You don't understand,' Dorigny le Dauphin said desperately. 'That would take a little time. They – would want the money tonight. François, for instance, is always short. He has this dream of leaving the army so he can write a book . . .'

'He's not the only one dreaming of getting out.'

But Dick was feeling less harsh than he sounded. As Dorigny le Dauphin hesitated he said: 'Tell me, apart from him, from whom did you borrow money? And why? Were you that anxious to gamble and that confident of winning?'

'Captain De Lacy,' said the young man. '*He* put me up to it. You see, I told him that I was an experienced player. He wanted you to lose. I was short of money myself and he said that, if I won and in the process humiliated you, he would not see me short . . .'

'But you lost and he wants his money back?'

'He says that he has powerful friends. I am a long way from Paris. I am staying with the Jesuits who are not exactly aggressive. Besides, neither my father nor my half-brother, Père Ignace, would take my part in this matter.'

Dick said: 'In terms of their muscles my friends are every bit as powerful as Captain De Lacy's. But let me see the painting. Then we'll talk again.'

His initial reaction was less erotic than disgusted: the creamy, plump, naked girl depicted in the painting was so damned young! So natural and so unaffectedly abandoned.

As the boy's own mother must have been, more than twenty years before. What had happened to *her*? he wondered. Used, at most, for a few nights' pleasure and then pensioned off.

While the boy . . . Was he officially recognized? Dick was not sure.

And meanwhile there was the painting . . .

'You are the art dealer. The man with the contacts. As you said yourself, soldiers, with the possible exception of men like Lord Clare, do not have access to unlimited funds. What if I take the painting from you and do not manage to find a buyer?'

'I'll find a buyer for you,' Dorigny le Dauphin said. 'But it might take a couple of weeks. It's just that – '

'You need the money now, and I have the rest of my winnings to keep me going. Well, I'll strike a bargain with you. I'll give you back the money you borrowed from Choderlos de Laclos – that only. Captain De Lacy can hang for his, as far as I am concerned. If he threatens you, remind him that I, too, have friends . . . As to the sale of the painting – your own integrity about that – I'll gamble on it. But it's the last thing I'll bet on. In fact, I suggest that the two of us give up gambling for good.'

2

WE, CHARLES O'BRIEN OF THOMOND, VICOMTE OF CLARE IN THE KINGDOM OF IRELAND, MARECHAL OF FRANCE, KNIGHT OF THE ORDER OF THE KING, COLONEL OF THE IRISH INFANTRY OF CLARE:

WE certify that Richard O'Shaughnessy has served in our regiment for eight years in all; that he has always behaved in an exemplary manner as a gallant gentleman; and it is with regret that we see him being forced to leave the service because of the severe English laws operative against the Irish who fight in the service of France . . .

Lord O'Brien had said: 'With that document as proof that you've left the army, the British won't arrest you if you're stopped at sea. When are you leaving for Ireland?'

And he had answered: 'As soon as possible. Whenever I can get a sailing.'

My Dearest Ellen,

. . . necessity to rebuild orders for cognac must come before all else since some of my customers are buying from my competitors and others, like Mr Thomas Creagh of Kinsale, are dead. So before I visit you I am going straight to Ireland . . .

Ellen, he thought, would surely understand.

Colm O'Neill, who had been granted leave, went with him to La Rochelle. Colm cheerfully agreed to deliver money and letters to Ellen and Liam before he went on to stay with friends in Angoulême.

260

'The letter to Crowley is vital,' Dick told Colm when the two men had stopped for an ice-cream in the Café de Provence and were watching the rich go by. 'He'll be buying cognac on my behalf while I'm in Ireland and these are his instructions.'

'I'll see that it gets there,' Colm said. 'Isn't it strange to think that the first inhabitants of this town were fishermen who settled on a rock in the middle of a swamp! They'd never believe it if they could see the grand houses the shipbuilders put up on the marshy land.'

'Or what's going on in business. Someone was telling me the other day that Pierre Barre is thinking of buying out one of the old crockery houses in La Rochelle. Of course it's not just in this town. At Jouy-en-Josas they've opened a factory for making coloured prints. It's a great country to be in if you are a man of commerce.'

The last remark reminded Colm that Dick was getting out of the army while he, who would also liked to have done so, was forced to continue his career as a soldier.

He said, sharply: 'Surely, above all, France is the centre of the civilized world? When you talk about La Rochelle you don't mention the academies for literature and music and art, and the research that's being done in medicine. You're a bit of a philistine, O'Shaughnessy – no wonder you sold that painting!'

Dick blinked, not troubling himself to respond. But in spite of this he and Colm managed to spend a pleasant enough day together during which Dick arranged a booking on a ship that would take him to Le Havre, prior to his sailing to Ireland.

It was when they were near the Académie Rochelais, where drama was staged, that Colm overheard part of a conversation between two young students.

'. . . Catherine of La Rochelle betrayed Jeanne d'Arc in court . . .'

261

'They were not friends?'

'Not at all. Catherine was opportunistic, urging King Charles to ask his subjects to surrender their treasures to the Crown in the hope that she could keep some of them for herself. The only similarity was that, like Jeanne, she fought in the army and heard mystical voices, but the two of them didn't get on well.'

'What became of Catherine Cantillon, Philip's sister?' Colm, put in mind of her name, asked Dick. 'Didn't she return here from Paris?'

'She did. In fact she lived in Cognac for quite a long time.'

'Lived? Do you know where she is now?'

'More than that,' Dick said. 'In fact, I shall be seeing her shortly. She moved to La Rochelle.'

So, in the early part of 1760, Dick retraced his steps of sixteen years before. To his surprise, the sea voyage passed without incident; he only encountered difficulties when he got home to Kilawillen.

First of all there was the inevitable shock on finding his parents grey-haired, with lines etched into their ageing faces; Willie heavier, balding; his sisters changed from young girls into women whose bodies had thickened after bearing children.

But that was a natural transition to which he soon adjusted. Without realizing it, though, he had changed during his years in France while, mentally, his relations had stayed the same. *His* mind had been stretched to encompass hundreds of new experiences, cultural, commercial and military, but when he told the family stories of the war, of friends in France, of the Charente and of his business, he saw their eyes glaze over with incomprehension.

He felt lonely at Kilawillen, and he suspected that

Willie, at least, resented him; regarded him an an opportunist who had gone off to fight a romantic war leaving others to do battle at home against the Penal Laws. Too late he realized that he should not have regaled Willie with the tale of his colossal win at cards, since it only underscored his brother's obvious suspicions about his own way of life in France.

Part of him sympathized with Willie. Ireland was in massive financial and economic distress, due to famine and trade depression. Banks were failing; the powerful secret society known as the Whiteboys, in attempting to offer protection to the peasantry from rack-renting landlords, was terrorizing whole districts; emigrants were leaving the country in their thousands, depriving it of industrious and valuable citizens.

Dick understood how Willie and other Catholics must feel, stifled under a blanket of frustration, and told himself that he should have nothing but admiration for all those who had resisted the temptation to emigrate, saying that they were too fond of their native land to ever leave its shores.

At the same time he felt irritated by what he felt was a lack of understanding.

'Look,' he wanted to say, 'I am one of you, even if I seem to be different. Do you really think it was any better – effortless, painless – for me than for you fighting for a living these last years?'

But even as he phrased the question in his mind he knew that the men who had stayed in the Blackwater Valley would have one unanimous answer: you, at least, had the chance to better yourself. We who remained had none.

And so he posed no questions except conventional ones, and in his approach was positive about the situation at home, telling Willie that the turnpiking of public roads

263

and the state-sponsored construction of canals were going to do wonders for Ireland.

Willie grunted. 'Isn't Parliament scheming to cut down coal and corn imports, by making it cheaper to transport from potential sources of supply inland to the coast?'

'I'm told that money has gone into inland and coastal navigation projects.'

'That was in the fifties,' Willie said gruffly, 'when Parliament had revenue to spare.'

'And I hear that a number of small farmers are beginning to do relatively well. They say there may be opportunities in grain.'

'*Who* says?' Willie demanded irritably. 'The prices have been low and are likely to remain so. And as for Irish iron production and timber processing, what can we do against cheaply smelted pig iron from Sweden and Russia, and cheap timber from New England? The country's in a terrible state and on top of it we have lunatic Frenchmen coming to take Carrickfergus. Not that it did them much good!'

'I thought it was an Irishman who headed that expedition,' Dick said, to get back at his brother's attempts to suppress him.

By contrast to Willie his mother's and sisters' wish was to over-cosset the homecomer and Dick soon had the feeling that they, too, were wrapping a blanket around him.

Still, once orders started coming in none of this would matter.

But *would* he get orders in this depressing climate? There was only one way to find out and that was to meet people, to move around the country.

'I'm going to Ballygriffin to see the Nagles,' he announced on his third morning in Kilawillen. 'They're bound to ask me for dinner so don't expect me home.'

'They'll be glad to see you – and to hear news of Ellen,' said his mother in an expressionless voice.

So after all these years she had not forgiven Ellen for being in his confidence prior to his departure from west Cork, or for running away to Paris dressed as a man in the company of a tramp.

He opened his mouth to tell her that Ellen had proved an invaluable asset to him in his business by keeping the books and that the tramp was now a skilled distiller, but promptly closed it again. It was pointless talking to his mother about his other life. She was interested only in how he related to her own existence at Kilawillen and that of his father and brother and sisters. Kissing her, he made good his escape.

Riding between the river and the Nagle Mountains he did not remember the dog that, at this place, had feasted off human entrails, having seen worse on the battlefields of France, and he did not visit the caves to relive boyhood experiences, but went on over the bridge and left towards Ballygriffin, with the Blackwater River meandering beside him and the ruins of Monaminy Castle at his back.

And ahead of him the likelihood of taking orders for cognac from his in-laws and, with luck, some of their visiting friends. After which, he thought, he would go in to Mallow and look up other connections and on another day to Glanworth and Ballyhooly and Castletownroche and Kanturk.

The Nagles welcomed him without the tensions that spring up out of the blood-tie, besieging him for news of Ellen whom her brothers obviously regarded with more admiration than resentment, all of them clamouring for descriptions of what life had been like in the Irish Brigade.

There was another man at the house who gave the impression of being genuinely interested in the life Dick had led in France, a tall, black-haired man with soft brown eyes and the long straight Nagle nose that Ellen had not inherited: her cousin Edmund Burke who he remembered from the hedge-school at Monaminy.

'But you were younger than myself.'

'By five years. I recall being much in awe of you. But then, of course, I went to school at Ballitore in Kildare and, afterwards, when I was fifteen, to Trinity College in Dublin.'

Which, having been reared as a Protestant, you were qualified to do, Dick thought, remembering that the Burkes had followed the custom of bringing their sons up in the Established Church so that they could avail themselves of the benefits Protestants got, while their daughters, who had no expectations beyond marriage, had been raised as Catholics.

'What are you doing with yourself now?' he asked Edmund Burke.

'I went to London ten years ago to keep terms at the Temple and conceived a strong distaste for the Law! I write. A necessity since my father conceived an equally strong distaste for the vagrancy of the profession of letters and withdrew my annual allowance! I practise oratory in the debating societies of Covent Garden. And I mix with the Bohemian society of the Temple.'

'He knows everyone. If you want to build up your orders for cognac stick close to the cousin,' Rory confided discreetly. 'And don't be deceived by the excitable manner he has. Under it all, he has a passion for order and justice.'

'You're set to go back to France, are you? It's a sad thing the way we lose so many good men . . .'

'You live in England yourself.'

'But I'm going to work for Ireland against the Penal Laws, against restrictions on Irish trade and industry and

266

landlord absenteeism,' Edmund Burke insisted. 'Still, I'd like to help you, if I can. My brother Garret has taken over Clogher estate near Shanballymore from the Catholic side of the family in order to protect their interests, and I'll be visiting him, and staying in Dublin for a while. After your visit here, why don't you join me? You could be taking orders further afield than the Blackwater Valley.'

For Dick, it was an extremely fortuitous day. In the afternoon when he and the other men walked around the Nagle estate Edmund Burke reiterated his offer to introduce him to people with an interest in purchasing cognac. His hitherto deflated spirits began to rise again.

'Who's that fellow you were telling us about, Edmund – who'd been at Trinity with you and is said to divide his time in London between writing poetry and acting the strolling player?'

'Oliver Goldsmith, Donagh. A gaudy but brilliant fellow . . .'

There were golden tips already on the gorse and the ivy growing on the low wall on which they stopped to sit was a rich deep velvety green instead of the mottled black-green of winter, and the crocuses were beginning to shoot.

Signs of a false spring? But what did it matter so long as you knew that the genuine spring would come?

It was raining heavily the evening Colm O'Neill reached Crouin, and he was not only wet but hungry when he arrived at Manoir des Yeux.

Foremost in his mind, as he knocked on the door, was the hope that Ellen would ask him to stay the night and save him the bother of having to ride into Cognac after their meeting and look for a suitable inn.

It was his first encounter with Dick's wife and as the maid showed him in he wondered idly what she would look like. As beautiful as Catherine Cantillon had been the last time he had seen her?

The answer was probably not. And more likely still, ugly and fat.

For otherwise why would Dick have been making a rendezvous in La Rochelle with the gorgeous Catherine?

At the time when Dick had announced his intention of doing that Colm had been surprised at his boldness. It was not the same at all as a man going off to visit a brothel, relieving his frustrations with a fallen woman when he was deprived of his own wife.

Planning to meet an old sweetheart – for Colm could remember that Dick and Catherine had been fond of each other in Paris – was very different. It indicated a real *affaire*, the kind of escapade that was happening all the time in the court. And, to him, smacked in a way he envied of luck and power and success.

All of which Dick already had in plenty . . .

Still maybe his wife was drab.

At that point in his cogitations the door opened and into the room stepped the woman he supposed to be Dick O'Shaughnessy's wife.

In the five years since the fire and Dick's return to the army, Ellen had resolutely pushed all thoughts of Catherine to the back of her mind, as being the only possible way to live with the memory of what she had seen on that fateful April evening, and she had shied away from all conversations about the other woman.

In the first few months of living in Crouin, so close to Catherine, she was haunted with the fear of a chance meeting – of the moment when their carriages would pass and she would be forced to look the other way; or when, shopping in Cognac, she would see a familiar figure ahead of her in the street and have to retrace her steps in case the two should meet.

Hélène never mentioned Catherine. Prying visitors invariably found that their efforts either to extract or impart information about the errant daughter had been parried and thwarted and the conversation deftly steered in another direction.

Then one day Liam, whose torrent of news about all and sundry was virtually impossible to dam up, announced that the Marretts had moved away from Cognac and Ellen felt that a great weight had been lifted from her back.

And still she said nothing to Dick about her discovery, while resenting the necessity to bottle up her hatred and her pain. For to reveal her emotions – to confess what she had witnessed – would be to relive that anguish again; although she might, ultimately, have confronted Dick had they seen each other more than occasionally over those five years.

Five years of sharing a home, not with a husband, but with understanding Hélène. Who had insisted that the fire had actually been beneficial to herself, providing her with company. Who had never shown signs of impatience with the children, whatever her secret feelings.

It could not go on forever, Ellen thought. But Hélène maintained it could.

In the last year, the pendulum had swung: for Hélène had not been well, had developed an unexplained swelling in her stomach, had complained of occasional pain, and Ellen felt that there was merit in her being at the older woman's side, to repay her hospitality with care and attention.

On the evening Colm O'Neill came to deliver Dick's letters, Hélène had been having one of her attacks and had gone to bed early and the children had soon followed her. Unaware that she was about to receive a visitor and motivated only by a desire to look attractive in order to reassure herself that she could still do so, in spite of being a mother of four, Ellen put on a fresh green gown and raised the front of her hair, which was dressed in rows of curls across the forehead, with a wad of combings.

The effect, she thought, was good: the horizontal curls helped to conceal the height of her forehead and gave balance to her face. She caught the hair at the back of her head and raised that too, tying it in a knot at the top.

And all this was to dine on her own! But then Brigitte, who had accompanied her to Crouin to assist with looking after the children, knocked on the bedroom door and said that a friend of Dick's had called.

To her annoyance, Ellen's heart thumped, as it always did when there was news of Dick.

'Tell him I'll be with him immediately,' she said, and augmented her new hairstyle with a big green plume.

All this titivation had its effects on Colm. Ellen, he thought, far from being fat and ugly, was lissom and comely.

She hardly paused to greet him before saying eagerly: 'You have a message from Dick? When will he come home?'

What was Dick up to, running around with another woman when he had a wife like this so anxious to see him? Colm's envy of Dick was endorsed by a sudden rush of self-righteousness and condemnation of his friend.

The fellow had no right to be behaving in that louche manner. If his wife knew what he was up to, the scales would fall from her eyes – Dick would tumble from the high pedestal on which he was standing now.

That was the sum total of the thoughts that were going around in Colm's mind as he and Ellen chatted. Finally, when he had handed over the letters and money, and given her a summary of the card game and its fortuitous results, he said: 'Dick was always lucky. Maybe that's why he's grown careless about looking after what should be closest to his heart.'

'What do you mean by that?' Ellen demanded immediately, sounding less friendly.

'It's only – he does things *I* wouldn't do if I were in his position . . .'

'Such as?'

So Colm repeated what Dick had said, about his intended meeting with Catherine. He imagined, briefly, that he was ingratiating himself with Ellen and even nurtured a passing hope that she might turn to him for comfort.

Instead, she stood up, scattering Dick's letters and money onto the floor and, as if she could no longer bear having Colm in the room with her for as much as another minute, she said coldly: 'Thank you for calling, Captain O'Neill. But no thanks for what you have told me. Excuse me. Brigitte will see you out.'

As the fire had blazed she had slept like a dead woman, worn out by emotion: after Colm had left the house she did not sleep at all.

In the morning the rain stopped and a lemony sun shone too brightly out of the pale grey sky.

'God is beating His Wife!' Brigitte said, as the Charentaïs said on such occasions, but Ellen did not smile.

'Look after the children for me. I have to go out.'

The next thing she knew she was on the road that led to Jarnac, near the village of Bourg-Charente, riding through the peat-brown wintry landscape, between tall leafless trees onto the emaciated branches of which clung clumps of mistletoe, looking like the empty nests of migratory birds.

271

When she rode by the river bank, in the place she had once believed to be *Magh Mel*, the same poplars and willows, looking down at the water, were swollen, dun and drab with the recent rain.

As she passed M. Merlet's wine-farm, the low lines of the brown vines looked like the skeletons of children, arms joined, executing a formal and gruesome dance. The earth seemed to be dead. When she dismounted from her horse, the fallen tree on which she sat, never to be fashioned into a cask, and the wet leaves under her feet, fuscous, *feuille-morte*, were sodden, too, from the rain.

The landscape offered neither solution nor consolation. Go home, she told herself. For what is the point of sitting morbid and dull and stagnant on a damp log watching the manic dance of the vines . . . ?

Go home.

But at the gates of the manor four small figures were waiting. Four faces were anxious.

'Maman, Father McMahon has been summoned,' James said seriously.

And over his brother's words Bawnie shouted: 'Grand-maman is ill.'

3

'All the time she is vomiting,' Yvette, no longer reticent in Ellen's company, reported grimly. 'It is bad, Madame Ellen. I can tell. We should send for Mademoiselle Catherine.'

'Madame Catherine is in La Rochelle,' Ellen said distractedly, not registering that Yvette, like her mistress, in referring to Catherine, did not give credence to the fact that she was married.

'A message will have to be sent,' Yvette insisted and Ellen knew then that Hélène's condition was very bad indeed.

'You're right, of course. Liam will have to be sent to fetch her. Except that we have no address for Madame Catherine . . .'

'Liam will find out where she is living. He knows everybody's business,' said Yvette, confidently.

'Then ask him to do so at once.'

She would not, not, not think about Dick and Catherine, Ellen vowed, sitting by Hélène's bedside while the older woman slept, in a temporary respite from pain and retching. Not now. Not when Maman was so ill. She would not allow herself to indulge in self-pity while watching the life of someone she loved run out.

Nevertheless as the days of vigil dragged on, visions of Catherine journeying from La Rochelle to Cognac infiltrated into her mind.

She was distracted by the unexpected arrival of Father McMahon, on one of his visits from Bordeaux. But

273

although the priest was a supportive presence, he was as pessimistic about Hélène's chances of recovery as Yvette had been, at the beginning of that week.

'It's just a matter of time,' he said, resignedly. 'Have you told her that Catherine is on her way?'

'Yes. She said she would not see her when she comes . . .'

'Ah sure, she'll change her mind yet,' the priest said in his reassuring way.

But events turned out very differently. Ellen was sitting in her usual position beside the sick woman's bed when Hélène moaned and turned agitatedly in her sleep before opening her brown eyes.

'I want . . .' she began, and retched, pathetically.

Her brow, under a tangle of hair, was covered in perspiration. I must fetch Father McMahon at once, to administer Extreme Unction, Ellen thought, jumping up.

'Ellen.'

'I want to call Father – '

'Don't go!'

Hélène's voice was surprisingly sharp.

'Father would want to be with you . . .'

'Wait. My affairs are in order, Ellen. My will has been made. It is all for you – everything. The house. Money . . .'

'Catherine?' Ellen said, bewildered. 'What about Catherine?'

'There is a letter for Catherine,' Hélène said. 'It explains everything. Now call Father McMahon. It is necessary to confess . . .'

The candles for the dying had been lit and then extinguished and the prayers for the dead were being chanted.

So much to organize, Ellen thought, sadly. The purchase of an oak coffin. Black silk or bombazine dresses

274

for Biddy and myself and black cloth-suits for the boys. Yvette and Brigitte and the other servants to be put into mourning as a mark of respect for Maman. Requiem Mass to be said . . .

'. . . mercy on the soul of Thy servant, and delivering it from the corruptions of mortality, to restore it to the inheritance of eternal salvation . . . Through our Lord Jesus Christ . . .'

'Amen.'

Yvette entered, whispered: 'Pardon – Mademoiselle Catherine is here.'

It was as if a brightly plumed and exotic bird had flown off-course into the house of mourning. Catherine was wearing a deep blue cape over a rose-coloured gown in the creation of which a *modiste* had been encouraged to express herself freely. *Échelles* of puffy ribbon bows plumped down the stomacher to be met by swags and flounces and loops. Enhancing the effect of ultra-femininity, Catherine's dark hair was piled high on the top of her head, allowing a few captivating curls to dangle at each side and at the back of her neck. There were pear-drop earrings in her pretty ears and the new lower-heel shoes, also in rose, on her tiny feet. She brought with her a strong waft of perfume.

But although she was as beautiful as ever, she was undeniably plump. All those chocolates, Ellen thought, gazing at her. She always did have a sweet tooth.

'All that rush and still I was too late,' Catherine said in a flat voice so that Ellen was not sure whether she was deeply distressed and trying to hide her feelings or was, in fact, detached.

'We sent for you the minute we realized how serious it was.'

275

'So Liam told me,' said Catherine, slipping off her cape and letting it fall onto the nearest chair.

Her gown was just that little bit too tight. In spite of the corset she must have been wearing there were tell-tale bulges above the waist.

'Did *she* ask you to send for me or was that your own idea?'

She must care, Ellen thought, or she would not have asked such a question, yet she makes it sound like a casual inquiry. How will she react when I tell her the truth?

'It was . . . She . . .'

To her own surprise Ellen, who for so long had wanted to hurt Catherine, to avenge the torment which Catherine had inflicted upon her – was still meting out – found herself unable to continue.

'She didn't want to see me,' Catherine said in her flat, matter-of-fact voice. 'I see. No, Ellen, don't try to make it better. Maman didn't love me – not then, nor at the end. It was good of you to send for me and foolish of me to come. Because, you see, I knew how she felt. I should have been more sensitive to her wishes.'

'Why should you?' asked Ellen uncomprehendingly.

She slumped wearily onto an ottoman, leaving Catherine standing, a position she would probably prefer, Ellen decided, in view of the number of puffy petticoats she seemed to be wearing underneath her gown.

From the next room came a murmur of voices – apparently those of Father McMahon and Liam.

Was it very bad, Ellen wondered, to think with longing of sleep? She was so tired that her whole body was aching with fatigue and the last vestige of her energy was centred on stopping her eyelids from shutting. She blinked, seeing instead of Catherine herself, a blurred image of the rose hue of her gown.

Unable to summon up hatred for its wearer at that moment, Ellen managed to rouse herself and show Catherine to her room for, after all, there was the funeral to attend. And with Hélène's body in the house, it was hardly appropriate to quarrel with Catherine even if she had been less exhausted and inclined to do so.

It was after the funeral that Catherine exploded her bombshell.

'I must leave immediately,' she said to Ellen. 'Marie-Geneviève will be missing me. I have never left her before.'

'Marie-Geneviève?'

'But haven't I told you? How could I have omitted to mention so important a thing . . . I have a daughter, Ellen. Is that not wonderful? She is almost exactly the same age as your Biddy. So you see that I must rush home to La Rochelle.'

A daughter almost exactly the same age as Biddy. Which meant that Catherine, like herself, had been pregnant on the night of the fire.

Pregnant by whom? By John Marrett? Or – which seemed much more likely – was Dick the father of Catherine's child as well?

I don't want to know, Ellen thought. I never want to know. I just never want to lay my eyes on Catherine again . . .

'Don't be grieving.' Liam, finding her weeping in the garden, concluded that her tears were for Hélène. 'Aren't they both better off up above, instead of down here suffering pain? Did I tell you, Miss Ellen, I had news of my father's death?'

'You did not.'

'Father McMahon is after telling me. There's no mistaking that it was him that was working down in Bordeaux.

And shouldn't I be crying myself, along with you this day?'

'I don't see why,' Ellen said, sniffing. 'Didn't you always tell me your father was no good?'

'I'm not so certain of that, either,' Liam said reflectively. 'I should have gone to see him, Miss Ellen, when I still had the chance. You can never tell about people, and him leaving me the bit of money he'd managed to save over the last few years. Heirs, that's what we are, the two of us – though you're the one with the power.'

But it is not the power I want, Ellen thought. The influence I desire has nothing to do with money, but with love, and there I am as powerless as ever I was. That potency belongs to Catherine.

Catherine who may be – must be – the mother of my husband's child . . .

Bury that thought. Bury it deep in the lowest depth of your mind, along with the vision of Dick and Catherine together. Intern it, imbed it with the same thoroughness as we, this day, have buried Maman's body in the earth. Speak to no one of these things – least of all, Dick.

In case he confirms your suspicions.

For if he does that, Ellen warned herself, you will be as Deirdre deprived of her love, and only death ahead of you on the rocks.

So do not voice your belief.

This is you, Ellen – you, who have always spoken the truth, have by and large had too much to say – a voice outside herself seemed to be asking: *you* will keep these things to yourself? Is it possible?

But she answered – it is not only possible but essential. For otherwise I *will* die, and Catherine will have won in the end.

* * *

278

'So you're off, are you?' Willie said. 'And with a load of orders taken for cognac from around the country I'm after hearing.'

'I've not done badly,' Dick said, trying not to grin lest Willie grew petulant about his success.

It was difficult having to conceal his pleasure in what he had achieved during his time in Ireland. Edmund Burke had proved as good as his word in giving him introductions to prospective customers and he had taken far more orders than he had envisaged, even at his most optimistic.

And it was hard, too, to curtail his impatience at the long trip ahead of him when all he wanted was to be back in Cognac, re-establishing his business.

He said as much to Nano Nagle and her brother Joseph when he broke his journey in Cork. He heard how Nano was risking imprisonment for running a school for poor children in a mud cabin in Cove Lane and another in a hut in Philpott Curran Lane, on the north side of the city, ventures of which Joseph had initially disapproved but now wholeheartedly supported.

'You're choosing an unlucky day for travelling,' Joseph warned when Dick was ready to leave. 'Don't we all know that the risk of being drowned is greatest on Whit Sunday? Could you not put off your journey?'

'I want to be getting back,' Dick said, trying to curb his own unease, aware that the drowned rose up out of the sea on Whit Sunday to coax and, if that failed, to force the living to join them.

People born on that day, he knew, too, to be the children of turbulence, prone to harm others, to possess the Evil Eye, or to die a violent death. The *Cingciseach*, such people were called, and you had to protect them from their own fate by making them kill a live creature, to nullify the evil.

'Do you remember, when we were young, the way you'd put a fly into the hand of a baby born on Whit Sunday, and squeeze his fingers together to crush it?' he said to the Nagles.

Joseph looked more serious than ever.

'Indeed, you have to protect such people from themselves,' he said.

Dick had bid his farewells and was on his way to Kinsale when he suddenly remembered – Catherine had been born at Whit.

And yet the sea stayed calm. He saw sight neither of enemy ships, nor the dead rising out of the water, only, at the end of his ocean journey, the haven of La Rochelle beckoning to him out of the deep bay.

He was home – or almost home! His love for France was great. At the same time, he thought that his feeling for Ireland had in no way diminished with time. It *was* possible to love both at the same time. There was no shame in it, although Willie seemed to query such a possibility, insinuating that, because he had built a new life in the Charente, he was shrugging off the old one. Yet in his own mind there were innumerable differences between the Charente and Kilawillen. If Willie took it in mind to visit him in his new home he would surely marvel at the similarities in landscape and weather.

The shared religion. The same volatility of people in both Ireland and France.

And the pathetic plight of the poor in both countries . . .

Well, he was not going to forget those who could not help themselves, he decided, his mind racing ahead to the time when the sale of cognac would make him a wealthy man. As he travelled from La Rochelle to Cognac his own money worries seemed a thing of the distant rather than the recent past. He thought of what he could do with his money for his family and for himself, as well as for others. He imagined the Château de Pericard once again restored – all of them living there. He thought a great deal about Ellen.

For a headstrong woman, he thought, she had been remarkably patient toiling all those years alone, while he had been in the army. All the same, that time had taken its toll of her, he concluded, so that too much of her natural exuberance had seemed to drain out of her, turning her serious before her time.

Well, that, too, would change – was bound to improve when she grew used to having him home.

He was still thinking about it when, in the dead of night, he finally got to Crouin.

Ellen was dreaming of water. She was in the land called *Tír fo Thuinn*, beneath the sea, where everything was much the same as it was on land except for the water above her head. There were animals under the water, horses and cattle, and although she could not actually see them, fairies who had been angels in Heaven before the revolt of Lucifer against God, and who, having been indecisive about which side they should join, had been cast into the sea.

It may have been the fairies who had stolen her clothes. Either they were responsible or she had discarded her garments herself and promptly forgotten about having done so, although it did not seem to matter one way or the other.

So she walked naked beneath the waves and under her bare feet was neither sand nor coral but the soft green grass of Ballygriffin, as vivid in its viridity as was the turquoise blue of the sea which lapped around her firm body and pulled her long dark hair out from her head as if it was strands of seaweed.

At the beginning of her dream she was acutely conscious of being happy but, quite soon, she became apprehensive, reminded by some exterior force that the invisible sea-fairies who shared her oceanic haven had, in their very hesitation, come under the influence of the Devil and were malevolent towards strangers.

She looked around uneasily, expecting to see an army of diminutive amphibious creatures who would attempt either to kill or abduct her, most likely the latter since fairy kings were known to lust after earthly women.

Reconnaissance yielded no sign of even a single fairy but out of the subaqueous depths swam a white shark and she spread out her arms, trying herself to swim away, because the half-fish half-man that it was intended to possess her.

'*No!*'

'You're all right,' said her husband in whose arms she was lying, still beneath the sea, and he kissed her gently three times, barely touching her tongue with his, and continued to hold her close so that they could both appreciate the way their bodies swayed in the water.

'Ellen . . .'

Somebody moaned softly. When he slid his finger between her legs she was part of the sea, he, rock-hard, pressing against her pubis. She arched her back so that her breasts could swell against his chest but he bent his head, kissing one of the bulging nipples.

'I love you.'

Her husband's words as he lifted her onto her back, entering her at once, the way she could be quite certain that she and the sea were one.

* * *

She was wide awake and Dick was lying across her, his blond hair hiding most of his face. She was no more in *Tír fo Thuinn* than she was in her old home, and she was facing the extraordinary fact that Dick and she had just been making love.

'Thank God I'm finally home,' Dick was saying in a jaded voice. 'I've had enough travel to last me a lifetime. I don't want to go even as far as La Rochelle again!'

'Not there . . . ?'

'There's no need to go there that I can see,' Dick said, and yawned widely. 'Everything I want is here – you, the children, my business. If there is travelling to do from now on, Liam can do it – and the boys, when they grow up!'

'What are you saying to me?'

'That I'm dead tired and I want to be in Cognac and nowhere else! Isn't that what I've just said? Oh, and that I want to restore the château, though that will take some time. We have to have more money for that.'

But *I* have the money, Ellen thought. Won't that surprise him? Only with that news goes the sad announcement that Maman is dead . . .

'You're not saying anything,' Dick said, sleepily. 'It's not like you, not to talk.'

He did not sound as if he minded too much about that, but rather as if he was already sliding into sleep.

'I've talked enough,' Ellen said, remembering her vow to suppress her suspicions about Dick and Catherine forever – not even when they were all old people and none of it would matter any more.

Or so she imagined . . .

And on such ground you hope to build a new life with Dick, the voice outside herself interjected; you, supposedly in love with the truth, will act out that kind of lie?

Ah, sure it's not a lie, Ellen said to the voice. I've told you before – I don't want to face the pain of truth.

And now, by some miracle – because Dick and Catherine have quarrelled; parted for good? – it seems that I can evade it. That, instead of death, I am being offered life. Dick has told me that he does not want to go to La Rochelle again – he has stated, quite clearly, that all he desires is here, in Cognac. On *that* I can rebuild.

Shutting out the fact that, in La Rochelle, there is a little girl the same age as Biddy, called Marie-Geneviève? the merciless voice went on. What does she look like, this little girl? Are her eyes very blue? What colour is her hair . . . ?

Be quiet, Ellen ordered the voice. Be quiet – be quiet – stop!

All right so, said the voice more gently. But let me tell you one last time, Ellen O'Shaughnessy, you are honest by nature and you should not move away from that.

The truth will catch up with you yet!

BOOK FOUR
1773–1778

1

In the way of brothers, the three O'Shaughnessys were either affectionate and supportive of each other, or irritated and contemptuous, dependent on what they were discussing. But there was one subject on which they unanimously agreed: that their sister Biddy was a pet, sweet-natured, loving and lenient, with a wisdom beyond her years.

But on this warm day in June 1773, Biddy's normally rosy vision of life was definitely clouded. She half-lay, half-sat on a pile of cushions in the tower toom of the O'Shaughnessy château, a tall, plump, blonde girl of almost seventeen, with large innocent eyes.

She had no right to quite such an artless appearance, for without a qualm of conscience she was eavesdropping on a conversation taking place in the adjacent parlour between her father and her eldest brother, James.

'The Dublin market collapsed in 1768 – *five years ago!*' James was saying heatedly. 'You're the very man who bemoans that – '

'Naturally.'

'But on the other hand you're not prepared to take the appropriate steps to save us from going downhill.'

'To take risks. That's what you're asking me to do.'

'I am asking you to open a branch of the business in what is now a major port. The La Rochelle market is growing thin, Papa. Bordeaux is the place that counts. Beef imports there are extremely high. New merchant houses are springing up to deal with that trade, and others. *We* should be there, to seize our opportunities.'

'To throw money away, more likely. From the house of the Devil to the house of the Demon!'

Biddy sighed, wondering which of them was right, Papa in his caution, or impatient, audacious James.

Papa had a fine reputation in Cognac as a well-to-do *négociant*. Yet to hear him talk you would think the whole family was on the brink of starvation instead of living in good if not extravagant style in a château which, after being almost completely razed to the ground, had long since been completely restored and refurbished.

On the other hand, to listen to James you would be convinced that it was an easy matter to outwit the clever shippers in Bordeaux who had already established themselves in the brandy trade, not only buying spirits but, in some cases, distilling it as well.

The way to regain the lost Dublin market, James was insisting, was to make an inexpensive brandy out of cheap wine which would still be superior in taste to domestic whiskey or to imported rum: 'That we should do from Bordeaux. And at the same time we should make an assault on the London market from Cognac. I know you're going to tell me that the market there is highly selective and extremely competitive, but there are Irishmen enough in London who would be willing to help if contact was made with them.'

'Go to Bordeaux and start up an alternative business!' Biddy heard Papa say in mock-despair. 'Travel to London and find Irishmen well-connected enough to enable us to break into the market! And run the House here at the same time! I suppose you'll be telling me next that, just because the Austrian Princess Marie-Antoinette is married to the Dauphin, we should take advantage of that connection and persuade the Austrians to buy brandy from us!'

Biddy closed her eyes, waiting for James to react

vociferously to Papa's scorn. I can't bear it if they fight, she thought miserably. The minute James starts to shout I'll get up and separate the pair of them . . .

But to her surprise, after a long pause in which, presumably, James struggled for self-control, her brother said in a comparatively normal voice: 'Will you at least *think* about my suggestions rather than dismissing them completely?' and Papa replied: 'Very well. But don't you be getting any fancy ideas into your head about setting up alternative businesses this year – or travelling abroad. The farthest you'll be going is to La Rochelle, to liaise with our usual shippers.'

Someone was getting to their feet, Biddy surmised. A door was shut, none too softly.

The danger of an altercation between father and son was – mercifully – averted, or, at least, temporarily contained.

I should have chosen a naval career, James thought hotly, as Dick left the room. After all, our navy has been instilled with new life, provided with so many well-equipped ships and frigates.

But he knew that he had no vocation for the navy, or for the army, either.

I am just like Papa, James thought resignedly. At heart I am a *négociant*, a merchant, rather than a service man. I am too interested in commerce to contemplate any other career.

And I am too aware of the catastrophic effects of war, too conscious of how the Seven Years War left what was potentially the greatest power in Europe humiliated and in financial ruins, to be impressed by the romantic aspects of soldiery.

An onlooker might well have remarked that James O'Shaughnessy resembled his father not only in choice of vocation but also in his looks. James, too, was tall and thin, and long-legged, with a broad chest and wide shoulders. And he had the same milky-blond hair, the same narrow face as his father and the same rather long nose, although James's was not crooked.

Only his eyes were different and in this respect James did not take after either his father or his mother, his being very brown.

James had beautiful eyes, Biddy thought, when she emerged out of the tower room to join him in the parlour.

'Well, you persuaded him to *think* about it, anyway,' she said to her brother, more to cheer him up than because she thought Papa would ultimately give way to the new proposals.

She moved closer to James, intending to give him a hug. But before she got that far James leapt up from his chair.

'I must go. I have to check our stock,' he said, and, much to Biddy's chagrin, the door was slammed again.

When Ellen peered into the mirror she could see nestling around her ears the appalling evidence that her hair was turning grey.

To be sure, it was only a matter of a few strands on either side, but a few grey hairs were enough to make her aware that she was forty-five years old, almost an elderly woman, at least in her children's eyes.

She did not feel old and when she contemplated her reflection, being severe on herself, forcing herself to be impartial, she decided she did not really look it, there being few traces of lines on her face and none at all on her neck.

But her hair . . .

Frowning, she separated the dead strands from the other living dark ones and with the tips of her fingers attempted to pull them out. It was a more difficult operation than she had anticipated. In spite of the care she thought she was taking the grey hairs obstinately stayed put and, instead, a little cluster of brown ones fluttered onto the floor.

'Ellen?'

'I'm here.'

Perhaps, when she was really grey, she could wear false hair, the way Madame du Barry, who had become the king's mistress after the death of Madame de Pompadour, did without inhibition.

'What are you doing?' demanded Dick, coming into the bedroom.

But she knew, seeing his frowning face reflected in the mirror, that he did not actually require an answer to this question, only an affirmation of her readiness to listen to whatever it was that was troubling him.

'I've just been talking to James,' said Dick before she could ask any questions herself. 'Or, rather, I have been listening to him. He has this idea . . .'

Ellen, in turn, listened.

'Would it be that risky to set up in Bordeaux?' she wanted to know when Dick had finished telling his tale. 'You don't require all that much in the way of capital to go into the brandy trade.'

'I don't feel like taking any more risks at my age,' said Dick bluntly. 'Even little ones. Jimmy must appreciate that.'

When you thought of how much had been lost in the fire, how much effort had gone into rebuilding the business later, Dick's attitude was understandable, Ellen thought.

But there was more to his hesitation than that, she decided, watching him in the mirror. James – only his father called him Jimmy – was a force with which to be reckoned; more ambitious, more effective than his more easy-going younger brothers, and perhaps something of a potential threat to his father.

'Where is James now?' she asked.

'He had been meaning to check our stock. That was before we started talking. I hope he doesn't get so carried away with his grandiose ideas for the future that he forgets what he should be doing now,' said Dick, rubbing his hand through his hair.

He has grey in it, too, Ellen thought – quite a lot. I'm not the only one.

Aloud she said: 'You know full well that James is dependable. Has he ever in his life let you down?'

'Well – ' Dick began, and stopped.

It was as near as he was going to concession. There was a long way to go yet before father and son agreed on the future of the business, Ellen thought, and frowned in the glass at her hair.

It was a Saturday, but that did not prevent James from riding into town to visit the warehouses, in order to check the casks in stock.

In owning the warehouses at all, he thought, his father had come a long way from the days when he had simply stocked his barrels on the quayside where they could be loaded onto the *gabares*, chancing to luck that, in the interim, they would not be taken by thieves.

In between those times, of course, and the present were the years when the business had been operated out of the château grounds, terminating only when Papa had decided that it was more professional, more accessible for his suppliers if he based himself in town. That decision having been made, he had been fortunate, his son thought, in securing not only his former office in the rue de la Richonne, but also that previously rented by his rival, John Marrett, so that James, too, could work in peace.

The O'Shaughnessy warehouses, three huge stone cellars stocked with ageing cognac, were conveniently positioned directly across the river.

'A dirty place!' Biddy had commented when first taken there to visit and, in a way, she had been right for the warehouses *did* seem to be covered in grime if you did not know the difference between that and the black fungus which thrived on the alcohol evaporating from the barrels of cognac.

'It's called the Angels' Share,' James had told his sister then, referring to the evaporated fumes, and for years, every time she came to the warehouses, Biddy had searched in vain for the presence of angels themselves.

James smiled, remembering, and pushed open the oak door, pausing in the entrance to light a candle before he ventured further into the cellars. At the same time he was thinking about the discussion – or argument, if you liked – with Papa.

Perhaps, rather than asking too much of his father at one fell swoop – a branch of the business in Bordeaux *and* an assault on the London market – he should concentrate on one of his schemes and (always supposing he could bring that one off) introduce the other later on, when Dick was more receptive to new ideas.

If that time ever came . . .

Oh come on now, he said, to himself.

Presume that Papa will decide to move with the times.

Ask yourself only whether you should press him to move into the London market, or to start another business in Bordeaux.

Holding the candle at eye-level he stepped into the first of the cellars, and looked around. In these warehouses, he knew, was cognac of a quality high enough to meet the demands of London, brandy which his father had been holding in reserve for years.

Like every wine-farmer, every *négociant*, Dick lived in fear and trembling of being put out of business by the failure of a crop.

Above all, they were frightened of frost.

Like the great frost of 1709, reports of which, handed down through the generations, were spoken of only in hushed tones.

Seven years ago, James recalled, shuddering at the memory, there had been another very bad frost in the Charente.

So terrible a frost that wine-farmers in the Borderies, the small zone running, due north of Grande Champagne, from Búrie to the tip of Cognac itself, had been almost ruined.

Prior to the frost, the sweet white wines which they had produced from the Colombard grape had been much prized by Dutch buyers. But, after it, the Borderies farmers had lost their market to competitors from Sauternes and Barsac.

After hearing these stories of woe Dick had held onto his stocks of good cognac more resolutely than ever, in anticipation less of a rainy than a frosty day.

As he counted the barrels, James took note, too, of the number of those casks which could be classified as superlative.

More than he had expected . . .

Enough for an initial assault upon the London market.

But only just enough.

Not sufficient to leave adequate stocks to keep his father happy.

But suppose we buy in against them, he thought, and his mind went back again to the wine-farmers in the Borderies. The wise ones had switched from producing wines for direct sale into distillation, making their own cognac, and thus increasing the number of suppliers in the field.

Many of them had become quite affluent, according to Liam Crowley. Although they were burdened by a law forcing them to harvest the grapes of the nobles, the *seigneurs*, before they could pick their own, the *ban des vendanges*, as this law was called, at least did not prohibit them from benefiting from fixed-money rents, from taking most of the profit.

How can I persuade Papa to avail himself of these new suppliers? James worried, holding his candle, biting his lip.

Because he was now clear in his mind that his first course was to attempt to inveigle his father into attacking the London market. Bordeaux could wait for a while – which, to James, meant a matter of months.

One thing at a time, he said to himself. Find these new suppliers. Then speak to Papa and see what he says.

He decided at once to make an excursion to the Borderies. He would ride out there tomorrow, first thing. There was no sense in letting grass grow under his feet.

Before he left the warehouse he remembered another bit of information Liam had volunteered concerning those farmers who had not survived the terrible frost. Some who had found themselves unable to distil their own wines had turned to drinking them and had lapsed into greater misery.

Such men could hardly afford to pay their rents. It followed that there could be land in the Borderies available for the letting.

What if, on that land, his family could grow their own grapes from which wines of their own making could be distilled?

It was an idea that appealed to him hugely. It was understandable that Papa, when he had rebuilt his business, should concentrate solely on buying cognac from suppliers rather than concern himself with what had largely been an experiment in distillation.

And yet . . .

Perhaps he was just being sentimental, James thought, in giving credence to the possibility of branching out in that particular way.

But what harm could it do if he wandered around in the morning and spoke to a few people, unearthed some information about what was going on?

And if he presented Papa with a list of new suppliers at the end of the day, who knew what he might not say about expansion?

The candle in his hand flickered a warning of its imminent demise and suddenly went out. He was left in total darkness.

'*Merde alors!*' said James crossly.

Still holding onto the candle – for who knew, even a warm wick might cause a conflagration in the warehouse if it made contact with a stray piece of paper or wood – he felt his way in the darkness past the rows of barrels, back to the oak door.

As he did so the beginnings of something else reported by Liam – information concerning the Marrett family who had been acquaintances of his parents – flitted into his mind.

What had that been all about? Something to do with cognac certainly, since John Marrett had been a rival of Papa's.

But for the life of him he could not remember precisely what Liam had said.

* * *

296

So on that Sunday James rode to the Borderies. A short distance from Cognac – indeed, in that part of the town which was on the right bank of the Charente – it was possible already to notice the difference in the soil from that of the Grande Champagne.

In the Borderies the vegetation was more diverse because there was less chalk. Here there were heaths on which it was fun to gallop a horse, and for a time he yielded to the temptation to do so.

He was close to one of the many wine farms when he heard a faint cry. A bird or an animal? There was plenty of wildlife in the area, concealed by the thick vegetation, drawn there by the added attraction of a nearby stream.

Meanwhile the crying persisted. James looked around, wrinkling his nose like a rabbit, a habit of his when he was trying to concentrate. And then, close to a group of trees, he found the source of the sound.

A short while earlier, three-year-old Edouard Helyot had been fast asleep, lying on his stomach on the kitchen floor of his parents' farmhouse, looking so comfortable, so secure that there seemed little likelihood of his waking for the rest of the afternoon.

So his father maintained, using it as part of his case to persuade his wife to go with him into the next room, in order to make love.

Mme Helyot hesitated.

'What if he does wake up?'

'He won't. I am certain of it,' said M. Helyot, coming up behind her and pressing himself against her generous bottom. 'He has eaten well. It is hot. No, he will continue to sleep.'

'You were going to fix the latch on the gate.'

But through the folds of her skirt Mme Helyot could

feel her husband's erection and she told herself that he was right, that Edouard would give them time.

'Afterwards,' said M. Helyot. 'Afterwards I will repair the gate. And do not worry about Edouard in the meantime . . .'

Mme Helyot stopped protesting. Leaving their small son sprawled on the kitchen floor, the two of them crept, hand in hand, into the other room, and closed the door behind them.

The door that led from the kitchen into the yard was wide open, offering an invitation to anyone to either come in or go out, but, preoccupied as the Helyots were, neither of them remembered.

Edouard, waking abruptly, sitting up and scratching his tousled head, was lured out both by the sunshine and by the conviction that his parents were out in the yard already.

When he did not see them there he was not unduly perturbed, being a placid and much-loved child. And when he noticed that the gate that led out on to the heath was ajar rather than, as usual, tightly-closed, he lost interest in the whereabouts of his father and mother.

He pulled at the side of the gate with his chubby fingers, peered out and gave in to his explorative instincts. By the time his father had brought his mother to a full climax little Edouard had disappeared onto the heath.

And Lucien Ducasse, who would normally have been out there at this time, was lying at home on his straw bed, as miserable as Edouard was glad.

For much of the year, Lucien earned a reasonable living trapping rabbits and birds which he sold in the Búrie market. The snares he set were simple slip-nooses made out of twine, designed to catch the victim by its neck, body or foot as it tried to pull away. When attached to a stout sapling which bent over and was prevented from

298

springing back by a crosspiece, they were very effective indeed. When a bird or a rabbit attempted to take the bait which Lucien left behind to tempt it, the crosspiece was invariably dislodged and the victim securely gripped by the noose.

The night before, Lucien had set all his traps as usual before going to bed. But in the morning he had woken with an excruciating toothache, in the light of which all else seemed to him an irrelevance.

He was a man far kinder to small children than to tiny mammals and birds and had he seen Edouard stumble into one of his traps he would have been deeply distressed, might even have rushed to the aid of his victim rather than continue to suck in and blow out his cheeks, in the hope of relieving his agony.

But Lucien remained unaware of little Edouard's plight.

'Papa – Mama!' wept Edouard, trying to pull his foot free from the noose and only succeeding in securing it more tightly, so that the twine cut into his ankle.

And then a kind lady came to his aid, easing him free from the snare, taking him into her arms, pressing her sweet-smelling cheek against his, saying over and over: 'Don't cry. Don't cry, my little one.'

But Edouard, even when the pain abated, saw no reason to staunch his flow of tears. If he stopped crying, he reasoned, the kind lady might terminate his cuddle, and that would be a shame.

So it was that James, in identifying the source of the cry, came across what he thought was a charming tableau – a pretty, although not beautiful, girl in riding costume, with her hair tucked under her high-crowned hat, holding in her arms a small chubby boy with a halo of dark untidy curls. They were seated under a clump of trees and a horse – obviously the girl's – was tethered nearby.

He glanced around, saw the trap and deduced for himself what had happened.

And when he spoke – rather loudly, to make himself heard over the cries of the child – the girl confirmed that she had been out riding on her own, and found the little boy.

'He must have come from that house, over there,' James said. 'Perhaps we should take him back.'

'I suppose we must,' the girl said.

She looked up at James and added, wistfully: 'I adore children. I am sorry to part with him.'

'This one seems to feel the same way about you,' said James, looking at little Edouard. 'Let me see his leg.'

And having ascertained that the injury was not as bad as Edouard's screams would indicate, he and the girl and the child went to the farmhouse in search of the absent parents.

By then, the Helyots had discovered that their son was missing. Reunited with him, they expressed their gratitude by plying James with Pineau, the aperitif made from ageing cognac and grape juice, and conversing with him and the girl at length.

Out of this meeting came not only the confirmation that the Helyots would be willing to supply cognac themselves to the O'Shaughnessys, but that they could persuade several of their neighbours to do so. And there was mention of a farm at Louzac which it might be possible to rent.

'But my father, too, would be interested in these matters,' the girl said after M. Helyot had promised to make further inquiries on James's behalf about the farm to rent. 'He is also in the business of selling cognac. Your father may even know him, Monsieur O'Shaughnessy.

His name is John Marrett and I am his daughter, Marie-Geneviève.'

And then James recalled precisely what Liam had said about the Marretts – that having lived in La Rochelle for many years they had recently returned to the Charente, and had settled in Saint-André.

At dinner he mentioned this fact, along with all the other matters, to the family at Chez Landart.

'In fact, I heard the Marretts were back from Liam myself this week,' Papa said. 'So what is the daughter like?'

'Is she beautiful?' Bawnie teased. 'Did she impress our big brother?'

'She's quite pretty,' James said, in a deliberately nonchalant voice.

Secretly, he had been impressed by Marie-Geneviève Marrett, by her love for children, her practicality and common sense, and the way she had, quite openly, rushed to protect her father's interests.

'You didn't mention to me that the Marretts had returned,' Mama said in what struck James as a distinctly strained voice.

He looked at his mother and thought that her expression, too, was odd – that her face was very pale.

'Did I not?' Papa said. 'It must have slipped my mind. We will have to write to them, of course – ask them to visit us . . .'

'Excuse me,' Mama said, got to her feet and virtually fled from the room.

2

Ellen's reaction to the subject of the Marretts faded almost immediately from James's mind since most of his thinking was focused on his plans for expanding the business. Dick sent him to La Rochelle and when he came back the grapes on the vines were ready for picking and for transporting in panniers carried by hand or strapped across the shoulders, for crushing in the presses.

It was a time of year James loved. The sun was still hot. With harvesting came celebrations and now that they were renting the wine-farm at Louzac he could join in with the pickers in the substantial meal that was provided in the farmhouse after the day's work in the vineyard was over.

Dick, too, was present at these gatherings and James's occasional frustration with his father was replaced by pride in the way the older man could bridge the gap between themselves and the people who worked for them, treating every man and woman the same, the way it used to be, James knew, at Kilawillen when his father was a child.

In the other activity in which he enthusiastically participated, when the harvest was over, there was no equality. Not only the humble were prohibited from taking part in the hunt, but also, in theory, merchants, artisans and bourgeoisie.

The O'Shaughnessys, James was aware, qualified for membership of the hunt because of their ownership of the Château de Pericard, and because they were descended from a noble Irish family, recognized as such in France.

302

The hunting laws of the Grand Roi were nonsensical, Papa said, a point of view apparently shared by the magistrates in Cognac since they turned a blind eye on *la chasse*. If they received complaints, the magistrates acted with leniency against offenders, rather than, as prescribed, fining them one hundred livres for a first offence, twice that amount for a second, after which a persistent huntsman risked three years' banishment following a spell in the pillory on market day.

None of this weighed on James when he joined the hunt early one morning with the object of hunting wolves.

Like himself, the men who were present carried short swords or hunting knives or even, in a few cases, guns, for the grey wolf, as some of them knew to their cost, was a savage and fearless predator quite capable of bringing down a horse and killing its luckless rider. Last season, James remembered, such a thing had happened to a man of his father's acquaintance.

'I didn't see you out with either the hare or the stag last season, young man,' said the formidable Comtesse d'Hiersac, drawing in beside him. 'Why is that, may I inquire?'

'I suppose I find hunting hares and stags less exciting than wolves or wild boar,' James began, but the Comtesse said, with a snort: 'Hare hunting is necessary in Lent when the weather is dry and fresh to keep the dogs in training and how you can maintain that stag hunting is unexciting I cannot imagine . . . My God, that man – over there. He is not only a merchant but a Protestant! He should not be present at the hunt!'

Following her gaze James saw a stocky, grey-haired rider with a young woman, mounted on a small brown mare.

He felt happier than ever. The young woman was Marie-Geneviève Marrett.

* * *

Dressing for the hunt, Marie-Geneviève had indulged in a rare fit of self-pity.

If only she were half as beautiful as Maman . . .

Her riding costume was severely tailored and constructed rather like a man's, at least as far as the jacket, with its back-vent and pleated side-vents and the contrasting waistcoat, were concerned.

The front skirt of her jacket was far more feminine in appearance, being joined by a seam at the waist to form a flare, so that it could fit more easily over her full petticoat skirt.

She wore a cravat, like a man, and her long, tight-fitting sleeves ended in closed cuffs and frills. And on her head was the most enchanting beehive-hat perched right on top of her wig.

But in spite of all this finery Marie-Geneviève did not feel confident about her looks, although they did not normally worry her and she had never previously felt that they would hinder her in the matter of gaining suitors.

Only recently.

Only in the last few months.

Ever since the day she had rescued little Edouard Helyot and made the acquaintance of James O'Shaughnessy.

All the way home and for weeks afterwards she had hoped that, since the two families knew each other and had much in common, they would call upon each other, or issue invitations. But to her disappointment nothing of the kind had occurred. And although she had allowed herself the luxury of a fantasy in which James, being enterprising, made it his business to find out where she lived and duly arrived on her doorstep, in reality he did nothing of the kind.

If I had been as beautiful as Maman, she thought,

getting ready for the hunt, I would not have been so easily forgotten.

'Marie-Geneviève, your father wishes to leave.'

'I am coming, Maman,' said Marie-Geneviève, smoothing out her frown with her index finger and forcing herself to smile.

At least, on the hunting-field I surpass Maman, she thought.

At least I look my best on a horse . . .

The forest, broken by villages, ran all the way from Cognac to La Rochelle. Far from thinking of it as a sinister place, as Maman insisted it was, Marie-Geneviève saw it as a modern Garden of Eden. She associated both the forest and the hunt with God Himself, having been enchanted by the story of Saint Hubert, son of Bertrand, Duke of Aquitaine, latter-day patron saint of *la chasse*, and a great killer of game. The very man who had been hunting in the forest on the day he had encountered a stag bearing a crucifix enlaced between its horns, and heard a strange voice calling to him from the midst of the steep Ardennes, summoning him to Christ.

'Now that your mother isn't here to be alarmed, I must warn you, Marie-Geneviève, to stay close to the hunt today,' John Marrett said to his daughter when they were assembled on the edge of the wood. 'I'm told that a large male wolf has been sighted in this place, an interloper which has not been accepted by the pack and is known to be particularly vicious.'

'Yes, Papa,' said Marie-Geneviève, not in the least alarmed.

It was a pity, she thought, that it was only November, too early in the year for breeding. Last season the hunt had come upon a den, and she had seen four tiny cubs, dark brown in colour, the way wolves were in their first few weeks of life, being suckled by their grey mother. A few weeks later, she had sighted the cubs again, pawing and licking each other, and chewing their mother's ears. How pretty they are in their play, she had thought, but when she had said as much to Papa he had drawn her attention to their implacable mask-like faces and had reminded her that these apparent balls of fur were fiendish killers at heart.

'Remember, there is a good reason why huntsmen carry guns and knives,' he said now, and Marie-Geneviève said: 'Yes, Papa,' and looked around her, noting how the nobility enjoyed vying with each other in the extent and quality of their equipage. The conversation was all about the latest additions to stables or kennels, and the women, she concluded, were able to put up as good a performance as any of the men.

Only hardy women hunted. Women like herself, and certainly not ultra-feminine women like Maman. Although few were as young as she was herself and some of them, like the Comtesse d'Hiersac down from Paris and looking quite wonderful in a green-and-black habit, seemed very old to her.

Although Marie-Geneviève admired the Comtesse for her courage in the saddle, she dreaded the imperious woman. Last season, the Comtesse had made a fearful fuss about Papa's presence on the hunting-field and had only been restrained from reporting him to the authorities by other members of the hunt. She was quite capable of doing so again, was, in fact, indicating to her companion, masked from Marie-Geneviève's view by the Comtesse's gesticulating hand, the spot where Papa was waiting.

Then the Comtesse lowered her hand and Marie-Geneviève saw the person to whom she was so animatedly speaking. It was James O'Shaughnessy!

Marie-Geneviève's hand went automatically up to her

hat to ensure that it was straight. She might have eaten a plate of butterflies for breakfast, rather than ham and cheese, the way her stomach reacted, and she was sure that all the blood had drained away from her face.

'We'll have to ride quite far in before we reach a pack,' Papa said, unaware of his daughter's condition. 'Stay close!'

'I will,' promised Marie-Geneviève, and then she saw with mixed horror and delight that the Comtesse, followed by James, was riding in their direction.

'Protestants!' the Comtesse said furiously to James. 'I shall go and tell the man precisely what I think of him for daring to be here!'

'I don't think you should do anything of the kind,' James said, but the Comtesse was already moving towards John Marrett and his daughter.

Dear God, prayed James devoutly, as he followed her, do not let this be a third offence by Marie-Geneviève's father.

'. . . no permission . . . merchants . . . Protestants . . . the Law . . .'

Marie-Geneviève smiled at him wanly as the Comtesse ranted on.

'Very well then,' said John Marrett, sounding calm and infinitely reasonable. 'I will leave, but you cannot force my daughter to do so since her mother, a Cantillon, does have noble blood.'

'Her mother married a *Protestant*!' the Comtesse said, in a haughty tone, but she was on uneasy ground, and well aware of the fact.

Already, hunters and hounds were beginning to move into the forest. The beaters were ahead, exploring the thicket for wolves.

'Don't forget what I told you about the need to stay

307

with the others,' John Marrett said to Marie-Geneviève. 'Will you see that she is safe, sir?'

'But, naturally, I will!'

At the beginning, Marie-Geneviève drifted rather than rode into the forest, with James O'Shaughnessy beside her, thinking of nothing more than the delights of being with such a handsome young man.

But after a time she began to think more soberly about her father. How dignified he had been, how shamefully he had been treated by that monstrous woman!

She looked around just in case Papa was somewhere at the back of the hunt but all she could see were chestnut trees which had marks on them like horseshoes. And indeed she felt so miserable about her father that nails from the shoes of horses might be driving into her heart.

How selfish she was, riding off into the forest, thinking only of herself and neglecting poor Papa.

None of this she wanted to explain to James. It would make Papa look silly – as if he was in need of her protection although, in fact, she felt he was, somewhere in the forest. She was sure he would not actually go home but would rather follow the hunt from a distance, to rejoin her at the end of the day.

But in the meantime she wanted to talk to him, to offer him support, to make him cheerful again, after which she could return to the hunt herself and enjoy herself, being with James.

'It's very kind of you to offer to ride with me but there are some friends of my father's I must talk with,' she said when the hunt had caught up with the advance party of beaters. 'I will rejoin you shortly.'

'Please do,' said James, and she was able to fall back, and discreetly retreat in the hope of finding her father.

* * *

But because her mind was half on the way in which her father had been humiliated, half on James, she managed to lose herself. Priding herself on her sensibility, she found it difficult to acknowledge the fact but in the end she was forced into it.

There was no trace of her father. After a while, instead of admiring the richness of the beech trees, the way they kept their brown leaves all through autumn and winter, holding on to them until they were literally pushed off the twigs by their first successors in spring; instead of revelling in the autumnal *ambiance*, taking pleasure in the orange and golden hues, Marie-Geneviève began to be aware of her surroundings in a more realistic way. The nearly-black evergreen oaks might provide a useful screen and shelter from wind and sun, but they were really very unattractive to look at and why had she never noticed before that there were so many nettles in the wood?

Far from being perfect she had the feeling that the forest had many pitfalls and eyesores and perils.

'Compose yourself,' she said to herself. 'You won't be lost for long. Either you will catch up with the hunt again, or you will come across Papa, or – '

At that point the little brown mare, without any warning, snorted and reared onto her hind legs.

Since her mind had been wandering and her hand had been slack on the reins, Marie-Geneviève was flung out of the saddle, mercifully flying over a large rock, to land stomach-downwards in a clump of brambles.

Her face and hands were superficially scratched and her jacket was badly split, but she was otherwise uninjured, and she lay gasping for breath, then reached out to clear a view-hole through the prickles and scrub, so she could scramble out.

But what she saw through the brambles made her stay where she was, not daring to budge another inch.

Now she understood only too well what had frightened the little brown mare.

In the clearing before her a huge grey wolf was standing, its white cheeks and muzzle highlighting its black lips, slightly parted, the corners of the mouth held back to bare the teeth in a hideous kind of grin.

Marie-Geneviève swallowed, conscious that she was wetting herself in fear.

The wolf snarled, narrowing its eyes, and she saw that its ears were tightly flattened backwards against the sides of its head.

The head lowered. The tail whipped from side to side, each time gaining momentum.

In front of the predator was its intended victim. Not herself, but the brown mare, standing perfectly still, transfixed, it appeared, as if under a spell.

Without any warning the wolf attacked, darting and biting at the mare's legs, going up for her throat.

'Fight back,' Marie-Geneviève wanted to cry out. 'A horse – even you, my little mare – is so much bigger than a wolf. Buck or rear or run . . .'

But she could not speak. Did not dare even to whisper, although under her breath she prayed.

There was blood on the mare's neck. Blood trickling down the mare's right foreleg as the powerful canine teeth inflicted crushing wounds.

Why was the little mare such a willing victim? Why . . .?

With a sickening thud the bigger animal crashed onto the ground and at once the wolf was back, darting, biting, wrestling, shaking its head incessantly.

Every so often it snarled. Otherwise the forest was silent, all action concentrated on the grotesque bout of wrestling taking place on the ground.

The brown mare lay on her side, pliant and exhausted.

Asserting its dominance, the wolf stood over her, forefeet on her shoulders before the powerful muscles went to work again.

Its hold on the brown head had tightened – its own head shook violently in a final and unnecessary attempt to prevent its prey from trying to bite. From where she knelt, Marie-Geneviève could see the flashing whites of the wolf's eyes.

It was over. The brown body was still. Extending its head, exposing its tongue, the wolf began to eat.

Where *was* she? James was beside himself with worry when he discovered that Marie-Geneviève was no longer with the hunt.

He had promised her father that he would look after her and she had managed to disappear, right under his nose, within half-an-hour of his vow.

James had no illusions about the forest. He knew it was filled with danger, not only from wolves but from wild dogs and boar and other predatory creatures. He berated himself at the thought of what could happen to a girl, to anyone, riding without a gun or sword for protection.

As he castigated himself for his deficiency in losing Marie-Geneviève he was already nudging his horse in the direction which she had taken. It was comparatively easy to track her, to follow the flattened grasses, moving as quickly as possible through the trees in order to catch her up.

He was still some distance away from the clearing where Marie-Geneviève was crouching in the brambles when he heard an extraordinary sound, as if a tree had fallen to the ground.

Or an animal – a large animal . . .?

At that instant it seemed to James, too, as if the forest had been silenced, encompassed by an aura of evil.

311

'If You will let me find Marie-Geneviève safely I promise You that I will look after her all my life,' he prayed, only half aware of the implications of his vow.

Then he rode into the clearing and saw to his horror the grey wolf, its ears still partially flattened, its eyes completely closed, gorging itself on the remains of Marie-Geneviève's mare.

Until reason returned, assuring him that wolves do not over-kill lest they destroy their own food supply, pointing out that this particular wolf was already feasting magnificently off its original prey, James was sure that Marie-Geneviève was dead.

'She cannot be dead. I love her,' he whispered, and in the extremity of the situation he knew that this was true.

Straight ahead of him the grey wolf had reopened its eyes. Its back arched in defence.

Yet there was no need now for fear – James knew that, understanding that the grey wolf had exhausted itself in this kill and would not willingly, at this stage, repeat its murderous performance.

Still, his hand instinctively felt for his knife. He looked around the clearing for Marie-Geneviève, again praying that she had come to no harm in parting from her horse.

And then he saw her in the bushes looking imploringly across at him and he edged towards her, his eyes imploring her in turn to be still, to stay where she was until he was in a position to reach down and pull her up onto the saddle.

The wolf's tail was down, a sign that it no longer felt in command of the situation. But wolves, he was aware, were acute observers, highly intelligent creatures, with a wide range of visual and audible signals to summon their fellow wolves.

What if this wolf was not, as he hoped, the outcast, but

312

a member of the pack which might assemble on hearing a mobilizing howl?

He had reached the clump of branches.

'Get up *slowly*,' he whispered to Marie-Geneviève, reaching for her wrist and hauling her up, so she could sit safely in front of him with her head against his chest, while the grey wolf watched.

Even in his concern for what might yet happen, maybe all the more because of it, he felt intensely aware that this woman, young as she was, was his partner in life and that she knew that, too.

Then a shot rang out to his left, and the grey wolf fell.

3

'Such a pity Mr Marrett was the one to shoot the wolf, James,' Biddy commented. 'I would have wanted *you* to do so!'

'And I!' agreed James.

But, on the whole, he thought, he had come out of the incident well. Far from blaming him for losing Marie-Geneviève at the hunt, her father had poured praise on him for finding her again; and later, when he was taken to Saint-André, her mother had done the same.

'Is she a nice lady?' Biddy wanted to know after James had regaled his own family with a description of the day.

'*I* think so,' said James, his mind on Marie-Geneviève. 'Do you know, she is almost exactly the same age as yourself, very young I know, but – '

'I meant Madame Marrett,' Biddy said. 'Papa says she was a friend of Maman's long ago.'

'That's not quite true – she was never my *friend* . . .'

'Oh Maman, you're spoiling the story again!'

What am I going to do? Ellen thought wildly. James, as usual, was making no attempt to conceal his feelings and it was perfectly obvious that he was more than interested in the Marrett girl.

Who might or might not be his half-sister . . .

Ever since she had heard that Catherine had returned from La Rochelle, ever since James and Marie-Geneviève had met, Ellen had been convinced that something dreadful was going to happen. All her old fears and horrors, buried for so long, began to erupt onto the surface of her

314

mind. And a surge of hatred for Dick welled up in her, along with the need to hurt him, as he had hurt her, and might well now damage James.

Because surely James had to be told of the possible danger before his involvement with Marie-Geneviève deepened?

I will have to tell him, and swear him to secrecy in the process lest other members of the family be damaged, she thought.

But if I tell him my suspicions James himself will be deeply hurt. He will hate his father for what he has done, not only to himself, but also to me.

And yet he has to be saved . . .

The family were dining in the kitchen that night, sitting, in the old French style, at only one side of the long narrow table which had been placed against the wall. Ellen, at one end of it, could not see Dick at the other for now the boys had moved on to an animated discussion of the economic state of the country, leaning forward to make their points to each other and to their father.

'. . . disaster – in spite of all the Controller-General's attempts at fiscal reform.'

'. . . Royal finances bankrupt because of the years of subservience to the will of the *parlements* . . .'

But perhaps there *is* an alternative to telling James what I fear, Ellen thought. This encounter of his surely has as its source nothing more complicated than a young man's need of passion. James barely knows this girl. He has only met her twice.

Marie-Geneviève, being Catherine's daughter, is bound to be beautiful, but she is not the only pretty girl in the world.

What if James is confronted with another attractive girl . . . or with several beautiful girls, one of whom is bound to distract him?

Her mind flashed to Count Patrick Darcy, with whom she had continued to correspond over the years, now a widower living in Ile d'Oléron, south of Ile de Ré.

A widower with two daughters in their middle and late teens, as well as two sons . . .

She could write to the Count and suggest that his family pay them a visit in the immediate future.

And there were other girls, nearer home, whom she could also invite, if she had a good excuse for doing so.

'. . . the price of grain is so low.'

'. . . *is* a new wave of reform . . .'

'. . . may be too late . . .'

Ellen said, quite loudly so that they all stopped talking and turned towards her:

'I want to hold a ball.'

'A ball?' echoed Dick, surprised. 'Why would you want to do that?'

But Biddy said, with glowing eyes: 'A ball – here in the château – Maman, that's a wonderful idea!'

'A ball,' Ellen repeated. 'And a display of fireworks in the gardens before the dancing starts. It's time that we had an entertainment for the children.'

'It sounds expensive,' Dick said dubiously. 'I'm not sure that I approve of spending money in that way when people are starving in the country, let alone when trade is bad.'

But Ellen detected a note of interest in his voice, in spite of what he said.

'We could have it at Martinmas, on the Eve of Saint Martin,' Ellen went on. 'And it could benefit the poor, as well as ourselves. You know that on Saint Martin's Day every Irish family kills some kind of animal. If they're rich it's a cow or a sheep and if they're poor maybe a hen or a cock so that the threshold of the house may be sprinkled with blood and the four corners as well, to cast evil spirits out from that place where the sacrifice is made.'

She knew she was saying too much, too quickly, in a slightly hysterical voice.

Biddy said sadly: 'The poor can't afford to waste a hen.'

'We won't ask them to do so. We'll give them the hens and the cocks that we have slaughtered for them, the way they can eat well themselves that night. In Ireland, it's expected of country gentlemen and strong farmers to share their sacrifice with the hovel-dwellers of the neighbourhood and the poor.'

'You can't possibly have it on the eve of Saint Martin's feast,' Dick said. 'That's the eleventh of November. There isn't the time left in which to organize a ball for then.'

'So we can have it at the end of November, or even in December instead,' urged Biddy. 'Papa, *please* let Maman hold her ball!'

After that, Ellen knew she had got her way, Biddy being Dick's favourite child.

'You will be surprised how quickly I will be able to organize it!' she exclaimed.

James was hardly listening. He was reminding himself that it was almost the weekend and that on Sunday he could visit Marie-Geneviève at Saint-André again.

'My dear good child, the way you have dressed your hair – it must be all of ninety centimetres in height!' John Marrett said to his daughter on Sunday morning. 'And what are all those strange things you've put into it?'

'Papa, it has taken Marguerite and me an age to achieve this effect!' Marie-Geneviève said indignantly. 'The wire support and the powder and the pomade and the ornaments . . .'

'Little plates of fruit and vegetables!' John Marrett said,

317

shaking his own head in disbelief. 'Where did you get such ideas?'

'Women all over France are wearing their hair this way. It is the style of Madame du Barry.'

'Why should my daughter follow an example set by the king's mistress? All women are mad these days. At dinner last Saturday evening our hostess looked less like a female than a hedgehog.'

'The *hérisson* style of *coiffure*,' Catherine told him. 'I like it, especially now that all colours of hair-powder are used. You are – you always have been – a stuffy old Englishman who does not want to move with the times!'

But there was affection rather than derision in her voice and she smiled at her husband as she spoke.

Marie-Geneviève was far more disconcerted by her father's opinion, for she trusted his judgement on most matters.

And it was so important that she look her best this day since James was expected at the house.

When Marie-Geneviève considered the condition she had been in when he had found her in the forest she went hot and cold all over with shame. It was bad enough that she lacked natural beauty but to be discovered in such a state . . .

And yet – that was the extraordinary thing – it did not seem to have deterred him. Otherwise why would he be coming to call this Sunday?

'It is a pity that we are leaving for Bordeaux and will not be able to greet James,' Catherine said. 'But you have Marguerite to chaperon you. Do not permit him to stay too late.'

'No, Maman,' Marie-Geneviève said, thinking how fortunate that her parents were going away so that she could be alone with James.

Marguerite could be persuaded to give them privacy.

The maid's own fiancé would already have heard of the elder Marretts' intentions and would be bound to present himself at the back door, the minute that they were gone.

Marguerite, opening the door to James, sighed, contrasting her own swarthy swain with this beautiful blond man in his white nankeen breeches.

When she showed James into the drawing-room, where Marie-Geneviève was waiting for him, she noticed that the otherwise sensible girl started convulsively at the mere sound of his voice.

She glanced quickly at James and came to the conclusion that the amount of time that had been spent on creating Marie-Geneviève's spectacular hairstyle was largely irrelevant.

For, judging by the expression on his handsome face, the blond man was already head over heels in love.

'Papa has taken Maman to Bordeaux for shopping,' Marie-Geneviève explained. 'She longs, of course, for Paris, but Papa says that Bordeaux is a compromise!'

'Does she miss living in La Rochelle?'

'That, too. That was why they went to live there, you know – because it was a more sophisticated environment for Maman. It inconvenienced Papa greatly with his business. He had to come so often to Cognac, to visit his suppliers. I sometimes came with him, not only to hunt, but also to keep him company.'

'He must love your mother very much to have done such a thing.'

'He does. But in the end the journeying was too much for him, so they had to come back.'

James stared at her, and Marie-Geneviève hoped devoutly that he was just a little impressed by what he saw.

But then he said, frowning: 'Do you have to wear your hair like that?' and she concluded that he was not.

'It's fashionable . . .'

'I prefer hair more simply dressed,' James said firmly. '*You* don't need all that ornamentation. You're much too pretty to bother with all that.'

'You think so?'

'I wouldn't say it if I didn't mean it,' said James, and Marie-Geneviève was flooded not only with happiness but with relief at the prospect of not facing a sleepless night with the edifice in her hair.

The minutes and hours fled while Marguerite left them discreetly alone. Marie-Geneviève was a good listener as well as a concise speaker who had been encouraged, from an early age, to put over her views without affectation. James, who would later discover that she was not entirely without fault, being impatient and, on occasions, intolerant of others, decided that she was perfect.

He needed no persuasion to stay to dinner, for if he did not, Marie-Geneviève pointed out, she would have had to eat alone.

They had consumed all the larks and thrushes which had followed the roast lamb and were about to proceed to the jams and sweetmeats when Marie-Geneviève told James that his father and her mother had once been in love.

'Maman told me the other day, after our meeting, how they had been young together, in Paris.'

'What an amazing thing!' said James, taken aback at the idea of Dick loving anyone else but Ellen.

Like most young people, he found it rather difficult to accept that his parents had ever been young and romantic.

Marie-Geneviève, however, seemed to experience no

320

such problem in envisaging the scene described by her mother and was apparently elated by it.

And when he listened to her James began to feel that this old romance somehow drew him closer to Marie-Geneviève, as if she was already part of his family.

'What else do you know about them?' he asked, as Marie-Geneviève finished telling him about the excursions in Palais-Royal which Dick and Catherine had taken together in the 1740s.

'That was all she told me.'

'And why did the romance finish?'

But Marie-Geneviève said she did not know.

'Ask your mother,' said James lightly. 'And I'll see what *I* can find out, at home.'

As a matter of course he invited Marie-Geneviève to the ball, and her parents as well. It was time the older generation was reunited, they both decided. It was only surprising that they had not themselves arranged such a meeting.

Pleased with himself, James went home and he never thought of mentioning to anyone, least of all his mother, that all three Marretts would be present at the ball.

Soon, he would engross himself in the business so thoroughly that he would not think of such minor matters as the old romance between his father and Marie-Geneviève's mother, but in the meantime he was curious about it, wondering what had gone wrong between the two of them. And he was naive enough to imagine that he could extract the story from Dick.

But when he was alone with his father in their offices in the rue de la Richonne he found that it was much more difficult to cross the dividing line between the generations than he had imagined, when it came to talking of love.

How on earth did you approach the subject with your

father? Did you talk around it, until something the older man said allowed you to ask a direct question, or did you come straight to the point, saying: 'Papa, Marie-Geneviève tells me that you were once in love with her mother. Would you please tell me what precisely happened between you?'

He peered over the top of an order book attempting to gauge his father's mood.

Perhaps he could risk a tiny probe . . .?

'Papa, you remember my telling you that I had met Marie-Geneviève's parents – '

That was as far as he got.

'Good God, look at this!' Dick exclaimed in fury. 'A letter from one of our shippers accusing me of owing him *three hundred livres*! Your mother would never have neglected such a matter. I must have instructed *you* to pay him.'

'I don't think so, Papa.'

'Who else could it have been? The man regards himself as a friend. Look, see what he says: "You are one of those whom I regard most highly . . . could not imagine *you* in default . . ."'

'I'll check the books to see if it is our error or his,' James said.

It was definitely not the time to pursue the subject of love.

'A *bal masqué*? – what will happen?' Biddy wanted to know as Ellen developed her plans.

'The guests will all wear masks and fancy-dress costumes,' George told her, but *what* masks, what costumes precisely? Biddy asked, perplexed.

Surely it was not a Charentais custom – or an Irish one?

'The Italians invented it,' said George in the manner of well-informed older brothers. 'It started in the theatre with comic plays based on the dramas of Plautus and Terence and upon Roman mimes, the *Commedia dell'arte*. People will dress as characters from Roman mythology, or from the various plays, and they'll call themselves Brighella, or Pulcinella, or Scarmuccia. Or perhaps they'll just be Harlequin and Columbine, or a flower-grower or seller.'

'But the masks – what kind of masks do we wear?'

George smiled wickedly: 'In the *Commedia* the players wear the most grotesque and terrifying masks – maybe made of heavy leather, with wrinkles and a beaked nose and a wart on the forehead!'

'Ugh – how ugly! I could not wear such a thing!'

'I don't think anyone will come to our ball in a *Commedia* mask,' said George, relenting. 'The ladies will have pretty little black ones that will just cover their eyes. You'll look very nice, my baby sister! It's going to be a big occasion and everyone will want to look their best.'

I shall dress as Diana, Marie-Geneviève decided, thinking of the ball. It seemed a particularly fitting role after her recent experience: Diana being mistress not only of domestic animals but also of forest creatures and the hunt.

Diana was also a fertility deity – pleasing since she intended one day to have a big family herself – and a protector of the lower classes.

So at the O'Shaughnessys' ball she would appear as a huntress, Roman style, carrying a bow and a quiver, and with her hair worn free of powder and ornamentation, according to James's wishes.

Having settled in her mind the matter of her own attire, she then turned her attention to what her parents should wear on such a grand occasion.

'You, Papa, must go as Jupiter, the chief god of the

Romans. He's also the god of light and a rain god and a god of the thunderbolt, according to what I have read.'

'A rain god . . . do I *have* to dress up in fancy costume?' her father asked, raising his eyes to Heaven. 'I should be far more comfortable wearing my own ordinary clothes.'

'Not at a *bal masqué*,' said Marie-Geneviève for she, every bit as much as Ellen, wanted the ball to be perfect in every way. 'All the guests will be in fancy dress, Papa. Surely you don't want to be the odd man out?'

'I think I do,' said her father slowly. 'Yes, the more I come to think about it, the more certain I am that I would feel ridiculous in a wig and curly beard. I'll leave the dressing up to your mother and yourself. Maman can go along as Juno, whom I seem to remember is the female counterpart of Jupiter, and I'll content myself with buying a new *jabot* for the occasion.'

'Oh, Papa!'

But Marie-Geneviève knew that it was pointless arguing with her father once his mind was made up.

Still, she liked the thought of Maman as Juno, saviour of women, female comforter. As Interducca, Juno, Marie-Geneviève remembered, brings the bride to her new home. As Cinxia Juno becomes the spirit of the bride's girdle. Perhaps the role that Maman was to play was an omen for James and herself?

Juno, symbol of women's sexuality, her father thought, seeing Catherine in quite a different way.

'Juno does sometimes exhibit military characteristics,' he said, smiling at Marie-Geneviève. 'But I don't think Maman would like to be depicted in that particular way.'

The O'Shaughnessys, too, pondered on their costumes, wondering whether to dress as characters from Roman mythology, or to take their ideas from the dramas of Plautus and Terence or one of the mimes.

'Maman could come as Terra, the earth goddess,' George, the expert on the *bal masqué*, suggested. 'Or Vesta, the hearth goddess.'

'Or, if I wear a Harlequin costume, she could dress as Columbine,' said Dick, caught up in the general air of excitement. 'What do you say, Ellen?'

'Yes, I could be Columbine,' Ellen agreed, absently, not minding what she wore as long as she succeeded in prising James away from Marie-Geneviève on the night of the ball.

Like his brothers, James felt that Roman gods were more dignified and manly than individuals out of Italian comedy.

'It's obvious for you to be Jupiter and for Bawnie and I to be Mars and Quirinus who were his associates,' George said to him. 'I'll be Mars, who protected his worshippers and their cattle.'

'And Quirinus – what was his particular function as a god?'

Caught out, George admitted that he did not know the answer to Bawnie's question.

'What does it matter – it's just an excuse to dress up.'

'It sounds too complicated for me. I'll just be a flower-seller,' Biddy told them.

All sorts of people were to be at the ball, she knew: not only those who considered themselves to be important – like the Comtesse d'Hiersac who would have been highly offended had her name been omitted from the list – but also local merchants and their wives and daughters and sons.

In fact, said Maman, anybody who could afford to dress up. And those who could not were to be fed anyway, if they came to the door.

A few days before the ball, many cows and sheep and turkeys and geese were slaughtered, and pheasant and wild boar, as part of the preparations for what was going to be a gargantuan meal. Maman and Brigitte held serious discussions on whether the perfumed *serviettes* should take the form of a shell or a mitre or a cross of Lorraine, and the silver-gilt services were spread out on the sideboard in the dining-room, prior to being placed on the tables.

It was all extremely exciting, Biddy thought, with only one drawback attached to it: the effect that this extra work was having on Maman's nerves. Even Bawnie, the least sensitive of the three boys, remarked that she was out of sorts and not her usual self.

What if it rains? Biddy worried. What if all the candles and torches and brands and flares that are to light up the avenue, as well as the house, go out in a puff of wind?

What if the Charente floods and all the smart people from Jarnac and Saintes and Angoulême cannot reach the grounds . . .?

'Then we'll have all that food for ourselves,' Bawnie teased. 'That will suit you, Biddy. You know how greedy you are!'

In the midst of the preparations Maman's old friend, Count Patrick Darcy, arrived from Ile d'Oléron, accompanied by his family, and Biddy went out to receive them. The two Darcy brothers and two sisters had auburn hair like their father and all five of them looked rather alike.

But Biddy only saw one of them. His name was Ronan and he was twenty and as soon as she saw him she lost interest in all aspects of the ball other than the opportunity of being there with him.

'You're not eating – what's the matter with you?' Bawnie asked her at dinner.

But Biddy felt as if she would never bother with food again.

* * *

Not everyone in the family was so amiable that week. Was it the frantic preparations that were going on that were driving Dick from the house? Ellen wondered. He even avoided meeting Count Darcy whenever he could, and when he could not he was polite to his guest rather than effusive.

The Count had aged well. His hair was still auburn with no discernible trace of grey in it and he looked to her much the same as the young man with whom she had sailed to France on *La Doutelle* in 1745.

'He was in love with you then and I'd say he still is,' Liam pronounced, and although Ellen laughed off his words she liked the way they raised her spirits.

Pleased about that, she was depressed about James's initial reaction to the Darcy sisters. While his brothers joked and chatted with them he remained detached.

And then asking her about Catherine, the last person she wanted to talk about – wanting to know how it was that Grand-maman Hélène had acted so unjustly in the matter of her will: 'Did you never feel bad about that, Maman?' he had actually asked. 'Did you not feel perhaps that you should have offered to *share* some of the money?'

'I did not,' Ellen said, thinking that he and Marie-Geneviève must have been talking about her inheritance – that they must be meeting regularly. 'Excuse me now, James. I have a lot to do.'

When James had been ejected in that way from the kitchen she leaned against the door and closed her eyes trying to blot all of it out.

There's time yet to rescue him, she said to herself.

Not for nothing have I scoured the Charente in search of suitable girls. If God is good, someone at the ball, other than Marie-Geneviève, is going to take his fancy.

But against her will came the thought – not issuing from

327

God, surely, but from the Devil, tormenting her – *what does that girl look like?*

The evening was clear, dry and cold: no wind blew out the flares as the carriages made their way up the illuminated avenue.

Out of them tumbled strange and amusing and elegant figures. As well as those predicted by George, there were others: El Capitano, Pantelone, Pedrolino, and a Zannis with beaked nose and wrinkles and wart.

James, buoyed by the prospect of spending the evening with Marie-Geneviève, was thwarted at the outset when she failed to arrive.

Or, at least, when she did not appear to be amongst those present. If she was in the hall then she was playing a silly game with him, hiding behind a mask and fancy costume and failing to make her presence known. He was irritated by this idea, having told himself that Marie-Geneviève was as direct and honest as his mother, which added to his enthusiasm for her.

Standing by the principal stairs with his mask in his hand so that Marie-Geneviève could find him easily, he wondered which, if any, of the masked figures could be hers. Even then, although identification would be narrowed down, it would not be completed since there was more than one Columbine, more than one Diana or Terra, present in the hall.

What was really worrying James was the possibility that the Marretts might not come at all that night. He had heard from Liam, not from Marie-Geneviève, about the way Hélène had drawn up her will in favour of his mother. It would be extremely odd, he thought, if Catherine did not resent losing her inheritance in this way.

In the first flush of gratitude towards himself for having come to Marie-Geneviève's rescue her mother might have tried to put out the fire of her resentment. But perhaps it was still kindling? Perhaps she had thought more clearly about his part in finding Marie-Geneviève and realized that he had not, after all, been so heroic? He had simply hauled Marie-Geneviève out of the bushes – her father had shot the wolf.

In which case Marie-Geneviève's mother might well decide not to come to the ball – or to allow her daughter to do so, either. The whole family might be sitting at home in Saint-André while Catherine explained to them how unjustly she had been treated.

She might even have come to the conclusion that James O'Shaughnessy, son of Ellen, was an unsuitable companion for Marie-Geneviève, and her husband and daughter, by now, might be feeling the same.

'What are you doing standing by the doorway instead of mixing with our guests?' Ellen said to him. 'There are so many pretty girls in the hall and the musicians are just beginning to play. You should join the dancing.'

'Just now . . .' James said.

For behind his mother's back he could see that three more people had entered the court and only two of them were costumed and masked. The third, in contemporary clothes, he saw with delight was Marie-Geneviève's father.

'George and Bawnie and Biddy are all there,' Ellen went on valiantly.

James bestowed upon her a most cherubic smile and, throwing his arms around her, hugged her so tight that her mask, too, fell off, and disappeared under the feet of the crowd.

'James!'

'Ellen, come and dance,' said a figure purporting to be of Roman origin, although Ellen knew who he was.

'Thank you,' she said, and still without her mask,

329

wondering why it was, all of a sudden, that James appeared to be so happy, she went to dance with the Count.

'Where have you *been*?' hissed James to Marie-Geneviève as soon as her parents had moved into the throng.

He took her by the arm to lead her inside the hall and realized that she was trembling.

'What's wrong?'

'That horrible woman,' said Marie-Geneviève, her voice shaking with anger. 'The Comtesse d'Hiersac. She had a summons sent to the house. She wants Papa prosecuted for having been at the hunt. We said he was out – that he would not be back tonight and so we had to wait until the messenger left before we could all come out.'

'Won't the messenger return?'

'I expect so,' said Marie-Geneviève. 'But Papa can go away for a week or so until it all blows over. It's happened before. Then the Comtesse goes back to Paris and everyone forgets.'

'But she's here – or I presume she's here. I don't think it would be wise for her to see your Papa. And he isn't in costume, or wearing even a mask. How many previous summonses has he had?'

'Two. James, if the Comtesse insists, Papa could be *banished* for what he has done.'

'We'll have to make sure the two of them don't meet. Your father is going to have to go upstairs to one of the bedrooms and wait until she has gone. Either that, or he must go home at once.'

'And have the messenger call again? I don't think that is wise.'

'Then let's get him away from the crowd before the

330

Comtesse sees him,' James said and felt her grow less tense. 'I'll take him to hide in one of the rooms upstairs.'

That was how it happened that, before the dinner and the fireworks display, Catherine found herself temporarily bereft of a husband.

She lost James and Marie-Geneviève quite early on and wandered through the *milieu* to see if by chance she could see the Comtesse d'Hiersac whose strident voice would surely ultimately betray her whereabouts. Her mind was totally occupied with the threat that was hanging over John, hanging over all of them since, if he was banished from Cognac, his wife and daughter could hardly stay behind. This would without doubt mean returning to La Rochelle but that was not what she wanted, whatever John might think.

If only there was less noise, she thought, taking a glass of wine from an adjacent tray and clutching its stem tight. Even without the music, the sound of so many voices raised in simultaneous chatter was enough to drown out that of a single speaker, albeit one as raucous as the Comtesse's.

But I'll have to track her down and stay close to her, Catherine thought. Otherwise we'll never know when it is safe for John to re-emerge. Let's hope that the wretched woman decides to go home early.

It was some time before she tracked the Comtesse down and she never learned that the woman who was causing so much trouble in her husband's life was attempting, ironically, to portray Venus, goddess of love; but, in the meantime, she sighted the unmasked Ellen in the company of a man in a Roman toga.

Dick? But the man had auburn hair under his laurel wreath so he had to be someone else.

How intriguing, thought Catherine, temporarily

331

diverted from her search for the Comtesse – Ellen, of all people, being flattered by the attentions of a man other than her husband. I must find out who he is.

She was neither so irresponsible nor so frivolous that she concentrated on this task rather than on her other, more vital pursuit.

But when she had finally discovered the whereabouts of the Comtesse and taken note, for future reference, of the colour of her dress, her eyes went back to Ellen and her partner, so absorbed in their conversation.

I shall get to know him, Catherine vowed. And the Devil got into *her* mind, too, and persuaded her to get up to some of her old tricks, although she told herself that, after the shock she and John and Marie-Geneviève had had that day, it was all for a bit of fun.

Blissfully unaware that Catherine was amongst those present, Ellen talked with the Count. Out of the corner of her eye she could see Dick, dressed as Harlequin, standing over by the minstrels' gallery, surrounded by other men. He looked over at her and she smiled at him, feeling herself, for once, to be in complete control. It was a pleasant and rather heady sensation. Instead of agonizing over Dick's proclivities, as she had done for so long in the past, she had the impression that he was slightly jealous of the attention that she was getting tonight.

And the younger O'Shaughnessys and Darcys were all getting along well together, George and Bawnie looking after the girls and Ronan apparently paying court to Biddy. Ellen no longer minded that James had absented himself from this group because he had finally found himself a girl – one of the three Dianas, although hers was by far the prettiest gown.

How right it had been to hold the ball; to rescue James from Marie-Geneviève just in the nick of time.

'Are you happy with your life, Ellen?' the Count wanted to know. 'Was it all worthwhile – your journey from Ireland long ago and all that has happened to you since then?'

'Oh, yes,' said Ellen. 'Naturally it has not always been perfect, but tonight I feel as if nothing bad can ever happen again.'

Biddy had scarcely eaten for three days with the distraction of having Ronan Darcy in the house. At dinner that evening she only picked at the turkey on her plate and ate nothing else, so eager was she to return to the dancing.

But when she rose from the table she realized that while the green polonaise – her rather too modern version of a medieval flower-seller's dress – was still in place, she had lost so much weight that she was in danger of losing her petticoat.

'Please excuse me,' she said to Ronan, trying, without making it obvious, to clutch at the offending garment through the folds of her gown.

'Come back quickly,' he said, delighting her, and she sidled towards the staircase and, out of sight of the guests, fled up to her bedroom, tore off her petticoat and threw it onto the floor.

And in the candlelight looked up to see a stranger – wide-awake – lying upon her bed.

Any other girl of her age would have been humiliated at being observed in performing so intimate an act and probably frightened, as well, but Biddy was so used to brothers invading her privacy that she did not mind too much. It was one thing to lose your petticoat in front of a handsome young man at a ball, she decided; quite another to be seen taking it off by a kind-faced man old enough to be your grandfather.

The stranger in her bedroom had thick grey hair and

deep blue eyes like Papa's although they were set much wider in his rather square heavy-jawed head, and a straight nose with nostrils that flared like a horse, and a mouth that curved into a slight smile and she felt quite bad about what she had done in front of him lest *he* feel embarrassed about it.

'I'm *sorry* – ' they both began at once, and the stranger added: 'You know, I have a daughter of about your age and she would be very, very upset if she found a strange man lying down in her bedroom.'

'Do you?' said Biddy, diverted. 'Is she here at the ball?'

'She is. I would be down there with her if there was not someone else present whom I didn't want to meet.'

'Who is that?' Biddy wanted to know.

She was so sympathetic that John found himself telling her about the Comtesse.

'You poor man,' she said when he had finished. 'I'll watch out for her, too.'

'Will you?'

'Naturally. And in the meantime I will bring you something to eat.'

James was also campaigning on behalf of John Marrett. He, too, had identified the Comtesse by the strident sound of her voice. She was seated quite close to him at dinner and he was therefore able to take note of how much and how enthusiastically she drank.

She was, he knew, a lady who, while purporting to despise merchants, was not above bargaining with them. A plan had occurred to him which might get Marie-Geneviève's father out of his current trouble.

'Wait here,' he commanded Marie-Geneviève when dinner was over and, having armed himself with a miniature cask of his father's very best cognac, he headed in the direction of the Comtesse, identified himself, and drew her into a corner.

'You must try this,' he said in his most persuasive voice and poured her a glass of *eau-de-vie*. 'Now, what do you think of it?'

'Wonderful,' the Comtesse said appreciatively. 'From your father's personal *paradis*, of course . . .'

'But available to one or two very privileged people at a very special price.'

'Which is what, exactly?'

Woe betide me if Papa overhears, James thought, stipulating so low a figure that the Comtesse, in mid-sip, swallowed and nearly choked.

But, no, Papa will not be angry – not when he knows the whole story of what I am trying to do, being the most altruistic of men himself.

'That's extremely generous of you,' the Comtesse managed to say.

'It is! There's just one little favour I would ask of you in return,' James said, refilling her empty glass. 'I understand that Mr John Marrett is at present under threat of prosecution . . .'

He left it there, watching the Comtesse sip again.

At last she said: 'No longer.'

'You mean – ?'

'I shall withdraw the prosecution. You are sure about that price?'

After dinner, Ellen lost the Count in the crowd. Since she did not feel in the least in love with him but was merely enjoying the novel sensation of being made to feel desirable by an attractive man, she was not distressed. At Dick's side she watched the fireworks which James and George and Bawnie set off, gratified to hear the voices around her exclaim at the reddish and greenish flames.

But when dancing recommenced she saw the Count again. He was with a very small, rather plump lady attired as Juno, saviour of womankind.

Ellen frowned, not because the Count's attention had been diverted from herself but because there was something about his tiny companion that reminded her of –

But, no, that was quite impossible. Not here. She was simply imagining things.

She shook her head at her own foolishness.

All the same, it *was* slightly irritating that the Count should be monopolized by Juno. I've lost my old admirer, Ellen thought ruefully.

She told herself that Count Patrick was a widower, and that, even if he had a fondness for herself, it was only natural that he should seek the company of a more available woman.

She reminded herself that she would rather be in the company of her husband than with any other man.

She went over to Dick to prove it to herself, although she needed no confirmation of the love she still had for him.

And *still* she was piqued about Juno's conquest of the Count.

Then the grandfather clock struck two chimes. The musicians laid down their instruments. The guests stopped dancing. It was time to unmask.

The Count and Juno were only a few feet away from Dick.

And Ellen was looking directly at Juno when, amidst the general laughter, the latter took off her mask.

Juno, saviour of womankind indeed, Ellen thought savagely – how did *she* come to be here? She is a stickler for convention in her way. She would not dream of arriving unasked.

336

Who invited her?

Only one person, surely.

And that, of course, must be, had to be Dick.

Biddy could not have been more pleased with herself as the guests began to unmask. Having paid another visit to her bedroom and found the nice stranger fast asleep on her bed she was now free to enjoy Ronan's company for the remainder of the night.

She caught sight of her parents in the crowd and was about to lead Ronan over to them when she noticed that Maman was looking distressed. What could have happened, she wondered, her own happiness beginning to ebb away in the light of Ellen's chagrin.

'Come,' she said, all the same, to Ronan, squeezing through the revellers in order to comfort her mother.

But James, she realized, was ahead of her, about to present to his parents the girl in the cream gown who had been at his side all night.

As Biddy came up to the group she heard him say, over the noise: 'This is Marie-Geneviève Marrett.'

These words, Biddy saw, seemed to stun her already shocked mother even more.

What could be the matter with Maman?

Or was there something odd about James's companion?

She surveyed the newcomer. James's lady looked surprisingly familiar – as if Biddy had seen her, or someone like her, before.

She had a straight nose with nostrils that flared like a horse, and a curving mouth, and a rather heavy jaw and large brown eyes, and her long, dark hair – shiny as pliant satin – fell loosely down her back.

'But she must be the daughter of the nice man who is asleep upstairs in my room!' Biddy thought, delighted with this discovery. 'If she is even half as pleasant as her father, I hope she'll be James's wife.'

4

God Himself might have been so delighted in His creation of John Marrett that He had gone on to make, in Marie-Geneviève, a female version of the man. But Ellen, although immensely relieved by the striking evidence of Marie-Geneviève's true paternity, remained depressed and apprehensive by the re-emergence of Catherine in her own life.

The image of Dick and Catherine walking arm in arm in the garden on the night of the fire still stuck in her mind, as did Colm O'Neill's report of their planned rendezvous in La Rochelle later.

The fact that John and not Dick was Marie-Geneviève's father did not rule out the likelihood, to Ellen, of Catherine having had an *affaire*.

Or *affaires* . . . Catherine, according to Hélène, had always collected men. In Cognac, prior to her marriage, she had been inhibited in this pursuit by the absence, through war, of suitable partners.

But who knew what she had been up to since? Look how she had made a set for Count Darcy at the ball while her husband was hiding upstairs.

Catherine was a powerful woman and men were enthralled by her – it was as simple as that, and as frightening. Given the chance, she would doubtless reassert her influence over Dick.

And not only for the sake of amusement. Not only, Ellen mused, to show power over myself, but because Catherine has a genuine feeling for Dick. I know this to be true.

It was equally accurate to say that Dick, at this time, did not appear to be giving any consideration to love.

Dick was worried sick by the depression in the brandy market. Again and again he reiterated that trade with Ireland was decreasing.

'I may as well become a plantation overseer in the West Indies,' was his response when the cost of the ball was totted up.

I wish we had never held it, Ellen thought, conscience-stricken. And what good did it do? James looked at Marie-Geneviève and no one else throughout the evening. And now it's almost certain that the two of them will be wed.

For the rest of her days Catherine will be woven into the fabric of my family. How can I cope with that?

'This is a serious matter,' John Marrett said to Catherine. 'How do *you* feel about Marie-Geneviève and young James?'

Catherine was in bed, reading *Alzire*. She looked down at her book, as if that and not the attraction between James and Marie-Geneviève was at the forefront of her mind.

'Voltaire is so *tragic*! He tries to introduce exotic notes into his work but he never quite escapes his classical training with the Jesuits . . . *Is* it serious?'

'You know it is! Don't look so tragic yourself! Are you going to be able to cope, when the two of them are married?'

'I won't have any alternative,' Catherine said, wide-eyed. 'Anyway, James is wonderful. What would we have done without him?'

'Been forced to leave in a hurry, I'd say! Is there room for me in that bed!'

* * *

339

In the next bedroom Marie-Geneviève was fast asleep already, dreaming of Ellen and James.

In her dream, Ellen had welcomed her to the château as a new bride, James and she having married at the ball.

Or was it Bawnie, James's youngest brother, who had become her husband, he having given up a girl with auburn hair in order to commit himself to her?

It was all rather indecisive, and the château itself was dim and obfuscated, since someone who did not like either herself or her new husband had blown the candles out.

'Where is James?' Marie-Geneviève heard herself call out.

Or should she have been looking for Bawnie? Whoever she had married had very inconsiderately taken himself off and Ellen, too, had mysteriously faded out of her dream, leaving Marie-Geneviève all alone in the darkness.

'But I thought you all liked me,' Marie-Geneviève said, hurt by this desertion, and, out of her need to find the O'Shaughnessys, she turned over in her bed and woke up with a start.

In spite of the confusing nature of her dream she felt happy. For, after all, she had not been abandoned, and there was no uncertainty in her mind as to who was the object of her love.

Wonderful James, she thought, echoing her mother's assessment of him. James the perennial saviour, firstly of herself, in the forest, and then of Papa from the awful Comtesse d'Hiersac.

James who appeared to be in love with her and was showing every indication that he would propose.

And if James himself was not enough there was the added attraction of his family. To an only child who had always longed for brothers and sisters, finding ready-made ones was enticing. And Biddy was the same age as herself!

Far from rejecting her, the O'Shaughnessys, she was sure, would welcome her with open arms, when she was James's wife. James's mother, instead of leaving her alone in the darkness, would approve of her as whole-heartedly as Papa and Maman commended darling James. Their two families would soon become one big, snug one.

Marie-Geneviève wriggled into a foetal position with her knees and breasts touching, and, looking forward to a delightful future, floated back to sleep.

'Has Marie-Geneviève been brought up as a Catholic or a Protestant?' Ellen asked James.

Much depended on the answer to this question. If Marie-Geneviève had been reared as a Protestant and, like her father, was unwilling to convert, marriage to James was surely impossible.

'I've never seen her at Mass at the Church of Saint-Léger,' said Biddy, understanding in part the implications of what her mother was asking.

'That's because she goes to Mass at the Church of Sainte Marie-Madeleine, in the rue Basse de Crouin,' James told them, unperturbed. 'I know her mother cannot take the sacraments but her father does not object to Marie-Geneviève being raised in the Catholic Church, only to being forced to become a Catholic himself.'

So that was that, simplifying matters in one way and complicating them in another.

Ellen told herself that she must not search for weapons with which to beat Marie-Geneviève off.

She seemed a nice girl. Her father was a perfect gentleman. It was perfectly feasible that in character as well as in looks Marie-Geneviève took after him.

Catherine did not resemble *her* mother at all; therefore why should Marie-Geneviève be like Catherine?

No weapons, said Ellen to herself – but she did not put down her shield.

The courtship process did not suit someone of James's temperament. He wished that he and Marie-Geneviève could be married at once. But, apart from the conventional dictates, women, he knew, did not like to be rushed. In order to make headway with them a man had to cajole and flatter and proceed with extreme caution when all he really wanted was to get them into bed with the minimum amount of fuss.

He would have been heartened had he known that Marie-Geneviève, too, was feeling impatient, as eager as he for love. It seemed entirely natural to both of them to embrace when James next called at the house in Saint-André. Marie-Geneviève was not wearing her laced corset that day and her *négligée*, a pink open robe made of particularly fine material, was also unboned. James was astonished at her softness. In contrast to himself – and it was, above all else, this contrast which appealed to him at that moment – he thought her unbelievably tender and supple, a creature made out of gossamer, he thought romantically, although she was, in reality, a good deal more solid than that.

He neither cajoled nor flattered her, since it was not necessary to do either, he realized gladly, but kissed her thoroughly until, as he had feared, the two small hands, the palms of which had been placed against his chest, pushed him firmly away.

'No more,' said Marie-Geneviève, intimating *not for the present* and, red-cheeked, backed away.

But not too far. Had James reached for her he could quite easily have pulled her into his arms. That was his first instinct. His second, partly the result of his need to protect her, partly out of the need to further his immediate cause, was to propose to her.

'That is what you want?'

'I wouldn't ask otherwise,' said James. '*Will* you marry me?'

'But, naturally, yes,' Marie-Geneviève said, and stepped back into his arms.

'Where are your parents?' James asked, neither of them having made an appearance.

'Out – '

But that was all James wanted to know and he promptly kissed her again. It was Marguerite – having decided that they had been left on their own for just long enough for their encounter to be interesting but not too daring – who knocked on the *alcôve* door.

'Dinner, mademoiselle.'

'Of course,' said Marie-Geneviève, adjusting her rumpled clothes. 'James, where will we live when we are married?'

James, having already thought about that, had his answer ready.

'But that is marvellous,' Marie-Geneviève said, and they started to kiss again.

'You would like to live *here*, with us?' Ellen said, after James had made his announcements. 'You're *sure* that's what you both want?'

'I always know what I want,' said James, truthfully. 'And Marie-Geneviève would like nothing more than to be really close to our family. And her parents, too, of course. You'll see them here much more often, I expect, after we are wed.'

* * *

343

'We would like to be married in the Church of Saint-Léger, rather than in Sainte Marie-Madeleine,' Marie-Geneviève said to Catherine. 'We've discussed it and we want a typically Charentais wedding.'

'The ceremonies of the Charente are grotesque and satirical,' said her mother, just as Marie-Geneviève had expected. 'In Poitou, for instance, during the fête of Verruyes, married couples have to jump into a pool of water! In front of people who laugh and mock their dirty clothes!'

'Oh, Maman!' Marie-Geneviève pleaded, laughing herself at her mother's pained expression.

It was a relief to laugh because May 1774 had been a grim month for France. At the end of April had come the alarming news that the king had been taken ill with smallpox. And then on the tenth of May the country had heard of King Louis' death.

At a time of national mourning it seemed almost irreverent to be happy – to discuss one's own plans for marriage, Marie-Geneviève thought.

But Maman was saying: 'And in Angoumois they play a game with a stick and ball *in the church*!'

'Only on Christmas Day and the two Sundays following,' said Marie-Geneviève, and laughed at her mother again.

In her white satin wedding-dress Marie-Geneviève arrived at the Church of Saint-Léger quite sure that her white silk fringed slippers had suddenly sprouted wings and were lifting her into the air.

When she looked up at the Gothic rose-window and the four round-arched voussures marking the portal she was convinced that she was on the same level as they were, well above the ground. Instead of concentrating on her status as a bride-to-be she found herself wondering what once, before the Wars of Religion, had been represented on the sculpted tympana of the two blind arcades. An Adoration of the Magi? Traces of three standing figures and a seated woman would suggest that she was right. And in the other arcade, on the right, the subject did seem to be the Holy Women and the Angel near Christ's Tomb.

The capitals of the portal were also somewhat mutilated but she was able to distinguish their decoration and the scenes which were represented – the struggle for life, depicted in number five . . .

I hope it will not be like that, said a small plaintive childish voice inside Marie-Geneviève's head, and she looked again at the absurd and vindictive foot-biter; the victim on the ground; the five defenders of a man in danger of being drowned.

Let life be kinder to James and me . . .

But now she was inside the wide nave, and her attention was diverted by another horror – by the hats perched high on the heads of Ellen and Catherine.

Marie-Geneviève's brown eyes, already wider and wilder than normal, grew truly huge with the shock of what she saw.

The hats were both of the type which Papa, she knew, would have described as extreme. She herself had felt that Maman, for once, had erred in making her selection for her hat was enormous, too big, in Marie-Geneviève's opinion, for a small person to wear. Its brim turned up at the back, and it was trimmed with ribbons and bows, although it *was* a very pretty pale pink, the same shade as Maman's gown . . .

Now she knew that Maman had made the wrong choice, and not only because the hat was too large for her.

Because – but how dreadful! – because Ellen's hat was almost exactly the same! It, too, was pale pink, the same colour as the trimmings on her dark blue dress, and it was huge, with a brim which turned up at the back, and it was also embellished with pale pink ribbons and bows . . .

Mon Dieu, but Maman will be *furious*, said Marie-Geneviève to herself, forgetting love, forgetting James waiting by the altar, and wishing nothing more than that her slippers really had wings and that she could be lifted out of the church, away from the furore to follow.

It's all my fault, she told herself. If I had not been too distracted by my own preparations I would have checked what James's Maman was planning to wear this day. I should have taken that interest . . .

Maman will never forgive me.

James's Maman will never, ever speak to me again . . .

And then James himself turned right around to see what on earth was keeping his bride, and he smiled, and the white fringed slippers did indeed seem to sprout wings again. James smiled at her and Marie-Geneviève lost sight of the matching hats and was no longer fearful of blame being heaped upon her head, and the urge she had to levitate out of the church faded away in the importance of floating up the aisle, to stand by James's side.

The ceremony of which Marie-Geneviève had spoken to Catherine was a tradition of Poitou and Angoumois and Châtillon-Sur-Sèvres, rather than peculiar to Cognac. Once, the smartly-dressed bachelors – swords at their sides, musicians accompanying them – would have been prospective knights, but even in their more prosaic form they were romantic, presenting a branch of an orange tree to the new bride before they asked her to dance.

Marie-Geneviève thought it a charming ceremony although, after the dance, she and James were required to lift a live sheep onto a table where it was obliged to consume some wine and bread.

Someone had handed her a switch which she hoped she would not have to use to force the sheep to turn around the table the obligatory three times.

'*Fessez le mouton!*' yelled George and Bawnie in unison. 'Marie-Geneviève – slap the sheep!'

They both thought that their new sister-in-law was a good sport to have introduced the custom, and had agreed to play their bachelor role on the following day, too, when they would arrive at the door and ask that she take part in the dance of the shepherdess.

'But you *must* wear white clothes,' Marie-Geneviève was warning the two of them. 'And after the dance you must follow James and me, in our wedding costumes, to a meadow where you must empty your glasses and race back to the château to be crowned the Kings of Youth!'

'She's so *young*,' said someone to Ellen and when she looked to her left there was Catherine looking wistfully at her newly-married daughter.

It was a part of Catherine Ellen had never seen before. In spite of herself she was moved by her enemy's softness.

'But James is so strong,' Catherine went on, 'I can feel confident that he will care for her well.'

She smiled up at Ellen as she said this, as if she was giving credit to her companion for having reared such a wonderful son.

'He *is* strong . . .' Ellen said, bemused.

Because, all of a sudden, she was toying with the most extraordinary notion: that she and Catherine were not only friends, but sisters. And (this was even more absurd) the fact that they were both wearing almost identical pale pink hats – something that had enraged her earlier on – now added, rather than detracted, from this fanciful illusion.

Bawnie lifted the sheep onto his back and pirouetted it around his head and Marie-Geneviève, turning away from

347

this sight, looked instead at her mother and Ellen, standing side-by-side, and her mind, too, promptly focused on hats.

Maman really did make a mistake in her selection, she thought again – that big hat is perfect for James's mother, and so wrong for mine.

And Ellen thought – Catherine looks so much prettier than I in that hat but at this moment I do not seem to mind . . .

'*Fessez le mouton . . .!*'

'What are you two ladies talking about?' Dick said, joining Ellen and Catherine.

At once, Catherine reverted to her more familiar self. There was nothing sisterly about her anymore – or motherly, either. Her maternal smile metamorphosed into the amatory and confident smile of a practised coquette. Her hands and arms and shoulders seemed, in their new suppleness, to speak of the power of love as she turned to talk to Dick.

So there it was – a reiteration, in a minor form, of the sense of betrayal Ellen had experienced in her previous dealings with Catherine. What a fool she had been to believe, even for an instant, that Catherine could change; that they could be friends or – sheer idiocy! – sisters, just because her son had married Catherine's daughter.

Madness.

But at least she was not stupid enough to imagine that she could compete with Catherine in the business of conquering men.

The whole idea of such a war irritated and repelled her at that moment. She wanted nothing more than to get away from the battle-ground.

Catherine was talking vivaciously, her eyes and lashes and hands all taking part in her one-sided conversation with Dick.

Without saying anything at all Ellen walked away from the two of them, away from the wedding guests, through the château grounds and out of the gateway, down to the river bank, where the sweet Charente, so gentle this day, meandered downstream to Tonnay-Charente and La Rochelle.

I am not frightened, she said fiercely to herself. What has been between Dick and Catherine is past. That decision was made long ago, and since then he and I have been happy.

He is a decent and honourable man, content with his family, deeply worried about the state of the trade in which he is involved, unlikely to seek out the inevitable disquiet of a resumed *affaire*.

I am not frightened.

Only –

Catherine, at heart, is amoral – impervious to the feelings of others, and she is shameless in reaching out and taking what she wants.

Catherine, in terms of Dick, will always be a threat.

Will always betray you.

Forget your sentimental image of Catherine and yourself as friends – as sisters . . .

Suddenly Ellen was seized with anger that was part humiliation, part disappointment – the anger that grows out of betrayal. With both hands she felt for the pins that were holding her pretty pink hat in place and pulled them out until she could prise the hat itself loose from her head.

Pink-faced with fury, she hurled the hat low and far across the gentle river and watched it land, like a rose-tinted swan, in the silver water.

Swans can bring you bad luck, she had once warned Catherine.

Well, bad luck to her old enemy then, for her innumerable betrayals. Bad cess to Catherine!

Marie-Geneviève was tidy by nature. That night, when the guests had gone home and the O'Shaughnessys had disappeared into their respective bedrooms, and James and she were in theirs, she folded up her wedding-gown, positioning each sleeve across the bodice at precisely the same angle and turning over the skirt drapes in the same meticulous way, before placing the dress in the box which she had instructed to be sent for that purpose out to Chez Landart.

Her white silk slippers she did not put away, or her matching petticoat for, although she would not wear her wedding-gown again, these other items which had been made to match it would be bound, she thought, to go with something else.

'Will you unlace the back of my corset?' she asked her new husband as if, James thought, they had been married for years instead of a day.

He had been observing the storage ritual with growing impatience. When, with some difficulty, he had managed to unlace the corset he irreverently tossed the irksome garment into the furthest corner.

'James . . .' protested Marie-Geneviève, about to retrieve it, as a matter of course.

But James was scooping her up into his arms and carrying her towards their bed. I'll put my corset away *after* we have made love, she thought automatically. The tidier everything was the more secure Marie-Geneviève always became.

But she always appeared self-sufficient and James, certainly, had no idea that she was feeling unsafe at that moment, like an animal lulled and coaxed out of its lair only to find itself caught off guard.

In the sanctuary of her own home she had longed to make love with James. But she was very young and her new surroundings seemed more inimical than friendly. As if they were fragments of pollen caught up in a whirlwind, her thoughts began to speed up and disintegrate so that James, the items in her trousseau, Papa and Maman at home on their own, the bed on which she was now lying appeared in her mind's eye as a jumble of words and letters.

Even after her body had begun to respond to her husband's love-making her real self was disengaged and at bay.

And then, out of the kaleidoscope in her mind one image emerged: of herself, with her head against James's chest, safe, while a grey wolf watched.

Safe . . .

And when he had entered her, after they were one, she did find safety, for the whirlwind had blown away.

Ellen decided that, in dealing with Marie-Geneviève, she would be polite but distant. As James's wife she could not be ignored. As Catherine's daughter she could be tolerated – just – but she could not be loved.

But it proved difficult to keep at arm's length someone as definite as Marie-Geneviève; someone who derived satisfaction from whatever task engrossed her and whose enthusiasm was so contagious it affected the whole house.

And it was hard, too, to be cold when you were by nature warm yourself.

And, on top of all this, there was Biddy singing the praises of her sister-in-law, saying how kind Marie-Geneviève was to her, with Ronan Darcy, to her grief, returned to Ile d'Oléron and unsure when he would see her again.

'How did we ever get on without her?' Biddy was wont to ask, pointing out how the girl was always doing

351

something useful around the house, either baking, or sewing, or exercising the horses, or dressing Biddy's hair.

Apart from being Catherine's daughter the second charge that one would have expected to be able to lay against Marie-Geneviève was that she must surely be spoilt.

But, Ellen had to admit, this was not the case, not unless you called selfishness her tendency to expect people to anticipate her needs and to behave accordingly.

After a month of having Marie-Geneviève in the house, Ellen was beginning to dislike herself for her prejudices more than the girl herself.

She seemed to be good for James, too. At the very least, the distraction of their marriage was a curtain concealing, for the time-being, the disparate business attitudes of Dick and James.

Then an incident occurred which, although it did not reconcile Ellen and Catherine, broke down one barrier.

Since the wedding George and Bawnie had continued to treat their new sister-in-law with respect. But they were both restless young men with too much bottled-up energy and uncertain futures. Under normal circumstances they could have looked forward to joining Dick and James in the business but the way things were going, their father said, there might not be a place in it for either of them.

In both of them was a tendency to tease with a touch of malice and, in their frustration, they gave way to it one morning after Dick and James had gone in to the offices in Cognac, leaving them behind.

'Tell me, Marie-Geneviève, how does your father go about practising the Protestant cult?' Bawnie began, being provocative out of sheer boredom. 'Does he have a secret chapel in a barn at the back of your house at Saint-André or do all the faithful gather at night in the woods to pray?'

Marie-Geneviève winced. Although neither George nor

Bawnie realized it, she was extremely sensitive about her parents' marriage and her own illegitimate standing in the eyes of the Church and state. All through her childhood she had secretly hoped that her father would convert.

'No, he doesn't have a chapel in the house,' she said, in a reasonable, controlled voice, sounding, from the boys' point of view, too unruffled for words. 'I don't know if Papa meets other Protestants when he prays or not. He always taught me to respect other people's privacy and I never asked him about that.'

'How self-righteous!' commented Bawnie. 'We're not a bit like that here. We like to know everything that is going on in the house – '

'And in the Charente, for that matter!' added Bawnie. 'You know, there used to be a chapel or an oratory at Jarnac. Perhaps your father attended services there in the old days? I believe they demolished the building later on. Troops were sent out to knock down the heretical temples . . . There was a fellow called Trouillier de Plonneuil – I'm sure your father would have heard of him – who was caught attending a service. All his goods were seized and he ended up serving His Majesty as a galley slave. For life! Isn't that so, George?'

'Yes, indeed! Cheer up, Marie-Geneviève. Don't look so glum. France is more tolerant these days. Who knows, perhaps we'll plant a cypress tree in the garden, as Protestants do, so that they can bury their dead in its shadow in the night. Just to show how tolerant we O'Shaughnessys are!'

He half-expected Marie-Geneviève to laugh. Either that or to flare up, which would be more fun, alleviating the dullness of the day. Maybe she'd shout and scream and throw her sewing into his face?

When she did none of these things he glanced quickly

at her and saw to his consternation that tears were streaming down her face.

'I'm sorry,' George said awkwardly. 'I – we are, aren't we, Bawnie? We didn't mean to upset you – '

But Marie-Geneviève was gone. And his mother, George realized, was in the garden, just outside the window, having heard what was going on.

'*Bullying!*' said Ellen furiously. 'Mocking that poor innocent girl! What's got into you boys behaving like wolves, tearing her apart, instead of like young gentlemen? Doesn't it occur to you that Marie-Geneviève must have suffered at the convent because of her situation?'

It had not occurred to Ellen, either, until a few minutes previously but she was not going to admit that to the boys. A wave of compassion for Marie-Geneviève had broken over her when she had been least expecting it and she was still recovering from the force of the surge.

'You wouldn't talk to the Darcy girls like that – or to Biddy. And this is your own sister-in-law.'

'The Darcy girls never minded being teased,' said Bawnie bravely. 'We had a lot of fun with the two of them. And Biddy – '

No one is ever unkind to Biddy, he was going to add. But that meant confessing his cruelty to Marie-Geneviève and he wisely retreated from speech, leaving George to mutter: 'Marie-Geneviève was never upset before.'

'She is now. Stay here. Don't budge from that room. I want to talk to the two of you again,' Ellen commanded.

To further terrorize them she scowled as fiercely as she could. Then she went into the house in search of Marie-Geneviève.

They don't like me, Marie-Geneviève was saying to herself. And their Maman is so cold . . .

At the thought of Ellen's coldness towards her, Ellen's

354

resistance to her demonstrations of friendship, her tears intensified into a cascade.

I've disappointed them, Marie-Geneviève thought despairingly. James's mother thinks that her son should not have married me and soon his father and James himself will come to the same conclusion.

At this prospect her stomach churned disconcertingly, and she clutched her throat, to stop herself being sick.

Why had she not given more consideration to the possibility that the O'Shaughnessy family, in whose well-aired cupboards no skeletons stood ready to tumble out when the doors were opened, might not have resented the marriage of the eldest son to an illegitimate child?

That was why Ellen did not respond to her – now it all made sense.

Perhaps she – the entire family – tried to talk James out of marrying me, Marie-Geneviève thought. Who knows what rows took place when he announced his intention of doing so. How brave he must have been, in the face of the opposition of his family, to go ahead with his plans to wed!

He must love me a great deal . . . For some obscure reason, thinking of James's bravery and love, instead of providing consolation, made her cry all over again.

'Marie-Geneviève?'

In her haste to get away from George and Bawnie she had left the bedroom door open behind her.

And now –

'Don't cry,' said Ellen in a voice that could never be described as cold, but rather as tender as that of Maman's. 'Those horrible boys. But they didn't mean a word they said.'

'But they must have done,' insisted Marie-Geneviève. 'They must be – surely none of you want the illegitimate daughter of a Protestant in the house?'

355

The wave of compassion rushed in and hit Ellen hard all over again.

I'll *kill* George and Bawnie, she vowed silently.

To Marie-Geneviève she said with total sincerity and a deep if newly-discovered affection: 'You silly girl. *Everyone* in the family wants you in this house.'

5

Several times during that year James had tried again to talk to his father about his plans for expanding the business. On each occasion Dick had procrastinated or adroitly fended him off.

These setbacks irritated him but they did not deter him from trying again. And in the meantime he had written a letter to Edmund Burke who had been of such good assistance to his father on his visit to Ireland in 1760. News of Burke's importance as a statesman had long since reached Cognac. James himself had heard that although the great man was indifferent to luxury he kept an open house. So what harm was there in asking him if he could assist with introductions which could lead to sales of cognac?

None at all, Burke seemed to think, writing back and suggesting that James journey to London and visit him soon after his arrival. Maybe even travel with him to Bristol, Burke added, he having just received the distinction of being chosen as one of this town's representatives.

Only Dick, when informed of these developments, saw something objectionable in what James had done.

'Bothering the fellow. A man in his position being approached by a young fellow like you instead of by myself.'

'He's ready to help, all the same. We *can* break into the London market, Papa, I'm certain of it. Maybe one day even into America, as well.'

'America! Have you forgotten that the Molasses Act virtually prohibits the importation of French-grown sugar

357

and molasses and rum into America, in order to protect the interests of the British plantations?'

'But we're not talking about rum – we're talking about cognac,' James said, sticking to his guns.

'It amounts to the same thing,' Dick said. 'The British won't encourage French exports into any of their colonies. And the colonies themselves are right under the thumb of their mother country. They're not even permitted to start businesses which could be seen as competing with British industry.'

'I know. And Englishmen are not allowed to smoke tobacco unless it's been grown in America or Bermuda. But all that must change. The Americans are tired of Britain and her tax demands. That incident last December in Boston when a cargo of tea was tipped into the sea was a war signal.'

'And when the battle is over maybe we *will* export to America,' Dick said, sounding as if their conversation, too, was about to terminate. 'In the meantime write to Edmund Burke and thank him for his offer of help. But I'm still not convinced that we should contemplate increasing our stocks or waste money and time going abroad, in the hope of success in London.'

'He won't listen to me,' James said to Marie-Geneviève.

'He will in the end. Maybe it wasn't tactful to write to Edmund Burke without mentioning it to your father first.'

'Maybe it wasn't,' agreed James. 'But I daresay that if I had told him about it, or asked him to write, he would have raised objections, as well. And in the meantime I look around me and I see other businesses expanding. I shall soon be forced to ignore Papa's wishes altogether and journey to London myself.'

'No, don't do that,' Marie-Geneviève said. 'Not yet

anyway. Because you might possibly be able to go *without* upsetting your father. What would you say if – '

But James's opinion came later. Before that, Marie-Geneviève had quite a lot to say herself.

'These high-falutin fancies about the London market!' said Dick to Ellen. 'I wonder how much of it has to do with Jimmy's own need to travel. You would have thought that marriage would have settled him. Instead of which the converse seems to be true.'

'I don't think that's the case at all,' Ellen said promptly. 'But even if it was, you wanted to travel yourself as a young man. If *you* hadn't had a few fancies there wouldn't be a business today.'

Dick shook his head as if to indicate that he was surrounded by the unthinking.

'Neither of you seem to understand that in my case there was no incentive to stay at home – no opportunity. I would have liked nothing better than to have remained in Ireland in as comfortable a situation as Jimmy is in now, but it was out of the question. Now, things seem to be easing over there.'

'You mean that Catholics are allowed to take a lease of a bog? As long as it's at least four feet deep, not less than half a mile from town, and that we undertake to reclaim half of it anyway, within twenty-one years! You call that easing?'

'Don't quibble, Ellen! It's the first actual relaxation in the Penal Laws. And at least taxes won't be levied on such bogland.'

'Only for seven years.'

'Ah! Leave Ireland for the moment, will you,' said Dick exasperatedly. 'I was talking about Jimmy.'

'You're too hard on him,' said his wife. 'I've told you

that before. You're lucky to have such a bright, hard-working son. The trouble with you, Dick O'Shaughnessy, is that deep down you're worried sick about the decline in the Irish market and our stake in it, and instead of saying so anymore you complain about poor James.'

'The trouble with me is that I need some peace,' riposted Dick.

He felt at loggerheads with everyone in the house since Marie-Geneviève would be bound to take James's part in this and any other altercation, Biddy would side in her head with her sister-in-law, and George and Bawnie were in a state of resentment with him for not taking them into the firm.

I need to get away myself, thought Dick, let alone listen to Jimmy talking about London and America. America! What else would the fellow suggest!

Pushing James out of his thoughts for the time being he reverted to the idea of escape.

Temporary withdrawal from his family. Evasive action while he sorted out his thoughts.

Paris?

A week ago a letter had arrived from Colm O'Neill telling him about the planned reunion of the Wild Geese which was to take place in the capital shortly.

Since peace had been declared the Irish Brigade had been far less militarily operative, but now Lord Clare had invited them *en masse* to rediscover their old friends and comrades.

When he had first read Colm's letter Dick had told himself that it was unrealistic to consider taking the time to journey north.

But even then he had wanted to meet again the men with whom he had shared so much trauma and suffering, as well as camaraderie and cheer. Although he told most things to Ellen, had tried to give her a picture of how his life had been in the Brigade, she could not be expected to fully appreciate what she had not herself experienced.

Unlike Colm.

Or even Roger De Lacy. His old enemy had been specifically mentioned in Colm's letter as having finally settled in Paris.

In a grand apartment, Colm had written, *much finer than my own, although I cannot for the life of me imagine how the fellow can afford it.*

Strange how even enemies, with time, turned into tolerated, even valued acquaintances, or so it seemed. Dick rather looked forward to the idea of meeting Roger again.

How would the fellow take the news that Catherine's daughter had married Dick O'Shaughnessy's son? Would it make Roger scowl – or smile?

But he was running ahead, anticipating a meeting which might never take place. He had not actually decided to go to Paris.

Yet he knew very well that he would do so, that he would write to Colm this very evening, accepting Lord Clare's invitation.

And his work in the meanwhile?

Jimmy can cope with it, Dick thought – with Liam to back him up.

Unbidden, the thought crept into his head: I'm lucky in having Jimmy as a son.

He had forgotten what a pleasure it was to travel on the good roads of France. When – *if* – Jimmy travelled overseas, he thought wryly, he would see the difference between journeying in a country where not only the roads but the canals were the envy of every foreign visitor and what it was like over there. English roads, he had been told, were a disgrace, with the supervision of them given over to unpaid parish officers. And as for the English canals – *they* did not exist!

Jimmy would be surprised!

But there he was, thinking about Jimmy and his ambition again, after telling himself that in going to Paris he was taking a respite from his family.

He found that it was easier to keep his vow to himself once he actually got to Paris. On the surface, the city was as vibrant and stimulating as ever. Outside the Louvre a marionette show was in progress. In the boulevards more people than ever seemed to be drinking coffee and showing off their beautiful clothes for, although it was October already, it was still extremely warm.

The reunion of the Irish Brigade was to take place the following day after which he would have plenty to talk about with old friends. A conversation which would not run out by the end of one evening which was why he planned to spend another week beyond that in Paris. A week in the company of the men of the Brigade would be bound to do him good.

Amongst whom – surely – would be at least one who also had problems with his son, or sons! They would be able to exchange confidences on the subject and, having done so, to laugh the whole thing off as absurd.

Meanwhile, there were his old haunts to visit – a nostalgic stroll in the city to the rue des Carmes, to call in at the Collège des Grassins, although all of the priests he had known there in his youth were either dead or dispersed to other houses.

And after that he retraced a path he and Philip had taken many a time along Boulevard Saint-Michel, past the thermal baths of Lutétia, over the river, and along to Palais-Royal.

As he walked, the memory of Philip was so vivid that it seemed as if the tall, very thin young man who had been

362

his friend was striding along beside him, managing, in spite of his apparent fatigue, to make such good time that Dick had to quicken his steps to keep pace with him.

'War is what matters, Dick,' Philip seemed to be insisting. 'I only went to college to please Maman. But I *must* follow in Papa's footsteps . . .'

But when Dick got to Palais-Royal it was Catherine who was monopolizing the conversation. Catherine as he had first seen her, a tiny goddess in a yellow wrapping-gown, gliding rather than walking towards him, so bewitching in her beauty that he thought of nothing beyond the hope of taking her into his arms.

'Do we *have* to talk about war?' she was saying. 'It's so tedious. So irrelevant . . .'

And Roger De Lacy, his brown eyes burning with jealousy, was assuring Dick that he would take the lady out of his life forever.

In a few days, Dick reminded himself, he would be able to verify how far Roger had moved from his old position of envy and hate.

On that day, around about the time that Dick had reached Port-au-Change, Marie-Geneviève was beginning to put her plan to relieve her husband's business frustrations into good effect.

The first part of this strategy entailed paying a visit to Catherine. Even this called for a plan within a plan. It was essential that she see her mother alone and while she had more than a suspicion that Ellen would not want to accompany her to Saint-André, Biddy, she imagined, would be hurt if she was not invited along.

Biddy thought of herself as Marie-Geneviève's real sister, which was how Marie-Geneviève also thought of her. There were few secrets between them: fond as Marie-Geneviève had grown of Ellen, it was Biddy she most loved in the family, after James – Biddy to whom she had this week confided that a baby was on the way.

But today I'll just have to tell her that it is necessary for me to talk to Maman alone, Marie-Geneviève decided. I'll tell her that she must not ask me questions for the time-being until everything is straightened out . . .

'But it's perfectly all right,' protested Biddy, reaching out for a second piece of the sweet cake Ellen had baked that morning. 'Why shouldn't you see your mother alone? I think it's perfectly natural.'

She had a slightly abstracted air about her, and Marie-Geneviève wondered what could have induced that particular kind of fey elation in someone who, although almost always happy, was usually down-to-earth.

Then Biddy held up a letter and said meaningfully: 'I heard from Ronan today,' and it occurred to Marie-Geneviève that Biddy was just as content staying home with her post as going to Saint-André with her.

She found her mother lying elegantly on an ottoman, eating chocolates and reading a book.

Although most people might have thought that Catherine was looking as attractive as ever, Marie-Geneviève came to the conclusion that her mother was now too fat.

I must persuade her to eat less, she thought – and Biddy as well, or what will Ronan think the next time he sees her?

But meanwhile there is this affair to settle . . .

'Are you on your own?' Catherine asked.

'Yes, so I could talk to you in peace,' said Marie-Geneviève, coming straight to the point. 'Let us have some coffee, Maman. No, I won't have a chocolate, thank you. I want to discuss Papa's business . . .'

So engrossed in this did she become that she omitted to mention to her mother the fact that she was pregnant.

* * *

'Good to be able to discuss our past,' James Mehegan said to Dick.

'Yours is very distinguished.'

'Colonel of a regiment of dragoons? I wonder.'

'My God, man, the king placed you at the head of the regiment of Royal Grenadiers as a result of the action you took at Minden – refusing to sign the terms of capitulation. *And* made you a count, to boot!'

'My brother was far more reputable – far more esteemed in his field. And yet, at forty-five, he was dead.'

In spite of this sombre note Dick was enjoying the reunion immensely.

'Alexander Maguire is here,' James went on. 'Baron of Enniskillen. Did you know that he accompanied Colonel Lally to India in '57 and distinguished himself in the campaign against the British? He's temporarily retired on half-pay.'

'He must have strong views on the appalling injustice that was meted out to Colonel Lally. To accuse him of betraying the interests of the king after fighting so bravely in India was outrageous. To execute him for it, vile beyond belief.'

'He will be exonerated yet. Before his death, I believe, Lally wrote to his son, charging him with the task of doing so.'

It was at that point that Dick saw, over the count's shoulder, Roger De Lacy, leaning nonchalantly against a table, talking to someone else.

So the fellow was here! How long was it again since they had met? Fourteen years? Long enough for Roger to have got rid of his hostile feelings?

'You must talk to Alexander Maguire about it,' said James, 'I believe Voltaire is also on Lally's side. I saw Alexander only a minute ago, over in that corner – '

He turned, looking into the crowd of laughing, chatting

men, clearing the ground between Dick and Roger De Lacy. As if manipulated like a marionette by an unseen hand, Roger also swung around and immediately spotted Dick.

He raised his hand in an ostensibly friendly greeting. But before, on Ile de Ré, he also simulated friendship and later tried to betray me, Dick recalled.

Still, he returned Roger's wave and nodded when the other man mouthed:

'You and I must talk.'

'Dick – there you are!'

Colm O'Neill had seen him and was pushing through the crowd.

'Isn't this a great day? Have you spoken to Lord Clare?'

'Talk on our own,' Roger had insisted when they had ultimately got together in the same group later in the evening.

Which was why Dick was now sitting on a straw-bottomed chair in the boulevard, absently watching the horse carriages and riders pass by, waiting for the man who had once been his enemy and might still be said to fall into that category for all he knew.

After living in the small town of Cognac he found it amazing to see again a street sufficiently wide to permit four carriages to ride abreast, most of them containing beautiful women taking the air and having a good look at the men who had ensconced themselves with cups of coffee under the double avenue of trees.

One of them, saucier than the rest, leaned forward and smiled at him and he rose and bowed to her from the waist. It was good to feel a man!

The lady went on her way and a few minutes afterwards Roger himself appeared, scurrying along the boulevard with a concerned expression on his face.

Like both of them, Dick thought, Roger had grown noticeably older. The dark red hair had faded and was liberally sprinkled with grey and as he drew nearer Dick noticed again that Roger had deep lines running from the corners of his eyes almost to his hairline.

'I'm sorry I'm late,' Roger said. 'The woman who cooks for me – an accident in the kitchen with the soup!' and he gestured with his long elegant hands as if to ask what on earth he could do.

'You needn't apologize. I've been enjoying myself. Coffee?'

'But of course.'

Was he going to launch into another discussion about the Young Chevalier and the lost cause of the Stuarts, as so many of their old comrades had done the night before? Only in Roger's case such a topic would be a red herring as he very obviously had something else on his mind.

Was he going to apologize for his monstrous behaviour in the past – was that why he wanted to get Dick on his own?

I would enjoy that, Dick thought. If Roger says he is sorry for what happened in Barré wood or on Ile de Ré, I will graciously accept his long-overdue apology and slap him on the back to show there is no hard feeling.

Rather to his disappointment, however, Roger did not cringe and beg for forgiveness. He waited instead for his coffee to arrive and when it did he stirred it thoughtfully for a long time before getting down to talking again.

And when he did speak it was of Catherine.

'I gather that her daughter has married your eldest son.'

'Oh, you heard that, did you?'

'From Colm O'Neill. Some time ago now. He said that you and he remain close friends.'

'We do. A good chap,' said Dick, innocent of Colm's past betrayal. 'One of my best and oldest friends.'

But Roger wanted only to talk of Catherine.

'I've never ceased to love her,' he said suddenly, dropping his defences. 'I never married because of her. All those years . . . Is she as beautiful as ever?'

'She's lovely – but hardly slim!' Dick said, grinning.

'And she's happy with this man Marrett?'

'So it would seem. A good fellow.'

'But much older than she, I'm told. How much older, would you say?'

'Fourteen – fifteen years. Something like that. He must be – oh, in his early sixties.'

'And in good health?'

'As far as I'm aware.'

'I always hoped that he would die and leave her a young widow – young enough for her to marry again and have more children. My children . . . Do you think I should write to her?'

What an extraordinary situation, Dick thought. After all these years, Roger, of all people, confiding in me, asking *me* for emotional advice?

But, damnit, the man, by his own admission, has never ceased to love – to worship – Catherine. He was constant, if nothing else.

'Why not? I'm sure her husband wouldn't object to your writing to her. He's an easy-going fellow. I'll give you her address.'

6

Engaging Catherine in serious conversation was a time-consuming affair, Marie-Geneviève discovered meanwhile. In the few months in which she had been living under the same roof as Ellen she had got used to direct questions and answers.

By contrast, Catherine's mind skittered off all over the place so that, having begun to talk about one thing – in this case, the subject which had brought Marie-Geneviève all the way to Saint-André that day – she rapidly moved onto discussing another which had nothing whatsoever to do with the first.

'But you do feel that Papa is over-doing things, that he is in need of a rest?'

'Undoubtedly,' Catherine said, nodding her still-dark head. 'But he has always worked too hard. He loves me so much, you see. He wants to ensure that there will always be sufficient money to enable me to indulge my little extravagances after he is gone. Which reminds me, I am thinking of having a *laiterie* constructed in the garden. There is a most charming one at Chantilly – circular, covered by a dome pierced with round windows. All around are little cascades which fall from porcelain masks and in the middle another spray rises out of a marble table . . .'

With some difficulty Marie-Geneviève succeeded in steering her mother back to the original theme.

'If he is so tired then he must either give up or get some assistance in the business. You say he's eager to make another trip to London?'

'No, darling,' Catherine said. 'He'd much rather stay in Saint-André with me. Although I always hope that I will be able to persuade him to take me to Paris for a *long* visit. Your Papa never wants to stop working for more than a few days at a time. I desperately miss the shops in Paris. Bordeaux and La Rochelle do not compensate in the least for – '

But Marie-Geneviève did not want to talk about the shops.

'I'll have a word with Papa,' she said decisively. 'In fact, I'll go and see him in town this very day.'

The slack in the Irish market having left Liam Crowley with time on his hands he had escorted Marie-Geneviève to Saint-André. She was a good girl, he thought, far better than her mother, of whom he still heartily disapproved.

When, having said goodbye to Catherine, she asked him to take her into Cognac to visit her father his curiosity was aroused.

'It must be an urgent matter, like?'

'It is.'

'I saw your father in town recently,' said Liam, 'I'd say he's working too hard. Not that he's given over for dead. But if he doesn't rest, I said to myself at the time, I wouldn't take a lease of his life.'

This remark, intended to lead into a confiding chat, yielded nothing more than: 'Yes, you're perfectly right.'

And her always so chatty as a rule, Liam thought, defeated.

Something was up. What could be preoccupying the girl to this extent?

She's pregnant, Liam decided. And she hot-footed it off to Saint-André to tell her mother before letting her father have the news of it from herself, as well.

Isn't that a great thing . . .?

To Marie-Geneviève he said only: 'Yes, he's a great worker, your father. He won't come out of that office of his till they take him out in a box.'

'Papa, I want to talk to you,' said Marie-Geneviève when she had kissed him on both cheeks.

'Oh, you do, do you?' John Marrett said, amused by the way his daughter's bottom lip stuck out when she had made up her mind to achieve something. 'Then I suppose I have no alternative but to listen to you.'

He was very pleased with the way his daughter had turned out. A first-rate young woman, he thought, married to the son of a man I respect and like.

'Then sit down, Papa,' she said to him, as if their roles were reversed and she and not he were the parent. 'I have a suggestion to put to you . . .'

Seriously and frankly she outlined what was in her mind. When she stopped talking John Marrett, although he was no longer smiling, nodded his head and thoughtfully rubbed his chin.

'There's something in what you say,' he said. 'But it's not as simple as that. You know nothing of business – or very little.'

'But you don't reject the idea.'

'I do not,' her father said. 'Far from it. It needs further thought, that's all. When did you say James's father is expected to come back?'

Travelling home, Dick mulled over the problems he had been experiencing with James and felt guilty about his defensive attitude towards his son.

The trip to Paris had not only relaxed and invigorated him, but given him a breathing space in which he could review his life and his worries in a broader sense.

In comparison to the misfortunes which had befallen some of the fine men he had known – foremost amongst them, the honest and faithful Lally – he could count himself lucky to face only comparatively minor dilemmas.

As he traversed the miles he moved from considering the background to his worries – the ailing Irish market – to James's suggestions for dealing with them.

Of the two proposals the scheme to sell standard cognac out of Bordeaux appealed to him more than attempting to break into the London market. He knew James was right when he stressed that the Irish community in Bordeaux was growing all the time in numbers and breadth of ventures. Not only were there families from Cork and Limerick living there, the Galweys, connections of his own, the MacCarthys, the Bonfields and the Meades, all of them in general trade, but also people like the Babes and the Byrnes and the Gernons, whose roots were in the Pale.

And as well as Catholic immigrants there were Protestants: the Gledstanes and the Forsters, powerful wine merchants, among that ilk.

Bordeaux could be an exciting town in which to start a branch of the business. Added to which the basis of it was there already: it was only a matter of rekindling it, by offering those customers who had fallen away titillating prices.

Whereas in London where they had, as yet, no basis of a market, they would be starting completely from scratch. Generous as Edmund Burke was, he was also an extremely busy man. Jimmy, in his enthusiasm, might not appreciate that the statesman could not devote all his time to boosting cognac sales, but with the demands that were doubtless being made on Edmund's life these days, whoever went to London might wait days before having the chance to even see him.

But maybe later . . .

Maybe after he – or Jimmy – got started in Bordeaux.

No, not Jimmy, he thought practically and without prejudice towards his son. Not Jimmy, not yet.

I would have to go there myself. Jimmy has the brains and the energy and he may surpass me yet, and good luck to him, but setting up a house to sell standard cognac is a job for the more experienced man.

Jimmy will have to look after the firm in Cognac.

That is, *if* I go.

He was back in the Charente by then, and his high spirits lifted even further as the familiar landscape stretched out before him. Angoulême, Hiersac, Jarnac – he was very nearly home.

He thought he should have called at the office in the rue de la Richonne to talk to James about work, but, instead, rather guiltily, he headed straight for Chez Landart and Ellen.

What would *she* feel about the idea of moving to Bordeaux? he wondered. For a short time – a few years at the most, just to get the business running, after which it would be a job for a younger man.

Or men . . .

George and Bawnie, he thought. Of course. They would be able to do it, if I laid the foundations for them.

If I go to Bordeaux.

Before he had time enough to clarify the Bordeaux scheme in his mind or, having done so, to talk to Ellen about it, Dick had a visit from John Marrett.

'I heard you were expected back,' he said. 'Are you busy or could we have a talk?'

'We can indeed,' Dick said, wishing that he would otherwise have been as occupied as John Marrett inferred, as he had hoped himself he would be, on his return from Paris.

But the Irish market had not taken a miraculous turn.

'I have all the time in the world for you,' he said ruefully. 'Sit down. What's on your mind?'

John did not mention Marie-Geneviève, or James, either. As if it was all his own idea he said: 'Would you be interested in a partnership? I need some of the weight taken off my shoulders, as far as my own business is concerned, and knowing how things are with the Dublin market I thought an *entrée* into London might be of some interest to yourself, and to James.'

'Good God!' said Dick involuntarily. 'Indeed I might be. Although – '

He started to explain to John Marrett the way his own thoughts had gone, on the journey back from Paris.

'I was getting used, in my own mind, to the prospect of moving to Bordeaux for a time. Although that would not necessarily preclude a partnership with yourself.'

'Far from it,' John said.

Marie-Geneviève had not mentioned Bordeaux to her father when she had given him the idea of offering Dick a partnership – it was never in her mind to do so and James himself had thought no further about it.

John, hearing of it for the first time, imagined it originated from Dick.

And Dick is the man who can bring it off, he thought. He has a way with people. The Protestant merchants in Bordeaux form a very close association. The Boyds are married into the Bartons who, in turn, are linked by marriage with the Johnstons. And there is a rumour that John Forster is fond of the daughter of Albert Gledstanes.

But Dick is the most lenient of men and people recognize that quality in him. He will become friendly with the influential Protestant merchants in no time and instead of being squeezed out as a *négociant* doors will open to him.

They began to discuss the possibility of a partnership in detail. James, they decided, would work alongside his father-in-law while George and Bawnie would be taken to Bordeaux on the understanding that they would ultimately stay on there.

'By the time you come back here I would be ready to retire completely,' John said finally. 'By then, if all goes well, you would be in a position to buy me out.'

'If all goes well,' Dick echoed.

But he did not find it in his heart to be even momentarily depressed by the chance of failure. On the contrary, he was confident, from the outset, that the proposed partnership with Catherine's husband would lead only to success.

'A partnership with John Marrett,' Ellen repeated, sounding totally bemused.

But since Dick was more concerned with her reaction to living in Bordeaux for a time than with her feelings about the actual merger, he went on to talk about that.

'I know you love our home, Cognac, having the children near,' he said eagerly. 'But I think you would find Bordeaux an exciting and interesting place to live in for a while. It's a very close-knit colony, and they live very well. You've heard about the carnival balls that are held there. I'm told that the atmosphere is quite different from Nantes which does not have the same sense of being a colony, in spite of the number of Irish families settled there.'

'Although they say there's more money in Nantes,' said Ellen, but in an uncharacteristically vague voice as if she was using that to fill in a gap in the conversation while her thoughts were occupied elsewhere.

How much closer to the Marretts can we get, she was really thinking, meaning – how much nearer, in every way, to Catherine?

At the same time she was adding up the benefits and losses resulting out of the new partnership.

As against the drawback inherent in this proximity was the advantage of living further away from Catherine's clutches.

But against that was the sadness of having to leave Chez Landart, albeit only for a while.

But if they went opportunities would be opened up, not only for the House as a whole, but also for George and Bawnie. They would no longer loll around all day, envying James and feeling resentful towards their father and cross with themselves, for being younger sons.

But then again –

'I would say Biddy would want to stay here,' Ellen said suddenly to Dick. 'She and Marie-Geneviève are so close and Marie-Geneviève will probably want her company all the more now that she's having a baby.'

'And then again Cognac is nearer to Ile d'Oléron than Bordeaux!' Dick pointed out, thinking of Ronan Darcy.

Nevertheless, when Ellen had done her sums she was in favour of the move. Dick was more elated than ever.

Ellen bought calico, newly-arrived from India, to be made into new dresses. Inquiries were made by letter about an office and a house to rent in Bordeaux.

But as the family prepared for the move they could not but be aware of the mounting tension within the country. The harvest had been poor. Scarcity of food led to bread riots. The *parlementaires*, Dick said to Ellen, were exploiting the legend that the dead king had speculated in grain to profit from the distress of his people.

'The people won't believe such tales,' Ellen said to this.

'They loved the king. They've never blamed anyone but the tax collectors for their suffering. The new king is the father of his people, just as *his* father was. I've heard in town that many are writing letters to King Louis, asking him to save them.'

'Much good that will do them,' said Dick cynically. 'By all accounts, the king has less power than the Chevalier d'Eon.'

Changing the subject he added: 'John tells me that Roger De Lacy, no less, is going to spend Christmas with them.'

'That fellow!'

'He's coming to see Catherine, of course. He told me in Paris that he had been in love with her all his life.'

'They deserve each other!' Ellen said before she could stop herself.

Dick raised an eyebrow and then changed the subject again.

Roger, Catherine was thinking, around that time, hugging the name to herself.

Although she knew that she had never been in love with Roger and probably never would be, his loyal affection kept her in good spirits.

Darling John had been so understanding about the sentimental letter which Roger had written to her after he and Dick had crossed paths in Paris.

Not that there was any reason for John to be jealous, but most husbands – say, for instance, Dick himself – would not be so reasonable about the re-emergence in his wife's life of a besotted old flame.

Let alone go along with her suggestion that, as the poor fellow seemed lonely, he should be asked to join them for Christmas and stay on in the house for several weeks.

Still, as well as being rational and wise about love,

John, she thought, rather enjoyed the spicy image he had of her as a *femme fatale*, an attitude which, to her way of thinking, had grown out of his repressed English Protestant background. In turn, she had always found John's shyness both charming and challenging.

How successful we have been, after all, as husband and wife, Catherine said complacently to herself.

She was less self-satisfied when she regarded herself in the mirror. How fat I have become, she thought. How very different I will appear, after all this time, to Roger. When he looks at me again he will be cured of love.

But she did not want Roger to make a speedy recovery from his *maladie* – or even to recuperate from it over a long period.

Surely, she thought, every woman should have in her life a man whose function it is to crave without reward; to suffer unrequited; to reinforce her knowledge that she is deeply loved?

Whose purpose, above all else, is to remind her of her power?

In that sense, Roger, in the past, had played his part to perfection. And since he was still willing to do so he should in no way be encouraged to relinquish the role.

Considering this, Catherine had also been looking at herself in the mirror from every possible angle and feeling no more reassured about her appearance than before. I shall have to deprive myself of food until Roger arrives, she thought sadly. It is already the nineteenth of November. If I do not eat until Christmas – or hardly at all – I will – I will *have* to be slim!

Catherine, Roger thought incessantly, conjuring up her exquisite face as it had been nearly thirty years before.

Thirty years, he thought – can it be so long? Have I really not seen Catherine since 1745?

By the same token he realized that he was expecting to find in Cognac in December the same unblemished beauty that he had worshipped in Paris long ago.

Still he could hope that something of the old Catherine remained. Dick had said she was still lovely. As he travelled down to see her again Roger had forgotten Dick's other comment about Catherine's additional weight.

It was his first visit to the Charente and the piercing sunlight burned into his eyes. How do people live in such luminosity? he wondered, rubbing his eyelids.

Seen from the coach, the landscape was slightly blurred. Lately, of course, his eyesight . . .

But he would not think of such depressing things. It was not as if he was old. As old, say, as Catherine's undoubtedly elderly husband whom shortly he would be forced to meet, who had apparently volunteered to meet him in Cognac and take him to the house on the other side of the river.

Tolerating the fellow was the price he had to pay for being with Catherine, just as he had put up with the dull company of an elderly and fortuitously single uncle who had lived far too long before leaving his nephew enough money to make up for the hours of boredom.

At his request, the coach dropped him in the Place d'Armes where a heavy, silver-haired man was waiting with the appropriate expectant expression on his some-what florid face.

'Monsieur De Lacy?' he inquired. 'I am very pleased indeed to finally make your acquaintance.'

An insincere statement, no doubt. John Marrett was very formal. Very serious.

And yet Roger was left with the distinct impression that Catherine's husband, under his dignified façade, was laughing in his face.

* * *

And finally, there she was.

Roger would never have any inkling of how Catherine had starved herself in the weeks prior to his arrival. As the skirt of her open-fronted *circassienne* was gathered into three large festoons which disguised the lower part of her body completely she need not have gone to such extremes in order to impress Roger.

But she was a determined woman and under the soft, pliant pastel-coloured fabric she was strapped so tightly into her corset it was a wonder that she was actually able to breathe, let alone utter a single word of greeting.

'Roger – how enchanting!' she, just, managed to say, at the same time stretching out a tiny hand towards the visitor.

She's *exactly* the same, Roger marvelled, bowing, and pressing the little hands to his lips. She was not quite the same, of course, but then neither was Roger's eyesight.

'Such a delight – ' Catherine started to enthuse.

But the effort was too much for her. Starvation and lacing had taken their toll.

Ellen would have felt slightly vindicated had she been present to observe what happened next but Ellen and Dick and George and Bawnie were already in Bordeaux.

Roger felt Catherine's hand slide out of his tremulous grip. With a barely audible sigh the woman he had loved for so long folded into the huge festoons of her dress, in a dead faint at his feet.

BOOK FIVE
1785–1789

1

Am I mad? Roger asked himself many a time, as he continued to write to Catherine, to repeat his Christmas visit to Cognac year after year until eleven years had passed since he had first stayed with the Marretts.

And all the time John Marrett, whom Catherine had described in one of her very early letters as feeling rather tired and conscious of his age, remained obstinately hearty and hale.

In his *seventies*, thought Roger crossly, and still going strong while my own life is ebbing away.

Today I am sixty-one!

Pleasingly, a letter had arrived from Catherine wishing him birthday happiness. He reread it eagerly, telling himself that it had indeed been written for altruistic reasons and not because the writer was looking for information about what was going on in Paris, in the boulevards and the shops and the court; asking him if the *opéra* was still moving from one theatre to the other, as it had continued to do for the last four years, since the fire in the hall of the Palais-Royal.

Over the years he had kept her informed about what he felt would interest her, omitting to comment on the latest attempt at reform by the Controller-General or news of renewed fighting between France and Britain, or even of the peace that had been signed at Versailles, but rather titillating her with details of how Queen Marie-Antoinette had been painted for the *Salon* with her hair unpowdered in a simple muslin blouse, and how the *comédie larmoyante* was extolling the virtues of 'back to nature' on the Parisian stage.

This day he had scintillating news to impart to Catherine. He could just imagine her expression – intrigued, eager to hear more – when she read that the queen had been charged with prostitution.

It would never have happened had not Cardinal Rohan found himself out of favour, Roger wrote in his precise, easy-to-decipher script. *Madame de la Motte, with the aid of forged letters, convinced him that all would be well if he pledged his credit to acquire a necklace for the queen. After which she paid a prostitute to dress as the queen and to meet the cardinal after dark in the gardens of Versailles . . .*

It is being whispered all around Paris that Queen Marie-Antoinette then changed her mind about the matter, he had intended to explain to Catherine. Instead, his hand stopped moving – his pen rested on the paper as his mind went over another aspect of his loved one's letter.

Why was it, every time Catherine wrote to him, she found it necessary to mention how well Dick O'Shaughnessy was doing in his business? It was almost as if she was trying to provoke him by emphasizing that the man who had once taken his place in her affections had been, after all, the better choice.

Over the years, without wanting any of it, he had been forced, by reading Catherine's letters, to learn how Dick's Bordeaux business had profited from the transient boom based on the Irish market; how there had been a sharp rise in the speculative brandy market in Bordeaux in the early 1780s; how the O'Shaughnessy-Marrett house in Cognac doubled their profits within the first two years of partnership; how Marrett had allowed himself to be bought out, in order to retire.

Most irritating of all was the information that Dick was

permanently installed in Cognac, leaving his younger sons to run the Bordeaux house, while he worked alongside the eldest one, James.

Dick, living in the Charente, related to Catherine by marriage, could see her frequently.

While he, Roger, waited in Paris for her ageing husband to die.

'*The queen has been discredited, even though she is innocent,*' he wrote. '*The affair cannot be good for France.*'

No more borrowing possible. The Royal treasury almost bankrupt again.

Taxes to hunt, to fish, to keep pigeons in your house.

Riots, seditious assemblies and minor revolts.

Here we are, in 1788, with *Parlement* suspended and rumours of heavier taxes still, Dick thought uneasily.

'And every prospect of a disastrous harvest into the bargain,' he said to Ellen.

It was sometimes difficult to get Ellen to himself, with James and Marie-Geneviève's six children continually under her feet. And later on in the month it would be even worse, since Ronan and Biddy and their three children would be down from Ile d'Oléron.

'It all goes back to the intrigues of the *parlementaires*,' Ellen said. 'They want to create the notion in the king's mind that the privileged classes are revolting against him, so that he will be truly under their power.'

'And to the *noblesses* the peasants do not exist, except for their benefit, so that the taxes which they pay can assist them with their debts,' Dick said, knowing that he was only telling Ellen what she already knew. 'You know what they say – the man who owes two millions is obviously twice as noble as the man who owes only one! But that does not stop them taking from the poor.'

385

'No one will ever be able to say that of us.'

'Ireland taught us classlessness. George said to me the other day that when he went there and looked around at the poverty, the tithes that were exacted on potatoes and country cess and church rates and hearth-money, in spite of the many times he heard the rising demands for reforms, he was acutely aware of that quality at the heart of Irish life – the conviction that, in the eyes of God, every man is equal.'

'It was a good thing that George went to Ireland in the end,' Ellen said with satisfaction. 'He felt that things had improved a lot from our day. Willie said to him that since the Irish qualify as subjects of the Crown these days, we should all consider coming home! The boys, he said, could all enlist in the British army!'

'And give up the powerful business we have built up over here!'

More and more, Dick thought, James was becoming the man responsible for that power. It was James who continued to expand the London market – James who took the unprecedented step of appointing an agent over there – James who recovered their debts when George and Bawnie had dealings with a tiny smuggling partnership in the County Dublin village of Rush, and talked them out of any subsequent rash acts.

The country is in a bad state but we, as a firm, are not, he said to himself and, as a defence against the chaos in the land, he immersed himself in work.

But he could not ignore the weather. Throughout October and November it rained incessantly.

Arc-en-ciel du matin, vent; arc-en-ciel du soir, pluie: rainbow in the morning, wind; rainbow in the evening, rain, went the old Charente saying.

Every evening there was a rainbow in the sky.

One particular evening when he rode down the rue de

la Richonne, Dick saw that the river was no longer green and tranquil in the meagre moonlight, but brown and angry and swollen. Further along, it had burst across its banks. The bloated bodies of small animals floated by, interspersed with débris.

The château is on high ground, thank God, he said to himself. At least we know we're safe from the Charente.

He reminded himself that all was well with the family at Chez Landart, with the business and those who worked in it, if not with the nation and the weather.

And he shivered, with a horrible sense of doom.

2

For John and Catherine the first of December 1788 had started out like any other winter's day, except for the unusually heavy rain.

They had moved back to Crouin the year before, after Catherine had complained about being so far away in Saint-André from her grandchildren, into a house very near the one in which they had started their married life.

And all was well, would be wonderful, Catherine had observed, except that when one looked out of the window at the rain falling one might suspect that the end of the world was imminent.

'Meanwhile, we shall be forced to live in boats – disgusting damp things,' she said from the depths of their bronze-green bed, with its painted and gilded headboard.

Catherine was very proud of their bed. Its canopy was draped with gold and green taffeta, as were the valances, and they were all finished off with gold and green fringes.

An appropriately decorative bed for an unusually beautiful woman, John sometimes said. But, this morning, all that he could see of the woman was the top of her head and her dark eyes peering at him over the stitched coverlet.

'You're obviously going to take refuge in there for some time,' he said, pulling on his black velvet breeches and fastening them with a ribbon. 'But I have to have some fresh air.'

'Fresh air!' the slightly muffled voice said from beneath the coverlet. 'I have never understood your passion for it. You are quite mad to go out on such a morning.'

'Maybe,' said John lightly. 'But you won't change me at this stage of my life.'

He bent over and kissed the top of her head.

'Stay warm, my darling. I promise I won't be long.'

In a few minutes he was striding towards Jarnouzeau on the bank of the swollen river. He had always enjoyed the curiously liberating sensation of walking or riding in the rain, his senses responding to the smell and feel and taste of it. The soft Charente rain seemed to him a misty barrier between other men and himself as if he, and not they, were cordoned off, at such times, and free to roam in the natural world.

But this rain, he had to admit, was different. The barrier was an impenetrable wall stretching all the way to Heaven and instead of feeling singled out and privileged he imagined himself isolated from his fellow men, they, not he, the lucky ones.

You're being fanciful and morose, he reproved himself. Old age is finally catching up with you. Senility, my old boy, is putting notions into your head.

Still, the rain was unusually heavy and by the look of the land and the river it had continued to fall incessantly throughout the night, showing no signs of easing off this morning.

Perhaps, as Catherine had said, he had been crazy to consider venturing out. No one else seemed to be doing so. All he could see in the way of life was a miserable and drenched horse huddling under a dripping poplar tree and two resentful cows which stared at him out of their great dark eyes as he strode past their field.

He was used to long walks, had taken what he called his morning constitutional every day since he had retired. But with the rain beginning to soak through his tricorne hat he decided, when he had gone no more than a mile and a half, to turn back. All of a sudden the canopied bed and the woman who had remained in it were more than ever an irresistible combination.

He was not sure what impelled him, at that particular moment, to look at the river. It was certainly not that he was drawn to contemplate its beauty for the Charente, normally so tranquil, at its most sportive a river which overflowed its banks only to add richness to the harvest or to permit the fishermen to catch trout and pike the more easily, was looking most unattractive, a muddy and murky receptacle for the ever-falling rain.

But look he did, and was instantly moved to pity.

Drifting towards him, desperately clinging to a tiny floating island made up of disintegrating tangled grasses and mud, was a scrawny black cat with a pathetic litter of kittens which, even in this precarious situation, were blindly attempting to suck.

A wild cat? It was hard to see clearly in the rain. If the creature was wild then any attempts he might make to save her could be fiercely repulsed and he could end up severely bitten for his pains.

But he was a kind man with a great love for animals and the plight of the cat and her kittens touched him. Their island home was quite close to the shore. As it came closer John splattered into the water stretching out a strong, blue-veined hand to grab at the drifting grasses.

He succeeded in arresting the path of the floating island. The black cat spat at him ungratefully, revealing two ridiculously long molars, her green eyes huge with fear.

'You're all right,' John said soothingly. 'I've got you – '

With a colossal effort he pushed the grassy island out of the water onto the edge of the bank.

It was a costly effort. Too costly. In making it, he lost his own balance and with a resounding splash fell sideways into the water.

Spluttering, he reached out with his left hand and felt it touch ground. Though the river tugged at his big body as if to insist that it required an alternative victim to the rescued black cat and her babies, it did not have its way. Somehow, he had swung most of his considerable weight back onto the bank, was rolling over onto his stomach in a most undignified way, hearing himself gulp and gasp for breath.

He was not sure how long he lay there, with the rain pelting down on him. Five minutes? Half an hour? Long enough, anyway, for the black cat to have taken her babies to a place of greater safety.

He sat up, looking for his black tricorne hat. But that, too, was gone, presumably lost in the river. The rain, in a sadistic frenzy, beat down on his grey head.

What on earth would Catherine say about his wet and muddied appearance? he wondered vaguely. After all, how wise she had been in staying in their warm bed this day.

Catherine, he thought wistfully. Their house in Crouin seemed very much further away from him than a mere mile and a half.

He wondered if he could walk that far.

But I must, he thought. I *must* go home to Catherine . . .

Soaked to the skin, shivering, he slowly set out.

'John, what on earth has happened to you? Come back to bed at once! Or, no, perhaps a hot tub – *Mon Dieu*, why did you have to go out? You're trembling all over . . .'

Before he knew it, John had been soaked in warm water, rubbed dry and put back into his night-shirt.

'I'm well,' he protested, and sneezed.

'You're not. You are to stay in bed all day.'

391

But staying in bed did not help. By six o'clock John had a pain in his chest and a headache and by ten a high fever.

'Your chest is all blocked up. Listen to your breathing,' Catherine said, concerned.

John had always been exceptionally fit and she sometimes found it hard to believe that he was more than a dozen years older than Dick. During their marriage she could not recollect one occasion on which he had been taken seriously ill.

And now here he was breathing so rapidly that she was frightened by that symptom alone. He was also coughing up a thick rusty sputum.

Added to which he was ashen pale.

'Stop fussing and try to get some rest yourself,' he said to her, and then gasped for breath again.

Even then Catherine knew it would be a long time before she had a restful night's sleep again.

The first James knew of his father-in-law's illness was three days later when he paid a call at the house in Crouin.

He found Catherine distraught and almost unrecognizable, with unkempt hair and dark shadows under her reddened eyes.

The story of John's tumble in the river and subsequent chill was quickly told. Looking grave, James heard that the older man's condition seemed to be getting worse.

'James, it is as if he has an abscess in here,' Catherine said anxiously, putting her hand on her breast. 'So much mucus is coming out.'

'Perhaps it's just the illness taking its course,' James said, trying to reassure her. 'It may be that he has to find a way to fight it.'

Catherine's eyes welled up with tears.

'I wish it was that,' she whispered. 'Peep in at him and tell me if you really believe that's so.'

James did as she asked.

'You see?' Catherine said afterwards. 'You see? Now can you really believe that he is able to fight it?'

Unwilling to answer truthfully, James put his arm around her.

'Liam Crowley is with me,' he said. 'I'll stay with you and I'll get him to go to Chez Landart and fetch Marie-Geneviève. That will make you feel better.'

My poor wife, he thought. The minute she gets here she will realize that her father is going to die.

Within two days it was over. On the evening of John's death James and Marie-Geneviève sat up talking for most of the night. Upstairs, Catherine, exhausted from weeping, had finally fallen asleep.

'We can't leave her,' Marie-Geneviève said. 'She depended totally on Papa. And it has been such a terrible shock.'

'Do you think if we were to stay with her for a week or two it would help?' James wanted to know.

'A little. But afterwards we would have to go home. We can't leave the children indefinitely with your Maman and we can't bring them to live in this house, even for a while. It was not designed for a large family! Maman would find it difficult to cope with all of them at the best of times, but now – '

'There's no question of that,' James said, his mind ticking over. 'And why should the children be asked to leave their own home – our home? We would all be very unhappy away from Chez Landart. No, the answer is not for us to move in with your Maman but for her to make a home with us at the château. There is plenty of room there.'

'Perhaps *your* Maman would object,' Marie-Geneviève said. 'We should ask her.'

'*I'll* talk to her,' said James decisively.

These days, what James O'Shaughnessy decided counted not only in the business world but also in the house.

That dear, good man John Marrett gone, Ellen was thinking when James accosted her and suggested that Catherine be invited to live in the house.

She was preparing to attend John's funeral and she was putting on her black calash as James, without preliminaries, came out with this astonishing proposal.

Ellen reached for the nearest chair and sat down on it abruptly, holding onto her cane hood with her left hand and hoping that it was concealing her expression from her son.

'She's in a very bad state,' James, working on her sympathy, carried on. 'Marie-Geneviève tells me that she's worried sick about her mother. Well, Maman, what do you say?'

'You've caught me by surprise,' said Ellen, playing for time.

She fiddled with the lace trimming around the front edge of the calash and tied the bow under her chin, aware of James's gathering impatience.

'Well?'

'How long would you want her to stay?'

'Forever. Of course,' James said. 'It would be cruel to have her here for a few months and then send her back to an empty house. You wouldn't want that, would you, Maman?'

I might, Ellen thought. I'm not nearly as nice as you imagine.

Or as kind as you're forcing me to be . . .

'I'll have to speak to your father,' she said, as a last resort. 'After all, it's his home, James, as well as yours and mine.'

'Oh, *Papa* won't mind,' said James, turning towards the door. 'He always fits in with your wishes in matters relating to the house and he will want to take care of Catherine. So that will be all right. I must get ready, Maman, and go back to Crouin – '

'Wait!' Ellen called after him. 'I haven't – '

Wasted words. James was gone, convinced in his own mind that Catherine was welcome in the house.

As a result of this Ellen found herself at John's funeral nurturing uncharitable thoughts not only about Catherine but also about James who, as well as being an exceptional son, was extremely bossy and manipulative when it suited him to be so. So his mother concluded.

Why did I let him outmanoeuvre me like that? she thought, looking away from the sight of Catherine at the graveside shaking with grief, huddling against her daughter.

But how could I have wriggled out of allowing the woman into the house, except by telling James about her relationship with his father, and that I could not do?

I did not even get time to talk to Dick before the die was cast because, by the time I got downstairs after dressing, James had made a general announcement that Catherine was coming to stay.

That very day, no less, after they had all gone back to Crouin with her to help her pack her things.

At that point, Catherine, in Ellen's opinion, behaved very strangely indeed.

'I want all your father's clothes and personal posses-sions to be taken away this minute and burnt,' she said to Marie-Geneviève as if the poor child was not upset enough without being given this gruesome task. 'Here are his shoes. And his high boots. And his rings – No, don't try to burn his rings. Give them to James.'

'Maman, getting rid of all these things won't take the pain away,' Marie-Geneviève said tearfully. 'I know that's why you're doing this but, believe me, it won't make any difference and you'll just tire yourself out. Why don't you just leave everything and come away to Chez Landart?'

'No, it must be done now,' insisted Catherine, holding a pile of frilled shirts and drawers in one hand and her dead husband's cape in another.

'Of course, I won't burn them,' Marie-Geneviève whispered to Ellen afterwards. 'I'll give them to those in need, except for Papa's gold watch-fob which I'm going to keep.'

How typical of Marie-Geneviève to think of the poor and needy, Ellen thought – and of Catherine not to consider the plight of anyone else.

It was disquieting to wake in your own home to the realization that your enemy was sleeping within its portals.

Or not sleeping. According to Marie-Geneviève, her mother spent night after night awake.

'She looks worn out,' Dick observed, an unfortunate remark, indicating over-concern, to make to a jealous woman.

'She always was a great actress,' Ellen said tartly, there being occasions when her own lack of histrionic ability let her down with a bump.

'It's unlike you not to show compassion,' said Dick mildly, and went into the garden to amuse his youngest grandchild.

On the whole, Ellen had to admit, Dick did not pay any particular attention to Catherine. One might have thought, almost, that he was avoiding her, or at least dodging her expressions of grief, as if he was unsure how to cope with their apparent intensity.

And, if she was to be truly honest with herself, Catherine was not being objectionable, was not making up to Dick. On the contrary, she was uncharacteristically reticent, seeming to be in a dark world of her own. When spoken to, she did not always react immediately, or even seem to hear. Quite often, those who addressed a remark to her had to repeat it once or even twice before Catherine, with a little shake of her head, finally responded.

And then there was that night when Ellen, waking well after midnight, found that Dick was missing from their bed.

Catherine, she thought instantly. And her old hatred came rushing back in a flood, all the stronger in the darkness, so that she wrenched open the bedroom door and rushed into the corridor expecting, even at this late stage in their lives, that she would ultimately discover Dick and Catherine in bed.

Instead, she chanced upon a cacophony of grief from two alternative sources. In one room she found her husband holding in his arms, not his mistress, but a sobbing baby, woken from a dream.

'Poor little fellow,' mouthed the adoring grandfather, over the baby's head.

Moved by the sight of the pair of them and thoroughly ashamed of her suspicions, Ellen resettled the baby into a more comfortable position in Dick's arms, and stroked his blond head.

'That's better, isn't it?'

With a sniff and a gulp the baby relapsed into sleep. Ellen went silently out of the room, leaving Dick to settle the child in his bed, and closed the door soundlessly.

That was when she heard the sound from Catherine's room.

The barely audible weeping of a mourning woman who believes she cannot be heard.

The cry of an unhappy, lonely woman for her dead husband to return.

Moved to compassion in spite of herself, Ellen stood hesitating outside Catherine's door, wondering if, after all, she should not knock and go in to offer consolation.

Then Dick crept out of the baby's room and turned to pull the door to behind him. Remembering the past, Ellen went on.

And in the morning she found that she had again steeled herself to resist any show of softness in Catherine, recalling the lack of leniency shown by Catherine when the advantage had been hers.

Meanwhile, Christmas was fast approaching. In her grief, Catherine had forgotten all about Roger De Lacy's annual visit. Others in the château were aware of his arrangement with the Marretts in a vague kind of way but, with one thing and another, it had faded from their minds.

But, to Roger, his pilgrimage to Cognac to see Catherine was of elemental importance.

There were those who said that the Faubourg-Saint-Germain had lost its character since so many large mansions had been constructed around Grenelle, but Roger De Lacy did not share their views. The addition of the mansions, he maintained to those who thought differently, gave the area an incredible and pleasing unity, as well as an air of elegance.

It might have been pointed out, and probably was on a number of occasions, that Roger himself rented an apartment in the boulevard and, under those circumstances, could hardly have been expected to express any other opinion.

Grenelle was certainly fashionable, which always counted with Roger. He was sure that Catherine would approve of it, and enjoy staying there with him one day.

The dream that she would ultimately do so sustained him from year to year. As he grew older, it became more and more obsessive – an unrealized ambition, an aspiration equivalent to other men's would-be military or commercial successes. Younger passers-by in the boulevard who scorned the visions of the elderly would have been astonished had they been able to enter the mind of the thin, grey-haired man who could be seen, from time to time, gazing at the Fontaine des Quatres Saisons, or contemplating the risqué décor of a certain house in the rue de Varenne where a scandalous courtesan was known to have her home.

Of that saucy lady other men fantasized: Roger dreamed of Catherine, dining with him, riding in a carriage beside him, sharing his bed at night.

That year, as he prepared for his journey to the Charente, his dreams were more vivid, more erotic than ever, the unconscious expression of an unrealized desire, a visual fallacy which, for a long time, had made his life worthwhile.

'Will you see Dick O'Shaughnessy in Cognac?' Colm O'Neill, with whom he maintained acquaintance, asked him.

'I doubt it. I haven't done so on my previous visits.'

'Pity to lose touch,' Colm said, for, in spite of what he had done to Dick, he was fond of him. 'I suppose he feels, as we all do, that the days of the Brigade are numbered now that Irish Catholics can enlist in the British army. It means the end of Ireland's loyalty to the Stuart cause, Roger. A sad state of affairs.'

'But realistic,' Roger said.

His hidden dreams would have startled Colm, too.

Buoyed by them, he arrived in the Charente shortly after the rains had ceased. The countryside, he noted, was sodden and still sorry for itself. In Angoulême, where he stopped for the night, the inn smelt strongly of damp.

As always, he had written in advance to confirm his date of arrival to Catherine. He had not been particularly concerned by her failure to write back to him. He presumed that she had done so, that her letter had gone astray as letters sometimes did. She was too precise, too mannerly not to have answered him. He had no way of knowing that Catherine, in her mourning, had not registered its arrival in her mind.

He was surprised when, fulfilling their customary arrangement, John Marrett was not waiting for him in the Place d'Armes as he stepped out of the coach. He stood around for the best part of an hour in the expectation that John would arrive, that he had been only temporarily delayed. When no one came to fetch him he testily hired a carriage to take him to Crouin, sure, by then, that it was his own letter which had gone astray in the post.

But, in that case, why had not Catherine, in her fastidious way, been aware of its absence and written, instead, to him?

Put out by the inference that, after all, she had not cared enough about him to have made inquiries about his dates, he began to wonder whether or not the Marretts would be expecting him.

What if they were not at home? His heart sank, envisaging a situation where John and Catherine had actually gone away for Christmas, perhaps to Bordeaux or La Rochelle.

Perhaps – this was a dreadful thought after his long

400

journey – perhaps John had taken Catherine on a shopping trip to Paris. Even now, for all he knew, the two of them could be knocking on his own door, hoping to surprise him.

Well, he thought ruefully, I will find the answer to that when I knock on *their* door, and proceeded to do so loudly.

After a lengthy and unnerving pause the door was thrown open by the hefty woman whom he remembered was Catherine's maid.

'Monsieur?'

She sounded puzzled. She did not look as if she had been expecting him. He sighed inwardly, anticipating a sojourn overnight in an inn and a journey back from whence he had come, beginning on the morrow.

Perhaps, on the way, passing John and Catherine, coming back.

Their coaches crossing, missing each other . . .

That would be my luck, he thought, immersed in self-pity.

Aloud he said: 'You knew I was coming?'

'Oh no!' the maid said, apparently shocked. 'Madame did not say.'

'She's here – at home?'

'But no,' said the maid again.

She paused momentarily, as if to collect her thoughts. Then: 'You have come from Paris, monsieur? Then perhaps you did not hear that Monsieur Marrett is dead?'

'Dead?' Roger repeated. 'John is – dead?'

It was just as well for the plump maid's peace of mind that *she* could not decipher his thoughts.

'*Who* is here?'

'Monsieur De Lacy – to see Madame Marrett,' Brigitte said, impressed.

Another suitor, she thought. At her age – and so soon after her husband's death. But then Madame Marrett – even now you could see it – was always attractive to men. It was too bad that she should have taken her husband's death so badly, spending hours sitting up in her bedroom with tears in her eyes gazing mournfully out of the window. Attempts to cheer her up – to remind her that, after all, his soul had gone to Heaven and they would be reunited later on, had so far lamentably failed.

'You had better show Mr De Lacy in,' said Ellen just as Brigitte, in her imagination, was marrying Catherine off to this thin, well-dressed suitor.

How like Catherine to encourage Roger De Lacy to come calling so soon after John's death, Ellen thought. Much as she disliked the thought of him, she was pleased about his arrival. She, too, toyed with the pleasing image of a marriage between Roger and Catherine – her old enemy plucked up and transferred to a Parisian apartment, living well out of the way, instead of right inside her house.

Roger, it was true, had an unpleasant reputation but was he any more than Catherine herself deserved?

What a sneaky face he has, Ellen thought, the minute Roger walked into the room.

He bowed low as a preliminary to kissing Ellen's hand and told her that he had heard a great deal about her.

'And I about you!' said Ellen in a voice that left no doubt in his mind of the nature of what she had heard.

'Who?' Catherine asked in a faraway voice, as if she had never in her whole life laid eyes on Roger De Lacy.

'You know,' said Ellen, disconcerted by Catherine's confused and aberrant attitude, so much at variance with her usual determined approach.

Maybe Dick was right when he insisted that Catherine

was suffering from shock. To her annoyance, Ellen found that she was feeling sorry for the woman she disliked.

'Roger De Lacy,' she repeated crossly, more exasperated, at that moment, with herself than anyone else.

She was actually fighting off an infuriating and incomprehensible impulse to put her arms around Catherine, to tell her that, one day, she *would* be happy again, even thinking of John.

What is the matter with me all of a sudden? Ellen asked herself when she had resisted this light-minded vagary. *I* must be suffering from shock.

'Roger,' Catherine said softly.

And then, like a pretty little bird shaking itself after a bath, she seemed to quiver and to return briefly to life.

'I won't see him,' Catherine said, looking up.

The big dark eyes were quite resolute.

'But he's waiting downstairs,' Ellen stressed. 'He's come all the way from Paris to see you, as he does every Christmas.'

'I won't see him,' said Catherine again. 'I don't want to see anyone at the moment but the family. I want to be with you and Dick and James and Marie-Geneviève and the children. Otherwise I need to be up in this room, remembering my wonderful life with John. *You* understand that, Ellen. You know what it's like to love.'

It was almost impossible to suspect her sincerity. But –

This is Catherine? Ellen said to herself.

And meanwhile, there was Roger De Lacy, waiting downstairs.

Roger De Lacy, who could, with luck, who wanted, surely, to take Catherine out of her house and life . . .

'But what shall I tell Roger De Lacy?' Ellen asked. 'Shall I suggest he stays at an inn and that the two of you meet tomorrow – or in a few days?'

Catherine looked surprised.

'Oh, no, Ellen,' she said clearly. 'I won't see him at all this Christmas. *Tell him to go away.*'

'Back to Paris without even being able to pay my condolences – without seeing her?' Roger asked, hurt and perplexed.

He was like a whipped dog, Ellen thought, an ageing Red Setter cast out from his master's house on a freezing winter's night.

'She's not in a state to see anyone now. Perhaps later on. Next year . . .'

'Back to Paris . . .' Roger muttered sadly.

And why not? said Ellen to herself. What else does he deserve but to put up at an inn in Cognac for the night and then off with him, back to Paris, out of everyone's life?

(But, hopefully, not, for always, out of Catherine's . . .)

Outside, a cold wind was blowing up from the river. In a short time Dick and James would be home.

'Not to see her at all,' said Roger, the dog lashed by the whip again.

'If you want to stay one night with us you're welcome,' Ellen heard herself say.

Dick, after all, might enjoy talking to the wretched man about the Brigade and times past.

And *then* he could go away.

Not to see her, Roger thought, tormented. To lie so near to her and not to be even able to look upon her face.

Like Catherine, who was sleeping so intermittently, he too, did not sleep well that night.

Waking at five after a brief slumber he was still half dreaming.

Thinking –

404

Maybe in time.
Perhaps next year.
When she has recovered from this experience.
Then she can be mine.

3

The rain, which had wrought such tragedy in the lives of
Catherine and Marie-Geneviève, had no adverse effect
whatsoever on the cognac market.

It was the weather of the first part of 1788 which, at the
end of that year, was concerning Dick and James, the fact
that it had been so cold then that the wine had frozen in
the cellars so that, all year round, distillers had complained about its poor quality.

With demand from England for cognac on the increase
since the introduction of the treaty which allowed free
trade, the euphoria that this induced was always tempered
by the nightmare vision of a future in which they ran short
of quality stock.

Nevertheless, James, in his pioneering way, decided to
travel to Sweden, Denmark, Prussia and Holland, following up introductions which could lead to additional orders.

Once he had set off to embark upon the *Bailly d'Aulan*,
which was loading for Gothenburg, Dick became more
immersed in work than ever. Marie-Geneviève was
already so involved with her children's lives, Ellen
thought, that she seemed hardly to notice that James was
not only absent from the château, but from the country.

Instead of the company of these two beloved people
Ellen found herself spending time with Catherine that
New Year.

Whether it was because she could weep no longer or
because she was driven by cold draughts to drift down to
the ground floor from her bedroom, Ellen did not know

but there Catherine was, dressed elegantly in black, sitting on a sofa, ready to chat.

What Catherine most wanted to do was to reminisce about their girlhood, beginning not with their first unfortunate encounter but with the – to Ellen – equally forgettable journey they had taken together from Paris to Cognac, and their early days in the Charente.

'You remember how we stopped at the cathedral of Saint-Pierre?' she would ask. 'Do you remember lighting a candle?' Or: 'Our wrapping-gowns, Ellen – you had one the colour of your eyes.'

And Ellen, who recalled squabbles and attempts, on Catherine's part, to be all-powerful, to make a mock of herself, answered noncommittally, saying: 'Yes.' or 'Did we really?' not quite snubbing Catherine, but hardly, she told herself, encouraging the creature to talk.

So how did it happen, she asked herself, that she still got drawn into Catherine's conversations?

Worse than that, she was actually beginning to enjoy them!

When Catherine caught a severe cold and was confined to bed Ellen, to her embarrassment, found that she was missing their little talks.

On the first day of Catherine's illness Ellen wandered out into the garden. Marie-Geneviève was in town with four of the children, Charles and Maurice having gone back to Douai college after the Christmas holidays, as their father and uncles had done before them.

It was because of the absence of her husband and daughter-in-law that she felt unfriended and forlorn this day – and because the children were not around to enliven a dark wintry morning.

That was behind her desolation. It could have nothing to do with Catherine . . . Naturally not.

When Marie-Geneviève returned, they ate together

after which Marie-Geneviève went into her room to write a letter to James, and Ellen, as she had often done before, took some sewing and prepared to settle down with the children.

For the first half-hour little Hélène and André and François and Pauline-Félicité behaved as if they did not mind that it was raining again, and that they were confined to the house. But after that somebody – François said it was Hélène and Hélène accused André – picked a quarrel and a wordy warfare ensued.

Ellen dispersed them with a few sharp words of her own, and decided that, much as she loved her grand-children, a wet afternoon in their company was not conversationally rewarding.

'But it *was* Hélène,' François essayed again, after a few minutes.

'Nobody ever brought peace but the woman who hadn't got it,' Ellen said, and went back to her side of the house.

Later that day she found herself carrying a tray up to Catherine's room.

She knocked on the door and, receiving no answer, she turned the latch and went in.

Catherine was asleep, as dainty and as neat in her unconscious condition as she was when she was awake. On the bed beside her a book lay face upwards, open at the page Catherine must have been reading before she had nodded off.

. . . *each is made for the other,* Ellen read, *each being is intimately related to the other beings . . .*

Voltaire's selfless philosophy which could not be expected to make any great impression upon such as Catherine!

'Mm?' Catherine murmured and Ellen supposed that she had woken up.

'I've brought you some food,' she started to say, wondering what had foolishly impelled her to be so altruistic.

Catherine did not say: 'Thank you,' or even sit up in bed.

'Mm,' she murmured again and then: 'I took after her. I was always much more like her in every way than Maman,' and Ellen realized that Catherine was still fast asleep.

What on earth was she talking about? Dreaming about?

And what in Heaven's name was *she* doing in the room, catching Catherine's cold . . .?

Then Catherine said something else and there was a funny little catch in her voice as if, once again, she was about to cry.

But not because of John.

'Oh, Ellen,' she said, in the confiding way she had been talking to Ellen of late. 'I wish I had known her. I wish she had not died.'

At Easter, Charles and Maurice came home from Douai by coach bringing tidings of bands of armed brigands roaming the countryside, terrorizing travellers and making demands for money and food.

'They stopped your coach?' Marie-Geneviève asked, her heart in her mouth, thinking of her sons.

'Not exactly,' Charles admitted. 'But we heard of others who had been stopped.'

'And a man at Angoulême got badly beaten up,' interjected Maurice. 'It may not be safe for us to return to school this year.'

Was that all there was to it, Marie-Geneviève wondered a boyish excuse to play truant from school or a true report of the facts?

Ellen said it was both, that in parts of the country

people were rioting for bread again: 'It can only get worse. You know yourself that the bad time, after the harvest like last year's, is the summer. Already there is just not enough produce left to feed people and we're months away from the new harvest.'

Dick nodded: 'There are disturbances in almost every part of the country already, Marie-Geneviève. You would get a good idea of the position if you watched how cargo is being moved on the Charente. Every town and province is trying to protect itself from starvation by purchasing grain.'

'But I've heard that grain is being exported,' Marie-Geneviève said, bewildered. 'How can that be true?'

'It's not. There's a false rumour in circulation that those who have a monopoly on grain are sending it abroad to create a shortage and increase their own profits but if you think about it, naturally it does not make sense.'

'Desperate people *don't* think,' said Marie-Geneviève, sounding desperate herself. 'All their energy goes into scavenging for food.'

'So the convoys of grain are being attacked by brigands, or hungry men, depending on how you look at them. Half the country is unemployed now and country people are pouring into the cities in search of work that isn't there. God knows where it will end.'

I wish James was home, Marie-Geneviève thought. will keep the boys with me in the meantime and whe James returns I will dissuade him from letting them trave again.

Roger, in Paris, thought not of the starving and the ang but only of the beauty in that city and, of course, Catherine.

Throughout the winter he had continued to write her. Her letters, concise, polite, had nonetheless appall

410

him, being devoid of Catherine's customary curiosity and fun. They were lifeless letters, written by a woman who seemed to wish for death herself.

He could only conclude that she was missing John Marrett so much that she was sunk in despair, a thought that did not please him.

For years he had regarded John as a token husband, a much older spouse whom Catherine had acquired, out of convenience, at a time when more eligible and more attractive young men – himself, for instance – had been taken out of her orbit by their duty in the Brigade.

He had, rather, been jealous of Catherine's interest in Dick O'Shaughnessy without ever understanding what had terminated their romance.

Now, to his annoyance, he found himself having to re-appraise Catherine's relationship with John. She appeared to have loved the man – or to have leaned upon him, most likely the latter. Had got used to the fellow, and was having difficulty in re-adjusting to life on her own.

Although since she was staying with the O'Shaughnessys, she was not technically alone. It would have been far more sensible, he thought – far better for his own case – had she stayed in Crouin, in a familiar terrain with trusted servants to see to her wants instead of allowing herself to be transplanted into alien and therefore disturbing surroundings at Chez Landart.

That compounded her unhappiness.

Made her unreasonable, which was why she had sent him away.

But, in April, Roger detected the first signs that Catherine, instead of resigning herself to death, was considering returning to life.

Her letters – he wrote to her twice a week; she replied almost immediately – became not exactly frivolous but indicative of a renewed interest in Parisian life.

The philosophical salon *that you told me Madame Necker founded, does it still exist?* she wrote, and *You used to tell me, Roger, that* she *was the power behind her husband all along.*

Good, encouraging portents, Roger thought. He wrote back eagerly, with all the gossip he could accumulate, making it appear as interesting, as enticing as possible in order to lure Catherine to Paris. He had a fine facility with words and he built up a vivid picture of life in the capital, the stimulating discussions, the new philosophies that came out of the *salons*; the surmise expressed in the cafés; the intrigues that permeated out of court circles – all of these things he related as if he had been present on each and every occasion instead of, all too often, on his own at home.

He was basically a lonely, even pathetic figure, but no one would have guessed it from the picture of his life that he presented in his letters.

And he was selective in his *reportage*: no one, certainly not a woman who had been out of Paris for a considerable time and who, in any case, liked only to look upon the glamorous side of life, would have thought, from Roger's letters, that there was an ugly aspect to the beautiful city. In the vision of Paris which Roger conjured up for Catherine there *were* no starving people; the populace had not been expanded by the hungry influx from the country; the city did not smell.

Roger did his best not to disturb his own sensibilities with unwholesome, disturbing thoughts and he had no intention of worrying Catherine with them.

For why should she, of all people, subject herself to any situation which reeked, even slightly, of squalor?

If she suspected that Paris could be grim – could be dangerous – then she might not want to come.

* * *

Many months had elapsed since Catherine had been back to her own house. In her absence the same servants had cleaned and dusted and polished the interior; the same gardener had toiled away outside. Everyone knew that Catherine would not return to live in Crouin and it was now time to tie up the loose ends, to arrange the sale of the house and to help the servants find jobs elsewhere.

'Come with me,' Catherine pleaded with Ellen. 'I don't want to go into the house on my own.'

The big dark eyes, not in the least faded, looked up into Ellen's green eyes. Catherine's fear of facing the void left by her husband's death was reflected in her eyes and Ellen once again found herself softening towards her.

'I need to go into town today anyway,' she said, in case Catherine noticed that she was weakening and took advantage of her kindness, 'so it won't be too much out of my way to go to your house.'

As Catherine said on the way, Dick and Ellen had seldom visited the Marretts' home: most family celebrations had been held at Chez Landart.

'So you have hardly seen my beautiful things,' Catherine said. 'Now they will all have to be packed up and taken to the château.'

This was what Ellen had known would happen sooner or later, but now that Catherine had put it into words she liked the sound of it even less.

Catherine stamping her personality on the château. Catherine introducing into her rooms the ornaments which clashed with Ellen's own taste.

This is a country house, not a palace, she had said to Catherine in the days when they were both hoping to marry Dick and putting forward their ideas on interior decoration.

And Catherine had spoken of luxury and opulence and

said that Dick, she was sure, would like to live in a modicum of style.

She will impose that mannered elegance upon my home, Ellen thought. How intrusive that will be.

And in that imposition she will challenge me once again, diminish me by making mock of my taste, by making it seem, by contrast, crude.

All this she thought as Catherine, after she had been welcomed warmly by her servants, began to show Ellen around the house, drawing her attention to a wooden table with a parquet top, representing flowers, to a wall framed in gilded borders, to Venetian brocade cushions and bedrooms gilded and painted and hung with satin curtains exquisitely corded with silk.

All the same, she continued, out of politeness, to follow Catherine from room to room until the latter, in a small, remote voice said: 'This was our bedroom,' and slowly opened a door.

There was the big bronze-green bed, its feet carved to represent eagles' claws, the canopy draped with gold and green, the gold and green valances.

'Such a pretty room,' Catherine said softly. 'I always loved the folding-screen. It came from the East. And look, Ellen, this looking-glass has a frame of walnut wood – isn't it attractive?'

In that very bed long ago, Ellen thought, did you and Dick make love?

When John was away in La Rochelle or in London did you lead my husband upstairs to this room?

When did your *affaire* with Dick begin and end?

What was there between you?

It shouldn't matter any more, said common sense. Whatever there was between them, it was terminated, resolved in *your* favour . . . Why torture yourself with what happened in the past?

But now the past and the present were colliding, that convergence being epitomized in the bronze-green bed that was draped in green and gold. The bed itself, along with Catherine's other possessions, was being moved into Ellen's home.

And afterwards Catherine, already showing signs that widowhood was not quite as unbearable as it had been, would – surely – begin to reassert herself; would revert to being her old inimical self.

'This flowered satin cushion has a violet background – such a pretty contrast,' Catherine was saying.

And Ellen was thinking: I don't want her in my home for ever.

Perhaps I will feel sorry for her again, quite soon.

Perhaps, of late, we have shared a kind of friendship.

Perhaps I have enjoyed her company more than I could have imagined.

But, deep down, I have not forgiven her.

Admit it, urged her inner self. No matter how close you get to Catherine on occasions, you are still afraid of the power that she can wield.

Marie-Geneviève said: 'James writes marvellous letters! He says that houses in Gothenburg are mostly built of wood which the inhabitants pretend to be much handsomer than stone ones and that several canals, running through the city, render it agreeable. But there's no society like ours: the women flock together or stay at home whilst the men go to play at the coffee houses! That would not suit you, Maman!'

'No, it would not!' Catherine said. 'See – I've had a letter, too. *Another* one from Roger. My goodness but I'm spoilt!'

'From Roger, eh?' Dick asked idly, stretching out his

long legs and settling into his chair. 'He writes often, doesn't he? What does he have to say?'

'Oh, this and that,' Catherine said vaguely, glancing over the pages. 'He, too, writes very well, but of Paris, of course. You would think that you were there. The *boutiques* . . . Do you remember the ones we used to visit, Dick? Monsieur Maille – Monsieur Sauvol . . .'

'Paris in those days was a delight,' Dick said, to Ellen's growing fury. 'I was completely beguiled.'

'It's still incredible, according to Roger. Oh, now this is interesting. He has read a most astonishing book which has taken all of Paris by storm. *Les Liaisons Dangereuses*. The story is most scandalous. Two people confide to each other about their *affaires*. Much sensuality, Roger says – a terrible book but one that you could not put down! I simply have to read it, even if I have to go to Paris in order to do so!'

Dick laughed.

'A long journey to acquire a book! Who wrote it, by the way?'

'Pierre Choderlos de Laclos. One piece of fiction he has written, that is all, and everyone talks about it!'

'One piece of fiction,' Dick said, shaking his head in amazement. 'This will surprise all of you – I knew the author when we were garrisoned on the Ile de Ré. He said then that he would be a great writer; that he would write something extraordinary that people would remember after he was dead. Well, well . . . What else does Roger have to report?'

'Something else – ' Catherine said, and made a little *moue*, looking down at the letter in her hand.

'More scandal?'

Catherine said: 'He wants me to join him in Paris. No, not just so I can read that book, Dick! He wants me to marry him! He says it's time he had a wife!'

* * *

'Are you seriously considering Roger De Lacy's offer?' Ellen asked.

Dick, surprised, she supposed, by this disclosure, had said nothing at all.

'Yes. No. I'm not sure,' Catherine answered, sounding like a little girl.

Under this childish façade, what is she really thinking? Ellen wondered.

Is she likely to say yes to this objectionable suitor?

Isn't this precisely what I have hoped?

'What would dissuade you?'

'But, Ellen,' Catherine said. 'John is so recently dead. How could I marry Roger after so short a time?'

'No one will be scandalized. You will be living in Paris, far away from this small provincial town where people tend to talk.'

'I wasn't thinking of the scandal,' said Catherine, looking bemused. 'It wasn't that, Ellen.'

'Then why not? John would not want you to be lonely in your old age.'

'I suppose not. Oh, Ellen,' Catherine burst out suddenly, ignoring everyone else. 'John was such a wonderful man. He was so kind and so good and so understanding. How could I marry again, after knowing such happiness? I could never hope to repeat it.'

This could not be an act, thought Ellen, gazing at Catherine. See how her eyes shine when she speaks of John – how her face lights up.

'But then I would not *want* to repeat it,' continued Catherine. 'Still, Roger does make me feel young again – isn't that silly? And then there is the lure of Paris itself. I always loved it so. All these years I have secretly dreamed of going back there to live. I always knew that John and I wouldn't do that. He may have been an Englishman by birth but he was a Charentais at heart. And he hated big

cities so I never told him how desperately I wanted to
return to what I have always felt was my true home . . .
I'll have to think about it. Ellen, you and I must talk
about it again.'

'Do *you* think I should accept Roger's proposal, Ellen?
What do you think of him? You always tell the truth. I
don't, you know. I don't have your courage. I used to
envy that quality in you as a girl. How weak I must always
have seemed to you, by comparison. How
unresourceful . . .'

'On the contrary,' said Ellen. 'You appeared to me to
be well able to cope.'

'In some respects. And now here I am, at my age,
asking for your advice. What would Maman say? I
wonder. No doubt she would be content to see me finally
married to a Catholic, ending up legally wed!'

'Did that never worry you over the years?' Ellen asked
curiously.

She had wondered from time to time how Catherine
coped with the implications of her marriage to a non-
Catholic, living in sin, in effect, since their contract was
not recognized by the Church. For every day of her life
since Catherine had wed John Marrett, she had risked the
loss of her soul.

Until she had been freed from her condition by John's
untimely death . . .

'Not really,' said Catherine easily. 'I cannot believe
that God is so inflexible, whatever the Church may say.
And most of the time, when I am being truly honest with
myself, I think that if I marry Roger, in church, in the
prescribed way, that, *then*, I would live in sin. Because in
my heart I will always be married to John. Do you
understand that, Ellen?'

How sincere she sounds, Ellen thought, more perplexed

418

than ever. To listen to Catherine you would think that she had been probity itself throughout her life.

Meanwhile Catherine was toying out loud with the idea of going to Paris on a holiday.

'There is apparently an apartment in the rue de Bourgogne which would suit me very well. Do you know that the footpaths have been paved, Ellen? Oh, I must go to Paris, don't you think? If only because of the shops!'

'And Roger?'

'Roger? Mm – that decision can wait!'

She was going. Clothes were being packed. Not mourning clothes – the black bombazine gowns which Catherine had worn during the winter were now being given away to the poor to be replaced by colourful brocades and cretonnes and lawn and a striped Pompadour silk.

'This is the nicest *and* the most popular,' said Catherine, holding up a length of pink cambric for Ellen's inspection. 'It came from Persia. I'm having it made up.'

Catherine's face and hands were made up, too, with scented starch, and she wore heavy perfume.

She was packing her trunks. She had acquired enormous hats with foolish names like 'Novice of Venus' and 'Cradle of Love'; hats to wear with plumes and feathers; a gipsy hat to wear over a ruffled cap.

As well as gowns and hats she was putting embroidered shoes with high heels set with jewels into her baggage, and an elaborate hand-painted fan, and sashes of many colours.

She was almost on her way, wearing a purple riding-coat dress with low *décolletage*, about to board the coach. Ellen was seeing her off, for Marie-Geneviève was pregnant again and was not feeling well.

'*Au revoir*,' Catherine said, and stood on tiptoe to hug

419

her. 'My dearest Ellen, I shall miss you terribly. Promise me that you will write.'

'I – ' Ellen started to say, and found she could not speak.

Catherine said: 'Please, please, come and see me in Paris. Persuade Dick to bring you,' and climbed into the coach.

It was very hot, standing in the street. Cool inside the coach, Catherine leaned forward to wave out of the window with a tiny white-gloved hand.

She had such delicate little hands.

'*Au revoir – au revoir*, Ellen.'

'Goodbye,' Ellen called.

And Catherine was gone.

4

Unable to believe his good luck, Roger checked again the details of the apartment which he had rented on behalf of Catherine, a place where she could reside until they could be married.

The apartment was small but delightfully proportioned, he thought, looking around complacently. The door handles were decorated with wreaths of roses and sunflowers and the window-fastenings were shaped like a flowering branch of lilies, touches likely to appeal to Catherine.

The furnishings were modern and therefore too simplistic for what he knew to be her taste. He had remedied that, to a certain extent, by adding an elaborately carved console which, when they were wed, would easily transfer to his own apartment, and an armchair covered with Beauvais tapestry which, although more recent, was so charming that he felt that Catherine, too, would not have been able to resist its purchase.

And she would have a pleasant view since the main rooms looked out onto a private garden which was now ablaze with summer flowers.

When he had satisfied himself that no further improvements could be made to Catherine's new but temporary abode he decided to take a short stroll by the river. It was a little too warm for his liking. In June and July one really should leave Paris, he thought, and no sensible person should stay here in August by which time it is bound, as always, to be insufferably hot.

Except that, where Paris was concerned, it was always difficult for a truly civilized person to be absolutely sane!

How could one consider leaving – even for a month or two – a city which offered so much?

Unless, as had been his own position in recent years, one was tempted away by the charms of a woman who herself had been forced to live elsewhere?

But all that was changed . . .

From now on, Roger thought, Catherine will be living in *my* city – *her* city, which she has always loved so much.

Liking the Palais-Bourbon, he paused briefly to look at the residence of the Prince of Condé before making his way to the *quai*. Despite the fact that the river smelt undeniably vile it seemed cooling walking alongside it. His energy began to return. What had begun as a short stroll turned into a brisk promenade.

Sometime later he found himself in the courtyard of the Commerce-Saint-André. At the rear, as he knew, a passage to the right led into rue de l'Ancienne-Comédie. Here was one of his favourite places, the Café Procope, established, it was true, not by a Frenchman but by a Sicilian, but nevertheless an interesting meeting-place for artists and authors and actors, patronized over the years by Diderot and Rousseau and Voltaire.

Catherine, he thought, would enjoy being taken there.

Although, lately, some of the people who frequented the place were not quite . . .

He scowled as a strongly-featured man with a sharply curved mouth and brilliant eyes blazing with inward passion pushed past him into the café, as if he was unaware of Roger's existence.

If I'm not mistaken, Roger thought, that's the advocate Danton.

'Ah, Marat!' the fellow shouted, rushing up to a table where another man was waiting.

Roger glared at them. They were not men with whom he felt in any way compatible. Marat, in particular, having achieved fame as a doctor, was now said to be publishing seditious pamphlets; was rumoured to have ambitions to start his own newspaper. In which, no doubt, he would continue to attack the leaders of France.

Seeing Marat and Danton in the café, he decided against stopping there himself for refreshment.

Ignoring the proprietor, who was waving him towards a table, Roger left the premises and made his way into the quiet rue de Jardinet.

Men like Marat and Danton and their other friend, Robespierre, were traitors to their own class.

Meddlesome men, unsettling the peasantry – giving them ideas beyond their reach.

And in the process reminding people like himself of that other Paris where nothing but squalor abounded.

Men of little consequence, it was true, but still an irritant.

On second thoughts, he decided, he would take Catherine elsewhere.

Catherine, who, by her own admission, was not as truthful as Ellen, had been guilty by omission when she had spoken of her reasons for joining Roger in Paris. Vanity had also played a large part in that decision – vanity and her avidity for power.

She did not lie to herself and admitted these motives quite freely in her own mind.

And what was wrong with them? she asked herself as the coach in which she was travelling drew nearer to Paris: from such sources women, being the weaker sex, drew a kind of strength which helped sustain them through the cruel rigours of life.

Most women . . . At that point in her musing it did seem that a faint but unmistakable female voice gave a derisive snort.

423

'Except *you*, Ellen,' conceded Catherine in silent response to the snort. '*You* are an exception. And it is true, as you seem to be indicating, that I was sheltered in my marriage from most of the cruel rigours by my darling John. And, yes, Roger, if I so wish, would pamper me again . . .'

Ellen, she felt, was not impressed by the 'pamper' and snorted a second time.

'Look after me, then,' Catherine substituted, but this alternative was greeted with equal scorn.

In order to drown out the voice and the derision Catherine recommenced her conversation with one of her travelling companions, a distinguished-looking man in his late fifties who regrettably had a wife waiting for him in Paris. Still, to keep, as it were, in practice, she flirted with him as a matter of course and had the satisfaction of noting his enraptured response.

'The same old Catherine!' Ellen's voice interrupted, just when the charming man was yielding to temptation and suggesting they meet for luncheon.

'I'm afraid that wouldn't be possible,' Catherine said. 'You see – ' and she told him about Roger, giving him the false impression that they were definitely going to wed.

'How regrettable,' her companion said, appearing to lose interest and shortly afterwards falling asleep.

'*You* did that to me, Ellen,' Catherine said accusingly. 'If you hadn't interfered I would at the very least have had someone to talk to – a little stimulation, on the way.'

'And what about all the things you did to me?' Ellen demanded in return. 'Look how badly you treated me, over the years. Let's discuss that first, shall we?'

'Not now,' Catherine responded. 'Not at this very minute. But later' – and she decided that, when she got to Paris, she would write to Ellen, to try to put everything right.

This put an end to the dialogue and shortly afterwards the coach reached the outskirts of the capital.

I'm here, Catherine told herself – finally, I am here.

But instead of a rush of elation there was no sensation at all. Not a spark.

It will be different when I get into the centre of the city, she told herself – when I begin to recognize the landmarks.

To her disappointment her mood did not change as she approached her final destination. She was feeling weary after her journey – that was why she was not responding to Paris in the way she had expected. The fact that she was at this particular moment not far from her old home in rue Vivienne, nonetheless, left her as unmoved as did the people who walked in the streets – the strangers. When, as arranged, the coach approached the Pont-Neuf, where she was to be set down, the entertainers who had once amused her in this place, the tooth-pullers who had set up shop nearby, did not attract her attention.

Roger, however, did. He was standing on the quai de la Mégisserie, a thin, grey-haired, anxious-looking man, sweltering in the summer heat, having very obviously stood there for some time, awaiting her arrival.

And quite right, too, Catherine thought. So should a man – suffering a little – greet the woman he loves.

Under normal circumstances this train of thought would have amused and stimulated her. Today it did not.

And the sight of Roger himself did not affect her one way or the other, either. She put a dainty hand up to her mouth to disguise a yawn and wished that she could go straight to bed instead of having to reassure the thin grey-haired man that she was pleased to see him again.

There was, naturally, no question about his delight in laying eyes on her. She would have been horrified had his brown eyes not burnt with the required ardour as she was handed down to him from the coach, but it induced no reciprocal feeling in her.

Meanwhile, Roger could hardly put two words together, so ecstatic did he become.

'Catherine, I – ' he began, and kissed her on both cheeks, placing his hands on her shoulders as he did so.

He's trembling all over, Catherine thought. Well, what else could I expect him to do? And once again the prospect of going to bed, on her own, loomed up and struck her as being of paramount importance.

'How brave of you to come all this way alone,' Roger said, finding his voice again. 'You must be quite weary.'

So at least she had a way out.

'I am,' said Catherine sincerely.

And Roger, most mercifully, said: 'As soon as you reach your apartment, I will leave you in peace so that you can rest.'

Having done precisely that, and slept soundly, Catherine convinced herself, when she woke in the morning, that she would feel quite different about Paris, about Roger as soon as she was out and about.

The apartment, after all, was every bit as charming as Roger had said in his letters and she was certain that in no time she would emerge from her temporary torpor and feel elated by what, after all, was a home-coming, a return to the beautiful and exciting city which she had missed so terribly during the years in the Charente.

But although she was certainly less languorous, less insensible when, having had her morning coffee, she peered from one of the windows into the street, she did not feel excited.

The apartment was situated on the corner where the rue de Bourgogne meets rue Saint Dominique. From this angle she could see, behind their monumental gateways, the façades of the great town houses which, at one time, had given her such pleasure. They were still beautiful but neither the stately residences nor the smart ladies and gentlemen leaving and entering them aroused her particular interest.

Perplexed by her own reactions, she poured herself a second coffee and drank it, sitting on her bed. Roger had engaged the services of a maid who, he had told her, would shortly appear and see to her needs. In the meantime, she had nothing to do but dress at her leisure and prepare to meet Roger for lunch.

Quite suddenly, she knew that this was the last thing she actually wanted to do. And it came forcibly to her that she, who had longed for so many years to return to Paris, was actually missing Cognac.

Instead of the smelly Seine she wanted to look upon the green Charente, in spite of what, in a perverted mood, it had done to darling John.

Instead of walking on smart pavements she realized that she would be happier tottering along on the narrow cobbled streets.

When, way in the distance, a church bell rang, she thought of Saint-Léger.

How ridiculous.

And yet –

Because it was not only Cognac itself that she was missing, but Marie-Geneviève and James and Dick and her grand-children.

And Ellen. That was the strange thing, when she remembered what enemies they had been as girls, the fact that she should miss Ellen most of all.

Ellen, she thought ruefully, was probably not even thinking of her, having the family for company and being in her own home.

If only she, too, could be with all of them now, instead of being here.

I'll go back, she thought wildly. Instead of meeting Roger for lunch I'll run away from Paris, back to the Charente.

Except that if I go back now, after one night in the city to which I told everybody that I wanted so desperately to return, I will look ridiculous; appear a fool in front of them all. I can't – not so quickly – admit I made a mistake.

But I could tell Ellen. Yes, I could reveal myself to her.

She remembered their silent conversation in the coach, her promise to write to Ellen, to apologize for her behaviour in the past.

There was all the time in the world before she had to meet Roger. She would write to Ellen at once.

'I'm sure Maman has made a great mistake in going to Paris,' Marie-Geneviève said worriedly to Ellen. 'She must be missing the children – and you, too, of course, as well as the rest of us. And on top of that I do feel that she's much too old for this change.'

'Old?'

'Not *very* old,' said Marie-Geneviève hastily, remembering that Ellen and her mother were much the same age. 'But at a stage in life where roots have been put down. When you think about it, what she has done is quite mad, dashing off to Paris, moving into a temporary apartment, leaving all her furniture here. And contemplating an offer of marriage so soon after Papa's death.'

'But it *is* from a man who has been in love with her all his life,' Ellen pointed out. 'And she is returning to her roots, having lived in Paris as a girl.'

'She was born in Cognac,' Marie-Geneviève said obstinately. 'And she is fonder of this town than she knows. As for the man, neither James nor I care for him. And I have a suspicion that, deep down, I think you feel the same.'

'But he *is* in love with her,' said Ellen, feeling pushed against a wall.

'But you don't like him, do you?' Marie-Geneviève asked her.

And when I say, as I must do: 'No, I do not like Roger De Lacy,' Marie-Geneviève will go further, will want to know if I said so to Catherine, Ellen thought bleakly.

And I will be forced to tell her that I, known for speaking my mind, kept silent on this particular matter, divulging nothing of what I know from Dick about Roger.

Because of my fear that Catherine would then change her mind about her move to Paris.

And stay here . . .

'Maman!'

Josette rushed into the room, followed by André.

'He rubbed soil into my hair!'

'I did not!'

God's help is nearer than the door, said Ellen to herself and leaving Marie-Geneviève to act as mediator, she managed to slip away.

James had just come home. When they had finished talking business Dick said ruminatively: 'Sometimes I wake in the night and wonder what is going to happen . . . I was speaking yesterday to a man who has just been in Paris. He maintains that armed brigands are preparing to march on Versailles. It may only be a rumour. The trouble is that the situation is so bad that one hears stories all the time. This same man insists that a group of intellectuals are inciting the people, feeding them with ideas drawn from republican Rome. He says Paris is flooded with pamphlets. He picked one up himself.'

James said slowly: 'Paris is said to be bursting with

discontented hungry people who have flooded in from the countryside. Could it get out of hand?'

'It might – and spread. It's unlikely to affect us, either as a family or as a business, if it does, since people here know our views. Let's hope that it is contained within Paris, and directed only at the administration there.'

'Let's hope so. At all events,' said James, putting into words what was in both of their minds, 'it's unlikely, surely, to spread into the Palais-Royal district – to affect Maman's stay . . .'

By the time Catherine had finished her letter to Ellen the maid whom Roger had engaged had arrived and she gave it to her to post.

Jeanne-Avril was a conscientious, hard-working girl – Roger would not have employed her otherwise – but at that time she, like many other people in Paris, was distracted by what was said to be going on.

Her own family – her two brothers – were involved in it, distributing pamphlets and telling their disbelieving parents that times were going to change.

Jeanne-Avril was thinking of what they had said as she took Catherine's letter and propped it up on the carved console which Roger had installed in the apartment, intending to post it later. For all her normal meticulousness, she balanced it at a bad angle.

'We have had enough of all of them,' her brothers had said. 'The aristocrats – the queen. The king . . .'

Jeanne-Avril began to dust, moving around the apartment, lost in her own thoughts. When she reached the carved console she stopped to remove a trace of dust from a nearby picture and her elbow inadvertently tipped Catherine's letter down behind the console and thereafter out of her worried mind.

The king?

But no – it could not be . . .

They are young, Jeanne-Avril said to herself, thinking of her brothers. Their heads are full of ideas.

The people, even when they are hungry, will be loyal to the king . . .

5

Jeanne-Avril was quite wrong for in Paris at that time
there was at least one man who had grown to hate the
king and all that he stood for.

Jean-Luc Lindet had not always loathed the monarchy.
On the contrary, as a boy in Arras he, like everyone else,
had thought of the king as being second only to God, a
deity himself, more divine than human, whose omnipo-
tence and wealth he would no more have thought of
questioning than his own family's semi-impoverished lot.

To be born rich or poor, he had then believed to be a
state into which God Himself had placed you, and if at
times it seemed strange that a God of love should vent
such misery as was now prevalent in France upon its
innocent people, he had accepted that no mere human
being could understand the mysterious ways in which the
mind of the Almighty worked.

But Jean-Luc no longer believed that to be hungry –
really hungry, going without any food at all for several
days at a time – was a condition in which God played a
hand.

He was not that sure that he even believed in the
existence of God anymore, although he was sustained by
faith and imbued with pietism. The difference was that
the object of his veneration was not an invisible god but a
most remarkable man.

Robespierre. Like himself, a native of Arras. Unlike
himself, a man from a comfortable background, the son
of an advocate who had been sent to the collège of Arras
and then to Paris, to the collège of Louis-le-Grand.

An advocate. A man of literature and – until he had seen the light – a frequenter of the *beau monde*.

A man who had secured the support of the country electors, and who, even though he was only thirty, had been elected fifth deputy of the *tiers état* of Artois to the States-general.

It was sheer coincidence that their paths had crossed. Arriving, like so many, in Paris, starving and with no hope, he soon discovered, of ever finding work, Jean-Luc had been on the point of despair.

At that time he had been hanging around near the Bastille prison. It was the last place he had expected to see a well-dressed man not, as he might have understood, walking quickly, having, perhaps, gone far out of his way en route to Notre Dame, but actually stopping and mingling with ordinary people, getting ready, it seemed, to deliver a speech.

And what a speech! Jean-Luc had never heard of Jean-Jacques Rousseau and therefore he did not know that the ideas which were being expressed by the well-dressed man – the notion that man was born naturally good; that discord and moral confusion came out of inequality of wealth; that a society of equals was not only a possibility but one for which it was perfectly possible to aim – had, in fact, been handed on to him by a French-Swiss moralist.

Jean-Luc did not understand everything the orator said, only the gist of it: that if he and the dirty, ragged, half-fed men and women who formed the rest of the audience found the courage to follow the speaker they would ultimately have access to a fair share of their country's wealth.

It was a heady doctrine to feed to a starving man and Jean-Luc devoured it eagerly. Squeezing through the rapt crowd like a devoted dog in search of its master, he managed to reach the well-dressed man. Then, weakened by hunger, he swayed, would doubtless have fallen only to be trampled upon as the crowd dispersed, had Robespierre not come to his rescue, catching him as he fell.

Much more was to follow. Jean-Luc was taken to Robespierre's apartment in the rue Saint-Honoré, fed and provided with money.

There were other men present of his host's ilk to whom he was introduced and whom he came to know on equal terms as Danton and Marat. He was asked to pass pamphlets around and he agreed to do so happily although, as he could not read, he was ignorant of their contents, as were many of the people to whom he gave them when he returned to the Bastille.

And yet their message, as with the half-understood speech to which he had listened with such attention on the first day, seemed to register with the angry, starving men and women who lived nearby.

Before he realized that it was happening, Jean-Luc found himself at the head of a small but tight-knit group, all supporters of Robespierre who, although they now had a little money in their pockets and could afford to indulge themselves in the rowdy dance-halls of the rue de Lappe, were much more concerned with venting their mounting anger on the monarchy and those around it.

All that week they had positioned themselves in the vicinity of the Bastille, watching the comings and goings; jeering as an aristocratic prisoner, said to be the Marquis de Sade, was moved out of the building to a lunatic asylum.

For the Bastille, a major symbol of royal absolution, was, they all agreed, to be the focus of their attack.

But when was that to be? They were all tired of waiting. Jean-Luc, like the other members of his group, was choking on his anger, furious that, for so much of his life he had been taken for a fool.

434

If only he had known that he was entitled to equality. And he thought with savage fury of the many times when he had paid homage to those with wealth.

Leaving the Bastille, striding along by the river was for Jean-Luc and his little group a gesture of defiance – a proclamation that they, too, could walk from an area of poverty to the riches of Palais-Royal without being prevented.

When they set out, it was no more than that. But they carried their anger with them, and the memory of their hunger and deprivation and humiliation at the hands of the rich, and passers-by in the streets, seeing their set expressions and blazing eyes, must have rated them dangerous men.

Catherine had been in Paris for eight days. The city woke early but she had made a point of staying in bed until eleven o'clock every morning and then taking her time about getting up in the hope that self-indulgence would lift her out of her depression.

It did not. And Roger's attentions – the luncheons, the suppers, the expeditions to the shops – failed in the same way.

What *am* I going to do? Catherine wondered. All week she had asked herself the same question: but now, finally, she knew that she had reached a decision.

She was going to return to Cognac. No matter how foolish she might appear in the eyes of the family she wanted to go home.

The decision, she knew, placed upon her shoulders the unenviable task of breaking the news to Roger. She groaned at the mere thought. He would be devastated. He would probably burst into tears but that would not change her mind, or even make her feel sorry for him.

Or help her to like him a little more.

Because she had come to the astonishing conclusion that she did not like him at all. Why had she not realized that before? In her youth? During the years when he had spent Christmases with John and herself in Cognac?

The fact remained that she had not opened her eyes to his true nature. It was only since her arrival in Paris, since they had been forced into an intimacy that now she did not want, that she had been able to view him clearly.

In this last week she had positive proof that Roger was weak, sly and vindictive. How could she ever have found him amusing? He poked fun, in a malicious way, at others, at those who were his superiors, at men who had achieved considerably more than he could ever hope to do.

He had mocked Dick for relinquishing a military career in order to become a merchant, as if this progression was a ladder down the social ranks which his old comrade had foolishly descended.

Catherine, naturally, had defended Dick against this attack, had pointed out to Roger the extent of Dick's commercial achievements, in so far as she was capable of enumerating them.

But after that Roger had been nasty about Ellen, reminding Catherine of what she had looked like when she had first arrived in France. He had culled this description from Catherine herself, which gave her conscience a dig, after which she rushed to Ellen's defence, leaving Roger puzzled.

In her annoyance with Roger Catherine lost sight of the fact that he was a man who now expressed himself best in the written rather than the spoken word: his personality was far less attractive than his pen.

And, in deriding Ellen, he was only telling Catherine what he believed she wanted to hear.

But even if Catherine had been able to accept all that

she would not have been able to forgive Roger for his treatment of Jeanne-Avril.

Catherine herself was courteous and considerate in her dealings with servants. So she was shocked to enter the apartment on one occasion, after a solitary expedition to the shops, to hear Roger shouting at Jeanne-Avril in a most ungentlemanly fashion, asking for this and that.

The demands themselves were somewhat unreasonable since Roger was putting in a request for chocolates, on the one hand, which meant an excursion into the street and beyond, and coffee, immediately, on the other but they did not upset Catherine so much as the tone of voice he used.

He is a bully, Catherine thought – he thrives on petty oppression. And she took pleasure in sweeping into the room while Roger was in full spate and praising Jeanne-Avril, quite oblivious that her letter to Ellen still lay in that very room.

'A boring, boring man!' said Catherine of Roger, as she prepared for one more interminable dinner with a man she did not love.

For that very reason, to raise her spirits, she had selected what she thought was the prettiest of her new gowns: the pink cambric polonaise, worn over hoops, which wickedly exposed her ankles. At least *they* were still slim, she thought gratefully. It was monstrous how weight, having been so painstakingly removed, managed to slip back on.

She looked with pleasure from her ankles to her tiny feet in their fashionable new shoes. How clever of the designer to have put simulated jewels in the heels! And such artistry in the making of the jewels themselves: people would think them real!

To add to all his other sins Roger, when he came to call for her, did not comment upon her shoes although, as

437

might have been expected, he did say that she was her usual lovely self.

'You have not been back to your old apartment in the rue Vivienne,' he said, when he had handed her into their carriage. 'So this evening I thought that we would drive there first, and you can look at it and remember our happy times before we go to dinner.'

In this Roger, although he did not suspect it, sinned all over again. Since coming to Paris Catherine had realized that she did not want to visit the rue Vivienne. For even the sight of her old apartment would force her to think too deeply of the people with whom she had shared it.

Because . . .

But she did not want to think about that. The rue Vivienne was quite simply the last place in Paris she wished to visit, least of all with Roger, but she could not tell him why.

Instead, she held her tongue and sulked, but not overtly. Roger, sitting beside her, had no idea of her feelings, either about his character, or their destination, or even how Catherine was reacting to the intense Parisian heat.

How stifling it is, Catherine thought crossly. It is quite impossible to breathe. And once again she thought wistfully of the green Charente countryside, of Cognac and the family.

And she was not pleased when Roger, thinking it would amuse her, suggested that they leave the carriage in the rue Vide-Gousset and walk to the Place des Petits-Pères and the Church of Notre-Dame-des-Victoires, on to rue Vivienne, the better to see the sights.

Did the man not realize that she was wearing new shoes in which it was difficult to walk a few yards let alone the distance he mentioned – no distance at all in most people's eyes but a long way to Catherine.

The fact that he had inflicted this walk upon her, albeit under the delusion that she would enjoy it, hardened her heart even more against him so that, as she trotted along beside him, she was rehearsing her farewell speech.

She would deliver it this very evening over dinner, she decided, and the angels who stood guard over the doorway of the nearby church seemed to smile in approval at her thoughts.

After all, it was pointless permitting the situation to remain static so that her own irritation and homesickness grew deeper by the minute.

And Roger, too, should be liberated from his unrealistic romantic dream.

Which was a boy's dream, not that of a grown man. Catherine no longer felt flattered that Roger should have idolized her for more years than she cared to remember. On the contrary, she thought him a fool for never growing up.

'Do you remember – ' he was saying when, after what seemed to her more like months than minutes, they turned into rue Vivienne.

Bleating like a sheep, Catherine thought, and stumbled on the cobbles, almost losing her balance which was deemed Roger's fault again. To think that she had seriously contemplated marriage to the man! She must have been quite mad.

' – almost there,' Roger said, and as if he was approaching an altar rather than a house in a quiet Parisian street he bowed his grey head.

They stood in silence in front of the fine-façaded mansion, Roger paying homage to those who had once lived inside it and Catherine – who had expected to feel a very much deeper and more unsettling emotion – simply pleased of the chance to finally rest her feet.

If only she could ease off her shoes, she thought, and

wriggle her poor pinched toes. But she could not do so without being observed by Roger, not in her shorter skirt.

Finally even Roger tired of paying his respects to the past and they retraced their steps back to the rue Vide-Gousset where the carriage was waiting on the curve.

'A most enjoyable stroll,' Roger pronounced as they went. 'All my life I shall remember the magic of this beautiful evening with you.'

You silly old man, Catherine thought disparagingly. But rue Vide-Gousset was probably the shortest street in Paris. Soon, very soon, in a matter of minutes, she could rest her feet again.

Jean-Luc and his followers had walked very much further than Roger and Catherine that evening, striding all the way along the river until they reached the half-Gothic half-Renaissance palace, constructed as a fortress on the banks of the Seine.

They stood there for a time, glowering at the building, and none of them thought of the military parades, the tourneys and the royal masques that had once been held there, as Roger might have done. They were ignorant of the fact that the palace apartments had been left empty when the court had repaired to Versailles and that the galleries had been occupied by artists and taverns and entertainers' shanties built up against its walls until plans were made to save it.

All they knew was that those plans were now being effected, doubtless at vast expense, and that infuriated all of them.

Money spent on restoring crumbling buildings while Jean-Luc and the others went poor . . .

'It should be razed to the ground instead,' Jean-Luc observed to his supporters. 'It is a symbol of the decadence of the rich.'

Although the others whole-heartedly agreed with him, they could not that evening destroy the palace, making that grand gesture which, all of them believed, would go a little way to restoring pride in themselves. A year, a few months, earlier none of them had known that they were entitled to dignity, that all men deserved respect simply because they were human. But they had learned quickly and well.

And in so doing they had arrived at a philosophy of their own. Having grovelled and bobbed and bowed and scraped throughout their miserable lives they felt they had given enough. They had no intention of proffering respect again, having used up their existing stocks.

From now on it was up to other men, and women, to render honour to *them*; to stand bareheaded in *their* presence, to genuflect and bow down to them.

That this was unlikely to happen as a matter of course was something they knew.

They were going to make it happen. Silently but unanimously every man present had arrived at this conclusion.

No bloodshed, Robespierre had stressed on several occasions during his public speeches. Without violence we will get what we want.

At the time they had concurred. Jean-Luc, in particular, thought that he was being given a new faith to replace that of the Catholic Church. When Robespierre spoke it was as if he was placing an alternative catechism in Jean-Luc's eager hands.

This catechism, unlike that from which his childhood teachings had derived, did not warn him that he would go to Hell if he were to break its rules.

There seemed, in fact, to *be* no rules, or any that he could spot, and no Hell, either, except on earth.

So when Robespierre, in his compelling way, urged no

441

violence, Jean-Luc did not feel that the new god of the soon-to-be-perfect universe was giving orders which his followers should obey, but rather predicting how men would live in this wonderful world in future.

But in the meantime their condition was far from ideal and they would have to proceed from that position.

'*Merde!*' he exclaimed, looking at the Palais du Louvre, and spat at the loathed walls.

His followers, to a man, echoed his sentiments, adding their own saliva before deciding to move on.

They had seen enough of the palace. Jean-Luc swung off to the right and then into the rue Croix des Petits Champs followed by the others. He had no particular objective beyond making his imprint as a poor man everywhere he went, rolled, like a ball, by the propulsion of his own considerable wrath.

In the Place des Victoires he and the others stopped again, this time before Desjardins' statue of the Sun King, crowned with laurels, standing high on a pedestal adorned with low reliefs and captives representing vanquished countries.

'*À bas le roi!*' Jean-Luc shouted, for he imagined the statue to represent the living king.

'*À bas!*' said everyone else.

'What's that noise?' said Roger.

He and Catherine were only just around the corner in the rue Vide-Gousset. The name of the street – pick-pocket street – should have been changed, in his opinion. It was a distasteful name, with unseemly connotations for a street in such a fine residential area. No doubt that was why, all of a sudden, he was nervous and uneasy, wanting to get away.

'What noise?' Catherine asked, as if she had been

away in her thoughts and had only just reverted to the present.

Before Roger could answer he saw, coming towards them, a group of rough men, not at all the sort of persons whom one would normally encounter in the vicinity of the Palais-Royal. His concern increased. The phalanx of men was now obscuring the carriage and although he realized with some relief that they were sober rather than drunk their expressions were not reassuring.

And as they drew near they did not, as one would have expected, step out of the way to allow their betters to pass but splayed out across the little street, blocking it, forcing Catherine and himself to stop.

Roger's unease turned into real fear. The leader of the group, the one the others were watching, was a brute of a man, dirty, hollow-cheeked, with huge hands and feet which were out of proportion to the rest of his body. And there were maybe a dozen men, in two rows, straggled across the narrow street, and no one else around.

'Allow me to pass.'

Catherine, small as she was, seemed to feel no terror. She was used to giving orders and these men were conditioned to being told what to do.

For a fleeting moment, all of them forgot about equality and they automatically cleared a path so that Catherine could walk between them to the carriage, leaving Roger behind.

But only for a moment . . . Afterwards, Jean-Luc was angrier than ever, part of his fury focused upon himself for having given way.

To these rich and imperious people. Instead of attaining dignity he had handed it away.

He stopped, holding out his hands to arrest his men, to motion to them to close ranks behind him, and swung around to look at the woman to whom he had given his self-respect.

She did not look back. Jean-Luc was left to contemplate her back view only.

He ran his eyes derisively over her fine clothes, mentally removing them, envisaging this wealthy woman walking naked in the street, humiliated, weeping, pleading for her clothes. The lewd image pleased him. He was about to describe it to his friends when, to his amazement, he noticed Catherine's intricately ornamented shoes.

Jewels! Once again, he was under a misconception, thinking they were real. At a time when men and women were starving this woman was flaunting her jewellery in a manner which struck him as obscene.

The rage was surging through him now, hot and fierce as liquor. A flood of terrible anger destined to destroy.

Catherine had reached the carriage. Jean-Luc, barely controlled, watched her climb in. Beside him, his followers waited uncertainly for their next instructions.

They were given their orders almost immediately.

'*À bas!*' Jean-Luc shouted hoarsely.

'*À bas! À bas! À bas!*' the others took up the cry.

Beyond them, in mortal terror, Roger cowered against a wall.

Catherine had believed Roger to be following behind her. She had barely time to seat herself in the carriage before Jean-Luc and his men surrounded it. She swung around to the window and saw outside it their bared blackened teeth, the cruelty in their faces.

'*À bas . . .*'

The carriage began to rock.

She might have been in a sailing vessel which was lurching and pitching and rolling in a devil's maelstrom wallowing and tossing and plunging before it plumbed the depths. And the angels who had fallen into Hell cried out: 'À bas! À bas! À bas!'

'Catherine! Catherine!'

That invocation was Roger's but he did not shout it out. His thoughts were whirling round and round in his head as the carriage shuddered and reeled. Hurtling Catherine from side to side in a crazy oscillation as the terrorized horse reared up.

They are only trying to scare her, said a voice inside Roger's head.

In a moment or two, when he is satisfied that she has been frightened enough, the leader will tell them to stop.

She is a woman. They will not truly harm her. It is I, as a man, who will become the focus of their wrath when they have rocked enough.

At the same time, he was taking a few steps backwards, feeling his way along the wall as if to draw strength from it.

If only Catherine had not incensed them, demanding that they let her pass through instead of wisely retreating as he would himself have advised, had he been given the chance.

If only Catherine had not marched ahead.

They will not hurt her, he said to himself, and his fumbling hand reached the end of the wall. To his left ran the rue du Mail. He paused at the junction, hesitating, watching the scene at the other end of the street.

When they tire of it, he told himself, they will remember me, and they will leave Catherine alone.

They will remember *me* . . .

And he thought fearfully: What will they do to a man?

And indeed, as he watched, Jean-Luc stood away from the carriage and shouted and made a gesture at his men to stop shaking it and one by one they obeyed.

Catherine is not really at risk, Roger told himself.

Whereas a man . . .

I . . .

Any minute now they would turn and see him and who knew, then, what they might do.

It would be so easy to slip away to his left while their attention was diverted elsewhere.

And –

Fetch help. In *that* way – far more sensible than offering himself as a victim – be of assistance to Catherine.

'Get out!' Jean-Luc shouted at her a couple of minutes later.

He sounded very much as if he might injure her but Roger, having slipped away, did not hear the shout.

Jean-Luc had wanted the rich woman to beg for mercy and when she did not he was disappointed.

But, at least, she was obeying his command, emerging from the carriage and standing in the street before him.

Jean-Luc looked at her and saw in her attitude, her clothes and her bejewelled shoes the epitome of everything he envied and hated. More than ever, he wanted to strip and reduce her. That was all he wanted to do. He had no more than that on his troubled mind when he said brusquely to her: 'Take off your shoes!'

Catherine stared at him, her expression registering none of the fear he craved to see on her face. He did not know that she was an expert at concealing her true feelings, that she had done so all her life in order to save herself.

But, then, her ability to dissemble merely increased her peril. She did as Jean-Luc ordered, taking off her shoes and standing, somewhat uneasily, in her bare feet, the first time in her life that she had appeared like that in public. She was not used to being without high heels at all, except in bed, and because they had been subjected

446

to encasement for such a long period her little feet had subtly changed over the years so she found it difficult to balance.

Wobbling slightly, but without losing her dignity, she looked at Jean-Luc in a manner that seemed insolent to him.

Pay respect to me, said Jean-Luc's burning eyes – give me back what I have lost.

But Catherine did not interpret this message, and she continued to stare back.

Maddened by her stance, Jean-Luc felt the last vestige of his self-control ebb away. Still, when he stepped towards Catherine his intention was to intimidate her, to have the pleasure of seeing her edge away, rather than to strike her.

But Catherine stood her ground. A scarlet wave of anger engulfed him. He hardly knew that he had raised his great clenched hand, felling her with the full force of his rage.

Afterwards, he stood stupidly over her body, wondering why she did not move. It was one of the others who shook his arm, who said that they must go, quickly – that the rich woman was dead.

6

'. . . fought desperately to save her but received only further blows for my pains,' wrote Roger to the O'Shaughnessys. 'Six of them pinned me down. One of the most brutal held a knife to my throat. Afterwards they must have knocked me unconscious for so I was found in the street, on the verge of death myself. By then the ruffians had fled . . .

'I am still in such pain. But far greater is the pain of her loss from which I will never recover . . .'

None of the people to whom this letter was addressed doubted its veracity. In any case, they were, each one of them, too distressed to concern themselves with Roger.

Over the next week the adults expressed their grief in different ways. Dick took several solitary walks by the river before joining James who was immersing himself more deeply in his work than ever.

Ellen ferociously attacked the weeds in the garden, and then decided to redesign the layout of several of the beds, in the process upsetting old Guillaume the gardener who liked them as they were.

Marie-Geneviève, on the other hand, stayed inside the house, re-organizing and tidying up, moving from room to room enhancing, until even she could see that there was no further scope for improvement.

She looked around, biting her lip, in search of some other object or corner which could do with neatening up before – partly out of compulsion to clean and embellish partly because she was forcing herself to come to term with her grief – she went into her mother's room.

It was already perfectly tidy, not a book nor a keepsake out of place.

But there are her papers, Marie-Geneviève reminded herself: Maman's documents will have to be examined and her affairs set in order, if this is not already the case.

Catherine's personal papers had been placed in an orderly manner in her escritoire. Marie-Geneviève lifted them out, being careful not to disturb their sequence, and began to look through them.

And then she found it – the letter which Hélène had written to Catherine shortly before she died, yellowing now, nearly thirty years later.

For a moment, Marie-Geneviève hesitated, wondering if, after all, she should read the letter, believing that it would upset her even more if she did. It was bound to castigate her mother for having married out of her faith – to say hurtful, uncomplimentary things about her father as well.

But she told herself that she should face the truth, that she should not spare herself, and instead of putting the letter aside with those documents which she had already examined, she forced herself to study it.

As she read, she bit her lip again. She had been ready to be hurt by the letter, even angered. But nothing had prepared her for the information Hélène had given to her mother, all those years ago.

'I have to talk to you,' Marie-Geneviève said, having tracked Ellen down in the garden.

She took her mother-in-law's arm and led her away from the flower-beds in the direction of the house, to the relief of old Guillaume.

'What is it?'

'It's this,' said Marie-Geneviève, and she thrust Hélène's letter into Ellen's hand.

How evocative hand-writing was! Ellen was struck by the familiarity of the neat script, remembering with clarity the kind-hearted woman who had taken a young girl into her home, before she actually deciphered the first few words:

Catherine, my husband's daughter . . .

'What – ?'

But Marie-Geneviève was motioning her to read the rest and Ellen began to do so aloud, as if voicing it would make more sense of what Hélène had revealed to Catherine: '*This may come as a shock to you although you perhaps sensed in your childhood that I had difficulty in loving you as a mother should. The truth is that you are not my daughter –* '

Ellen's voice faltered. But –

'Go on,' said Marie-Geneviève softly. 'Go on . . .'

' *– not my daughter, but the result of an* affaire *which your father had with my sister, Danielle. She died in giving birth and I did what I felt to be my duty and offered to bring you up. I must confess to you that I found it a great strain, almost unbearable, all those years, looking at you growing up, resembling your mother, reminding me in that way of what had happened . . .*'

'And I suppose no one likes to live with a continual reminder of their own failure in passion,' Marie-Geneviève said into the silence that remained after Ellen's words trailed off. 'Would you say that my *grand-mère* – that Maman's aunt – was perhaps a little puritanical – maybe self-righteous, as well?'

'But kind,' Ellen said. 'To me, immensely kind.'

They had reached a stone staircase that led up to the kitchen door. With the letter still in her hand Ellen sat down abruptly on the bottom step wondering what had compelled Hélène to ever tell Catherine the truth, after having concealed it for so many years. A need to purge herself – or a long-repressed urge to punish the girl who was living evidence of her husband's unfaithful love?

Or simply an explanation for leaving Catherine out of her will?

We will never know, Ellen thought. It is much better that we do not know, that I can just remember Hélène's unblemished kindness to me, years of love, her role as a mother to me, that lasted from our first encounter right up to her death.

She gazed back down the garden. Guillaume, grunting to himself, was stumping off without having carried out her orders. But Ellen had lost interest in redesigning the layout of the flower-beds.

I was treated like her real daughter, she thought again, considering Hélène. She often told me that, to her, that's what I was – that I must have been named in Heaven, after her. Catherine sneered at that.

But I wonder what Catherine was really feeling all those years.

'You perhaps sensed in childhood that I had difficulty in loving you,' her adoptive mother had written.

But Hélène had experienced no problems in mothering Ellen, in smothering her in love.

Deep down, Catherine must have resented me, Ellen thought, bemused.

How much of her attitude to me stemmed from her own deprivation?

I will never know the answer to that, either, thought Ellen sadly, sitting on the step.

But in that – as she was soon to discover – Ellen was proven wrong.

Roger had been accurate in one of the statements he had made to the O'Shaughnessys: he was indeed devastated by Catherine's death. But it did not stop his ordering the removal of the Beauvais tapestry armchair and the handsome carved console from the apartment in the rue de Bourgogne to his own rooms.

As she struggled to push the heavy console across the floor Jeanne-Avril found Catherine's unposted letter, and blushed scarlet with shame. According to what she had heard from the concierge – who had been informed by Captain De Lacy – Madame Marrett had been set upon by assassins.

Jeanne-Avril felt personally involved in her death. It was because of men like her two brothers that the pretty lady for whom she had worked for barely a week had so tragically died.

She took the letter to the post at once, asking the Virgin Mary to intercede on her behalf, that she be forgiven for her laxness, and her brothers for believing that her Son did not exist.

As she handed it over for posting, Jeanne-Avril wondered for the first time who the letter was for.

Madame Marrett's daughter, perhaps. She had mentioned that she had one.

Or perhaps, Jeanne-Avril said to herself, it's a letter to a friend . . .

Catherine is alive – she has written – Roger has made a mistake! So, for a minute, Ellen told herself when the letter duly arrived.

But she knew full well that these were wildly optimistic thoughts even before she tore open the envelope and saw that the letter was dated the week before Catherine's death.

It was a long letter – several pages. How extraordinary that Catherine – who had not communicated with Marie-Geneviève – should have written at length to her at a time when she was supposed to have been enjoying herself in Paris.

Ellen was alone in the house. Dick and James had gone to Bourg-Charente to discuss business with distillers there, and Marie-Geneviève and the children were out visiting friends.

But with Catherine's letter in her hand Ellen had the curious feeling that she was no longer on her own, that Catherine, far from being dead, was sitting beside her, ready to have a chat.

If only they really could . . . Since learning of Catherine's death Ellen had found that her hatred was gone; it no longer seemed to matter that Catherine and Dick had once, apparently, been lovers. All that recently seemed important was the quality of the conversations Ellen and Catherine had shared.

Now, in a way, Catherine was going to talk to her again . . .

I owe it to you, Ellen, to write, and apologize to you for all those years in which I tried to prove that I was better than you. The real truth is that I was jealous of you, of your independence and your courage and your strength, and of the respect that these qualities engendered in everyone else . . .

There was no mention of Hélène in the letter. As Ellen scanned the pages she was forced to accept the fact that Catherine had not so much been envious of the affection Hélène had lavished upon her but of what Catherine had seen as Ellen's superior nature.

More than that, of Ellen's success, not only as a human being, but as an immensely attractive girl.

A woman who had not been, after all, Catherine's inferior in the game of love but one who had surpassed her.

*Everyone admired you, Ellen, even my darling John
. . .*

And Dick, Ellen might have thought then – what about Dick? What do you have to say about him?

But there was no need for Ellen to interrupt Catherine with questions about her husband because Catherine was considering Dick herself. Had much to say about him, had devoted three pages to the subject, not always sticking to the point, for that was Catherine's way.

Except that Ellen could extract from those pages the main and relevant points.

Dick, with whom I believed myself to be in love, was himself in love with you, wrote Catherine with obvious sincerity.

I always knew that, but it did not stop me, on principle, trying to outdo you. . .

. . . Dick is a faithful man . . .

'In which case,' demanded Ellen, not at all angry now, simply wanting to know, 'what was he doing walking with you in the garden that night in April long ago? What, if he was faithful to me, was he doing in La Rochelle?'

The possibility that Catherine might have been attempting to present herself in a good light in writing the letter did occur to Ellen – that Catherine had been playing another kind of game.

But even as the thought crossed her mind she knew that this letter had come from the heart – that its contents had to be true.

As methodically as she had picked out the salient points relating to her husband in the letter, so Ellen considered the possibility that Dick and Catherine had not been lovers at all.

That her suspicions and agonies over the years had

been for nothing and about nothing. That she had been a victim of her own fears.

'Dick is a faithful man . . .'

There was only one way to find out whether this was a truthful statement.

To ask Dick himself.

'When I have his answer,' said Ellen in her mind to Catherine, 'I will know just how culpable *I* have been, in what I have done to you.'

The week in which Catherine had died the vines, as if to stress that life must go on, had burst into their very brief flowering: the new grapes had been born.

And now the undulating plains of the wine-farms were yellow-green, dotted with distant figures, weeding, and pruning the leaves to concentrate growth in the right places. Every so often one of the figures stopped working and wiped his brow with the back of his hand, avoiding the direct glare of the luminous summer sun.

Dick and Ellen could see the workers from the road, as they drove along in the carriage, with Liam at the reins.

It was the day after Catherine's letter had arrived and Ellen had not yet spoken to Dick although she planned to do so this very afternoon, as soon as they were alone.

'Do you the world of good to get out of the house, instead of brooding about Catherine,' Dick had said, when he had suggested the excursion.

There was much to remind both of them of that day, before they were married, when they had first driven together to Bourg-Charente: then, as now, the conditions had been idyllic for a drive, warm and serene, the trees green down to their very roots, and their branches laden with pheasants.

'I think we may as well eat first, don't you?' suggested Dick when they turned off on the Jarnac road. 'Perhaps we could take our food down by the river and sit in the shade of the trees?'

Once again, they were retracing their steps, and Liam knew it, too.

'Ah, sure, God bless them,' he thought, and took it into his head to leave the two of them together and wander along the bank.

Dick, taking a look at Ellen, decided that she was more affected than she realized by the news of Catherine's death.

'Sit down there,' he said tenderly to his wife, throwing a blanket onto the grass. 'And stop fretting. It will not bring her back.'

He spread out on the ground the contents of the basket which Marie-Geneviève had packed for them – ham, cheese, bread and a bottle of red wine – and rummaged in the basket again, looking for a knife.

'Are you feeling hungry?' he asked but instead of answering Ellen asked a question of her own.

Out of the blue she demanded to know: 'Were you and Catherine lovers?'

'*Lovers?*' echoed Dick.

How blue his eyes still were, Ellen thought, bluer than the unclouded sky above them, undimmed by time. Dick seemed to her to be hardly changed at all from the young man who had sat beside her in this place long ago, speaking of his ambitions. The shadow cast by the tree under which they were sitting, blurring his image, softened the lines upon his face, assisting this delusion.

'Lovers?' said Dick again.

He blinked, his hand still in the basket.

The poor fellow, he must be wondering what got into you to ask him such a question at this stage of his life, said a voice in Ellen's head. And, indeed, Dick was looking bewildered.

'You must be asking yourself why I should bring this up now,' said Ellen, in deference to the voice. 'But I'll tell you that afterwards . . . In the meantime, *you* tell *me* the truth about yourself and Catherine.'

For a minute or two, no one spoke. Dick renewed his search in the basket and finally found the cheese.

'Well, I'll be damned,' he said. 'Ellen . . . This is a fine time to be worrying about a thing like that, I must say. Still, I'll tell you the truth – all of it.'

'There was a time when I was infatuated with Catherine,' said Dick, looking back. 'I thought her the most beautiful creature I had ever seen, and indeed she was in those days. And at the beginning, when I was equally enamoured of Paris, the two of them were inseparable in my mind, she the epitome of young sophistication in that sophisticated city.

'But in due course I began to see through Catherine. I realized that she was not quite as certain of herself as she liked to pretend. That in itself would not have put me off, but her tendency to gain confidence by trampling over others, that certainly did.

'Afterwards, I learned that there might be a reason for her unattractive behaviour but, by then, I had got over my infatuation . . .'

On the other side of the river a young couple appeared walking hand-in-hand, errant servants perhaps, sneaking away from the château de Bourg, to spend time under the trees.

'I was well cured,' Dick said, 'before I went to war. But then Philip confided in me. He knew, you see, that Hélène was not Catherine's mother. He was only four when the baby was brought to the house but then and for several years afterwards he heard his parents arguing about what had happened. Later, as Catherine herself grew old enough to understand, the arguments petered out.'

'He never told her?'

'No. Even as a child he must have understood how hurt she would have been by the truth. He was convinced that it would break her. He begged me to keep it to myself in case the story reached her. I couldn't even tell you. But it affected my life as well. Philip made me promise that if anything were to happen to him during the battle, I would look after Catherine. I think – I *know* he hoped that I would marry her.

'But we were young and full of life and I could not imagine either of us dying . . .'

Across the river the girl broke away from her lover and ran laughing along the bank. But Dick's thoughts were far away and he himself was frowning.

He began to cut the cheese, passing it to Ellen, not eating himself.

He said: 'But Philip died and I was left with the memory of my promise to care for Catherine. It seemed of little consequence in comparison to the guilt I was carrying for simply being alive and for a long time it was that, and nothing else, that concerned me.

'But when my mind began to recover – when I thought seriously about marrying, that promise got in the way.'

'No!' cried the girl across the river, evading her lover's grip, and doubling back, to tease him. 'I don't believe in your love . . .'

'So, you see, after Fontenoy it was not love I felt for Catherine, but a sense of responsibility. I understood her nature already but even if I had not done so before the battle, I would have done so afterwards, because I was no longer a romantic. She was very kind to me, she had matured – a little. And I knew very well that I did not want her as a wife.

'Whereas you . . . By comparison to her, you were pure and fresh and real. But I was under an obligation to Philip and I was not sure for a long time how free I was to choose.'

So, you see, there are two tellings to every story, said the voice in Ellen's head – and only afterwards is everything understood.

'But you *did* choose. What made you choose in the end?'

'Sanity made me choose,' Dick said. 'Sanity and the realization that I could not live with red satin chairs and gold-lacquered commodes! Do you remember the day you and Catherine came out to the château to advise me about furniture and you said, "This is a country house, not a palace", and told me how you would put the colours of the earth and the flowers and the sky into our future house? I knew then that I had no alternative but to marry the girl I loved. But even then it was not easy to live with my guilt. And when I went to propose to you, Hélène made it worse by telling me that Catherine was engaged to Roger De Lacy, of all unsuitable people! But I was freed by then, and I had to leave her, as I thought, to her fate.'

But that was *then*, Ellen thought – before we were married. Thrilled as I am – surprised as I am to hear these things, it leaves me with the unanswered, vital question – what happened later on, not only when Catherine was living here, in Crouin, but also in La Rochelle?

Why bother the man at all with your questions? the voice in her head asked. Would it not be wise to leave well alone, after what you have learned?

459

Didn't the man love *you* all that time, and wasn't it you he wanted to marry in spite of all his guilt?

Does it matter so much to you that he might have strayed once or twice in the past with a woman he did not love?

But it *does* matter, Ellen replied – and what is important is that I have the courage to ask him, after being afraid for so many years . . .

'Tell me the rest of it,' she said, but Dick had already begun to speak: 'It would have been so much easier, as time went by, had *you* liked Catherine – we could have cared for her as a couple, when the need for caring arose. But you made it plain you disliked her and so I didn't encourage her to enter our lives after she was married. I saw her from time to time when she called upon John in his office and once, when he was away in England on business, a messenger came with a note from Catherine saying that stones had been thrown at the house and that she was frightened of anti-Protestant action. She was exaggerating, as it turned out, but she was pregnant at the time and far from well, worrying about the possibility of yet another miscarriage. And so I forgave her when the cause of the disturbance turned out to be, not anti-Protestant extremists, but two small boys, neighbours' sons, running amok, who were not a threat at all. I remember walking with Catherine in the garden that night after I had found this out, putting my arm around her, trying to comfort her, and all the time my mind was creeping guiltily back to my work and I was wondering when I could get away. It was work – the notion of building a great cognac house – that was of paramount importance to me, Ellen. Never other women!'

The couple across the river had been reunited. The boy was pulling the girl into his arms, bending his head to kiss her.

In this place, Ellen thought, Dick and I were once transported into the clouds by the fairy people.

Dick's words seemed to be having the same effect on her now as the *Sidh*'s action then.

Not a threat, said a lovely godly voice – maybe that of Dagda himself – *not a threat at all*. But Dagda – if indeed it was he – was talking of Catherine, not of stone-throwing boys.

'I say "that night" as if the date was irrelevant, but it was the night of our own fire,' Dick said, breaking the bread into several pieces, taking a bit of ham, as if he was picnicking by the river and not leading Ellen by the hand to *Magh Mel*, the legendary Plain of Honey. 'With all that happened afterwards I forgot about the incident but when I was back in the army it crossed my mind that if it hadn't been for Catherine and her fears, if I had finished my work and gone home as planned, I might have been in time to prevent the damned thing spreading. Still, I could hardly hold it against Catherine. I kept in touch with John and herself when I was in Ile de Ré and saw them in La Rochelle. But, in all honesty – and maybe, at the back of my mind I *did* blame her for the fire – there were times when I felt that I did not like her very much. It was Philip I loved, as a friend.

'Ellen, what in God's name put it into your head that she and I were lovers?'

'It was your conception of Catherine that was the trouble,' Dick said later when much had been explained. 'Not Catherine as she was . . .

'And, no, don't feel guilty. Don't tell me again that you could have prevented her from going to Paris if you had expressed your opinions of Roger. She would have gone anyway, and that, too, is the truth.'

On the other bank the two young lovers were lying on

the ground, locked in a passionate embrace, oblivious of their audience.

Dick reached for Ellen's hand with one of his and laid it palm downwards in the other, looking at it reflectively.

'I've always loved your hands,' he said. 'They're like you – strong and practical and true. You're a great woman, Ellen. The right one for me.'

Aware that the young couple were now uninhibitedly making love, he averted his eyes from the spectacle. But its eroticism had crept into his mind.

'Come here,' he said to Ellen, and pulled her into his arms, the way Liam, coming back to them, along the bank, was forced to turn away.